A PRINCESS FOR
Christmas

A PRINCESS FOR
Christmas

A Novel

Jenny Holiday

AVON
An Imprint of HarperCollinsPublishers

HarperCollins books may be purchased for educational, business, or sales promotional use. For information, please email the Special Markets Department at SPsales@harpercollins.com.

FIRST EDITION

Designed by Diahann Sturge

Princess crown illustration © Paulaparaula / Shutterstock
Gift boxes with bows illustration © AnastasiaSonne / Shutterstock

Library of Congress Cataloging-in-Publication Data has been applied for.

ISBN 978-0-06-295207-3

20 21 22 23 24   LSC   10 9 8 7 6 5 4 3 2 1

For my dad, aka Mr. Hallmark Christmas

A PRINCESS FOR
Christmas

Chapter One

Talking to kids was easier in cars. Leo might be making a hash of everything with Gabby, but that was one thing he'd learned in the two years he'd been trying to pinch-hit on the whole parenting thing.

Talking to kids was easier in cars. Not *easy*. Easier. Usually only marginally to imperceptibly. Like today when, despite his best efforts, he could not extract any information about how the middle school production of *The Wizard of Oz* had gone.

"Did Aidan remember his line today?" At yesterday's show, number four of the weeklong run, the boy playing the head of the Lollipop Guild had forgotten his line—the line that came before Gabby's—so the whole production had ground to a halt, Gabby unsure whether she should wait for him. The result, she reported, had been "extreme and utter mortification" when the teacher cued her to go ahead, thus making it look like the flub had been her fault.

Or so he'd been told yesterday, when Gabby had been infinitely more chatty than today.

Today, getting her to speak was like trying to arrange an audience with the great and powerful Oz.

She didn't answer, just performed a kind of girlish grunt as she looked out the window in the back of his taxi.

Did Aidan remember his line or not? he wanted to shout. But a person didn't shout things like that at his eleven-year-old sister. Especially when *Did Aidan remember his line or not?* was really a proxy for *Please tell me you're okay.*

Also: *Where is your winter hat? It might not be snowing yet, but it's December, and I don't care about your hair. I care about your ears not getting frostbitten.*

But Leo didn't know how to say any of those things. One day Gabby was all smiles and stories and "extreme and utter mortification," and the next she was closed up as tightly as the clams Dani brought back from Long Island.

He didn't know if the way she ran so hot and cold was normal. The parenting books he read suggested it was, but he thought it was early for her to be like this—he'd been expecting this moodiness to arrive later, to be more of a teenage thing.

But on the other hand, she had always been socially advanced. And she was a lot smarter than he was. He had never used phrases like *extreme and utter mortification* when he was eleven. Or in the fourteen years since, for that matter.

"What does that mean?" he said in response to her grunt. "Did the Lollipop League boss come through? I'm on pins and needles, here, kiddo."

"It's the Lollipop *Guild*, Leo."

And, oh, the disdain she managed to infuse into that single

word. His heart sped up like it always did when he felt like he was on the brink of fucking things up irrevocably.

Who knew he was capable of getting so worked up over *The Wizard of Oz*?

But hang on, now. This was important, yes, because it was important to her, but confusing the Lollipop Guild and the Lollipop League wasn't fucking things up irrevocably. He needed to keep some perspective here.

No. What he needed was a vacation. But that wasn't happening anytime soon.

So he cleared his throat as he turned onto First Avenue. "Right. Lollipop *Guild*; Lullaby *League*. Got it."

There was a long silence as he navigated the snarl of traffic on the few blocks between them and their destination. But then Gabby said, "You're for sure coming tomorrow, right?"

There. That's what these rides were about. She never would have asked him that so directly at home. But he could hear in her tone how much she wanted him there. And how much she'd missed the fact that he hadn't been yet.

"You can count on it." He still felt terrible about missing today's show. He'd told her he would be there, but Mrs. Octavio in 2C had run a bath and forgotten about it, causing it to overflow into the unit below hers.

He should have been there like he promised. He should have been on hand to witness the "extreme and utter mortification." That he hadn't was edging closer to "fucking up irrevocably" territory. Leo worried sometimes that all his small mistakes, his oversights and omissions, while not large enough individually to do any real harm, were invisibly accreting. That they were some-where *inside* Gabby, dormant for now, but that one day, when he committed one too many, there would be a kind of tipping point. That all his little fuckups would add up to one giant one that *actually* harmed her.

"I'll let the building flood before I miss it," he vowed.

He was watching her in the rearview mirror, so he caught the way her brow knit. "Well, maybe don't do *that*. I'm just Lollipop Guilder Number Four. I only have the one line."

He hated that an eleven-year-old knew where their household priorities had to lie. Knew that his second job as their building's on-site super was the only way they could afford the rent. Knew that flooded apartments had to take precedent over school plays.

Hell, he hated that their priorities had to line up like that to begin with. They had never been rich when Mom and Dad were alive, but things were a lot tighter now.

"Already done, kiddo. Dani's gonna work from home tomorrow so she can be on call as backup in case any building nonsense crops up."

"Don't call me kiddo."

He glanced in the rearview mirror again, and this time he liked what he saw. She was trying to tamp down a smile as she lodged her objection. He relaxed a little. They were okay. For another day, anyway.

"Okay, *kiddo*"—he stressed the endearment—"today you and Max are in for a treat. We are going to . . ." He rolled his tongue and drummed on the steering wheel. He was *trying* to irritate her now. He was still her brother, after all. Normalcy was important. Routines created stability. And Gabby needed to believe that there was a purpose to their little drive-arounds other than trying to, like, ensure her long-term emotional well-being.

He turned on the singsong, lecture-y tone she purported to hate. "And here we are! The United Nations Headquarters, designed in 1952 by Oscar Niemeyer, one of the pioneers of modern architecture. So like I said, you are in for an exciting time. And you, too, Max. Get ready, my friends."

At hearing his name, Max started barking. Or yapping, because what Max did could not properly be called a bark.

"See? Max appreciates my genius even if no one else does."

Gabby snorted. But she was openly smiling now.

He had beat back the forces of chaos for a little longer.

When the applause broke out, Marie almost started crying.

Which was not rational. There would have been many more logical instances in which to cry today. Perhaps *before* she gave a speech at the General Assembly of the United Nations? When she'd been standing up there looking at all the dignitaries and translators—a literal subset of the *entire world*—she'd felt like she was floating outside her actual body and therefore would have to call in absent to the speech she'd been practicing for so long. Would have to call her father and tell him he had been right. That she had been foolish to try to tack this speech on to the New York visit.

But, no, somehow, as she'd made her way up to the podium and looked out at that sea of faces and been sure that she was about to float away—sail up past the murals on the side walls and up and over the press gallery—she'd managed to get a hold of herself. Reach up and anchor some small shred of her being, like capturing the string of a runaway helium balloon just before it floated away forever, open her mouth, and talk.

Once she'd gotten going, it had actually been fine. She knew this material. She *cared* about this material. She was giving a speech about the ongoing European refugee crisis. She owed those people her best. And she was fairly certain she had delivered.

But, oh, afterward, the *relief*. It was all-encompassing. Like when you woke from a nightmare and it was still playing in your head, but then there was that glorious tipping point when enough of reality—your bed, the outline of your armoire—kicked in and triggered that wonderful notion: *it was just a dream*.

Or, less dramatically, like the feeling she used to get as a girl after she was done with her weekly dancing lesson. Six days of freedom until she had to do it again! Or like that one time Monsieur Lavoie went away for the summer and they decided to give her *three months off* instead of replacing him.

The startling liberation of a heavy responsibility suddenly lifted.

It made her giddy even as she wanted to weep with relief.

She had done it, her father's naysaying be damned.

But, as she navigated a crowd of well-wishers after the session was over, both the giddiness and the relief faded. Because she wasn't done yet with this epic day. It was the reason she was leaving so soon after her speech, instead of staying to take questions and talk policy.

In some ways, her father was right. Her next task *was* more important than the speech had been, if less public.

It was certainly as nerve-racking. She didn't fear that she was going to float away like an escaped balloon this time. More that she might, suddenly and with no warning, be violently popped. Be left with nothing to show for herself but a sad handful of broken latex.

She had tried to tell her father the party was not the place to do this. That an ambush would not go over well. But, as he had pointed out—reasonably, she had to admit—they really had no choice. Philip Gregory was attending the party, and what they needed to do—their last resort—was to charm Philip Gregory.

Charm.

Not something Marie possessed a lot of, despite her ongoing efforts.

Charm. Grace. Classical beauty. All the things that someone in her position was expected to have, Marie lacked. Her mother had had those things.

Instead, Marie was cursed with a surfeit of other qualities, things like anxiety and an overabundance of caution.

Which probably explained why she was in the bathroom at the United Nations changing into her party dress.

Mr. Benz had tried to insist that they had time to return to the hotel for her to change, and that plan might have worked if it had merely been a regular party. A party on land. But the boat was leaving at seven o'clock sharp, and even though anyone else would probably wait for her if "her people" asked, tonight's hostess most decidedly would not. She had only invited Marie because it would look odd if she didn't.

Marie, ever conscientious, had done her homework. A session with Google Maps had informed her that it was a twenty-minute drive down and around FDR Drive from the UN buildings to the marina. And while Mr. Benz, who *so very much* did not want to stand by while she changed in a restroom at the United Nations, might be technically correct—they *might* be able to get up to the Plaza and back down to catch the boat—that was cutting it too close for her liking.

Marie didn't have room in her life for *might*. She hated being late at the best of times—being late only confirmed the worst stereotypes about people like her—and this wasn't the best of times. This was important. This was work. This was duty.

"You should have had Verene make the trip with you." Mr. Benz's tone, as Marie emerged from the bathroom as polished and pulled together as she was going to get on her own steam, would have sounded neutral to outsiders. Marie, however, heard the nuance. She heard the slightly clipped consonants that signaled his disapproval.

She might be somewhat sheltered—she would admit to that—but even she knew that traveling with someone whose sole job was to pin her hair and steam the wrinkles out of her clothes was not a good look when one was trying to be casually charming. High-profile American people did not have these sorts of visible assistants. The Kardashians, for example, probably had armies of people spraying and fluffing them behind the scenes, but the key was that they made it look effortless. Americans enjoyed pretending they lived in a classless society, one where social mobility was as easy as a walk to the corner store. But she couldn't explain that to Mr. Benz, who refused on principle to even attempt to understand the ways of Americans, much less bend to them.

"There was no need to pay for another person to make the trip," she said with artificial cheer, falling back on the economic argument she'd made at home. And it was true. She was here to try to shore up the economy at home, not leech off it.

Mr. Benz sniffed. He preferred to pretend that they still lived in a world where the family did not need to concern itself with things so pedestrian, so crass, as money.

"Regardless, I'm perfectly capable of dressing myself."

Which might not actually be true, judging by how much trouble the back of her dress had given her. It laced up corset-style, and the pink ribbons it was threaded with weren't long enough for her to reach around and tie herself. This had been a poor choice, but of course she hadn't thought through the sartorial details the way Verene would have.

But she was not about to ask Mr. Benz for help or, worse, let him see that she was setting out for the party with the back of her dress undone. She would have to find a sympathetic partygoer to discreetly help her.

So she adjusted her cape to better hide her back, pasted on a smile, and said, "Shall we go?"

When they emerged on First and East Forty-Second, the agreed-upon meeting place for maximumly efficient extraction, Torkel was there shaking his head and speaking urgently into his phone.

Torkel was usually the epitome of cool. A man of few words and no outward emotions, he let his big, beefy muscles and his mirrored sunglasses—oh, she'd had such a crush on him when she was a teenager!—speak for him.

Usually.

Today he snapped, "Consider yourself fired," into the phone, curse-whispered, "*So ein Schmarrn!*" to himself, and turned to them with a grim expression.

Seeing *any* expression on Torkel's face was such a novelty, it distracted Marie for a moment.

"The car isn't coming," he said.

"I beg your pardon?" Mr. Benz's neutral-on-the-surface-of-things tone was now shading into alarm.

"It broke down."

Mr. Benz blinked a few times. "Pardon me?"

"It broke down."

"The car *isn't coming*?" Goodness. Mr. Benz rarely emphasized one syllable over another. This must be his version of panic. If Marie hadn't been sharing in that sentiment, she would have been amused. "It wasn't supposed to go anywhere," Mr. Benz went on. "It was supposed to wait for us and meet us here when I texted, *which I just did*."

Oh, he had emphasized *four* words there!

Marie felt badly. Torkel would be taking this to heart. He'd chosen the car service because, after extensive research and interviewing, he had determined it could best accommodate their security protocol. He had swept the car and conducted extensive background checks on their driver.

"Our vehicle is currently broken down on the Queensboro Bridge." A vein bulged in Torkel's neck. "Apparently drivers on UN detail congregate at the home of the Costa Rican ambassador while they're waiting to pick up."

"All right," Marie said. They didn't have time to waste. "It's not the end of the world. No one's dead."

"This was why the speech—" Mr. Benz cut himself off. He'd been going to say, *This was why the speech was a bad idea.* A frivolous indulgence. But of course he wouldn't actually *say* it.

He might be right, though. Not about it being frivolous, but about Marie's prioritizing it over the meeting with Gregory.

"I've ordered another car," Torkel said.

Marie shook her head. "We don't have time for that. We'll summon a taxi."

Mr. Benz gasped. Torkel growled.

She extended her arm out in the direction of the street before the inevitable volley of objections could be launched. She had never attempted to hail a taxi before, but that was how they always did it on *Sex and the City*. She started waving her arm around for good measure.

She could feel the disapproval radiating from both men. She didn't pull rank very often. She usually let them . . . handle her. It was their job, after all.

But it wouldn't be their job to tell her father that she had missed the boat—literally, though she was familiar with the American idiom—and with it her only chance to talk to Philip Gregory.

No, that would be *her* job.

She lifted her chin and tried to make the face her mother always used to when Grand-mère came to their apartment for tea. Recalled her mother saying, *If you want someone to listen to you, don't yell. Yelling signals desperation. Speak quietly but firmly. Assume you will be heard.*

All those dancing lessons might have been for naught, but *some* of her training had stuck.

Marie also remembered her mother hugging her, grabbing the remote control, and cuddling up next to her to watch some "deliciously dreadful American TV" after Grand-mère left.

She lifted her chin. "Gentleman. We are getting a taxi. There will be no further discussion."

She missed Maman so very much.

"So, EVEN THOUGH they started out at odds on the project, it's interesting that the final plan was a combination of their visions. Now, I'm not sure how happy Niemeyer was about that. He may have just given up and let Le Corbusier have his way."

"*Super*interesting," Gabby said.

Leo was executing a complicated U-turn to put them in the direction of home, so he couldn't check her out in the mirror, but he could *hear* the eye roll in her tone. He decided to lean in, to further antagonize her in the hopes of getting her to laugh. "The *other* interesting fact about the UN Headquarters is that the Secretariat Building—that's the tall one—was the first skyscraper in North America to use a curtain wall. It was—"

"I got my period yesterday."

Wait. *What?*

He was drowning. Plunged into dark, swirling, freezing water. His body might appear to be sitting placidly in the driver's seat of his cab, but he, his real, inner self, was a block over, sinking like a stone in the East River.

Jesus, Mary, Joseph, and all the saints—what?

He started sweating—like, his body just started shoving perspiration out of his pores—and Max started yapping. Probably because he could sense Leo's panic. Leo couldn't think through all the racket. He was going to die, and the last thing he was going to hear would be that glorified rat.

But no. He couldn't die. He was all Gabby had left.

Okay. Think. Gabby got her period. She was too young for that. Wasn't she?

Well, obviously not, Einstein.

Also, his sister liked to give him shit, but he found it hard to imagine her joking about something like this.

So, he needed to acknowledge her news. To say *something*.

He cleared his throat. "You mean like your first one?"

"Yeah."

Fuck. *Fuck, fuck, fuck.*

It wasn't like he hadn't known this was coming. But Gabby was *eleven*.

Oh god, maybe there was something wrong with her.

He rolled his neck to try to work out some knots that had taken up residence in it and made an effort to sound casual. "So I guess we should go to the doctor?"

The doctor for which the copay was four hundred dollars.

"I don't need a *doctor*, Leo. I'm not sick."

But what if you are? What if you have some terrible disease that causes little girls to—

"I just need some money to buy supplies."

Right. Supplies. *Right.*

Oh, *fuck*, he wished Mom were here.

"Yeah, of course. No problem. We can stop on the way home."

And then they would have to talk, right? About her feelings on the matter, if not the mechanics of things? They had already covered the mechanics during various excruciating versions of the birds and the bees talk in the past two years, Leo reading robotically from a script he'd modified from library books on how to talk to your kids about this shit—because the library had no books about how to talk to your much younger sister about this shit.

Was he supposed to say something here? Something profound and speechlike? *Congratulations, Gabby; you've become a woman today.*

But not today. *Yesterday.* She said she got her period *yesterday.*

"So, uh, this happened yesterday? What have you been . . . doing?"

Using? Wearing?

"I went to the school nurse, and she gave me some maxi pads," Gabby said matter-of-factly. "But I'm out."

Maxi pads. Leo's vision started to swim.

"She said I was too young for tampons."

Oh, Jesus Christ, *tampons.* He opened his eyes as wide as they would go and forced himself to concentrate on the road in front of him rather than the blurry blobs congregating in his peripheral vision.

All right. They just had to get out of Manhattan. Stop at the store for . . . supplies. And maybe some takeout. They would get her favorite, pasta from Ralph's. Which normally he hated doing, because she only ever wanted penne with marinara, which he could make at home. In theory. Not that he ever did. But their mom's recipe was better than Ralph's, so it bugged him to spend twelve bucks for subpar pasta from down the street.

But all he could think to do right now was figure out what would make his sister happy, and make it happen. "So, kiddo, what do you say we stop at—"

"Oh my god!"

"What? What?" Leo was already so enervated, that was all it

took for his adrenaline to spike, making him white-knuckle the steering wheel so he wouldn't fly away like an overinflated balloon. His chest hurt.

"Look at that girl! She's trying to hail a cab! Stop for her!"

"I'm not on duty." *Also, I'm having a fucking heart attack.*

"She looks like a princess!"

She did kind of look like a princess. She was even flanked by a tall, slim man looking very ill at ease in his old-timey suit, and a beefy, sunglasses-wearing bald guy looking very ill at ease in his new-timey one.

"Pick her up!"

"I'm not on duty," he said again. *Also, I'm still having a fucking heart attack.*

"Then just give her a ride. She looks like she really needs one."

She did. She was literally jumping up and down, waving her hands in the air like she was a runway worker at La Guardia trying to signal a plane gone rogue. She was wearing a shiny, white dress that puffed out like a parachute each time she jumped. She looked like a wedding cake topper in an aerobics class. It would have been funny if Leo had any humor to spare.

"Leo! Stop! You can't just leave her there."

He could, though. He would have exactly zero qualms about doing just that. He had other stuff to worry about. Maxi pads and pasta, to be precise. And heart attacks—the copay for heart attacks was probably a hell of a lot more than four hundred bucks. "Traffic is terrible, Gab. If we stop, it'll be forever until we get home. And we can't keep Max crated that much longer." Probably. He didn't really know. Normally, he ignored Max. But normally, he wasn't driving Max back and forth from his starring role as

Toto in the Bronx Technology Charter School production of *The Wizard of Oz.* "Also, it's going to start snowing any minute." The sky was a heavy, telltale gray.

"She's never going to get a cab."

Gabby was not wrong. It was six o'clock, it was about to snow, and the traffic was horrendous, especially over here because FDR Drive was closed. Miss Cake Topper was going to be jumping for a while.

Which, okay, maybe he felt a *tiny* bit bad about. He didn't like turning his back on a damsel in distress. But he was currently in possession of an eleven-year-old damsel who was taking up all his bandwidth. He wasn't taking new clients right now.

"*Please*, Leo."

Well, *shit*.

He heaved a sigh, pulled up in front of the woman, and lowered the passenger-side window.

He'd been going to ask where she was headed. To say something about how he was off duty, but if she wasn't going far, or was going straight uptown, he could take her.

But she got right in the front and, without even making eye contact with him, twisted around to face the back seat and said, "Can that thing go in the trunk so my . . . associates can sit in back?"

Leo did not care for that tone. Not at all. It was cool and entitled. And coming from someone who hadn't even made eye contact with him yet.

"That *thing* is a dog, so no, he can't go in the trunk."

Funny how quickly Leo had become Team Max.

His passenger's brow furrowed as she looked at the crate—it

was huge and took up half the back seat. Max was small like Toto, but, as the beneficiary of Dani's complete over-the-topness when it came to her canine companion, he had an enormous kennel they were using to transport him between school and home.

After silently assessing the backseat situation, the woman transferred her attention to her companions, who, given their extreme physical divergence, kind of looked like a nursery rhyme come to life—if Jack Sprat was a competitive body builder and his spouse was a stuffy professor of philosophy. "Well, you two are going to have to stay behind—which is fine."

"I can't allow it." The proper man, who was, upon closer examination, not as old as his formal attire had initially suggested, spoke with what sounded like a German accent. "You need Torkel at least for the party."

"I don't. I'm not taking him on board with me. You will recall that I'm attempting to be casual. To circumvent all the formal meetings Gregory won't take with us."

"You can't go alone."

"Well, I'm not taking Torkel on the boat. I never was." She looked at the beefy guy. "My apologies, Torkel. You would be a . . . what do they call it here? A down bringer?" Her brow knit slightly, then quickly smoothed as she found a phrase she apparently liked better. "No, a mood killer."

The man—Torkel—nodded. It was a strange, deep nod that almost looked like a bow.

The other man sighed and opened the back door, like he was about to get in. "I'll come, then." He directed a "move over" motion to Gabby. "This young lady and I shall endure these tight quarters."

"Hang on, now." Leo spoke to halt the man's progress, but he directed his words at the woman. "Rewind."

She looked at him, really looked at him, for the first time since she'd gotten in his car.

His mind had made the cake topper bride comparison because of the voluminous white dress, and maybe because her dark hair was twisted into a low bun that seemed sort of formal and wed-dinglike, but up close, she did not look like a cake topper at all. Cake toppers were made of plastic and wore generically bland expressions.

This woman's face was the opposite of generic. It cycled through a rapid-fire slideshow of emotions: confusion gave way to annoyance, and there was still a touch of that entitlement he'd seen earlier. It got his hackles up. She had dark blue eyes fringed with eyelashes so long they looked like cartoons—like someone had drawn them on with a Sharpie—and full, pink lips that also looked kind of cartoonish in the way they formed a heart on top.

It was good she was so snooty underneath all that beauty. That made it easier to say, "Did you not notice that the 'Off Duty' part of my sign was lit up?" He pointed to the ceiling.

"It was?" The entitlement slid off her face. It was very satisfying.

"Yeah. We're headed home, so if you're on our way, we'll take you."

"I'm going to the North Cove Marina."

"In Battery Park?"

"Battery what?"

"Park?"

"Well, I'm getting on a yacht on a pier in the North Cove Ma-rina. It's down around the tip of Manhattan. Is that Battery Park?

You should be able to take FDR Drive around, and it should take twenty minutes. *Exactly* twenty minutes—that's not me rounding up or down."

"That might be true if FDR Drive was open."

The cascade of emotions continued: dismay, panic, and, he was pretty sure, outright fear.

That did something to him. Whatever this lady's deal was, she apparently *really* needed to get to Battery Park.

"FDR Drive is closed?" she whispered.

"Yep. For resurfacing. Between here and the Manhattan Bridge." When she didn't say anything, he added, "So you'll have to go straight across, which, this time of day, will probably take you at least forty minutes."

She looked at her watch. It was big and chunky and seemed out of place with the fancy, poufy dress she was wearing. She blew out a staccato little breath, like she was steeling herself for something, and turned to him. "I so appreciate you stopping for me. I will pay you any amount of money you name if you will get me to the North Cove Marina by seven o'clock."

He barked a laugh. Any amount of money he could name? Maybe four hundred bucks so he could take Gabby to the doctor to talk about her period? Or, no, maybe whatever amount it would take to hire a shrink for him so *he* could talk about Gabby's period?

Or maybe just thirty-five bucks for a case of Moretti.

"Of course we'll take you," Gabby said from the back seat.

The woman turned to the serious man, who was still frozen half in, half out of the car. "Really, Mr. Benz, there's no need for either of you to come. I'm getting on the boat by myself anyway."

Mr. Benz looked like he was going to object, but the woman lifted her chin a good two inches, turned to Leo, and said, "It will just be me, thank you." Then she turned back to her companions and said it again, more emphatically. "Just me."

That last "just me" sounded like an order, but it also sounded like maybe this woman wasn't in the habit of issuing orders.

"You can sort out the car service and send someone to pick me up," she added in a mollifying tone.

The man's nostrils flared, but he backed away from the car. "I must insist on collecting your name and contact information," he said to Leo.

"Hang on, now." Leo wasn't really sure what was happening. He had not agreed to take this woman to Battery Park. If he did that, it was going to be three hours before they got home. They had maxi pads to buy and pasta to eat. And the mutt was going to need to pee—Leo had only been going to pick up Gabby and Max from the play, dip down for a quick architecture tour/sibling bonding sesh, and head back home. Dani would be home soon, and she would start worrying about the damn dog.

Which with anyone else Leo would give a fuck about, but they needed Dani. She was the closest thing they had to family.

The woman with the not-plastic face looked at him and said, "Please." She whispered it so quietly, he was pretty sure Gabby couldn't hear. Certainly her dude-posse outside the car couldn't. And after she said it, she bowed her head and covered her face in her hands. Almost like she was already giving up.

Shit.

Damsels in distress. They did it to him every goddamn time.

He tipped his head back and sighed.

Both Gabby and Miss Cake Topper must have interpreted that sigh as the surrender it was, because they both started exclaiming, thanking him like he had just saved a kitten from drowning or some shit. They didn't understand that this afternoon, *he* was the one drowning.

But, resigned, he pulled out his phone so he could text Dani before they set off—and also to figure out where they could stop to let Max out to pee after they dropped their posh passenger at her yacht since it was going to take them approximately a hundred years to get home.

"You've saved me. Thank you." She spoke loudly enough that she drew the attention of the man she'd called Mr. Benz. He had moved away from the back door of the cab, but now he stuck his head fully in the open window on the front passenger side. He looked at the woman for a long moment and transferred his gaze to Leo.

"I think it important that you know the identity of your passenger, sir."

Yeah, he wanted to say. *That would be good. Because I'm guessing Miss Cake Topper isn't actually her name.* The woman started speaking rapidly to Mr. Benz in German, but he ignored her, raising his voice so Leo could hear him over the woman's protests—you didn't need to speak German to know she was annoyed. "You are transporting Her Royal Highness Marie Joséphine Annagret Elena, Princess of Eldovia."

There was a squeal from the back seat.

"And in case it matters," Mr. Benz went on, "I shall inform you that Eldovia has always embraced absolute primogeniture."

"Absolute what?" Gabby asked.

"It means the firstborn inherits the throne, regardless of gender. No tinkering with succession laws necessary in *our* country." He sniffed and performed the slightest of shudders. "Her Royal Highness has been heir to the throne from the moment she was born. Which means, my good sir, that you are transporting the future Queen of Eldovia."

Gabby started shrieking.

For his part, Leo rested his head—it was suddenly too heavy to hold up—on the steering wheel and groaned.

Chapter Two

She had almost made it!

If Marie were a different sort of person, she would have cursed here. *Goddammit,* she'd almost made it!

She wasn't naïve enough to think she could pass as a normal person. Not with Torkel and Mr. Benz hovering over her like a pair of helicopter parents at kindergarten drop-off. But she had hoped her rescuer would classify her as merely a run-of-the-mill rich person.

But, really, what did it matter? This man was going to drive her to the boat, and she would never see him again. She had nothing to be ashamed of. She had just given a speech at the United Nations, for heaven's sake! And done a rather fine job of it, too.

So she straightened her spine and lifted her chin. "It is vitally important that I reach the North Cove Marina by seven o'clock."

"So you can go to a party on a boat," the taxi driver said flatly. He was not impressed.

She could try to explain that it wasn't merely a party, but

actually, if things went well, a stealth trade meeting. But, again, what was the point? Mr. Benz's wildly unnecessary little speech had probably already cemented this man's opinion of her. So she merely said, "That is correct."

He didn't bother hiding his disdain as he reached across her and handed Mr. Benz a business card through the open window, and as they pulled away from the curb, his lip physically curled upward.

His other passenger didn't seem to share his disregard, though. "Are you really a princess?" she exclaimed.

Marie turned to look at the girl though the open window in the clear plexiglass partition that separated the front seat from the back. "I am."

"Eeee! That is so *amazing!*" The girl threw up her hands. She must be the driver's daughter. They had the same thick, dark hair, though hers was in a ponytail and her dad's was a shaggy mass of waves. Matching light-brown eyes were topped with heavy, unkempt brows. Thick, pillowy lips that would make the girl a knockout when she got older made her dad . . . a knockout currently. His were surrounded by a beard that was a little too long to be called stubble, but only just. She found this tendency of some American men to hover perpetually in limbo between clean-shaven and bearded rather vexing.

"What was the name of the country again?" the girl asked.

"Eldovia."

"I've never heard of it."

"Lots of people haven't. It's a small nation located between Switzerland and Austria."

"Near Italy, or up closer to Germany?" the man asked.

She was impressed. Most Americans thought of Europe as one indistinguishable mass. They knew the UK and perhaps the boot of Italy, but that was usually as far as their geographical knowledge went.

"Germany—we're north of Liechtenstein."

"Eldovia." He snorted. "It sounds like one of those fake Hallmark Channel countries."

"Leo!" the girl protested. "That was so *rude!*"

Marie smiled. She was pretty sure that was *exactly* what most people thought, but she'd never met someone who actually said it to her face.

Also: *Leo*. The girl had called the man by his first name. Was this perhaps *not* a father-daughter relationship? She glanced at the man's—Leo's—hands on the steering wheel. No ring.

Not that that mattered in any way.

"It's a real country," she assured them. "It has a long, rich history. But it *is* absurdly picturesque. The Alps will do that."

"And it has a princess!" came the voice from the back seat.

"And a king, too," Marie said, enjoying the girl's unbridled enthusiasm. That wasn't an emotion she had a lot of experience with, at least not lately, and it seemed . . . like fun. She twisted in her seat again so she could see the girl.

"Is he an evil king who tries to thwart your happiness at every turn?"

Marie startled herself by laughing. She wasn't normally easy with laughter. She also wasn't sure how to answer the question. Her father *was* thwarting her happiness, but he wasn't doing it on purpose. And he wasn't evil.

"Or! Is he a kindly king?"

"I think he's a sad king." It was out before Marie could think better of it, but it was true.

The girl scrunched up her face as if *sad* was not an entry in her mental reference book under *Kings, types of.*

"Why is he sad?"

"Because my mother died." And with her, any opportunities for unbridled enthusiasm.

Normally, Marie would never speak like this. But these people seemed safe. They were so far from her life at home, both geographically and in every other way, that she felt like she could tell them the truth.

"Oh! I'm sorry." The girl opened her mouth like she was going to say more, but closed it.

The man was looking in the rearview mirror. He'd been doing that a lot, and Marie was fairly certain, given the length and frequency of those looks, that it wasn't traffic he was examining. "Why don't you introduce yourself, kiddo?"

"Right!" The girl arranged her face into a parody of seriousness and said, "I am Gabriella Ricci, and I am pleased to make your acquaintance, Your Majesty." Then she placed her hands on the sides of her skirt, moved the fabric out, and dipped her head. She was trying to curtsy while buckled into the back of a cab.

Marie bit back a laugh. "You don't have to bow or curtsy, you know. Or call me anything like that."

"Because I'm not your *subject*?" The unchecked delight from the back seat was back.

So was the disdain from the front: the man—Leo—snorted again. Marie refrained from saying that technically, it was her father who had subjects.

"Stop being rude, Leo!" Gabriella rolled her eyes at Marie like they were sharing a secret. "This is my brother, Leonardo Ricci." She sniffed—she could give Mr. Benz a run for his money on that front. "Leo's not very . . . refined."

Brother.

Well.

That was interesting.

Someone laid on a horn, and it jolted her back to reality. Reality where it was *not* interesting that Leonardo Ricci was Gabriella Ricci's brother and not her father. Because it was neither here nor there.

Reality where—she glanced at her watch, the very symbol of her mission this evening—she had exactly thirty-four minutes to make it to the boat before Lucrecia, a kind of neo-Euro Lady Gatsby ruling over her boatful of beautiful but empty revelers, lifted a champagne flute and trilled *bon voyage!*

Goodness, she was anxious. No, *scared.* Full-on scared. Her pulse started hammering in her neck so hard it made her throat ache.

Part of her wanted to miss the boat. To have tried her hardest but failed.

But then she conjured her father's face at the cabinet table—his scowl.

The sad king.

"How much longer to you think it's going to take? Can you go any faster?"

WHO THE HELL *was* this lady?

Well, Leo *knew* who she was—a literal *princess.*

He extended one arm, palm up, toward the gridlock visible as far as he could see out the windshield. "Does it *look* like I can go any faster?"

Jesus. Just when he'd started to think that Her Royal Highness—she was an actual fucking *Her Royal Highness*—with her sad father and her kindness to Gabby, had a human side, she'd reverted to form. She'd gotten all stiff and prissy and entitled. Or maybe she was just delusional. Maybe she thought a fairy godmother was going to appear, harness some magical flying horses to his cab, and off they would fly to catch the yacht.

"It is vital that I reach that boat before it leaves." Her tone was clipped. Prim. Dripping with privilege.

He was driving a *princess* to a party on a *yacht*. That was not something he had a ton of patience for. "God forbid you should miss your night of champagne and caviar, Your Most Exalted Majestyness."

He was being mean, but he didn't care. There were people in this world for whom twelve bucks for pasta on a Thursday night was a splurge. How dare she elbow her way into his cab—his *off-duty* cab—and start ordering him around?

She pressed her lips together and looked out her window.

Fuck. That was the problem with him—he *did* care about being mean. Not a lot. But enough for a splinter to work its way under his skin—his mother had raised him too well.

But *not* enough to apologize. So he just kept driving. There was a shortcut they could take around Washington Square Park.

"Leo! Give me your phone!"

"Why?" He tried to limit screen time. Dani had told him that too much of it fried kids' brains, and Dani knew about that stuff.

Other than *Minecraft*, which he and Gabby played together—he couldn't help himself; it satisfied his frustrated architectural ambitions—he gave her an hour a day.

"I want to look up Eldovia."

Sighing, he tossed the phone through the partition.

A few minutes later, she was reading aloud from Eldovia's Wikipedia entry. "'Though not diversified, Eldovia's economy is robust. It is dominated by manufacturing—of luxury watches primarily, but also of power tools.'"

He chuckled. Power tools and Rolexes? Maybe this woman's huge watch was a homegrown specialty.

"Then there's a whole bunch of stuff about winter tourism, but it all says 'Citation needed.'" Gabby laughed. "I could totally update this right now. I'd be like, 'Source: Actual princess of country.'"

Gabby chattered happily for a while, not noticing that the princess was growing increasingly agitated. She was trying to hide it—she had her right hand resting over the watch on her left arm, and she'd shift to the side and subtly peek at it from time to time.

Leo should keep his mouth shut. Gabby was happy—and talking, which was a minor miracle. But eff him if he didn't suddenly want this princess chick to be happy and talking, too. "You gonna do any New York Christmasy stuff while you're here? Skating at Rockefeller Center?"

She looked startled. "No. I don't think so."

"Not a skater?"

"Actually, I'm quite a good skater. I just don't think I . . . will have time."

"Too busy yachting?" He said it teasingly this time.

She smiled, but it was a pathetic one. "Something like that."

A sad princess to go with the sad king?

Well. Not his problem. He turned south on Sixth Avenue, reasoning that he might be able to shave a few minutes off their trip if he wound his way through Greenwich Village—he knew its maze of nonstandard streets like the back of his hand. Her Most Royal Prissiness didn't know what good service she was getting here.

Soon enough, they were crossing the West Side Highway with five minutes to spare. He slowed to a halt as they reached the end of the road. You couldn't drive right up to the docks from here, so she would have to walk the rest of the way.

As Leo watched the princess heave a shaky breath before getting out—he would have thought, given how impatient she'd been, that she'd have leapt out of the car—he realized she was not looking forward to this party.

"We'll walk you the rest of the way." He got out and opened the back door for Gabby. Max barked. "Not you." But then he rethought that. There was a little circular park ahead of them, and the beast could pee there. "All right. Come on, everybody."

He leashed the dog, locked the car, prayed his illegal parking job wouldn't earn him a ticket, and they set out, walking briskly.

"I don't have any money," Princess Marie said, loping along beside him. "But do you have a card with your direction? I will ensure that you're compensated."

Your direction? What century was this woman living in? "There's no need to pay me." Though if he got a ticket, he was totally sending it to her. So he took the card she produced from the world's tiniest purse, a diamond-encrusted thing that dangled from a strap around her wrist.

He didn't like the idea of her alone in New York with no money. "Do you have a credit card?"

She shook her head. "I wasn't planning . . . I just have my phone."

He heard what she wasn't saying. She wasn't a person who normally had to sully herself by carrying cash or credit cards.

They'd reached the park. He handed Max's leash to Gabby and pointed down the path to where a big boat was visible. "Gabby, make sure Max pees. I'll be over there, and then I'll be right back."

"Bye!" Gabby's farewell was drowned out by a foghornlike noise. Despite being dragged out to Long Island on the reg by Dani, Leo didn't know boats. But to him, that sounded like the kind of noise a really big boat might make before it departed.

Marie must have thought so, too, because she squeaked in protest and started jogging.

He matched his pace to hers, even as he dug in his pocket for a card. He carried cards with his cell number on them. He had a handful of regulars—passengers he'd hit it off with and who called him personally when they needed a ride.

He had *not* hit it off with the princess, but he pushed a card into her hand anyway. "You call me if you need a ride home or if you get into any trouble."

"Thank you." It was more breath than words—she was panting from the running.

"You know which boat it is?" he asked.

"It's called *Lovely Lucrecia*."

Was he mistaken or did he detect a hint of derision in her tone? Like she knew Lucrecia and found her not very lovely?

"There." He pointed. The *Lovely Lucrecia* was still docked. It was glowing with lights, and laughter and conversation spilled from its deck.

"Thank you so much," she said again, her voice all quivery. She gave him a little wave and set off toward the boat.

He was about to turn away, but he noticed the back of her dress was gaping. It looked like it was supposed to be tied up with a pair of pink ribbons that were hanging loose. She'd worn some kind of fur cape thing in the cab, but she was currently carrying that over one arm, leaving her back exposed. Almost bare.

"Wait. Your dress."

"Oh! Oh, I forgot!" She ran back to him and turned around. "Please, can you do it up?" Her voice was even shakier than it had been before, and as she lifted one of the ribbons as if to hand it to him, her hands trembled.

This was definitely not just a party. Something else was going on.

"It's like an exercise shoe," she said. "Tighten the laces and tie a bow at the top."

She was misinterpreting his inaction as confusion. And it was, in a way, just not over the mechanics of how her dress worked.

He was confused by the fact that she was apparently so afraid of whatever awaited her on that boat that she was shaking like an abandoned baby bird. But also by the sight of her almost naked back, covered with a fine sheen of sweat despite the cold evening air.

Clearing his throat, Leo moved to tighten the ribbons. He tried not to touch her skin. His clumsy hands were too rough for her. But he couldn't entirely avoid it.

Goose bumps rose on her back when his hand brushed her spine. Goose bumps *and* sweat. That was . . . something.

He tied off the bow, hoping he'd done a decent enough job. There was probably some kind of royal knot he didn't know about. "There you go." His voice had gone low. Husky. It was those goose bumps. They were fucking with him. But those goose bumps only meant she was cold. His brain was moving slowly for some reason, so the realization was belated. He sincerely hoped the boat was heated. Who had yacht parties in the winter?

Absurdly rich people, apparently.

He took the fur cape from her and settled it over her shoulders. Then he patted her back—which was now covered with silky fur. Somehow, nonsensically, that fur didn't seem as soft as her actual back had been.

She didn't move, just stood there under his hand, breathing hard.

The boat made another of those jarring hornlike noises.

Galvanized, she smiled at him—*really* smiled. And unlike when they'd been seated side by side in the car, he was looking at her straight on.

She had dimples. Two of them.

"Thank you, Mr. Leonardo Ricci. You saved the day."

Before he could think how to respond, she whirled, hitched up her skirt, and took off running.

He watched her run all the way down the dock and leap onto the *Lovely Lucrecia* just as it started moving.

He stood there for a while, watching the boat begin to inch out of the marina.

Hell, he probably would have stayed there until it was out of sight had Gabby not appeared beside him, Max yapping excitedly at her feet.

"That was wild. Also, I'm starving."

"Let's get Ralph's on the way home."

"Yay!" She slipped her hand into his—which was not something she did much anymore—as they walked back to the cab. Oh, his heart. His heart could not take any more of this little-sisters-growing-up business.

He squeezed her hand as hard as he dared.

Chapter Three

*A*n hour and a beer later—he *had* stopped for some Moretti; that was *his* treat—Leo was feeling a little more in control of things.

Gabby was almost done with her pasta, Dani had demolished a big salad—they always brought their own dinners to Thursday-night K-drama—and Leo was eating random bits of leftovers from the fridge at his place.

"You guys done?" Dani paused the show. "Ice cream time?"

"Yes!" Gabby said. "What kind?"

"I have Half Baked, Triple Caramel Crunch, and"—she made a face at Leo—"Vanilla."

Gabby and Dani shared an affection for ice cream with tons of crap in it, and they both mocked Leo for his simple tastes.

"You are so *boring*, Leo!" Gabby said.

"I don't like stuff in my ice cream!" he protested. "You can't even taste the ice cream through all the texture in yours! Is it ice cream or trail mix?"

Dani served Gabby a huge bowl that was half of each of the

crazy flavors and gave herself a small serving of each. Then she emptied nearly the entire pint of vanilla into Leo's bowl and began scooping hot fudge she'd heated in the microwave onto it.

Leo used to protest the elaborate ice cream course that always followed their Thursday-night dinners—those pints of fancy ice cream were pricey. And when that didn't work, he tried to bring his own grocery-store-brand vanilla, insisting that his taste buds didn't know the difference. But Dani wouldn't hear of it. She just kept serving him Häagen-Dazs Vanilla Bean topped with hot fudge that came from a mason jar with a cutesy, hand-lettered label on it that almost certainly came from one of the bullshit new shops in an area a little south of here that idiot gentrifiers persisted in calling "SoBro."

Eventually, Leo had stopped protesting the ice cream situation. He'd been worn down by Dani's cheerful stubbornness, her fancy hot fudge, and her Korean dramas.

"Thanks," he said as Dani slid him his bowl. Then he said it again. He had no idea why. "*Thanks.*"

Dani must have known why, though, because instead of giving him shit, which was their usual mode of expressing their friendship, she tilted her head, looked at Leo for long enough to make him uncomfortable, and said, "You're welcome."

Leo was, officially, the super of this building, but without a doubt the real caretaker of his little family of two was Daniela Martinez. His second-cousin-in-law. Soon to be *ex* second-cousin-in-law—just as soon as she managed to finally get rid of her shitty estranged husband. About the only thing Leo's second cousin Vince had going for him was that it was through him they'd met Dani. It had been Dani who'd pulled strings not only to get Leo and Gabby a place in the building, once it became clear that they weren't going to be able to hang on to the family house, but to arrange the super gig to help them afford it.

He owed her so much, it made his throat hurt.

"So what's with this robot?" he asked, settling in to his role as K-drama skeptic. Their latest show was bonkers. "Is she actually a robot?" He was guilty of not having paid one hundred percent attention. The subtitles on this one were small, and his brain was tired. It kept zooming back to . . . pink ribbons.

"Well, she's pretending to be a robot, but there *is* actually a robot, too," Gabby said.

"Imagine the love triangles that could ensue!" Dani said.

Gabby and Dani high-fived. The two of them were romantics, though Dani, whose horrific divorce-in-progress had inspired her to swear off love, would never admit it.

"Leo's going to hate that!" Gabby said gleefully.

Whatever had made Leo add that weird, extra thank-you to Dani squeezed on his chest again, making it hard to take a full, deep breath. He lived for Thursday nights—for this. For unstructured time with his sister and their neighbor. Leo could make good money if he'd wanted to drive Thursday nights. And Gabby and Dani didn't need him for their soap operas. But these nights had come to mean everything to him. On Thursday nights, they kicked back, joked, and ate ice cream. On Thursday nights, he stopped worrying—temporarily.

He even liked the shows they watched, though he pretended not to because it amused the other two. Their current was called *I Am Not a Robot*. It was ridiculous. But he was sucked right in to the tale of the boy who was allergic to skin contact and the girl who was pretending to be a robot, or . . . something. He needed to start paying attention to this episode, or he was going to get left behind.

"Tell me again about the princess!" Dani commanded when the episode was over, and that was all it took to set Gabby off. She gestured wildly as she retold the tale of their afternoon adventure.

Leo's chest was still doing that squeezing thing. This was not how he had ever foreseen his life turning out. For so long after his parents died, he had been focused on what he had lost—his parents, college, his carefree youth. His existence had become about stanching the bleeding the accident had caused in their lives. About surviving and making sure Gabby not only survived, but thrived. Dani had been part of that first aid kit, initially. She still was. But now she was a true friend, too. A best friend, though they didn't talk about their relationship in those terms. They didn't talk about their relationship at all, which Leo frankly appreciated.

The point was, as hard as the past two years had been, he and Gabby were lucky. They had each other. They had Dani.

They had their ridiculous Korean soap operas and objectionably elaborate ice cream.

He remained uncharacteristically sentimental as the evening wound down. It wasn't until after he'd tucked Gabby in that Leo remembered they'd forgotten to stop for her . . . supplies.

Dammit. Just when he was feeling like he had things moderately under control.

"Kiddo," he whispered. He'd been sitting on a chair next to her bed. On nights he wasn't driving, she liked him to sit with her while she fell asleep. Though she was probably too old for that, he indulged her. She'd had nightmares after the accident, and this was such an easy thing to give her. It didn't cost anything. And it was good for *him* to sit there after she fell asleep and listen to her steady, strong breathing, surrounded by her girlish clutter. It reminded him what was important.

She wasn't quite asleep yet tonight, which was the only reason he'd spoken to her.

"Hmm?" She sighed. She was so sleepy.

"We forgot to stop for maxi pads." He congratulated himself on getting the words out without his voice doing something weird.

"It's okay," she whispered. "I wadded up some Kleenexes. I'll be okay until the morning."

Jesus Christ on a cracker. She *wadded up some Kleenexes?* Why hadn't she reminded him?

Probably because despite her casual delivery of the news, it had taken a lot for her to tell him in the first place. And then, with the ball in his court, he'd done nothing.

He debated getting up and asking Dani to come over while he ran to a bodega. Or maybe Dani herself had some supplies she could donate to the cause. But Gabby was almost asleep. So he stroked her hair and said, "Okay," even as he beat himself up for forgetting something so important. He would get up before she did tomorrow and get some from Dani or from the store.

HOURS LATER, LEO was nodding off over one of his mom's old mystery novels—like her, he preferred his fiction with a side of murder rather than the romance Gabby favored—when his phone buzzed.

Well, eff him. It was Her Majesty, the cake topper. **Hello. This is Marie. You collected me earlier and drove me to the marina?**

As if he could forget. As if he picked up princesses every day and delivered them to yachts. Also, *collected*? He typed a reply. **Everything okay, Your Royalness?**

She sent an eye-rolling emoji. Apparently even though her vocabulary was that of an octogenarian, she knew emojis. It was quickly followed by a question. **Did you mean it when you offered to pick me up?**

Well, shit. He'd meant it at the time, when he was face-to-face with her fear. Or face-to-face with her unnaturally soft, goosebumpy back. Or maybe both.

Did he mean it at eleven thirty after a strangely emotional day he just wanted to be over?

He sighed. He wasn't the kind of guy who made false promises.

> **Leo:** Sure. It will take me a while to get there, though.

> **Marie:** That's fine. I'm still on the boat, but we're headed back to shore.

> **Leo:** Enjoy your champagne. It will probably take me forty minutes, maybe a little longer.

> **Marie:** No champagne for me. I was working, and now I'm hiding in the bathroom.

Hiding in the bathroom? Huh? Another text arrived before he could think what to say in response. **Thank you, Mr. Ricci. You are a good man. I will meet you where you dropped me off.**

Luckily, Dani would still be up and would come over and sit

with Gabby. Dani was an English professor who, as far as Leo could tell, worked pretty much all the time including into the wee hours of the morning. So he heaved himself out of bed, got dressed, and went across the hall to knock on her door.

He had a princess to rescue.

Again.

MARIE WAS HIDING in the bushes.

Hiding. In. The. Bushes. The way Americans sometimes wrote sentences with a period after each word in order to convey the gravity of a situation used to seem excessive to her. She was beginning to understand.

She tried to tell herself that hiding in the bushes was better than hiding in the bathroom. In the bushes, you could cry without anyone seeing.

She'd cried in the bathroom on the boat, after Philip Gregory informed her, in no uncertain terms, that Gregory Inc., the largest independent watch retailer in North America, would not be reconsidering its decision to drop the Morneau brand from its inventory. And that, moreover, if she and her people didn't leave him alone, he was going to have to pursue legal action. He'd had too much to drink, even though the boat had just departed, and he'd started ranting about restraining orders. She had watched enough American legal shows with her mother to know that she had done nothing to warrant a restraining order—a *restraining order*, for heaven's sake—but his vitriol had stung nevertheless.

And of course Lucrecia had heard everything. Witnessed Marie's humiliation.

And said some choice things to her friends while freshening

her makeup in the same bathroom Marie was hiding in. She'd *known* Marie was in there—Lucrecia didn't miss anything.

It's a pity her mother is dead. She was a lot more at ease at these sorts of things.

That one barely stung. It was true, after all.

But then they'd moved on to how no one would have her except poor Maximillian, who *had* to have her.

Can you imagine? Someone like him marrying someone like her?

You're forgetting that she'll be queen one day, Lu.

Of that ridiculous little country. Honestly. At least Max looks the part.

Marie was stuck in her stall, feet pulled up so they wouldn't recognize her pink pumps. She'd selected them to match the pink ribbons in her dress, but on the ground here in America they seemed girlish and unsophisticated. Like the kind of shoes someone who was pretending to be a princess would wear.

At least here in the bushes, she didn't have to listen to any of that. There was only the ambient noise of the city, soothing in its anonymity.

And the sound of a car pulling up, an engine being cut, a door slamming.

Was it her knight in a yellow taxi?

She rose from her hiding place—and he was *right* there. A foot from her.

"What's wrong?" he said urgently.

"Nothing. I was merely . . . hiding." She tried to laugh. It didn't work.

"You've been crying."

"No, no." But why lie? This man didn't know her. And she had already, bizarrely, told him about the sad king. "Yes."

He didn't press her, just led her to the cab, opened the back door, and gestured for her to climb in.

"May I . . . sit up front with you?" She didn't want to be a passenger, or at least not the anonymous, sit-in-the-back kind. She wanted to sit next to him and notice things about him, like how he wasn't wearing a ring and how deftly he navigated the city streets that were, to her, an endless maze of urbanization. That was part of why she had called him instead of Torkel.

She wanted him to spirit her to the hotel, to make her white lie to Mr. Benz—*He's driving me back to the hotel after the boat docks*—be true. Mr. Benz had no doubt assumed she meant Philip Gregory, but she hadn't technically lied.

Because *he* was here. Mr. Leonardo Ricci was here.

He shrugged, slammed the back door, and moved to open the front one.

She slid in as gracefully as she, *not* her mother's daughter in this regard—Lucrecia had been right about that—could, given the volume of her dress. It took some wrestling with the thing for her to get settled in.

He pulled away from the curb. "Where to?"

"The Plaza." She braced for more of his disdain but none came.

He simply said, "Rough night?"

"You could say that."

He nodded, seeming to accept her vague answer as evidence that she didn't want to talk about it.

This was also why she had called him. She had known, somehow, that he would be silent. Let *her* be silent. He would not pepper her with questions or crush her with his unarticulated disappointment. No, that would come later.

He was wearing a red-and-gray flannel shirt, and the sleeves were rolled up to his elbows. Even though the car was an automatic, he rested his right hand on the shifter. He had a very nice forearm. It was muscular and lightly dusted with hair the same rich dark-brown shade as on his head. And it was very . . . veiny. Which was an odd thing to find appealing, but she did.

Soon she began recognizing landmarks that suggested they were almost back at the hotel. "Would you mind stopping so I can get something to eat? I . . . wasn't able to eat at the party." *On account of all the crying in the bathroom.* "There's a sandwich shop that's open all night on the next block. The concierge recommended their pastrami on rye, and I have never tried pastrami on rye."

"Can't stop there," Leo said gruffly.

"Why not?"

"I don't do Fifth and Fifty-Eighth."

"You don't *do* Fifth and Fifty-Eighth?" She laughed incredulously. What a curious man.

"I can drop you off a block up, and you can walk back down."

He was in earnest. "Isn't that rather hard in your line of work? To boycott a major intersection?"

Leo's face remained utterly unchanged as he said, "My parents died in a car accident on that intersection two Christmases ago."

He might as well have slapped her. Tears—they were still so close to the surface after the evening she'd had—gathered in her throat. She opened her mouth, and closed it.

But why not just tell him? She had told him a great deal already today, including that her mother had died, just not when or how. "*My* mother died *three* Christmases ago. On December twenty-second. Breast cancer."

That got his attention. He looked at her sharply. "That's why your father's sad."

She nodded. "Though it doesn't look like sadness from the outside. I'm not sure why I called it that before."

"What does it look like?"

"Anger." *Paralysis.*

He nodded like her answer made sense to him. "Is he going to be angry at you about what happened tonight?"

"Probably. Or disappointed, which is actually worse."

"You want to talk about it?"

She started to say no, she didn't want to talk about it. But to her shock, that wasn't exactly true. So she found herself telling him about the meeting gone bad. About how much Eldovia needed the Gregory account.

He listened and asked nonsnarky questions. "So this Philip Gregory guy owns a big watch store chain?"

"He owns twenty shops nationwide, which perhaps doesn't sound big, but the luxury watch industry isn't like others. It's so expensive to produce these watches that we rely on orders from retailers to fund production runs."

"So you download the risk onto the little guy."

His grin showed he was jesting, but he wasn't wrong. "You could say that, except Philip Gregory is not a little guy. When we had his account, it was seventeen percent of our GDP. We'll lose a thousand jobs without it. And that's out of a population of two hundred and twelve thousand."

Leo whistled.

"Indeed. He didn't want to meet to discuss his decision, so I was supposed to . . . ambush him, if you will. He was not pleased about it. Not only did I not get to talk to him, he made a bit of a scene."

"How did you know he'd even be at the party?"

"There's a Euros-in-New-York crowd. Everyone knows one another. He's not European, but he's Euro-adjacent, and the hostess of the party—that would be the Lucrecia the boat was named after—is a major society figure within the New York scene."

"Lucrecia. That's not a name you hear much on this side of the pond."

"Lucrecia von Bachenheim. Her father is a cousin to the Austrian archduke. Also, she's a total bitch."

Marie almost laughed with glee. A day ago, she would never have uttered those words in front of another human being. She wouldn't even have allowed herself to *think* them. But there was something about being with Mr. Leonardo Ricci in a taxi in the middle of the night that inspired boldness.

"Lucrecia von Bachenheim?" he echoed. "Does she have one hundred and one Dalmatians?"

"Excuse me?" That must be a pop culture reference she wasn't getting.

He shook his head. "So this Gregory guy snubbed you, Lucrecia von Bachenheim is a bitch, and you were stuck on a boat where everyone was being horrible to you."

She laughed. "Yes, that about sums it up."

Marie didn't feel so bad about it all anymore, though. Talking to Leo, an outsider who wasn't tied up in either her mission or what was or wasn't proper for her to be doing or saying, had been therapeutic.

When the hotel was in sight, he slowed down. "This pizza place is good. Let me get you a slice."

"Let me get *you* a slice. It's the least I can do."

He pulled over and parked the car—the street was relatively empty this time of night. New York City had given her the impression that it was always wall-to-wall with people and vehicles, but that wasn't the case right now.

"Actually . . ." He was leaning over the center console and peering out her window, staring rather intently at something called "CVS." It seemed to be some sort of pharmacy, albeit an absurdly large one. He was close enough that she could smell him. He smelled like . . . oranges. She always associated oranges with America. The California trips of her youth.

He pulled back abruptly. She missed the oranges, suddenly and sharply.

"Can you do me a huge favor?" he asked.

"Yes." She was startled by the immediacy of her answer. Normally, she didn't trust easily. She did her duty but hesitated over giving more than that.

An even more startling realization?

She would do pretty much anything Mr. Leonardo Ricci asked her to.

AND SO LEO found himself perusing the feminine hygiene aisle in a Midtown CVS at one in the morning with the princess of Eldovia.

"Gabby got her first period this week," he said as they slowed to a stop in front of a bewildering display of products. "She needs, uh, supplies. I should really take some home for her. I tried to google earlier to figure out what to buy, but there was so much . . . choice."

Marie's dimples came out, and they were just so fucking *cute*.

She scanned the shelf. "There are so many different products, it can be confusing even for those of us who've been doing this awhile." The skin between her eyebrows wrinkled and she started walking, seeming to dismiss the area immediately in front of him. "I'm going to say she probably doesn't want tampons yet."

Jesus, Mary, and Joseph. Could everyone just stop saying *tampons* in front of him?

"I think the best thing to do is to purchase an assortment of pads and liners, and she can see what she likes. There *is* a lot of choice." She pulled a box off the shelf and turned it over. "More than at home. And I don't know all these brands—we have some different ones in Europe." She was concentrating like he'd asked her to diffuse a bomb. He couldn't help but appreciate the seriousness with which she was approaching her assignment, even as it amused him.

After a minute or two of silent perusal, Marie picked a few items off the shelf, some in boxes and some in plastic bags sort of shaped like boxes. "This should be good to start."

She led him to the checkout, plunked her booty on the counter, and when he got out his wallet, said, "Let me buy them."

"You don't have any money," he reminded her.

She expelled a little breath of frustration. The dimples came back out, but they were fake dimples this time. Not the same ones she'd flashed at him earlier. He didn't know how he knew the difference—he just did.

"Good evening," Marie said to the clerk. "I don't suppose if I told you that I am a member of the Eldovian royal family and am staying a block up—at the Plaza—and pledged to return tomorrow to pay for these items that you would extend me credit this evening?"

The cashier rolled her eyes.

"She's an honest-to-God princess," Leo added, not because he was going to let her pay. He wasn't. But he was enjoying watching her try to conduct a retail transaction on royal credit. She had even turned up an accent that Leo had only heard flashes of before. Previously, she had spoken mostly unaccented, if slightly formal, English.

"We don't take princess credit at CVS, honey." The clerk examined her manicure as she spoke.

Laughing, Leo laid his credit card down.

"I'm sorry!" Marie exclaimed as they emerged onto the street, where it had just started to snow. A big, fat flake landed on one of her absurdly long eyelashes. "I can't even buy you a slice of pizza." The dejection that had crept into her tone would have been comical if it hadn't seemed so sincere.

But she quickly perked up. "Oh!" It was hard keeping up with her. Her mind moved fast, and her expressive face reflected the rapid cycling of emotions she seemed to engage in. Princess Marie did *not* have a poker face. Leo settled in to try to get a read on her current mood. Her eyebrows were high. She was buoyed by whatever thought had popped into her head. "You could come up to my suite, and we could order room service!"

He didn't answer right away—because it was tempting. Which was ridiculous, because whatever kind of food she would order at the Plaza would not be his kind of food. It would be like Dani wasting the fancy ice cream on him. And anyway, he needed to get going so Dani could go home.

He had been silent too long, though, because Marie gasped as if a horrible thought had just occurred to her. "I didn't mean . . ." She looked at the ground.

"You didn't mean what?"

Leo had a pretty good idea what she was thinking, given the way she was looking everywhere but at him, but bastard that he was, he wanted to hear what she, with her prim, formal way of speaking, would say.

"Well . . . I understand from American television that the late-night invitation to visit one's quarters can be a . . . euphemism for other activities."

One's *quarters*. He bit back a laugh. "Really?" He schooled his face to look confused. "What activities?"

She blushed. It was apparent even in the diffuse glow of a New York night.

"Ohhhh . . ." He let the single syllable stretch out over his tongue. "You mean a booty call." He remembered those. Barely. That was another thing that had mostly fallen by the wayside since his parents died. He opened the pizza parlor door for her, but she made no move to enter.

"A *what* call?"

"Booty call. *Booty* being American slang for *ass*." He let his eyes drop. Her dress was too puffy for him to see hers, but he let his gaze linger in the general vicinity anyway. Princess Marie whatever whatever—she had a lot of names—was a very pretty woman. Those dimples. Those eyelashes. If he were a betting man, he'd say everything under that dress was probably equally enticing.

He would also bet that she never got told that. That people deferred and kept her at arm's length. Or were catty bitches like Cruella De Vil Von Whatever.

It was nice sometimes to be appreciated for one's . . . assets. So he let his gaze linger even longer, and because Marie was oddly innocent—he wasn't sure if it was because of her royalness or her non-Americanness—waggled his eyebrows to make sure she got the point. "You'd better get your royal booty inside, Your Splendidness. We're letting all the cold air into this fine establishment. I'm sorry to say I'm going to have to pass on the booty call, but pizza's on me."

He wouldn't have thought it possible, but she blushed even more. And the dimples—the real ones—came back as she brushed past him.

At the counter, she treated the dilemma of what kind of slice to get like it was an exam question. In the end she settled on one pepperoni and one mushroom, which he approved of. She'd surprised him. He would have thought she'd go for vegetarian, or some chicken-with-white-sauce nonsense.

"Will you join me?" she asked as the guy behind the counter heated her slices. "We can sit in the window and watch the snow."

He really wanted to. Which was a little unsettling. But it didn't matter, because he couldn't. Responsibility was something he could have a tiny vacation from, but that was the extent of it. "I have to go home. I have a neighbor sitting with Gabby."

"Oh, yes! How selfish of me! I'll take my pizza to go."

Outside, the snow was picking up. She paused in the middle of getting into the cab and looked up at the sky.

"You like winter?" he asked.

"It reminds me of home."

That wasn't really an answer. "Are you homesick?"

"That is a complicated question, Mr. Ricci." She flashed another of her sad-princess smiles. "But I do love the snow. It's different here, against the backdrop of the city, but lovely in its own way."

When they pulled up to the hotel, Marie stuck out her hand for him to shake. "Mr. Ricci. You rescued me twice today. And what's more, you've made it so I've ended this evening on a pleasant note. I would not have thought that possible. Thank you."

She was so formal in her speech but so earnest. He took the proffered hand.

It was really fucking soft. Just like her back.

He nodded meaningfully at the CVS bag. "Thank *you*." Then he lifted her hand to his mouth and kissed the back of it.

Because why not? A cabdriver from the Bronx didn't have that many opportunities to spend the evening with a princess, and when he did—especially if she was a sad princess—he should probably seize the chance to kiss her hand.

The moment passed, and as she took her hand back, she peered out her window at the hotel. Something about the way she held herself changed. She stiffened a bit. Then she did the chin-lifting thing he now recognized as one of her signature mannerisms. Except whereas before he'd thought it signaled snootiness, now he suspected it was more about steeling herself. Working herself up to duty.

He knew that feeling.

She reached for the door handle, but he held out an arm to stop her. "Hold on. Wait here."

"Why?"

"Because I'm going to come around and help you out." He jogged around front, offered her an arm, and helped marshal her dress. She'd had trouble getting out of the car at the pizza place, but she'd triumphed over the voluminous fabric before he could help.

When they were standing face-to-face, she asked, "Did you help me out of the car because I am a princess?"

Uh-oh. Was she going to get pissy? Had he offended her feminist sensibilities? He was a sucker for a damsel in distress, but it wasn't like he thought women actually needed men to help them out of cars and through doors and shit. If he had ever harbored such an antiquated notion, five minutes of eavesdropping on Gabby and her friends plotting world domination had cured him of that. No, it was just a reflex. Manners.

Leo had a sudden memory of his dad pulling up in front of Our Lady of Mount Carmel on Sunday mornings. He would always drop them off before parking, and he would run around the car to help Mom out, taking extra care with her church dress.

The princess was waiting for an answer, so he told her the truth. "Nope. I don't give a crap about the princess stuff. I just did it because my dad always did that for my mom. Especially when she was dressed up."

She huffed a small laugh that seemed to signal delight. It was cold enough that a puff of steam accompanied it. It called to mind a dragon. If dragons had dimples.

"Mr. Ricci, I have a proposition for you."

Chapter Four

*I*n the light of day, the princess's proposition seemed ludicrous. It was like she'd put the whammy on him. Which was funny, because in fairy tales—Gabby still made Leo read to her from a compendium their mom had given her—the princess was always the one being passively manipulated either by an evil stepmother or by a prince kissing her awake or some shit. In stories, the princess was never the one doing the whammying.

But here he was pulling up to the Plaza on a Friday morning to pick up the goddamn heiress to the throne of Eldovia like he was one of those frogs turned into footmen.

But not, he told himself, because there had been any whammying. He was *not* under her spell or anyone else's. It was the cash. She'd offered him five grand a day to be her chauffeur. For three days. That was a *ridiculous* amount of money. Enough for him to get caught up on their bills, buy Gabby some nice Christmas presents, and still have a chunk left over for her college fund. Or maybe they'd throw caution to the wind and take a vacation—he'd just been thinking how much he could use one. Gabby's last day of school was today, and she didn't have to be back until after New Year's, so maybe they'd head down to Florida and heat their bones for a week after Christmas.

Marie was waiting out front as she'd said she would be—she had insisted he not park and come inside to get her. Leo was impressed: a self-sufficient princess. She'd been that way last night, too, when she'd dismissed her handlers.

But hang on, now. There was no call to get carried away admiring a freaking princess because she could take an elevator in a luxury hotel downstairs by herself.

She hadn't seen him yet—she was probably expecting the taxi. It didn't seem right to honk at her, so he got out of the car.

"Oh!" she exclaimed. "Good morning!"

She hurried toward him. There was no formal gown today. She was wearing a royal blue . . . dress? Coat? It was like it was both at once—a dress made out of heavy material that was belted like a coat. She had a huge brooch on one shoulder, a green stone the size of a Ping-Pong ball surrounded by diamonds. She also wore black tights, black leather ankle boots, and black leather gloves. The sleeves of her coat only went to her elbows, but the gloves were long, fancy-lady ones.

His first thought was that she looked amazing. The dress-coat thingy, which was fitted on the top and had a swingy skirt, was the same color as her eyes, and it made them pop. As she took his hand and smiled at him as he guided her to the passenger side of the car, it was like looking into a pair of sapphires.

Okay, maybe he *was* in danger of being whammied if he was comparing her eyes to gemstones.

But no. Because his second thought was eminently practical:

she wasn't dressed warmly enough for the weather. Last night's snow had brought with it a serious dip in the temperature. But it probably didn't matter. For all he knew, she was going to be inside all day. He had agreed to act as her chauffeur for the rest of her trip, but he hadn't inquired as to what that actually meant.

"Let's go!" She seemed a little on edge.

"Just you?" He had half expected the big beefy guy to be tagging along.

"Yes!" She seemed surprised by her own answer.

But she was also incorrect, because Jack Sprat and the Terminator suddenly appeared.

She glared at them.

They glared back. Well, the butler dude did. Mr. Benz—Leo remembered his name because he'd wondered if he was related to the fancy car brand. The bigger one whose name Leo did not remember—he suspected he was the princess's bodyguard—was busy scanning their surroundings.

It seemed that the butler and the princess were having a staring contest. She lost. After she looked away, she allowed herself to be led a few feet away, where the two of them had a short, whispered argument in German. Mr. Benz must have won it. He marched back over to the car and, without speaking to Leo, opened the backseat door and slid in. Marie huffed a defeated little sigh. Leo wasn't sure why she didn't just dismiss these dudes like she'd done yesterday, but, hey, not his problem. He was just the chauffeur.

Even though she didn't have a big poufy gown on, he helped her into the car under the big guy's watchful eye. After the bodyguard, too, had gotten into the back, Leo turned to Marie. "So, where to, Your Loftiness?" She rolled her eyes but smiled a little, even as there was a distinct sniff from the back seat. "Erickson's on Fifth Avenue at East Fifty-Third. It's a watch shop."

"But not Philip Gregory's watch shop." He probably wasn't supposed to know about Philip Gregory, but since she was carrying on as if they didn't have an audience, he was gonna do the same.

Another, louder sniff was issued by the butler. She turned and glared at him.

"Maybe I should have come in the taxi," he said. "We could have closed the partition."

"If you"—she pointed over the seat—"are going to insist on being here, I must ask that you remain silent." Her words were right, but her tone was all wrong, if her aim was to assert her independence. Her voice was soft, and she sounded like she was asking, not telling.

But again, not his concern.

Marie returned to Leo's question. "Erickson's is not owned by Philip Gregory. I'm going to spend the morning visiting some of the other retailers that stock our brand. I have appointments at three establishments between now and noon. So that should leave enough cushioning for you to make your two o'clock engagement, I believe?"

"Your Royal Highness," the butler said, "we have another car. We don't need to—"

She turned around, looking very much like a mother about to issue an *If you two don't stop, so help me, I will pull this car over* threat. It was kind of funny the way the two of them seemed to communicate with no words.

When she won that round, Marie repeated herself, more

firmly this time. "I wouldn't want you to miss your two o'clock engagement."

His two o'clock "engagement" was *The Wizard of Oz*. When the princess had made her proposal last night, he'd told her he could clear his schedule of everything except Gabby's play this afternoon and counterproposed that she pay him only for half a day. She'd refused. He was planning to argue it with her later.

"All right then." He started the car, and off they went.

"What happened to the taxi?" Marie asked.

"I don't own it. The medallion belongs to a family friend. So I drive it, but I effectively pay for the right to do so." It was owned by one of their old neighbors on Belmont, in fact, an old drinking buddy of his dad's.

"Like rent?"

"Exactly. He gives me first dibs on schedule, so I can have the cab whenever I want, but I have to pay him whether I'm using it or not. If I'm not using it, someone else can drive it." In addition to first crack at the schedule, Leo suspected that Mr. Bianchi was undercharging him, though he insisted he wasn't. One of these days, Leo was going to have to push the issue. While he'd been willing to swallow his pride enough to take the handouts necessary to get him and Gabby on their feet after the accident, he wouldn't live on charity forever.

"So this is your car."

"Yep."

He eyed the backseat passengers in the rearview mirror, irrationally wondering if they could see through the lie. The big guy was looking out the window, but the butler was staring right back at him.

The car was a rental, but he didn't want to get into it with her—she'd probably insist on paying for it. He'd calculated that renting a car would cost about the same as what he'd have to pay for the use of the taxi, and the black sedan seemed . . . classier. More fit for a princess.

Not that he cared about any of that shit. "So are these meetings going to be stressful like last night?"

"Oh, no." She did seem more at ease today, despite her annoyance over her royal babysitters. "These are courtesy calls. I'll chat with them about upcoming orders, see if they have any concerns or technical questions."

"You can answer technical questions about watches?"

"I can."

Leo racked his brain to think of one. He wasn't sure why. "Is it true that some people have weird magnetic fields that make watches stop?"

She laughed. It was more gratifying than it should have been. And it was getting a little easier to ignore her handlers since the butler had quit his sniffling. "I can't answer that one. Our watches don't have batteries."

"They don't?" He'd never heard of that.

"High-end watches don't. You have to wind them. They're powered by a spring and a series of gears."

Well. He felt like an idiot. They had an old clock in the apartment that had been his great-grandmother's, and it needed to be wound—which was why it was always stopped. "Wind the clock" wasn't something that ever made it to the top of his to-do list.

"But it's a good question. And actually, you don't have to wind all our watches. Some of them are self-winding. They have a rotor that captures energy from normal movement and transfers it . . ." Just when it seemed like she was ramping up, she trailed off. "Sorry. I get carried away. I studied engineering at university."

A princess *and* a brainiac. It figured. "Where was that?"

"Oxford."

Of course.

"Did you attend an institution of higher learning or undertake any postsecondary studies?"

He swallowed a chuckle. The formal way she sometimes spoke tickled him. "Nope."

That was another lie. He'd spent four years working toward a bachelor's degree in architecture at the City College of New York—which he'd chosen over the other, more prestigious colleges with architecture programs in the city because it was much cheaper. He'd only been going part-time, though, so when the accident happened, he only had two years' worth of actual credit. He couldn't see his way through to sticking with it. He had student loans already, which was one thing when it was just him, but he couldn't have a negative income *and* keep a roof over Gabby's head.

Maybe someday he'd be able to return, although at twenty-five he already felt too old to be an undergrad.

Anyway, it wasn't like he'd been very good at it to begin with. He'd been holding on by his fingernails, his status as the first Ricci ever to attend college the only thing keeping him going some days.

He didn't want to get into it with Princess Smartypants,

though. Especially with the audience in the back seat. He didn't need her pity. He didn't need *anyone's* pity.

Leo deflected Marie from talk of "institutions of higher learning" by pointing out a few landmarks along the way to her first appointment.

"I wish I had time to do all the New York things," she said with a hint of wistfulness. "Eat all the New York food."

When he pulled up in front of the watch shop, and the back-seat passengers unbuckled their seat belts, the princess's battle with the butler resumed. "I'm going in alone."

"But Your Royal Highness—"

"If you come in with me, it looks like I need a babysitter." Mr. Benz started to say something—Leo was pretty sure he was poised to argue that she did, in fact, need a babysitter—but she held up a hand. "Is that the message we want to send about me in my role as the business representative of the Morneau brand? And do I have to remind you that right now, that's what I am?"

"Why don't you text me five minutes before you want us to pick you up?" Leo said, suddenly wanting to help her cause. He leaned over her lap to open her door for her. He would have gone around to help her out as a proper chauffeur should—he was probably scandalizing her butler—but he reasoned that would just give Tweedledum and Tweedledee time to get out, too. He made a little "hurry up" motion only Marie could see.

The dimples came out, and she was out of the car before the butler could issue another objection.

So was the bodyguard, though. Damn. But he could hear him assuring Marie that he was going to stand outside the store.

Well. Leo had done his best. He hit the gas.

"Where on *earth* are we going?" Mr. Benz asked.

"We're going to get the princess a bagel."

THE MORNING STARTED well enough, despite the fact that Marie hadn't managed to elude Torkel and Mr. Benz. In retrospect, she'd won their early-morning argument regarding her chaperonage way too easily. She'd been naïve to think they would simply let her drive away with Leo.

Still, once she had Mr. Benz settled down, she'd enjoyed talking with Leo. And she was on familiar ground today. Work was a lot more comfortable for her than parties. When she called on a store owner as a representative of the Morneau line, they had an automatic topic of conversation. There was a social aspect to these calls, of course, but their primary purpose was business. It was important, her father believed, for the family to make occasional appearances in the shops of their retailers. He used to do it himself. Before he became the sad king and stopped doing anything besides peevishly issuing orders.

Marie was also happy to be alone in the shops. While it was true she'd never done these kinds of calls before—her father had still been doing his job last time there'd been a New York trip—she knew the Morneau line inside and out. Literally: she could pop one of those suckers open and talk crowns and mainsprings. Or if the retailer wanted to discuss marketing, or demand forecasting, she was well versed in those areas, too.

Having Mr. Benz, or worse, Torkel, hovering called attention to the princess part of her role—the unearned part, in other words. She truly believed she was serving the mission better by presenting herself as a knowledgeable businesswoman who happened to be a princess and not vice versa.

After their fraught first stop, they got into a routine, one that Mr. Benz begrudgingly accepted. She'd go in, Torkel would stand sentry outside, and Leo and Mr. Benz would drive off—to get her a treat! That was the astonishing part.

It had been a cup of coffee and a bagel after the first one, and after the second one, a big biscuit Leo called a black-and-white cookie, which was apparently a signature New York treat. He, it seemed, had taken to heart her wish to "eat all the New York food."

In addition to doing good work, Marie was having *fun*. Leo was charming and easy to talk to. He had a kind of . . . not optimism— he was too grumpy for that—but a good-humored stoicism that was contagious. She was even letting herself forget the ugly confrontation with Philip Gregory from last night. Letting herself believe that perhaps there was a solution they hadn't thought of yet. Or at least allowing herself to ignore the problem for a while.

And driving between appointments, Leo had been a wonderful tour guide, pointing out iconic buildings but also dispensing interesting anecdotes about their history. With some extra time before her final appointment of the morning, he took her to nearby Madison Square Park. They strolled with Torkel and Mr. Benz following a good distance behind them. It was *almost* like being alone.

"Is Madison Square Garden around here?" she asked as they passed a large Christmas tree set up in an empty fountain. "It's one of those iconic American buildings you always hear about."

"It used to be, but the modern incarnation of Madison Square Garden—which, incidentally, is its fourth—is in Midtown. I can drive you by it if you like, but it's not much to see."

"It's funny how sometimes the most famous places aren't."

"But if you're into iconic New York City architecture, this is a good spot." He pointed over her shoulder. "That's the Flatiron Building."

"Oh, I know the Flatiron Building!" She turned.

"Most people do, even if not by name."

"No, I mean I studied it. My degree specialization was in solid materials and mechanics, but I took a course in the history of civil engineering. Apparently wind load was a challenge for this building, because it's so narrow."

"It was one of the early steel-frame skyscrapers," Leo said. "Apparently there was a lot of interest from the public as it went up. It's also kind of unique in that it's limestone on the bottom and terra-cotta on the top."

"How do you know all this?"

He shrugged and stuck his hands in the pockets of his jeans. "Architectural history is kind of a hobby of mine." He pivoted ninety degrees. "Check out this one—the MetLife Tower. It was built in 1909. It was originally clad in marble but was refaced in limestone in the sixties."

"It would have been something to see them getting the marble up there in 1909."

"It would, wouldn't it?" He spoke to her but he was still looking at the building. "Supposedly the architect was inspired by the bell tower on the Piazza San Marco."

She considered that. "I don't see it. Yes, they're both towers, but isn't the St. Mark's tower made of brick?"

"Yeah."

"Have you been? You're Italian, yes?"

"I am—well, Italian-American. My grandparents on both sides were the first generation. So my parents spoke Italian, but Gabby and I just know slang and swear words, mostly. But, nope, I've never been to Italy." He looked almost wistful as he gazed at the tower. Was he thinking about his parents? Or about the ancestral homeland he'd never been to? "The light from this tower is on all the time," he went on. "The old MetLife advertising used to say it was 'the light that never fails.'"

What a delightful little fact. "Mr. Ricci, I'm not sure I believe you when you say that architectural history is a hobby of yours." That dislodged his attention from the building. He shot her a bewildered look. She grinned. "I think the situation is better characterized by saying that you are complete architecture nerd."

He barked a startled laugh. "Guilty as charged. But what about you, Your Royal Watch Engineering Highness?"

She smiled. The titles he made up for her were highly amusing.

"Anyway, the reason I brought you here is that the MetLife Tower was one of the only buildings with a clock face on each side. It still is. Even watch nerds don't see *that* every day."

What a treat—and more evidence of Leo's thoughtfulness. "I imagine those clocks are digital now, but given the era of construction, I suspect they would originally have been powered by an electric motor that would have been mounted near the clockworks. There was a New York–based clock company, in fact, that was . . ." Leo was smirking at her as she was ramping up her self-winding clock lecture. She tried not to smile as she pretended to be offended. "I for one think enthusiasm over topics one cares about is an attractive trait."

"I agree."

"You might call it nerdiness, but people with passion are much more interesting than those without it." She was still teasing him, but she actually believed that.

"Still not arguing." He held up his hands and grinned. "And *you're* the one who called *me* a nerd, remember?" He bumped his shoulder against hers, and she ignored the little noise of disapproval Mr. Benz made from behind them. "I think maybe it takes one to know one."

She gave up her mock outrage and smiled at him. When was the last time she'd teased someone and been teased in return? Certainly not since before Maman died. It was rather wonderful.

And so it was on a cloud of satisfaction that she strode into her last appointment of the day—at Marx on Madison.

And experienced the karmic correction to all that good cheer.

She could tell right away it wasn't going to go well. She introduced herself to a clerk who disappeared into the back. When the woman returned, she announced that Bernard Marx, the owner, would be a few minutes. That itself was a red flag. Although Marie had said earlier that she preferred to be seen in this context as a businesswoman and not a princess, people usually deferred to the princess part. She was typically ushered immediately into a private office and, well, fawned over, to be honest.

Here, she was left to drift around looking at watches under glass—for quite a bit longer than "a few minutes." She found the Morneau section. It was . . . small. She'd thought this store stocked four models, but she saw only two. Hmm.

"Your Royal Highness." Mr. Marx finally emerged from the back, his face unreadable.

She extended her hand for him to shake. "Please call me Marie."

She had no idea how her father handled this bit of protocol, and Mr. Benz would be having a heart attack if he could see her, but the Americans, despite their obsession with fame, had thrown off the monarchy, and she wanted this man to see her as a colleague.

"I'm afraid something has come up, so I only have a few minutes to speak with you."

"That's quite all right. I'm here primarily to see if you have any questions, to discover if everything about the Morneau product line is proving satisfactory."

"I have seventy percent of my stock available online. I'd like it to be one hundred."

She blinked. He was going to get right into it, was he? Many of the luxury brands didn't allow third-party retailers to sell their products online, Morneau included. It was impossible to guarantee the authenticity of the product unless they were sold through licensed dealers. There were probably ways around that—like selling direct-to-consumer themselves, but her father wouldn't budge on the matter.

"Rolex will never allow it," she deflected.

Marx shrugged. "I never thought Rolex would make a smart watch, either. We're trying to make some room for luxury smart watches, so we're trimming our traditional inventory."

She sighed. She couldn't give him the things he wanted. Only the sad king could make those kinds of promises, and he never would.

Marie tried to smooth things over, to be diplomatic, but soon the uncomfortable appointment was cut short when Marx announced they would only be ordering two models, not the usual four, next year.

She had been foolish to think she could shrug off the Philip Gregory debacle. Gregory had been a major blow, but this was part of the same trend—a real trend, not a blip. And one her father, with his blind insistence on tradition, refused to acknowledge.

Which would make it her fault. She hadn't tried hard enough. She hadn't made them see reason.

She emerged from the store blinking back tears. It was a beautiful day, cold and sunny. She forced herself to take a deep breath of the chilled air and tilted her head back. A little bit of blue sky was visible between the buildings. The same sky as at home, even if you could only see a thin slice of it here.

Torkel was by her side in an instant. "Is everything all right, Your Royal Highness?"

She didn't want him. She wanted—

"What's wrong?"

Leo. Who was here. "You were supposed to text me," he said as he jogged up. He looked annoyed. "You were supposed to give me a five-minute warning so I could drive around."

Yes. They had agreed on that protocol because he couldn't always find a place to park nearby.

When she didn't answer right away—she was too busy forcing back those tears that were threatening—he jogged around to stand in front of her. She tried to look away, but he kept moving, tracking her gaze with his body, and eventually crouching down so he could get right in her face. In the bright sunlight, his eyes were the color of American pennies. "Hey," he said quietly, low enough so that Torkel and Mr. Benz, who was hurrying down the sidewalk toward them, couldn't hear. "What's wrong?"

She cleared her throat. "Nothing."

"Bullshit."

Marie sucked in a startled breath. No one spoke to her like that. She laughed a little. Because how absurd was it that no one ever said anything negative in front of her? But then, to her mortification, a rogue tear escaped, and then another, because she was going to have to tell Mr. Benz, and ultimately her father, that not only had she not gotten the Gregory account back, but Bernard Marx was planning to halve his order.

And those things were probably just the beginning.

What was she going to *do*? It was one thing to be facing these problems, quite another to be facing them alone.

And she was alone, in this, and in . . . everything. Her father was happy to issue directives, but since her mother had died, he'd simply stopped working. He spent most of every day in his library, but Marie had no idea what he did there. He talked a lot at meetings of his advisory council, but he didn't actually *do* anything. She had been trying to pick up the slack, since she'd come home from university, but she constantly felt as though success was slipping through her fingers.

"You know what? I suck at this emotional shit," Leo said, arresting her rising panic. He pulled her away from Torkel and Mr. Benz, waving them off when they tried to follow. He steered her under the awning of a restaurant next to Marx's and lowered his voice to a whisper. "But I *do* know there's a fantastic deli not too far from here that serves pastrami on rye."

She smiled and swiped at those mortifying tears. She begged to differ on his claim that he wasn't good at "this emotional shit." He seemed very good at it, in fact, judging by how he had read her face, and by the way he'd treated his sister yesterday. But she didn't want to embarrass him. And . . . "I'm still dying to try pastrami on rye."

"Any chance you can get rid of these guys?" Leo jerked his thumb at Torkel and Mr. Benz. "Frankly, they're making me nervous. Have you ever tried to buy cookies at Dean & DeLuca with a butler?"

She stifled a laugh, even though she didn't know what Dean & DeLuca was. "He would hate to be called a butler. He's my father's equerry."

"I have no idea what that means."

She pondered his question: Could she get rid of her handlers? Technically, of course she could. She'd done it last night by channeling her mother. It was just that last night, she hadn't really thought about it. In her panic to get to the boat, she'd just *done* it.

This morning, she was back to her usual self: the girl who tried to do her duty in all things. And perhaps also the girl who didn't want to anger her father. Mr. Benz would obey her, when it came down to it, but he was loyal to her father above all. Everything she did here was being reported back to him, of that she had no doubt.

But how much worse could Mr. Benz's report get? She'd already failed with Philip Gregory, hired a stranger to drive her around, and failed to talk Marx out of reducing his order. By comparison, a little lunch seemed like nothing.

And she really wanted to have pastrami on rye with Leo Ricci. So she lifted her chin and answered his earlier question. "Yes. I will dismiss my associates."

He grinned. "That's the spirit."

What followed was an entirely predictable argument she could have had in her sleep.

"It's merely lunch," she said when they—even the usually silent Torkel didn't like the idea of her going off without them—began to object. "It's no different from walking down the hill to eat at Angela's." Which was something she hadn't done in ages, come to think of it.

"Begging your pardon, Your Royal Highness, but it's not like that at all," Mr. Benz said. "You can't expect the freedom you have at home to be available to you here."

"But no one knows me here," she countered. "Most people here have never even heard of Eldovia."

"It's not 'most people' I'm worried about," Mr. Benz said, and he and Torkel swung their attention to Leo, who was watching the face-off from a few feet away.

"Oh, for heaven's sake. If Mr. Ricci wanted to kidnap me or murder me and throw my body in the river, don't you think he would have done so in the middle of the night last night?" She turned to Leo and called to him, "Are you planning to kidnap me or murder me and throw my body in the river?"

He smirked. "Well, now that you mention it, I *could* do with some ransom money."

That set Mr. Benz off again.

All right. Enough. She shouldn't have allowed herself to get drawn into arguing, as if she were a teenager begging for a curfew extension. She raised a hand to halt Mr. Benz's monologue and notched her chin a little higher. "Gentlemen. Given that my schedule is clear for the rest of the day, I will be having lunch with Mr. Ricci. He will escort me back to the hotel, and I will see you there later. Good afternoon."

She turned and hitched her head slightly to Leo to signal that they should start walking. He was trying—though not very hard—to suppress a grin.

He waited until they were a little ways down the block to say, "I didn't want to mess up your dramatic exit, but the car is actually in the other direction."

She laughed. Because that was funny, but also because she was *free*. For just a little bit, but that wasn't nothing. It was a sunny winter day in New York City, and she was going to have lunch with a grumpy-nice man. How normal. How unremarkable. How *wonderful*.

"Are we going in the right direction for the sandwich place?" she asked. "Do we have time to walk there? I'm sure they're standing there watching me, and I'd really rather preserve my triumphant exit."

Leo chuckled. "We're going the right way, but you're not dressed warmly enough. It's a good four blocks."

"I'll be fine."

He took off his hat, which was a black, knit toque with ISLANDERS embroidered on it in white.

"No, no, I can't take your hat. I assure you—"

He jammed it on her head.

"I'm from the Alps!" She tried one more protest. "I'm hearty."

"I'm from the Bronx," he countered. "I'm heartier."

She had no argument for that. He was definitely . . . heartier than she was. So when he held out his arm and said, "Your pas-

trami on rye awaits, Your Honorable Ladyness," all she could do
was take it.

"So what's the verdict?"

He should probably have let her take more than a bite before
he started pressing her. Or at least given her a chance to properly
chew and swallow her first bite. But Leo found himself wanting
the princess to approve of his deli. As much as he hated to admit
it, he'd been thrown for a loop to find her on the verge of tears
outside that last shop. He'd wanted to cheer her up.

It was worth remembering, though, that cheering up princesses wasn't in his job description. They would finish up here,
and he would take her back to the hotel and head up to Gabby's
play.

When she'd conquered her bite, Marie set the sandwich down
and looked at it skeptically. "It's very good, but it's so big. You
Americans always put so much meat on everything."

So big. So much meat. He chuckled. He couldn't help it. As
much as he'd had to grow up in recent years, he still had an inner
thirteen-year-old.

"What is amusing?"

Leo shook his head. "You are." Marie was such a strange mix
of competent and innocent. Smart and oblivious. Some of it was
probably due to the fact that English wasn't her first language—
though she spoke it perfectly—but some of it, he suspected, was
just her.

She frowned. So, not wanting her to feel self-conscious, Leo
said, "So what happened at the last store? Do I need to go back
there and kick someone's ass?"

Marie's forehead smoothed as she smiled. Mission accomplished. "No. I was merely upset because I found out we're losing some more business."

He had achieved his goal to make her smile. And he didn't really give a fuck about the Eldovian watch industry, so he had no idea why he opened his mouth again and said, "You want to tell me about it?"

It turned out she did.

The luxury watch industry, he learned as they ate, was facing some trouble. Production runs, as she'd mentioned before, relied on preorders. That made sense to him. You weren't going to want to manufacture really expensive products unless you knew there was a market for them. The rest? Not so much.

"So why not make a smart watch?" he asked. "Something classier than the Apple Watch. Every idiot has one of those these days."

"My father thinks it's a fad that will pass. He sees it as sullying the brand. Morneau watches have been made entirely in our country via traditional methods for more than two hundred years. He takes pride in that."

Leo could see it, and oh how he wished Apple everything was a fad. New York was full of zombies too lazy to take their phones out of their pockets, marching through the city staring at their wrists. But . . . "I don't think smart watches are going anywhere. But anyway, do you have to make them? Can you license the Morneau name? Like, you know the Fitbit?"

She nodded. "It never really took off in our country—I feel as though when you have the Alps, you don't need a device to tell you how much to walk—but I know it."

"My mom had one of the early models. She thought it was ugly, though. But there were these Kate Spade band things. Like a container you wrapped around the actual Fitbit. She thought one of those would class it up. But they were expensive." Well, they were expensive to the Riccis. For all he knew, Kate Spade was actually a ghetto brand when you were a royal. But his point stood, so he pressed on. "My dad kept telling her to go ahead and buy one, but she said she couldn't justify it. She told us to go in on it for a Christmas present for her. But then—"

Ah, *shit*.

This was why he avoided talking about his parents. He could force himself to keep his shit together to do it with Gabby because he knew it was important for her to be able to talk about them. But on his own? No. He just didn't go there.

Because it made his throat close up.

Her hand was on his, suddenly. She was wearing nail polish. He hadn't noticed that before. It was super pale pink—almost beige. It was an ugly color, actually.

A princess with ugly nails. The thought anchored him. Stopped the drowning.

She was going to say something. Something kind, probably. He didn't want that, so he rushed to finish the story. "One day—just a normal day; it wasn't a special occasion—my dad came home with one for her."

"Oh, that's so—"

"The point is"—he hated to interrupt her, but he couldn't let her get all moony over his parents, or he'd embarrass himself by joining her—"the addition of the Kate Spade part made all the difference. I don't know if it was the brand—the idea of it—or if it made an actual aesthetic difference to her. But she wore that thing every day until she . . ."

"Until she died?"

Leo was too tired, suddenly, to fight Marie's quiet empathy, so he nodded. "I almost had her buried in it, actually. But then I thought maybe Gabby might want it. But *then* I thought . . ."

Gah. Shut *up*. Why was he babbling like this?

"Then you thought what?" she prodded gently. She was looking at him like she genuinely cared about the answer.

"Well, I don't know. She was only nine. Who puts a Fitbit on a nine-year-old? They're supposed to run and play because they like it, right? Not because they need something to remind them to get up and move their bodies. So I thought I'd save it for later, but . . ." Well, fuck it, he'd come this far. "She's older now, but the last two years have been kind of a crash course in parenting a girl in the modern world. I see all this . . . shit she tries to live up to. Already! Like, she wants to wear all this makeup. For what? So she can look like she's twenty-five? We had a major blowout this past Halloween because she wanted to be an angel and I stupidly agreed, not realizing that what she actually wanted to be was a *Victoria's Secret angel*. She's eleven! Where is that coming from?"

"The patriarchy."

He barked a surprised laugh but she was right. He wouldn't have said it like that, but watching—watching closely—as Gabby grew up had opened his eyes to a lot of shit he had not seen when he was just her semiabsent big brother. "So anyway, with the Fitbit, I thought no way am I giving her anything that's so . . . prescriptive, you know? That tells her to be a certain way or to do things a certain way?" God. He needed to stop talking. "Listen to me. I'm—"

"A good brother. A good surrogate father."

The ugly-nailed hand was back on top of his, squeezing this time.

He'd been going to say "an idiot," but hell, he'd take her assessment, even if she was incorrect. He was *trying* to be those things. Did that count?

Leo cleared his throat and pulled his hand back. "Anyway. We were supposed to be talking about your watches. Maybe you should consider making a smart watch."

Marie nodded. "And selling our products online. Or at least letting retailers do so. That was another thing Marx was upset about."

"You don't sell your watches online?" That was hard to believe.

"Most luxury brands don't."

"Is that some kind of weird exclusivity thing? Because no offense, that's just dumb. I'm the last guy to climb on board any tech trend. I still read the physical newspaper and listen to records— and not in a hipster-ironic way. But I'm not your market. How much do your watches cost?"

"They start at around ten thousand US."

He snorted. "And where do they end?"

"The top model right now retails for four hundred thousand US."

He blinked. This was where the term *sticker shock* came from, he supposed. He had an idea that there was a category of watches—like Rolexes—that were really expensive, but he'd had no idea. "Well, to my mind, not selling your stuff online is stupid. Stubborn-mindedly ignoring a huge market. It's like . . ." He cast around for a metaphor. "I don't know, it's like the Islanders not selling Islanders merchandise." He pointed at his hat, which was lying on the table next to her.

She burst out laughing. He laughed along with her. It felt good.

He simply wasn't capable of wrapping his mind around spending so much for a watch, even if you had that kind of money to burn. "No offense, Your Exalted Loftiness, but in my opinion, this is all a load of shit." He reached for her hand. He'd noticed earlier today that she was wearing the same big watch as yesterday. It was a good-looking watch, silver—platinum?—with a few small diamonds on the face, but not worth anywhere near what it no doubt retailed for. "This is a watch, not the cure for cancer. You can't just—oh, shit. How did it get so late? I have to go."

Goddammit. It was nearly quarter to one. He had to get up to Gabby's school. He was cutting it close, but if he left right now, he'd be fine. Probably. Thankfully, Dani was on Toto chauffeur duty today, so he didn't have to stop home first.

"Of course." Marie pushed back from the table. Leo felt bad that she'd barely made a dent in her sandwich, so he hustled to the counter for a take-out container and boxed it up for her. Outside, he paused, trying to think what the most efficient way was to get her back to the hotel. Uber there, drop her, and then go back for his car? Or go to his car first?

His indecision must have betrayed his anxiousness, because she said, "I'll get a cab from here."

"No, you won't." It wasn't her fault he'd gotten carried away rambling about Fitbits and age-inappropriate Halloween costumes. "Come on. The car's on our way. I can drop you and probably still make it."

"Probably?" she echoed. "No, thank you. You can't miss this play."

Her bossy tone was sweet but also a little irritating. "I won't. Come on."

Marie dug her heels in as Leo tried to take her arm to get them moving.

So much for sweet. In fact, she was back to radiating that entitled snootiness she'd been wrapped in when she first got into his cab. He rolled his eyes. "Listen, Princess McRolex, unless you want to attend an extremely amateur production of *The Wizard of Oz* in which *all* the actors are Munchkins, do me a favor and—"

"I do."

Huh? "You do what?"

"I do want to attend an extremely amateur production of *The Wizard of Oz* in which all the actors are Munchkins."

He hadn't actually been inviting her. She must have realized that.

"I have no competing engagements, and it sounds like a delightfully normal way to spend the afternoon."

He opened his mouth to argue, but closed it. Fuck it. It was easier to just take her. Faster. Plus Gabby would love it.

"Well, then." He held out his arm and she took it. "We're off to see the wizard."

Chapter Five

They pulled up in front of the school with five minutes to spare. His phone rang—again—as he parked haphazardly.

"Hi," he said, picking up Dani's call as he held the passenger-side door for the princess. Dani had been calling for the past twenty minutes, but without a Bluetooth system in the rental, he hadn't been able to pick up while driving. "I'm here, I'm here."

"Okay, good. I was starting to fear you weren't going to make it."

"I'll be there in two minutes."

"I've saved you a seat. On the left about halfway back."

He glanced at Marie, who was looking around like she was a tourist in Times Square instead of on an unremarkable street in the Bronx. "I need two seats." He was met by silence, so he added, "I, uh, brought a guest."

"Oh my god, you brought the princess of Eldovia, didn't you?"

"I did not," he said as he grabbed the very same princess and started towing her toward the entrance.

"Oh my *god*!" Dani went on. "I can't believe—"

He hung up, turned to Marie, and said, "Remember when you were running for the boat?"

She nodded.

"This is my version of running for the boat."

And bless her, she nodded again, more vehemently this time, and took off ahead of him toward the door.

Inside, Leo spotted Dani right away. She was standing near the back—she must have moved from her original spot—guarding three chairs. The silver lining of their late arrival was that he didn't have to do more than quickly introduce the two women before the lights went out. And even that he didn't really have to do because after he'd said, "This is my friend, Daniela Martinez," Marie preemptively stuck out her hand and said, "Marie Accola."

The lights went out, and after some scrambling and whispering from backstage, some high-powered fans started imposing a "tornado" on Kansas.

The show was pretty great, and not just kid-great. The school was a technology magnet, so Leo hadn't had high hopes, but whatever the play lacked in terms of show-biz skills of its actors, it made up for in production values. Beside him, Marie gasped audibly when Dorothy woke up and a cool trick of light and engineering saw the black-and-white sets of Kansas replaced by the splendor of Oz.

He was acutely aware of Marie's reactions to everything, even though most of them were more subtle than that gasp. She clapped and laughed, and when he sneaked a glance at her, she was rapt. He would have thought she'd be accustomed to . . . he didn't even know. Opera? Ballet? Whatever it was rich people did when they wanted to be entertained. But it seemed that this modest, home-spun production truly delighted her.

And then the Lollipop *Guild*—not League—appeared along with the rest of the Munchkins. And there she was, his Gabby. It was probably all the mucking about he'd done the last two days in memories best left undisturbed, but something turned over in Leo's chest. He was so fucking proud of her. Which was dumb, because it wasn't like this was an actual achievement. She was just on the side of the pack, dressed in neon colors holding an oversized piece of cardboard made to look like a lollipop.

She was just standing there.

But, she was *standing there*. Alive and thriving—mostly. Smiling through the nerves that were clearly visible—to him, anyway—on her face. Growing up so fast.

The one thing he hadn't been prepared for when it came to his role as a pseudodad was the wrenching contradictions that came with the gig. He wanted her to grow up, yet he didn't. She was a child, yet not a child. She'd had her first period, yet there she was, part of a crowd of Munchkins, looking younger than her years.

As the Lullaby League wrapped up their welcome to Dorothy, that Aidan punk stepped up. Leo leaned forward in his seat. There was a pause.

Say it. *Say it.*

"We represent the Lollipop Guild."

Leo expelled the breath he hadn't realized he was holding. Then Gabby, smooth as anything, handed Dorothy her lollipop and said, "And on behalf of the Lollipop Guild, we welcome you to Munchkin Land."

His hands shot up into the air. He wasn't sure if he meant to clap them over his head or to pump his fists in victory, but of course neither was appropriate for this context. This wasn't an Islanders game. The show had moved on and there were people behind him, people who were probably just as excited about their own kids' theatrical triumphs.

So he lowered his arms, trying to be smooth. And failing, judging by the fact that both Dani and Marie were looking at him with amusement. Dani actually snorted.

The rest of the play was boring. What could he say? Other people's kids were boring.

But at the end, even though the play had been a nonmusical version, everyone came out and sang "Somewhere Over the Rainbow." Gabby was back, smiling and singing and waving the cardboard lollipop she must have gotten back from Dorothy.

When Leo leapt to his feet along with the rest of the crowd in a standing ovation, he had never meant anything more.

As the applause died down, Marie leaned over and whispered to Leo, "Can we keep the princess thing quiet?"

He turned to her but didn't answer. His eyes raked over her body in a way that made her feel . . . funny. "We can try," he finally said.

Was she not dressed appropriately? She'd tried to dress more businesslike than princesslike this morning, but it seemed that coat dresses were not quite the thing in America.

"I don't want to upstage your sister, or any of the other children," she whispered, and it was true—or part of the truth. The rest of it was that she was having so much fun. The students' enthusiasm for the play, the parents' pride—it was all contagious.

And, goodness: Leo. He could be such a grump, but he was practically oozing love for his sister.

"Yeah, well, my sister is the one likely to bust your cover. She hasn't had the easiest time socially since she started middle school, and having an honest-to-God princess come see her play is probably the best thing that's happened to her all year."

Daniela handed Leo a bouquet of flowers. "We're supposed to meet them in the lunchroom."

"Thank you for this," Leo said, his tone fervent. "I should have thought of this."

"That's why you have me." Daniela must be Leo's girlfriend. Marie had been so fixated on the fact that Leo was Gabby's brother and not father, but of course why would a handsome man like him not have a girlfriend?

And why was that disappointing?

Marie reminded herself that Leo's romantic attachments or lack thereof were no concern of hers, had absolutely no bearing on her life.

Some awkwardness settled as they made their way to the lunchroom. Munchkins and flying monkeys and all manner of creature were milling around, reunited with proud parents. Marie's awkwardness wasn't only that she didn't want to out herself as royalty, but that she felt her otherness. Her apartness. She wasn't a parent. There were no children running up to hug her—and she probably wouldn't have known how to act if there were. There was no place for her in this circle of warmth and goodwill.

She tried to tell herself this was nothing new. She was accustomed to feeling like she didn't belong—like she wasn't charming enough, or graceful enough, to meet people's expectations. It happened all the time. At parties—like last night on the boat. Anytime she had to dance. When she was trying to get her father and his advisers to let her allocate some time and capital to what they snootily called her "do-gooder projects."

But it actually made sense that she felt like an outsider *here*, at this middle school in the Bronx. She *was* one, objectively speaking.

So why did that fact make her so sad?

Marie watched Daniela approach Gabby. She had the dog that had played Toto—and that had been in the taxi the other night—on a leash. They embraced, and soon they were talking easily. Dani didn't have a child here, either, but she had an ease about her that Marie envied.

Her brooding was cut off by the appearance of Leo by her side.

"There you are. I was starting to wonder if you'd turned into a pumpkin."

She tried not to smile. She didn't want to be so easy for him to amuse. "I think it was the carriage that turned into a pumpkin, not Cinderella."

"Whatever." He hitched his head toward the center of the gathering, where Gabby and Daniela were still smiling and laughing. "Come on."

"I don't want to intrude."

"Are you kidding? She would murder me in my sleep if she found out you were here and she didn't get to say hello. Actually, no, she wouldn't wait for me to fall asleep. She'd just do it here, in cold blood. Do you want my blood on your hands?"

"I do need someone to drive me around this weekend."

"Follow me." Leo cut a path for them through the crowd, nodding at the occasional parent. As they passed Dorothy, who was huddling with Glinda the Good Witch, he leaned over and spoke low in Marie's ear. "Contrary to appearances, Dorothy and Glinda are first-class bullies."

"Is this the source of the social trouble your sister is having?"

"I think so. She seems to want to be friends with them, but I'm not sure why. They seem awful."

"Like the Plastics."

"Like the what?"

"From the movie *Mean Girls*."

"I haven't seen it."

Marie was tickled that she could pull out an American pop culture reference Leo didn't know. "The only thing to do, really, is to wait it out. Grow up and have your revenge."

"Is that what you did?"

"What do you mean?"

"I mean Lucrecia von Bachenheim," he said without hesitation.

She was surprised he remembered her actual name, given that he'd been calling her Lucrecia von Whatever yesterday.

"Well, I'm not sure I really achieved revenge. I guess my revenge is more in my position, but I was born to that, so I can't really take credit for it."

"Did Lucrecia von Bachenheim address the United Nations yesterday?"

She was saved from having to respond, because they'd reached Gabby, but she took his point. In fact, his point made her smile to herself.

"I told her you were here but that you wanted to keep things locked down," Leo whispered.

"Hi!" Gabby whisper-yelled. Then she started to curtsy. It was impossibly cute and completely unnecessary, so Marie, before she could overthink it, intercepted her with a hug. See? She *could* do this.

"You were wonderful!"

"I can't believe you came!"

Marie glanced at Leo. It wasn't like she'd been planning to come.

Leo winked at her. "She said she couldn't miss it."

"Gabby, you were so good!" A voice from behind Marie caused her to turn, but not before she'd caught sight of the look on Leo's face.

It was Dorothy, with Glinda by her side. Hmm.

Gabby stiffened. "Oh, I only had one line. You guys were the ones who were so good!" Her enthusiasm was clearly forced. Marie had no idea precisely what these girls had done to Gabby, but she found herself inclined to dislike them on sight. That inclination was ratified when Glinda outright ogled Leo in a way that was entirely inappropriate for an eighth grader to look at a grown man. "Hi, Leo."

"*Girls*," Leo said, and Marie wondered if he was stressing the word to remind them of the age gap.

"I don't believe we've met," Dorothy said to Marie, the formal phrase making her sound like a little girl impersonating an adult.

"This is my friend, Marie," Leo said quickly, and though she appreciated that he was rushing to introduce her like that so her cover wouldn't be blown, Marie had changed her mind on that front. What was a little unwanted attention if it would earn Gabby some social capital?

So she lifted her chin, tried to channel her mother, and said,

"Good afternoon. I am Marie Joséphine Annagret Elena, Princess of Eldovia, and I'm a friend of Gabriella's."

WELL, EFF HIM. Leo didn't know whether to laugh or to whoop in victory. The bomb Marie had dropped on Rosie and Allison, aka Dorothy and Glinda, literally struck them dumb, something he would have thought impossible.

Marie took advantage of their silence, waiting only a few beats before turning to him and saying, in that snootily regal tone of hers, "Gabriella, Leonardo, Daniela, shall we be going?"

"Why yes, Your Royal Highness," he said—no fake honorifics this time—"I think we shall." He held his arms out wide, intending to encompass all three of the amazing women he had in his charge this afternoon, and gestured toward the exit. He caught a glimpse of each of their faces before they turned to leave. Gabby, with her eyes wide and jaw dropped, looked like the surprised-face emoji. Dani was clearly holding back laughter. Marie had notched her chin even higher and was positively radiating regality.

Neither her face nor her bearing changed as they wound their way through the crowd in the lunchroom, drawing stares. It wasn't until they were outside on the relatively sparsely populated sidewalk that she became more herself. Dani started outright laughing, and that cracked Marie's facade. She smiled, and the dimples—the real ones—came out.

"I like you," Dani said, and Max yapped happily, as if to signal his agreement. "This is Max," she said, gesturing to the mutt.

"Oh!" Marie exclaimed. "I met him yesterday!" She smiled. "I know a Max. A human one. This one is much cuter."

Suddenly there were more people. People with phones taking

pictures. Leo could see why Marie hadn't wanted to blow her cover, though he appreciated the hell out of the fact that she had. "All right." He shooed the women and the beast down the sidewalk toward where he was parked. He needed to get Marie out of here. "Do we need to get Max's crate?" he asked Dani.

"Nope. Let's get it later. I think it's best for us to make our grand exit right now."

And so once everyone was buckled in, they did.

"I hope I didn't overstep there," Marie said. "Those girls just seemed like they could use some . . ."

"Moral correction?" Dani supplied cheerfully.

Marie laughed. "Yes."

Leo turned to her. "If you don't mind, I'll drop Dani at our building before taking you back to the hotel."

He thought for a moment that Marie was going to argue, probably something along the lines of she could make her own way back, but he shot her a look that successfully quashed whatever it was she'd been about to say.

They rode in silence a ways until Marie surprised him by twisting around to look at Gabby in the back seat. "Would you like to come to tea at the Plaza Hotel tomorrow afternoon?" Then she gestured to him and to Dani. "All of you. I would love to have you."

"Oh my gosh, like Eloise!" Gabby said.

"Like who?" Leo asked.

"There's a famous book set at the Plaza," Dani said. "About a girl named Eloise."

Must have been before his time. It was strange sometimes, to be so enmeshed in the minutiae of Gabby's life now but also to have these big holes in his knowledge of her past. He knew what she was reading today—*Wonderstruck* and that book of fairy tales their mom had given her. She never seemed to grow out of that. But he'd missed Eloise and everything that came before the accident. It wasn't that he blamed himself for that, particularly. He was four-teen years older than she was and hadn't lived at home for years by the time of the accident. But the gaps in his Gabby-knowledge felt like shortcomings all the same. He added this one to the list.

"Oh, can we, Leo? Please?"

He sort of felt like he should say no. Would having tea with Marie at the Plaza be like taking charity? He sure as hell was go-ing to feel out of place. He glanced at Dani in the rearview mirror. She always knew what to do.

"I would adore tea at the Plaza," she said, spearing him with an intense look.

"Sounds great," Leo said, the fact that he had to clear his throat to get the sentence out torpedoing the casual delivery he was going for.

"If you like, you can invite your . . . friends," Marie said to Gabby.

Leo knew what she was doing, offering more of her princess-ness for Gabby to use as currency at school. He hoped Gabby would say no. As much as tea at the Plaza was not his thing, having his sister's teen tormenters there would guarantee that *nobody* would have a good time, not Gabby and not Marie, either. Marie would be in princess-performance mode, which made her project a stiffness and snootiness that wasn't really her—though it was a little startling to realize he knew her well enough to say that.

"No thanks," Gabby said. "I think it will be more fun if it's just us."

Atta girl.

A few minutes later, Leo was pulling up at home.

"I don't have anything planned this evening if you want to stay with me rather than go with Leo," Dani said to Gabby.

He could see Gabby waffling. On the one hand, the drive into Manhattan and back would take a ridiculously long time. On the other hand: princess.

"We can watch some more of *I Am Not a Robot*," Dani added.

Gabby got out of the car. "Yes!" But then she paused and looked back at him. "But we should wait for Leo to watch."

Oh, this girl and her big heart. She was going to kill him.

He'd insisted on Thursdays for their formal K-drama nights because he hadn't wanted to tie Dani up on weekend nights, in case she wanted to go on dates or out with friends. But Dani's social life was about as exciting as his was, and she didn't have guardianship of a tween and impending financial disaster as excuses. Still, it gratified him to know that their little ritual meant as much to Gabby as it did to him. He cleared his throat. "Don't wait for me to start the show. I'll bring home pizza."

"Oh, we're waiting for you," Dani said.

"How else are you going to know what happens to Seung-ho and Ji-ah?" Gabby said teasingly.

"I'm sure you'll fill me in."

"We're waiting," Gabby confirmed, and he could not argue.

"Leo." Marie placed a hand on his forearm. "I am going to call a car to take me back. That way you can—"

"Nope." She was paying him a ridiculous amount of money to drive her around, and drive her around was what he was damn well going to do. That aside, Leo definitely owed her for what she'd done for Gabby today. Marie Joséphine Annagret Elena, Princess of Eldovia, was getting a ride back to the Plaza whether she wanted it or not.

"But I don't want you to have to postpone—"

"Will you *hush*?"

She hushed.

It was very gratifying.

She didn't *stay* hushed, though. As soon as they got on the road, she started interrogating him. "It sounds like you're watching a television program with Daniela and Gabriella? Is it one I would know?"

"Probably not. It's a Korean drama. A soap opera, basically. Dani got us hooked on them."

"I've heard about those! I should try one. Do you have any recommendations?"

He must have looked as puzzled as he felt—it was hard to wrap his mind around the idea of the princess doing something as mundane as watching TV—because she said, "I watch a lot of TV."

"You *do*?"

"But only American TV. I should branch out."

Leo chuckled and shook his head, because, again, he wasn't seeing it. Ice skating in the Alps, yes. Bending over watches with one of those eye things jewelers wore, okay. But sacked out watching *Real Housewives*? Not so much.

"My mother was educated in America, and she developed quite a fondness for American TV," Marie said. "When she came to Eldovia—she was French, but she married my father right after her graduation from Yale—she brought a trunkload of VHS tapes and DVDs with her, and she continued to order them."

"And you watched with her."

"Yes."

"Is that why you don't have an accent?"

She laughed. "I don't think so. If I'd learned diction from American TV, I would totally talk like a valley girl, like oh my gosh." She had attempted—and failed—to deliver that last line with a valley-girl accent. "My mother's favorite show was *Beverly Hills, 90210*."

"Well, I'll be."

"But I should switch to something else," she said with an odd sort of vehemence.

"Why?" Even if *Beverly Hills, 90210* hadn't been from before his time, he was pretty sure it wouldn't have been his thing. But he wasn't one to shit on other people's choices.

Marie didn't answer right away. She turned her head to look out the window, in fact, so he thought she was dismissing him. So he was surprised when she said, very quietly, "Because watching them without her hurts too much. And yet I can't seem to stop."

"Ah."

"Do you have anything like that? Any routines that are part of your life that remind you of your parents?"

He sure did. Reading the fairy-tale book with Gabby. Looking at his mom's handwritten recipe cards. Driving past buildings he'd worked on with his dad's crew. "Yeah," he said, his voice having gone all gruff. "Though I mostly try to avoid them."

"Like Fifth and Fifty-Eighth?" she asked gently.

"Like Fifth and Fifty-Eighth," he confirmed, feeling a bit sheepish. "But you know what? Not that I'm an expert, but I don't think it matters whether you face those things or try to ignore them. It hurts just the same. So I say, watch *90210* if you want to."

She didn't speak for a while. Maybe he'd overstepped. Really, who was he to give lessons on grieving? He didn't know shit.

But then the quiet voice was back. "I think you are a very wise man, Leonardo Ricci."

He wasn't sure he agreed with that, but hell, he'd take it.

"Is your butler going to be mad at you for being gone all afternoon?" he asked as they crossed into Manhattan.

"He's not a butler," she said with a laugh.

"So you keep saying." Leo shrugged. "Looks like a duck, walks like a duck."

Marie looked out the window. "Yes, he will probably be angry with me. I texted him that I was going to the play with you, but he's . . . displeased. The larger issue, though, is that *my father* will be angry with me."

"He's going to tattle to your father?"

"He no doubt already has. He's my father's equerry, not mine."

That was the second time she had used that word. Leo made a mental note to look it up when he got home. "So let me get this straight. You had nothing else to do, so you weren't shirking any duties. But still, going to a school play is gonna get him mad at you."

She huffed a small laugh, as if she realized how silly that sounded. "That is correct."

Well. "I hope it was worth it." He was kidding. There was no way the Bronx Technology Charter School production of *The Wizard of Oz* was worth the wrath of a king.

When she didn't laugh at his little joke, he glanced over at her.

"It was." She smiled at him. "It was worth it."

Chapter Six

$\mathcal{S}$aturday morning Marie hosted a breakfast in her hotel suite for friends of the crown. This was an older crowd, people who were friendly with her father. And most of them had known her mother, too. Some of them shared reminiscences, and the morning turned out to be both more enjoyable and more emotional than she'd anticipated.

After that, she had two more appointments with watch retailers, and Leo had taken her to those.

And, more remarkably, Torkel and Mr. Weiss had not accompanied her. She hadn't even had to push very hard. When she'd said she was going alone, they'd grumbled but acquiesced. Perhaps they had finally come to trust Leo.

"Well?" Leo asked when she emerged from her last shop. He'd inquired after every meeting, no doubt spooked by her vast overreaction—crying, for heaven's sake—to yesterday's final appointment.

"Oh, fine." Marie waved a hand dismissively as he opened the passenger-side door of his car for her. "Today's retailers are smaller ones. The stakes are lower."

Leo narrowed his eyes like he didn't quite believe her. It was oddly charming.

"I actually got one of them to increase his order by ten percent over last year," she said laughingly.

It wasn't nearly enough in the grand scheme of things, but it seemed to appease him. He stepped back so she could get in the car.

"Where to next?"

"That's it for today. My next engagement is tea with new friends but not for two hours. So why don't you take me back to the hotel and I'll see you all later."

"You're paying me too much."

"I beg your pardon?"

"I've taken you to two appointments today. It took all of ninety minutes. You can't pay me five grand for that."

"Well, you also had to commute down and back—and you'll have to do so again if you're picking up Gabriella and Daniela for tea."

He shot her a look. "Come on."

"We had an agreement. If you suddenly find the terms too favorable, that's your concern, not mine."

Leo rolled his eyes and started the car, but soon Marie realized they'd gone farther south than the hotel—she was becoming familiar with the local geography. "Where are we going?"

"Skating."

She had her mouth preopened to protest—Leonardo Ricci seemed to inspire reflexive protest. But then she closed it. Because she *really* wanted to go skating. "At Rockefeller Center?"

That was one of those New York things she'd wished she could do while she was here.

"Yep."

A frisson of excitement ran through her. She tried to dial back her smile by several notches, but she did not succeed.

He flashed one of his own, a very self-satisfied one.

As they waited in line, Leo said, "What are we getting into here? Are people going to recognize you? Are there going to be paparazzi?"

"Oh my goodness, no. Thankfully, we don't have the public profile the Brits do."

"What about all those people taking pictures at Gab's school?"

"Don't you think that was merely because word had gotten out about me rather than because someone actually recognized me of his or her own volition?"

He shrugged. "You do have a way of drawing attention."

"I do?" Marie looked down at herself. She'd tried to look more American today, and under her coat, she was wearing a simple black day dress, though she supposed the very concept of a day dress wasn't American. The coat itself, though, was bright pink, belted, swingy, and decorated with black wool piping. Princesses didn't really do parkas. And she was wearing Grand-mère's emerald brooch. "It's the clothes, isn't it? The clothes are all wrong."

He looked at her for a long time without saying anything. The line was outside in the cold, but his gaze heated her from the inside. Embarrassed her. He did that so easily. "No," he finally said. "The clothes are just fine." He drew out the vowels in the last two words: *juuust fiiiine*. She did not know what that meant, but it caused more of that heated embarrassment.

Soon enough, they were easing themselves onto the ice. Marie felt her shoulders relax, and the vestiges of her discomfiture faded as they took their first few strokes.

"You're very good!" she said, and indeed, Leo had an easy grace as he matched his pace to hers.

"I played organized hockey as a kid and was in and out of rec leagues after I graduated from high school." He sped up and rapidly spun around so he was skating backward in front of her, grinning from ear to ear. The move was so well executed that she laughed in delight. "I haven't been on the ice in years, though. Not since before—"

She knew what he'd been about to say. "I imagine you gave up a lot more than hockey after your parents died." She had seen firsthand the way he took care of his sister. That kind of guardianship didn't come without a cost.

He shrugged as he fell in beside her again. "It's worth it."

"I'm sure it is. But that doesn't mean there aren't sacrifices."

His face shuttered. She had said too much. Poked at a topic he clearly didn't want to discuss. She should have known better—the private life of Leonardo Ricci was none of her business.

She was trying to decide if apologizing would only exacerbate matters, but he cleared his throat and said, "You're not too bad on the ice yourself, Your Royal Mostness. I suppose everyone in Eldovia has to learn to skate, like a citizenship requirement?"

She smiled, thankful for the new topic. She picked up speed, and he matched her. "Something like that, but I did have lessons as a girl." Somehow, they'd taken in a way the dancing lessons hadn't. It made no sense that she should be lighter on her feet on ice than inside in a ballroom. Perhaps the difference was that no one ever watched her skate. No one was *judging* her skating. "I'm actually fairly accomplished at most winter sports."

It was her turn for a trick. She skated away and built up speed for a single axel, which was as far as her lessons had taken her. She wasn't sure she would land it—it had been years since she'd attempted one, and she was just as likely to land on her . . . booty, to use the American term she'd learned this week. But she was successful. She enjoyed a sharp prick of satisfaction, entering her like a needle and diffusing like a drug, as her blade sliced against the ice as she stuck the landing.

Leo whistled and clapped as he caught up with her. They grabbed hands. She wasn't sure if he grabbed hers or she grabbed his, but something like a shiver ran up her arm when they made contact, even though she was wearing gloves. It was a *warm* shiver, though, which should have been a contradiction but somehow wasn't. He spun them around once before letting go and saying, "You're really good."

"My mother loved skating." Marie took off on a lap around the rink, a slower one this time, and Leo fell in beside her. "We had this pond in the woods near . . . our house."

"You were going to say 'the palace' or something, weren't you?"

"I was not!" she lied, but her laughter was giving her away.

"No?" he teased, his brown eyes twinkling. "The *castle* then?"

Now she couldn't *stop* laughing. There was something about the crisp, cold air, the familiar, comforting zing of metal blades on ice, and Leo's good-natured teasing that made her . . . laugh.

"The *estate*?" he continued, physically poking her this time, lightly against her side. She batted his hand away and tried to skate away from him, but he was too fast, too light on his blades. He caught up with her so they were both racing around the rink. "The *grounds*? The . . . I don't know. I fold. I'm not a thesaurus."

She stopped suddenly, and he hadn't been anticipating it, because he crashed into her.

"Shit!" He grabbed her before she fell. She was still laughing, though, and he must have realized she wasn't hurt. And after some to-ing and fro-ing where she wasn't sure if they would tumble to the ice, he stabilized them and joined in her laughter, his knowing chuckle a bass line that snaked through her, alchemizing her amusement into . . . something else.

They stopped near the center of the rink, staring at each other, both of them breathing hard.

Gradually, she realized other people were staring, too. At them. At her?

She stood by what she had said before. She was almost certain no one was looking at her thinking, *There's the princess of Eldovia.* But they *were* staring at her. She stood out. She was visually identifiable as someone who did not belong. She hated that.

The last vestiges of laughter left her body like helium out of a balloon with a pinprick in it. She looked down at herself. This silly coat. New Yorkers wore big, puffy parkas that said "Canada Goose" on them. She needed to get one of those.

"Hey."

Leo's fingers came to rest under her chin. They were warm, even though he wasn't wearing gloves. He tilted her chin up and forced her to make eye contact with him.

"It's *not* the clothes."

IT WASN'T THE clothes. It was the dimples.

Leo had been thinking about them all afternoon, on the drive back home to get Dani and Gabby as well as on the train ride back into Manhattan—without a princess for a passenger, they'd done the sensible thing and taken the subway in.

That smile, the way it lit up her entire face to such an extent that you couldn't *not* look at her. He wasn't the only one. That was why, as they'd twirled on the ice, people had watched. Yes, she wore kind of fussy clothing. That bright pink coat drew the eye. But still, that wasn't why people stared. It was her face in its delighted state.

It was those dimples.

And here they were again as she greeted them at the door to her suite.

But they weren't the real ones at the moment. She was smiling, but only with her mouth. The dimples were there, but they were only physical indentations in her cheeks. The mechanical result of her moving the corners of her mouth upward.

She was nervous. His interpretation was verified by the way she opened the door to her suite only a foot, stood there stiffly, and mouthed, *I'm sorry.*

The door swung fully open to reveal the *equerry*—Leo had in fact looked up the word and learned it referred to a kind of fancy personal attendant. He didn't get how that was different from a butler, but whatever. "Good afternoon, Mr. Ricci. Miss Ricci. Ms. Martinez."

"Actually, it's *Dr.* Martinez," Leo said, just to be contrary, as he gestured at Dani.

"My apologies. Dr. Martinez," Mr. Benz corrected as Dani

waved away the formality. "I'm sure you will all understand the need for a minor security screening before your visit commences."

"Isn't it a little late for that?" Leo asked. "I could have kidnapped your precious princess at any point over the past couple days. Did you know we went ice skating today?"

He didn't react, and the other man, the bodyguard, stepped forward. "Mr. Ricci, we've already run background checks on all of you." He didn't even have the nerve to look sheepish. Leo was irritated, but he didn't do anything beyond raising his eyebrows, because Marie looked mortified. "If I could ask all of you to remove your coats and temporarily surrender your bags for inspection."

"I'm so sorry," Marie said as they complied. "They know I'm safe with you, but they get nervous about people coming into my space."

"While you are in America, this suite is an extension of the palace," Mr. Benz said. The exaggerated patience in his tone as he spoke to Marie annoyed Leo more than being searched did. "I won't have anyone who doesn't have your best interests at heart intruding."

Once again, it was Marie's obvious chagrin that kept Leo from saying something snarky. And the truth was, this guy was right to be suspicious. Marie was charming, lovely, rich, and royal—a combination that was bound to attract grifters or worse. So he emptied his pockets—he didn't have a bag like Dani and Gabby did.

"I'm sorry," Marie said again.

"Don't worry about it. Your butler is only doing his job." And, yeah, he used the wrong word on purpose.

"I'll have you know that I am in fact equerry to the king of Eldovia," the man said.

Leo just smirked. The bodyguard had finished his examination of everyone's bags and nodded at Mr. Benz, who performed the tiniest of eye rolls.

Leo was back to being annoyed.

"Ma'am, we will be in the adjoining room if you have need of us," said Mr. Benz.

The bodyguard handed her a small box with a button. Jesus, Mary, and Joseph, a panic button?

The men retreated, and there was a beat of awkward silence, but Dani, bless her, covered it by saying, "What a beautiful suite. May I have a look at the view?"

"Please do." Marie waved them deeper into the suite. "I took the liberty of ordering tea to be served here. I thought it might be more comfortable than in the Palm Room."

She was looking at Gabby as she spoke, and Gabby's reaction to the suite suggested she'd made the right call.

Leo had to agree. It was insane. Enormous, to begin with. Easily bigger than their entire apartment and Dani's put together. Full of fabrics and light fixtures and wall treatments that telegraphed restrained, old-world luxury. Fit for a princess, one might say.

Once they'd finished admiring the view of Central Park and beyond, they gathered around a coffee table in a sumptuous living area. Leo had had the vague idea that when a princess proposed "tea," it didn't mean just tea. He had expected finger sandwiches, maybe. And to be fair, there *were* finger sandwiches—several dozen of them on a tower of plates. But there were also cakes and cookies. Deviled eggs, olives, and nuts. A cluster of teapots sat to one side, each flanked by a card identifying its contents: Earl Grey tea, peppermint tea, coffee, and hot chocolate. On ice was a bottle of champagne, a decanter of lemonade, and—God bless the princess—several bottles of some kind of fancy craft beer.

"Oh. My. God," Gabby said.

Dani, who was standing behind Marie, who had moved to sit, mouthed the same thing at Leo, making an exaggerated face of astonishment.

After they were settled in with their tiny, perfect foods and their beverages of choice—Leo was double-fisting it with coffee and beer—Marie turned to Dani and said, "So it's *Dr.* Martinez. Are you a physician?"

"No, no. Not that kind of doctor. I have a PhD. I'm an English professor at Fordham."

"I minored in English literature myself."

Wow. And that was in addition to the engineering major.

"What is your particular area of expertise?" Marie asked Dani. She seemed pleased to have found this thing in common, but she was being weirdly stiff. He would have thought she'd have become more comfortable once her handlers disappeared.

"Early-twentieth-century American literature by women," Dani said.

"I'm afraid I'm not very well read in that area, but I did very much enjoy *The Age of Innocence*."

"I did my PhD dissertation on Wharton! Particularly on representations of women and work in her novels. And I'm working on a book now on Kate Chopin."

Well. This party was going to be a total snooze, then, was it? Leo sighed and took a long pull on his beer—he'd declined a glass and was drinking straight from the bottle, not caring that that probably wasn't "done" at high tea. For some absurd reason, being confronted with so much visual evidence of the economic gulf between Marie and him compelled him to double down on expressing his working-class roots. He looked around the room, only half listening as Dani and Marie talked and Gabby inhaled so many miniature cupcakes she would be up half the night.

Until Marie dropped a little bomb: "How long have you two been together?"

Together? What? Who was she talking about?

Then Dani started laughing, and he figured it out.

"We're not . . ." Leo couldn't even finish the sentence, so he waved his hand back and forth between himself and Dani and shook his head.

Dani joined in the nonverbal denial, shaking her head, too, but she was still laughing as she did so.

The princess looked between them, confused.

"First of all," Dani said when she'd finally recovered, "I'm married to his cousin."

Marie's eyebrows shot up.

"*Second* cousin," Leo corrected, because he didn't want to take any more credit for Vince than he had to. He ordered himself to stop staring at Marie's eyelashes. It was just that they were so long, and the way her eyebrows had reacted to Dani's statement had called attention to them.

"But they're getting divorced because Cousin Vince is a jerk-face," Gabby piped up, and Leo congratulated himself that she'd internalized the "jerkface" designation, which meant that he and Dani had successfully kept their more colorful descriptors for Vince confined to conversations at which Gabby had not been present.

"Leo and Gabby come from a big Italian family, and I had only met them a couple of times when their parents died. But I always liked them. When I heard they were . . . looking for a place—"

"When she heard we'd lost the family house," Leo corrected, because his pride did not hold with euphemisms, "she hooked us up with a unit in her building."

"My soon-to-be ex and I were already separated at that point."

"And then she started taking care of us and stuff, and now she's our best friend," Gabby said with the innocent forthrightness she still possessed despite the efforts of Dorothy and Glinda the bad Good Witch to stomp all over it.

Leo chuckled. He wouldn't have said it like that, but . . . "That's exactly right."

"We probably *should* get married when the divorce is final," Dani said. "It would make everything a lot easier. You could get my health insurance, and we could knock down the walls between the apartments and actually have some space to spread out."

She was clearly joking, but Marie must not have understood that. "I thought Americans didn't get married for anything less than true, all-consuming love?"

Her wistful tone—as if she admired Americans for their commitment to true, all-consuming love—made Leo want to ask why Eldovians got married, but for all he knew she was going to be married off to some evil prince who would keep her in a tower until her hair grew long enough for someone to climb up it and rescue her.

"Well, then I'm never getting married again, because I'm *done* with love," Dani said. "Anyway, love aside, Leo's like my brother, so . . ." She wrinkled her nose. "Gross."

"Well, thank you very much," Leo teased, though he agreed with the sentiment. If Dani ever got over her aversion to men, she would make some guy a fantastic girlfriend or wife, but it was never going to be him.

"And do you have a girlfriend, Mr. Ricci?" Marie asked.

"Nope," he said. He didn't have to look at Dani to know she was probably giving him a subtle eye roll. But it was true. He *didn't* have a girlfriend. He had an ex-girlfriend—way, way, ex; they had dated briefly in high school—he sometimes hooked up with, but that was all he had going on in that department. Dani thought he should be "putting himself out there," whatever that meant. It was a weird blind spot she had. He already walked around feeling like he was failing Gabby half the time, and Dani wanted him to add a girlfriend to the mix? Someone else he could fail? No, thanks. "No girlfriend," he said again, probably a little too vehemently.

"I see," Marie said serenely. But she turned away as she spoke, seemingly to pour herself more tea, though her cup was already full. She seemed like she was trying to hide a smile.

The real dimples were back, and wasn't that interesting?

Chapter Seven

*T*he problem with the princess was that Leo was starting to view the actual job part of his interactions with her as something to get through before he could get to the *hanging out with her* part.

As he drove Marie to appointments Sunday afternoon, he had to remind himself that this was it. There would be no more hanging out. No more skating, no more tea parties, no more pizza slices and maxi pad shopping. No more driving around talking about dead parents. She was going home tomorrow. And he was going back to his regular life.

She got back into the car—he'd been waiting for her outside Deutsche Bank—and held out an envelope full of cash.

He was going to back to his regular life fifteen grand richer.

He wasn't sure what he'd expected. A check, maybe? A small chest full of golden coins?

His instinct was to refuse the money. He had hardly done anything. She'd only had two appointments today. She'd given Gabby the time of her life. And despite Marie's odd formality and her occasional lapses into prissiness, Leo had had a pretty fantastic time with her, too. The run-up to the holidays was hard for the Ricci siblings, and Marie had lifted their spirits. It felt wrong to take fifteen grand for that.

But no. If he refused the money, that meant . . . all kinds of things he'd rather not think about. She had hired him to do a job, and now she was paying him for services rendered.

And things were getting awkward, with her holding the envelope out and him not taking it.

"Thanks," he said gruffly, sliding the envelope into his back pocket. He started the car and pulled into heavy traffic made worse by the fact that it had been snowing steadily all day. He'd have a lot of shoveling to do when he got home.

Marie sighed, and Leo glanced over. She was looking out the window, and she didn't look happy. Which was a little odd, because he'd found that snow delighted her, generally. She'd been exclaiming the past couple days about how picturesque a New York City Christmas was.

"What's wrong?" he asked.

"Oh, nothing." She turned to him and fake-smiled so that the empty dimples appeared.

"Bullshit."

That got a real smile, albeit a small, wistful one. "Well, if you must know, I don't want to go home. Despite the fact that I'm not bringing the best news home economically speaking, this trip has been a . . . surprisingly refreshing break from reality."

A surprisingly refreshing break from reality. That was it. That was what had him so weirded out. He'd been fantasizing lately about taking a vacation. Vacations weren't part of his life right now, but these last few days had kind of felt like one. Maybe he *would* spend some of his windfall to take Gabby to Florida next week.

Cheered at having figured out the cause of his ennui, he said, "At least it's Christmas when you get back. Do princesses get a Christmas break? Gabby's practically levitating with excitement over being off school."

"My mother loved Christmas."

That didn't answer his question, and someone who didn't know the princess might think she was trying to change the subject. But Leo heard what she wasn't saying. This was a hard time of year to be missing people, especially if those people had died close to Christmastime.

He had no idea what to say, though. So, fuck it, he reached over and took her hand. Squeezed it.

She turned to him, and he could feel how startled she was. He wanted to keep holding her hand, to feel her relax, to have his touch be the thing that made her relax. But this was just supposed to be a quick, reassuring squeeze. A solidarity squeeze. So he made himself let go.

It was hard.

"I have to work a few days next week," she said, going back to his question, "then I'm formally on break."

What did that mean? The concept of "work" didn't really jibe with his concept of "princess." But what had she been doing all week if not working? Pretty hard, too. And it was work that seemed to weigh heavily on her, given the consequences for the economy of her country.

She must have heard his unarticulated confusion, because she elaborated. "Eldovia is a constitutional monarchy. It has a Westminster parliamentary system."

He had no idea what that meant.

She continued with the whole reading-his-mind thing. "Which means that the crown's power is mostly symbolic. As it should be. But my father has always had a strong advisory role. He has a cabinet of sorts made up of people who help him shape his legislative agenda."

"And you're on it."

"Not formally."

"But you want to be?"

"If I'm going to do my father's job, it would be nice to have formal recognition of that fact." She sucked in a sharp little inhalation, as if she'd spoken too fast or too openly. As if she'd surprised herself.

If I'm doing my father's job. Leo had so many questions. He opened his mouth, intending to voice the foremost one—*What does that mean?*—but Marie kept talking. "I've also been trying to work with parliament informally to steer the country's reaction to the refugee crisis in Europe. But that's something of a side project."

"That's what the UN speech was about."

"Yes."

"Well, damn, here I thought the job description of *princess* would be more like getting your nails done and ordering room service."

"I suppose it could be, if I wanted it to."

She didn't though. She wasn't the kind of person who expected to get a free ride. Which was a weird thing to say about a princess, but it was true.

"What are you up to this evening?" she asked.

She was changing the subject, and not very subtly.

Which . . . fine. What did he care about royal politics or Westminster whatever in Eldovia?

"Shoveling." He snorted. "So much shoveling. Followed by that most gourmet of meals: grilled cheese sandwiches and Campbell's tomato soup."

She sighed again, one of those wistful ones. "Sounds lovely."

"Are you kidding me? Manual labor and grilled cheese? It's not exactly high tea at the Plaza."

She performed a little shrug as she turned to look out the window again, one he didn't think he was supposed to see.

Well. Wasn't that something? The princess of freaking Eldovia thought grilled cheese in his shitty apartment sounded like a better time than whatever she would order up in her giant luxury suite at the Plaza.

That suite was a lot of space for one person.

A person alone. A person who would eat scrumptious food but probably do it by herself.

Or maybe with that asshole butler—Leo refused to call him anything else, even in his mind—who treated her like a child.

Yeah, Leo might be eating cheese on Wonder Bread this evening, but he wasn't doing it alone. He'd be doing it with the world's greatest eleven-year-old. And possibly the world's greatest thirty-one-year-old, if Dani was around. Which she almost certainly would be on account of her stubborn refusal to move on after Vince.

Well, shit. Before he could overthink it, he just asked her. "You wanna come over for dinner?" After tonight, he would never see her again anyway.

Marie gasped audibly in what he was pretty sure was delight, and shit, that . . . did something to him. So, to keep himself in check, he added, "There's one condition."

"And what is that?"

"You have to help me shovel. I bet you've never done that."

"Untrue. I did it . . . once."

"Once?"

"It's a long story." She frowned. "It's . . . not a happy memory."

What he wanted to say to that was, *Tell me*. It was an urgent want, to hear about her unhappy memories and store them away in his mind next to his own. What he *actually* said, was, "Fair enough." He turned on his blinker and changed lanes so they could head uptown. "Let's get the hell out of here."

When they parked back at home—one of the perks of being the on-site super was a dedicated space behind the building—he started thinking about how shabby and messy his place was. Shabby he couldn't do anything about, but . . . He craned his neck so he could see up to Dani's apartment. The light was on.

Marie was about to get out of the car. "Sit tight for a minute, if you don't mind. I just need to . . . deal with something." He got out his phone. Can you do me a huge favor and go over to my place and clean up the living room? Get Gabby to help you. Just shove everything into my bedroom.

Marie would never see his bedroom.

Dani: Why?

Leo: We're having a guest for dinner.

Dani: Are we now? And who might this guest be?

She followed that up with a string of crown emojis. Leo didn't bother replying, knowing that as much as Dani enjoyed watching him squirm, she would do what he'd asked in this case.

So, okay, onto manual labor with the princess.

"Oh, how unfortunate that there's only one shovel," Marie teased when Leo opened a shedlike structure nestled against the back of the building to reveal a variety of garden tools but only one shovel.

Again, she was struck by how unusual it was for her to be teasing someone. She didn't tease people—except maybe Max and even then, not that much. But Leo was just so . . . easy to tease. Plus, he was good at it himself. She'd probably learned it from him.

"Hold your royal horses." He shoved aside a big bag of salt to reveal a second, smaller shovel. "I usually make Gabby help me. Lucky for her, today I've conscripted a princess."

She waited for him to make some remark about how the child-size shovel was a perfect fit for her, but he didn't. Leo's teasing, she realized, was never truly mean. It wasn't about attributes she had no control over, like her stature.

They walked around to the front of the building. "You start here," he said, pointing to the edge of the property. "I'll start on the far side, and we'll meet in the middle."

She did as she was told. It was a beautiful evening, the snow still drifting down in big, fat flakes. It was only five thirty, but it was already dark, the yellow glow of the streetlights filling in for the absent moon, painting everything in a golden glow.

Soon, she was out of breath. Her muscles were protesting, but it was a good kind of protesting. A good kind of breathlessness. The aches and shortness of breath meant she was using her body to do something useful. Something concrete. She felt a satisfied pride in looking back at the cleared section of sidewalk behind her—although it was already dusted over with a layer of new snow.

"Hey," Leo said, and then he was there, right in her space. "Don't hurt yourself. There's a lot accumulated. Take it off in two layers." He demonstrated, digging his shovel in and scooping but not going all the way down to the pavement. Then he made a second pass to clear the bottom layer. He worked quickly and efficiently, with a grace she wouldn't have expected.

"You're not doing it that way," she pointed out. "You're scooping it up all at once." She'd been aiming for more of that earlier playfulness, but she feared the accusation came out sounding more petulant than anything.

But somehow, he knew what she meant. He lifted an arm in a biceps-flexing gesture and said, with a joking flourish, "That is because I am a big manly man."

"And I'm a weak little princess?" she filled in.

But she must have gotten it wrong, because he blinked rapidly, surprised. He had snowflakes on his eyelashes. "No," he said quietly. "No. You're just not used to doing this."

She was such an idiot. Hadn't she *just* been thinking about how Leo never made fun of people for traits they couldn't control?

But it was too late. The damage was done. She'd made things awkward.

Leo turned to go back to his spot. The sight of his retreating back did something to her chest. He was leaving without understanding. He was leaving with things all wrong.

He was *leaving*.

She was leaving. After tonight, she would never see him again.

Her body took over, bending her knees so she was crouching near the ground. Her hands gathered snow, formed it into a tight, icy ball. Her knees carried her back to standing. Her mouth turned up at the corners.

And, finally, her arm retracted—and she let it rip.

"Ooooff."

Was that . . . ?

Leo whirled—and was promptly hit in the face by a second snowball.

Holy shit. The sight of Marie, she of the fancy pink coat, huddled near a snowbank outside his shitty apartment building, was so incongruous that it froze him in place for a moment, made his mind slow down. Was the *princess of Eldovia* really throwing snowballs at him?

A third one thwacked his solar plexus, summoning an involuntary gasp.

Yes, yes she was.

And her aim was *perfect*. And she was laughing like a hyena.

Well, princess or no, that could not be allowed to stand.

That laugh again, a cackle really, and it was like it somehow traveled across the thirty feet of shoveled sidewalk between them, reached inside his chest and pulled out one from him.

A matching set.

But he swallowed that laugh as soon as he could, unfroze his clumsy body, and ducked to avoid the next incoming missile. "You are going to regret that, Your Magical Regalness."

"I doubt that!" she called back. "I told you I'm very good at winter pursuits."

Which she demonstrated by evading his first several snowballs. It was that same lightness on her feet she'd had at Rockefeller Center.

"I'm also quite talented at archery," Marie taunted, and she landed another hit while he was temporarily disabled, stunned really, by the image of her with a bow and arrow, poised to vanquish her enemies with merely a finely honed arrow and her perfect aim.

But, okay, *get a grip, Ricci.* He lifted his hands into the air and started walking toward her, pretending to surrender. He hit her with a grin—not that he had to fake it. "Clearly, you win, Your Right Honorable Heiressness."

When she threw her head back to laugh in victory, he moved like lightning and gathered an armful of snow. He didn't shape it into a ball, just unceremoniously dumped it on her head.

"Ahhh!" she shrieked. "Not fair!"

"Oh," he said, stooping to gather some more snow. "Are we observing the Geneva Conventions here? My mistake." He got her again, but she got him just as good. "Is this not how you do snowball fights in *Eldovia?*"

He'd made a more traditional, formed snowball while he was baiting her, and he retracted his arm to let it fly—gently because she was right in front of him and he wasn't a jerk, or at least not that kind of jerk. But she did this strange leaping thing, and suddenly she was hanging off his arm, trying to block his throw.

He cracked up as he tried to shake her off. He had to hand it to her—she was giving it her all. She was like a small dog, like Max, trying to play tug-of-war with a great big mutt.

Or maybe . . . not like Max.

She stepped back, panting and smiling. Her cheeks were pink, and her hair was a total mess.

Oh, shit. He was in trouble.

He knew it. Which was why he didn't make a move, not exactly. It wasn't like he thought *I'm going to kiss her now.* He would never have done that. He didn't think she would have, either. But he saw the moment she figured it out, what was going to happen if neither of them stopped it.

Neither of them did.

And then the smiles were gone, all their joking replaced by a kind of focused seriousness that had them grabbing each other as their mouths crashed together.

If Leo had thought about what kissing a princess would be like—which he most decidedly had not—he would have thought of proper, restrained kisses. Of pecks on cheeks or maybe even on the backs of hands.

There certainly wouldn't be tongue.

Or moaning.

Jesus Fucking Christ, his tongue was in her mouth. He wasn't really sure how that had happened, but she was *into* it, judging by the low, breathy noises she was making as she grabbed onto the front of his parka, like she wanted to make sure he couldn't escape.

He did not want to escape. So he surrendered to this madness, this beautiful madness. This *wanting.* Let himself melt, as heat shot through his body despite the cold. It had been so long since he'd kissed anyone, and having that heart-shaped mouth under his was so improbable and, frankly, it was making him crazy. So was the no-holds-barred enthusiasm with which she was returning his kiss.

So he was just going to stand here and kiss her forever. He brought his hands up—he'd gotten overheated while shoveling and had pulled his gloves off and hadn't had time to put them back on before she declared snow-war on him—and clamped them down on her cheeks as he continued to work her mouth.

His aim had been, in a mirror-image gesture of her grabbing his coat—she was still holding onto it as if for dear life—to make sure she stayed. To do what he could to make sure this kiss *never ended*.

But his hands were too cold. Or too rough. Or too something.

Because they hadn't been settled against her cheeks for an instant before she gasped—not a good gasp this time—and let go of him. Marie stepped back, shock written on her face: her eyes were wide, and her mouth, red from his ministrations, rounded into an O.

Leo held up a palm, because she was going to start talking, and no good would come of that.

But it didn't work. "I can't kiss you!" she exclaimed.

"Okay." She was right, of course. He'd thought maybe for one second there that they could enjoy a fleeting moment of pleasure, but he'd been wrong.

"The thing is . . . I'll have to . . ."

"It's okay, really." He took a step back. "Let's forget this happened. I'll finish up the shoveling. Why don't you go upstairs? Or if you'd rather, I can take you back—"

"I have to marry strategically."

"*What?*" What the fuck did *that* have to do with anything?

"I have to marry someone with whom an alliance will advance Eldovia's interests."

Leo's brain was back to moving slowly. What Marie was saying wasn't computing. "What the fuck does *that* have to do with anything?" She blinked in confusion, and he was pretty sure he did the same thing back. Unless . . . "Hang on." Oh, Jesus, Mary, and Joseph. He didn't know whether to be flattered or offended. Probably offended was the right call here. "Princess, I assure you there is no universe—*no universe*—in which I want to marry you."

"I know that," she said, taking a step toward him.

He threw both hands in the air. It was, on the surface of things, the same gesture he'd made as he'd walked toward her pretending to surrender but secretly planning his snow-attack. But this time it was protective. *Self*-protective. What did she think? That he was some kind of gold digger on a long con? "It was just a kiss." Leo let some derision seep into his tone, even though part of him knew that was a dick move.

"Right," Marie said quickly, too quickly, as her face shuttered and she took a step back. "Of course."

Sighing, he let his head fall back. Despite his Catholic upbringing, he wasn't at all sure about the whole God thing, but he could use some divine intervention right about now. Ideally, a celestial rewind button.

The window of his place opened, and Gabby stuck her head out. "Leo!"

He had to laugh. If God existed, it appeared he—She? Probably she—had a sense of humor.

"The sandwiches are ready!" Gabby shouted. "What's taking you so long?"

What is taking me so long is that I'm having snowball fights and making out with a goddamn princess instead of doing my actual job.

"I should go," Marie whispered. "I'll get a cab, and you can—"

"Your Majesty!" Gabby laughingly called. "Is that what I'm supposed to call you? I googled, and I think it's actually Your Royal Highness because your dad is the Your Majesty? Anyway! I'm *soooo* excited you're coming for dinner. I made you a special sandwich! Wait till you see it!"

Leo turned to Marie with his eyebrows raised. He'd like to see her get out of this one. She stared back at him, and he could see the princess returning and her bearing grow stiff. He recognized that posture as defensive. She was in survival mode.

Well, so was he. He actually wanted her to leave. Kind of. But he wanted her to leave less than he wanted to go upstairs and tell Gabby that Marie had changed her mind. "What do you say, Princess? You're not going to let a meaningless little kiss scare you off grilled cheese on the wrong side of the tracks, are you?"

"Hi! Hi! Come in! Come in!"

Marie could see what Leo meant about Gabby being happy about her school break. She *was* vibrating. Bouncing up and down on her toes as she took Marie's coat and herded her toward a sofa where Daniela was already seated. "I'm so happy you're here! I want to show you—"

"Ahem." Leo, still standing in the entryway, drew their attention. "What am I? Chopped liver?" He tilted his head, leveled a mock-annoyed stare at Gabby, and pointed to his cheek.

Grinning, she skipped over to him and made a show of kissing his cheek. He must have thought that was going to be the end of it, because he took off his hat and started to pull away, but Gabby threw her arms around him. Leo was clearly startled, but he hugged her back, picking her up off the floor in the process. "Merry Christmas, kiddo." His voice was raspy, and Marie's throat thickened. It was seeing them together—the easy love between them. But also seeing how little it took to make Gabby, who had lost so much, so happy.

"Should we eat in front of the tree?" Daniela suggested when the siblings separated.

"We stuck apple slices in the sandwiches!" Gabby exclaimed. "Dani said that would class them up."

Leo made a face, and Gabby wrinkled her nose at him. It was like they had a secret, nonverbal language. Marie didn't have that with anyone. Not anymore. She and her mother used to do that. Maman would hold up DVDs when they were trying to decide what to watch and Marie would opine on them with merely her facial expressions. She'd forgotten about that. The memory made her smile.

"I don't understand why a thing can't just be what it is," Leo said as he helped Dani set the coffee table. "Why do you have to put apples in a perfectly good grilled cheese sandwich? Why do you have to put candy in ice cream? If it ain't broke, don't fix it."

Gabby rolled her eyes at Marie as she set a plate in front of her. It was a small, private display, meant just for Marie—like Marie was in on the joke. It was more thrilling than it should have been. "My brother has such simple tastes," Gabby said. "Do you know that his favorite kind of ice cream is *vanilla*? Plain vanilla!"

"Maybe it's not simple taste so much as classic taste," Marie said. "A well-made vanilla is subtle, but if you're paying attention, hard to beat."

"*Thank you.*" Leo plopped down next to her on the sofa, and oh, she was in trouble, because he was looking at her with an almost violent sort of intensity. Like she was the world's tastiest vanilla ice cream that he alone appreciated.

It only lasted a moment, and he was on to making sure everyone was situated around the coffee table.

But the effect of that look lingered. Leo had moved on, but Marie had not. She wanted to kiss him again, and wasn't *that* interesting?

He scooted closer to her to make room for Gabby. He was *almost* but not quite touching her, which was somehow worse—better?—than actual contact would have been. There was perhaps an inch of space between the edge of her skirt and his jeans-clad thigh. He'd taken off the ubiquitous flannel shirt and wore only a short-sleeve T-shirt, which meant his arm was bare all the way up to the middle of his upper arm. That was . . . a lot of arm. She let her eyes slide over the familiar forearm with its veins and muscles. He'd worn his flannel shirt rolled up while he'd driven her around, so she'd spent a lot of time looking at his forearms. But because it was winter, upper arms were uncharted territory. His were, unsurprisingly, as nice as his forearms. They were . . .

And, oh. Oh no. She didn't just want to kiss Leo again, she wanted that arm. To have it draped casually over her shoulders, like it belonged there. Or, worse, to pick it up and arrange herself beneath it, to burrow under it and hide from the world, like she had the right to do that.

Her ears were on fire. Her whole face was on fire. She was hyperaware of every inch of her skin. Of the boundary between her body and the world. The hole in her tights that her big toe was making worse. The spot where the tag of her dress rubbed against the back of her neck. It didn't hurt or itch. It was just . . . there. A small sensation suddenly magnified a thousandfold.

The spot on her arm where her sleeve—her dress was three-quarters sleeve—stopped and her bare arm was exposed to the air. If she concentrated very hard, she could feel the heat from his arm radiating across the inch of space between them. Energy from his body making contact with her skin.

What if she moved her arm so it touched his? It would only take a slight shift. An accident.

And it probably would have gone unnoticed if she hadn't hissed a sharp, involuntary inhalation the moment she made contact with him.

He turned toward her and in so doing ended the contact between them.

"You okay?"

"Yes," Marie squeaked, aware that she probably did not look okay, but rather like a red-faced lunatic.

An arm. It was merely an arm. Goodness. She was like a nineteenth-century gentleman tied into knots over the sight of an unexpectedly exposed ankle. "It's . . . been a long few days," she said lamely.

She ordered herself to pay attention to what was happening, which was that Dani was carrying over plates from the kitchen. Soon they were enjoying the fancy sandwiches, which were delicious—Marie made sure to tell Gabby as much—and steaming cups of soup. She looked around as she ate. The apartment was modest but homey. It was furnished with what she suspected had been the furniture from the house Leo grew up in—big, solid, wooden pieces and worn sofas and chairs with quilts over them. It was comfortable and warm and lovingly decorated for Christmas right down to a homemade, cardboard fireplace and hearth trimmed with garlands. Two stockings lay on the floor next to it, waiting to be hung.

"Your tree is lovely," Marie said. Every square inch of it was covered in ornaments, lights, and tinsel.

"It's probably not as fancy as an Eldovian tree," Gabby said. "But, look! There are a bunch of princesses on it!" She pointed out the Disney version of Snow White and Cinderella and a couple more figurines in the same style that Marie didn't recognize. "My mom loved fairy tales, right, Leo?"

"She did. She used to read them to you at night before you went to bed."

"And I used to tell her I wanted to be a princess when I grew up. But then . . ." She trailed off, clearly wanting Leo to continue the familiar story. Perhaps this was their way of remembering their parents.

"She would say, 'Princess of our hearts is about the best you can hope for—unless you marry extremely well.'"

"You must miss her," Marie said, feeling a little awkward stating the obvious but also like she needed to acknowledge the loss.

"Yes," Gabby said. "Every day. Do you miss your mother?"

"Every day," Marie echoed.

And there was Leo's hand again. A quick squeeze, and then it was gone, as in the car earlier. It didn't mean anything. It was merely a gesture of empathy.

"Tell us about Christmas in Eldovia," Daniela said from her armchair on the other side of the coffee table, but not before her eyes flickered down to where Marie's and Leo's hands had been joined.

"Christmas is big business in Eldovia. We have an annual Cocoa Fest on Christmas Eve day. Restaurants and pubs participate, and so does the palace. We make big cauldrons of different kinds of cocoa and serve them outside on the grounds."

"Are you *kidding* me?" Gabby demanded.

Marie laughed. "I am entirely in earnest. And there's a Cocoa Ball in the evening—though that's not for children." She wasn't sure why she added that qualifier. It wasn't as if Gabby, whose eyes had grown comically wide, would be around to be told she couldn't attend the ball.

"Oh my god, you *are* from a fake Hallmark country," Leo deadpanned.

Gabby reached around Marie, who was sitting in the middle spot on the sofa, and punched her brother in the arm. "Don't be *rude*, Leo." She turned to Marie. "That is the *best thing* I have *ever heard*."

Marie smiled—that kind of unbridled enthusiasm was hard to resist. "It is rather wonderful." Not the dancing—never that—but Christmas Eves at home were something special. Or at least they used to be. Before her mother fell ill, there had always been an uncommodifiable spirit about the holidays. A sense of shelter and peace and safety underneath all the hustle and bustle.

Much like here.

Exactly like here. "I like the fireplace." She pointed at the homemade hearth. "There must be a story there."

"We have a family tradition of making wishes every year when we hang our stockings," Gabby said. "Last year was our first year in this apartment. There was nowhere to hang the stockings, so Leo made that."

Of course he did.

"Do you have stockings in Eldovia?" Gabby asked.

"Yes. When I was younger, we always put stockings up for my parents and me in our private quarters. There's a public section of the palace, with a big tree and elaborate decorations, but we always used to have a tree in our apartment, too—the real tree, as I used to call it, because that's where Santa left my presents. And we'd put stockings up over our fireplace there." She paused, thinking back to the Christmas her mother died. They hadn't gotten the stockings out that year, because they'd practically been living in the hospital. But when they came home a few days before Christmas, shell-shocked, Marie had hung them—well, she'd hung hers and her father's and wept as she'd put her mother's away. She'd planned on filling them the way her mother always had, but when she crept out of bed early Christmas morning to do it, she found that he'd taken them down. She swallowed a lump in her throat, forcing the memory down. "We don't do that anymore, but there are some lovely stockings hanging on a grand fireplace in the main entryway of the palace, with the formal tree." Although no one had ever filled those stockings. They were purely for show.

"I bet it's beautiful." Gabby sighed. "I bet it isn't made out of cardboard." Then she looked stricken. "No offense, Leo."

He smiled. "None taken, kiddo."

"It is . . . beautiful," Marie said.

"Don't sound so convincing," Leo teased.

The fireplace she was thinking of was enormous and tiled in creamy white marble topped by a cherry mantel carved into an elaborate scene of cherubim playing. In the center hung a portrait of her mother, one Marie wasn't partial to because it was formal and stuffy and captured little of her mother's spirit. The whole thing *was* beautiful, in an imposing sort of way, and it was a centerpiece of the public space in the palace, but . . . "I like this one better."

"Are you *crazy?*" Gabby exclaimed. "How can you like this one better?"

"I just do."

It was the truth. And here was another truth: she didn't want to leave.

It was hard to say good-bye.

Leo didn't like to think of himself as a sentimental person. He had accepted the fact that he was when it came to Gabby, but that was because they were related. He was her de facto parent. She didn't have to get under his skin because she was already there. She *belonged* there.

But damn, it seemed like the princess had somehow wormed her way in there, too.

She was prissy and uptight and entitled, he reminded himself as they all stood awkwardly near the door. She had insisted that her handler dudes pick her up, firmly rebuffing Leo's offer to drive her back to the hotel.

He held her coat for her—the ridiculous pink one—then reached for his, intending to walk her downstairs, but then Mr. Benz appeared in the hallway.

"Your Royal Highness." He inclined his head. "Are you ready?"

Right. It was a good reminder. Marie was a person people literally bowed down to. She was a person who had a fucking *manservant*.

Leo would admit that the last few days had been, to quote Marie, a surprisingly refreshing break from reality. By god, he'd had a snowball fight with a princess and kissed her. But a break was just that: a break. Reality still loomed on the other side of it.

Marie turned to Dani. "I'm sorry we didn't get to talk more about literature, but I so enjoyed meeting you, and I wish you the best. I can't wait to read your book."

Dani smiled, and the women shook hands. Then it was Gabby's turn to receive the royal blessing. "I so enjoyed meeting you, too, Gabriella, and attending your play. Thank you for your hospitality this evening. Your sandwiches were delicious."

Gabby and her big heart responded by throwing her arms around Marie. Mr. Benz sniffed.

Well, fuck that. As soon as Marie parted from Gabby, Leo grabbed her and wrapped her in a big hug. He did it to annoy Mr. Benz. Or at least that's what he told himself.

She was small and strong, and she made his chest hurt. He bent down to whisper in her ear. "Keep your chin up, Princess."

"And you as well, Mr. Ricci."

And then she was gone.

The break from reality was over.

He spared a moment, as he, Dani, and Gabby started clearing the dishes, to wonder if he could text Marie. Just once, late tomorrow, to check that she had gotten home okay.

But that was dumb. She had a snooty butler-manservant and a shredded bodyguard whose sole tasks were to make sure she got places okay. She didn't need him.

Back to reality.

Except . . . fuck it. The way the school calendar fell this year meant Gabby didn't have to be back at school for more than two weeks, and he literally had fifteen grand in his back pocket. "What do you say we go to Florida?"

A dish clattered into the sink as Gabby swung to face him. "What? Like for Christmas?"

"Yeah. Why not?" He made eye contact with Dani, who looked as surprised as Gabby. "We can leave tomorrow. All of us."

"Um, first of all because it's expensive?" Gabby said. "And second of all there's no snow there, and you have to have snow for Christmas."

"Right." She was right. He looked around for something to distract himself. "Hey, what do you say we hang our stockings?" He picked his up. In the old days, he used to wish for stupid shit like the Islanders to win the Stanley Cup. Last year he'd wished for Glinda the Good Witch to be attacked by flying monkeys. What about this year? The first thing that popped into his head was—

A sharp knock drew everyone's attention.

Holy shit. Leo felt like his soul was floating above his body as he moved to answer the door, like there was a mismatch between his physical, embodied self and the runaway thoughts inside his head.

It was her, as he had known it would be. The sight of Marie had the effect of immediately reuniting body and mind. He felt righted, suddenly, like the edges matched up. She would only be here because she'd forgotten something—a purse, maybe—but it felt like a reprieve all the same.

He stepped back wordlessly to let her in even as he surveyed the apartment for whatever it was that had drawn her back, when she said, "Come to Eldovia for Christmas."

He didn't hear the next thing she said, because of Gabby's shrieking. Or maybe it was the rush of blood in his ears.

"All of you," she was saying when he managed to tune back in. She was gesturing toward Dani as if to include her in the extraordinary invitation.

"That's so kind of you," Dani said, "but I have a two-week date with my book manuscript. If I don't get this thing done, I can kiss any hope of getting tenure good-bye."

"I have a . . . dear friend who is spending the holidays writing his master's thesis, so I understand," Marie said.

"Wait." Leo needed to impose some order on this conversation.

"Oh, but we can FaceTime you!" Gabby said to Dani. "We can show you the big fireplace and the cauldrons of hot chocolate."

"Hang on," Leo tried again, but no one heard him. They'd launched into a discussion of the time difference between Eldovia and New York and when they could call Dani for her to get the optimal view of the Christmas festivities.

He stuck his fingers into his mouth and whistled, high and shrill, like he used to do at Islanders games back when his life still included things like Islanders games. That did it. Three pairs of wide eyes turned to him.

"We can't go to Eldovia for Christmas."

Right?

"Why not?" Gabby demanded, and before he could answer, she followed that with, "You were *just* saying we could go to Florida. This is better than Florida. Way better."

"Yeah, but we can't just—"

"Leo." Marie walked over until she was standing right in front of him, and for fuck's sake, he needed her not to be so close so he could think clearly. "I know this is an impulsive invitation. But I have a feeling that none of us has done anything impulsive for far too long. Christmas in Eldovia is lovely, but I will admit that the last few have been terribly lonely. Since my mother died, things have . . . not been the same. I would truly love to have you and your sister as my guests."

Oh, that forthright honesty, that vulnerability. It was like a paper cut: minor on the surface of things, but after a beat to absorb it, stealthily sharp and stinging.

"I can't," he said automatically, the words a defensive shield against her earnestness. "I'm the super of this building. I can't be gone for a chunk of time in the middle of the winter. I have to shovel, and—"

"I'll shovel," Dani said. "It will be good for me to get a little exercise amid all the hunching over the computer."

"But—"

"Anything else, I'll call in the professionals. You're allowed a vacation, Leo. I'm pretty sure that's even in your contract, yes?"

And Marie, damn her, kept going. "I've had so much fun with you these last few days." She turned to Gabby, as if to include her in the sentiment, and then back to him. "I just thought . . ."

Oh god, he had no defenses against her. The way she seemed to lose her nerve and trail off sheepishly. Well, he would have given her anything in that moment, opened a vein and bled for her, and all she was asking was that they come for a vacation in a literal palace.

Could they . . . do this?

". . . you would really enjoy it." Marie was speaking to Gabby now, and Leo had the sense that that wasn't how she'd initially meant to finish her sentence. *I just thought . . .* she'd started out, and she'd been talking to *him*. He wanted to know what she'd thought.

"There's skating and hayrides and—"

"A ball!" Gabby exclaimed.

"But not for children, I'm sorry to say. My father is very strict on that front."

"But I can watch you get ready, maybe? See your dress?"

Marie smiled. "Yes. I would love that. I secretly hate balls—I'm a terrible dancer—so I'd love the company to calm my nerves."

Dani caught Leo's eye as the other two kept chattering as if the decision had already been made. Very slowly, her eyebrows lifted, like she was issuing a dare.

And as if they had somehow heard Dani's wordless challenge, Marie and Gabby fell silent. They both turned to him. Gabby's face was an almost comical plea. Leo could tell she desperately wanted to burst out with a barrage of words to get him to agree but somehow sensed that was the wrong approach.

And Marie. She smiled. Those *fucking* dimples.

He sighed. Because apparently he was going to spend Christmas in a palace with a goddamn princess in a country he had never heard of before this week.

"I'm *not* going to any balls, though."

Chapter Eight

*T*his had been a mistake.

The first hint was the palace itself.

It looked like the result you'd get if you did a Google image search for "castle in the Alps."

It shouldn't have been that jarring. Leo was doubly qualified to deal with the concept of a castle. He had half an architecture degree, and he was Gabby Ricci's brother and therefore well acquainted with the concept of fairy-tale palaces.

Still: *holy shit*.

The thing was perched on top of a steep, treed hill. It appeared, from a distance, to be white, but he suspected it was actually constructed from yellow limestone or something similar. He counted three turrets, the asymmetry of which annoyed him. He checked himself. He had no business being offended by the placement, number, or mere existence of turrets on the royal palace of Eldovia.

They had been steadily gaining elevation since they got off the plane. He'd been cheered—falsely, it turned out—by the fact that they had flown commercial from New York to Zurich. But then a private plane had puddle-jumped them to a small airfield a short drive from "home," to use the princess's understated term for the monstrosity in the distance. And now they were being driven in a huge SUV, Marie and Mr. Benz in the second row and Leo and Gabby in the third. Torkel was riding shotgun.

The slope increased as they entered the palace compound through a gate. The guard, like the driver before him, and the pilot before *him*, had seemed genuinely happy to see Marie. They'd all offered a perfectly correct but warm, "Your Royal Highness," and she had greeted them all equally warmly by name.

Marie glanced over her shoulder at him from time to time as if she was expecting him to say something, but he had been silent since they'd gotten off the second plane, the fact of which was less awkward than it would have been thanks to Gabby's incessant chattering interspersed with amazed exclamations.

The car wound its way up the road from the gatehouse, climbing the hill on a series of switchbacks. He kept twisting around to see the castle as they approached. It was, objectively, ridiculous. But it was so . . . *vehemently* ridiculous that it was hard not to be impressed by it, even as it simultaneously inspired mild revulsion.

"Can you hike in these woods?" Gabby asked. "Oh! Can you ride horses in these woods? I've never ridden a horse. I think I might be afraid to, but I've also always kind of wanted to try."

"Mr. Benz is an avid horseman. I'm sure he'd be delighted to take you riding," Marie said. Mr. Benz looked anything but delighted at this suggestion, but he did not object.

The car moved slowly, laboring as the slope increased, and Leo felt a little like he was being driven to his own execution. When they finally reached the front door—was that the term? Did palaces have front doors?—there was a lineup of people outside.

Not people, or at least not regular people. Servants. Some of the women even wore black dresses with white aprons and caps—like "sexy maid" Halloween costumes minus the sexy part.

"Oh dear," Marie murmured. She turned to Leo. "There is going to be a bit of silly pomp and ritual right now. Just smile and ignore it, and we'll soon be done."

"Smile and ignore it? Have you met me?" He couldn't help the retort, but she grinned, so he doubled down. "I'm not bowing to your father. Or to anyone." He was teasing, but not really.

"Of course not. You're not his subject."

He refrained from pointing out that he wasn't anyone's subject and never would be. That it wasn't his citizenship that kept him from bowing; it was that *he didn't bow*.

There were several opportunities in the ensuing minutes to feel once again like he had made a mistake. But he bucked up and endured the "pomp and ritual" as a butler—so apparently Mr. Benz truly wasn't one—greeted Marie. Gabby provided distraction just by being her credulous self and was properly fussed over by the housekeeper, whose name was Frau Lehman.

Mr. Benz and the butler started conversing in German.

Marie, who had been chatting with Frau Lehman, suddenly whipped her head up. "Is Father in Riems?" There was some alarm in her tone.

He had noticed that Marie always spoke English when he and Gabby were around, even when she was speaking to her associates about matters that didn't concern them. He supposed it was her innate politeness—she didn't want them to feel excluded.

"Indeed, he is, ma'am." The butler, following her lead, had switched to English. "He and the duke had business to discuss." He turned to Mr. Benz. "And to answer your question, he is not yet returned. He is en route, though, and expects to be back in time for dinner."

Marie pressed her lips together like she wanted to say more but was holding herself back. Something about the situation was unsettling her, but Leo couldn't ask. Not here.

Mr. Benz, apparently not seeing the need for the palace guests to feel included, said something curtly in German, did one of those bow-nods to Marie, and left.

Soon, Leo and Gabby were being shown to their rooms by Frau Lehman and a man he could only describe as a footman. Leo insisted they all go to Gabby's first because he wanted to be able to find it in case of . . . what? The need for an emergency exit in the event that the king decided to eject the commoners when he got home?

As he looked around at the enormous portraits of fancy, old-fashioned people that lined the wood-paneled walls of the seemingly endless corridors they traversed, it seemed like a distinct possibility.

"I'm sorry your rooms aren't closer together, but I thought we'd put Miss Gabriella in the nursery wing," Frau Lehman said as they arrived at a room and the footman opened the door.

"Oh, I don't need to be in the nursery," Gabby said. "I'm eleven, so—"

Yep, Leo would have been struck dumb, too, if he'd been talking. The room was like . . . a giant marshmallow. It was painted white, and the bed was covered with one of those flowy netlike things. Why did rich people always want their beds covered with what was basically fancy mosquito netting? Wasn't that what you resorted to if you didn't have air conditioning or, like, walls? There was an enormous dollhouse—one of those nearly life-size ones you saw in places like FAO Schwarz. Even though Gabby had recently declared herself "too old for Barbies," she gravitated toward it with an "Ooh."

Frau Lehman smiled. "That belonged to Her Royal Highness when she was a girl." She bustled around the room fluffing pillows. "We're all so glad to have a visitor who appreciates it." She walked over to a small table at the foot of the bed. On it was a small potted pine tree strung with lights. "Miss Gabriella, I thought perhaps tomorrow we could decorate your tree. We have an ornament room, and you can choose what you like."

Gabby turned, her eyes wide. She hadn't registered the tree in her enthusiasm for the dollhouse. "Oh, yes, please! I've never had my own tree! And an ornament *room*? I can't believe you have a whole room for ornaments!"

Leo met Frau Lehman's smiling eyes over Gabby's head. This lady was all right.

"Mr. Ricci, if it meets with your approval, I will stay and help Miss Gabriella get unpacked and dressed for dinner, and Thomas can show you to your room."

He wanted to tell her that unpacking Gabby's small duffel would take about two minutes and that her version of "dress for dinner," might be different from the Riccis' version, which was basically, "You should be dressed," but Leo agreed, leaving Gabby in raptures over the Juliet balcony that overlooked a courtyard lit with what looked like millions of tiny white lights.

His own room was more masculine. Its centerpiece was a massive, mahogany four-poster bed. There was an ornate writing desk, a pair of wingback chairs in front of a fireplace, and the walls were covered in dark-green fabric.

"Shall I light a fire, sir?" the footman—Thomas—asked. "It can get rather drafty in the palace in the winter."

Leo's inner architect wanted to ask about the central heating the palace appeared to have. It must have been a feat of engineering to retrofit. But maybe that was a topic best saved for the king. They'd have to talk about *something*, and if the man was at all house-proud, there was a topic Leo was actually interested in. As to the fire, the room was cold, but he was ready for some solitude. And a concrete task—doing something for himself, with his own hands—would be a welcome corrective to the past twenty-four hours. "No, thanks. I can do it myself."

That was the incorrect answer, judging by Thomas's slightly raised eyebrows, but Leo stood his ground. Raised his own eyebrows. Thomas opened his mouth like he was going to protest but got control of himself, nodded, and murmured, "You'll find the fireplace already laid with firewood and kindling. There are matches in the box on the mantel." He moved to the door but stopped to point out a velvet rope that was hanging out of the wall there. "Simply ring if you need anything."

And Leo was alone. Finally, blessedly alone.

Which was when it happened. The thing that definitely, conclusively, absolutely told him he had made a mistake. That he was way out of his depth here.

He tried to eat a piece of soap.

In his defense, there was chocolate everywhere. He'd noticed it in Gabby's room, and Marie had told them on the flight to Zurich that the Christmas chocolate theme in Eldovia extended beyond cocoa. Various artisanal chocolate makers made truffles and other treats to celebrate the season. A box of those truffles rested on the bedside table.

He had eaten every one of them, and they were freaking delicious.

Then he'd moved into the bathroom, intending to wash his hands and face after the long journey. There were more truffles in the bathroom, laid out in some kind of crystal bowl.

Well, when in Eldovia . . .

And . . . fuck.

There was a knock on his door while Leo was rinsing his mouth out. The phrase "rinse your mouth out with soap" came to mind, but what did you call it when you were rinsing your mouth to try to get rid of the soap that was already in there?

He swung open the door to reveal Marie. She was wearing jeans. He had to blink several times in order for his brain to process the sight of Casual Princess. Though she wasn't really *casual*-casual. Those were what he would call fancy jeans and she was wearing a blouse and blazer on top, and her hair, which in New York had either been down or twisted into a bun, had been styled into an elaborate Princess-Leia-style over-the-head braid. But, still, a princess wearing jeans. Skinny ones. Leo let his gaze slide down, but only because they were alone, and because he'd gotten the sense, in New York, that Marie liked it when he checked her out.

And because she was so . . . check-out-able. "You look good," he said, because it was true.

Hello, dimples.

"So do you," she said.

"No, I don't. I look like a schlub from the Bronx who has been on planes for eleven hours." *And who can't tell the difference between soap and chocolate.*

"My father is on his way home and has texted to invite us for predinner cocktails in an hour's time, should you care to join us."

Should he "care to join them." Leo could think of few things he would care to do less, but he didn't really have a choice here, did he? You didn't come to the Eldovian royal palace and refuse a summons from the king. "Will there be more pomp and ritual?" he asked.

"Not really. It will just be us."

He suspected her definition of "pomp and ritual" was different from his, but he merely asked, "Will there be beer?"

"There will, in fact, be beer. I've made sure of it. I have an old friend who owns a pub in the village, and she's started some small-scale brewing. We also have various Oktoberfests and Hefeweizens on hand."

Leo had been kidding, of course, with the beer question, but he was oddly touched that she'd gone to the trouble.

"And," Marie went on, "I am told that the cook, who is a lovely woman who thrills to new challenges, is outdoing herself concocting nonalcoholic creations fit for young New Yorkers with discerning palates."

"You are a good egg, Princess." He had the sudden, ridiculous urge to rest his hand on her cheek, but of course he checked it.

"And if you're not too tired," she said, "after dinner I can take you down to the village and show you around. That way you'll know how to escape when you need to."

"And where do you go when you need to escape?"

It was out before he could help it. He was fairly certain she *didn't* escape. That duty and the sad king and the beautiful but impersonal palace were the boundaries of her universe.

But she surprised him by grinning playfully. "I'll never tell."

WHAT WAS THE *matter* with her?

Had Marie's time in New York made her forget everything about her life?

About her father?

He made his displeasure over the fact that she'd returned with guests known immediately upon his return from Riems.

"You didn't tell me you were going to see the duke," she said as he strode into her sitting room, a footman trailing him because he hadn't even taken off his coat.

"You didn't tell me you were bringing Americans home for Christmas," he shot back.

Fair enough, but that was because if she'd "told" him, he would have interpreted it as "asking" and would have said no. "They're my friends. They've had a difficult few years, and they're alone for Christmas."

"I won't ask how you made friends with a couple of—"

She channeled the spirit of her mother and glared at him. Her mother had always had a way of tempering her father's sternness, his most aristocratic instincts.

It must have worked, because he said, "New Yorkers" even though they both knew that wasn't originally how he'd intended to finish that sentence.

"That's the appealing thing about New York," Marie said with studied mildness. "It puts you in the path of people you otherwise wouldn't meet."

"And you also met Philip Gregory, I understand. Or should I say *didn't meet*?"

Clearly Mr. Benz had already filled him in.

"It didn't go well," she confirmed. There was no point in dissembling.

"And the other retailers?"

"Shall we discuss this at a more opportune time, when we don't have guests waiting? I have some ideas on that front."

Ideas he would shoot down, she was certain, even though he was doing nothing himself to address the problem.

Mr. Benz entered. Bless him, even though he and Marie didn't always see eye to eye, he was forever trying to help pick up the slack caused by her father's . . . what? She would have said grief, but three years had gone by. It seemed that what really animated him these days was anger. She feared her mother had had more of a tempering influence on him than they knew.

"Your Majesty, Your Royal Highness, I've called the cabinet to come tomorrow and the next day. We can debrief the New York trip"—Mr. Benz glanced grimly at Marie—"and I'd like to discuss strategy for the MPs' breakfast on the twentieth."

"That sounds fine," Marie said. "I'd like to add an agenda item, if I may."

Both men raised their eyebrows at her. "The UN speech went extremely well. I'd like to discuss follow-up strategy, including raising the number of refugees we accept. And if we come to an agreement, we can informally raise the idea at the breakfast and encourage parliament to take it up in the new year."

"We're a small country," her father snapped. "How many people do you think we can accept?"

Marie took a deep breath and checked herself from deploying her usual arguments: they couldn't leave the rest of Europe to deal with the crisis. Had he not seen the terrible pictures from the Mediterranean?

Did he not have a heart? Had it died along with Maman?

She knew from experience that those arguments didn't work. And she had a new idea. "I've been doing some reading. I believe our smallness can actually be an asset in this context." She was going to suggest that they have individual villages come together to sponsor families. She'd gathered some information on American church groups doing that, and she suspected the tight bonds of Eldovian villages could be leveraged in a similar fashion.

Her father was starting to ramp up, but Mr. Benz stepped in to smooth things over. "I'd be happy to put your project on the agenda for the first cabinet meeting in the new year if that suits? We've told everyone two half days of meetings this week. Then the MPs' breakfast. Then we'll break for the holiday, so I'm wary of overloading the agenda."

He was putting her off. He was just being nicer about it than Father, who would say that she wasn't on the cabinet anyway. She could go to New York and do his job for him, but he didn't see any need to listen to her ideas. It made Marie's blood boil.

"Why don't we discuss *my* trip briefly before cocktails?" her father asked, and the question diffused some of her frustration.

"Yes. I had no idea you were making such a trip." She was glad he had, though. Her father and the duke were close, if unlikely, friends. The Houses of Accola and Aquilla had battled over the

Eldovian throne centuries ago, and though there hadn't been hostilities for generations, there *had* been a long-standing chill between the two noble families. Riems, the seat of the House of Aquilla, was on the other side of the country, over a mountain ridge, and other than waging political battles by proxy in parliament, the royal and ducal families had essentially ignored each other's existence—until her father's generation. The future king and future duke had gone to boarding school together and become friends. As they'd grown up and risen to power, that friendship had extended to include their wives and children—and had become an alliance that was playing out in parliament and that had the potential to see the two houses collaborate economically.

"How is everyone?" she asked.

"Maximillian has announced his desire to take a PhD."

"I beg your pardon?" She'd spoken too sharply, betrayed her surprise, so she tried again. "I thought he was staying in Cambridge for Christmas." Like Dani, Max had professed a need to hole up over the break and write—in his case, his master's thesis. Knowing Max, she wasn't at all convinced that writing was what he would fill his holiday with, but she didn't ask questions. As much as Marie adored Max, his absence—over the holidays, and in general—suited them both.

Because that new alliance between the Houses of Accola and Aquilla? Her father and Max's had a plan for strengthening it, for making sure it outlasted them. A plan she'd known about for as long as she could remember—but one she preferred not to think about.

"Max is in Cambridge for the holiday, yes. However, he has

recently informed the duke of a newfound fascination with the social history of the Blitz and therefore a desire to stay on in Cambridge for a PhD. Aquilla asked me to come discuss the matter with him."

She couldn't have been more shocked if her father had slapped her.

And happy. Shocked and *happy*. That would buy them, what? Three years? "And how did that discussion go?" She tried to pitch the question as if she were indifferent to the answer.

Her father narrowed his eyes. "Shall we take this up at, as you say, a more opportune time? We must dress for dinner."

Well, she could text Max herself. He was a more reliable source anyway. "Yes. I'll see you shortly. I've asked for cocktails to be served in the green parlor."

He nodded and turned, but he paused with a hand on the door and looked back at her. Smiled. His old smile. "I'm glad you're back. I missed you."

She sucked in a breath. Thought of those years after her mother died when she was still in university and wanted nothing more than to quit. To come home. She had missed him so much then, but he'd given her no indication that he felt the same. She'd been starving for a kind word from him, but all he'd done was force her to stay in school. They'd grieved apart, and a gulf had grown between them, one she never knew how to cross.

Now, though, he looked so much like her old papa that she was moving toward him before she could overthink it. She reached up and hugged him, even though he was still wearing his snowy coat. "I missed you, too."

They parted, and he left. Mr. Benz started to follow him—

where the king went, generally his equerry did, too—but paused
and looked at Marie for a beat. She thought she detected sympathy
in that look, but that must not be right. Mr. Benz did efficiency,
not sympathy.

By the time everyone had assembled for cocktails, Marie's father
was back to his usual cranky self. She had described him to Leo
and Gabby as the sad king, but she actually had no idea where
that phrase had come from. Like his mother before him, he was
a master of passive aggression when he wanted to be. He could
convey an entire cornucopia of negative emotions, irritation and
superiority chief among them, without actually saying anything.

Like the way, after she'd introduced Leo and Gabby, he let his
eyes slide down Leo's body and then raised them a tiny bit too
high on the way back up. You couldn't call it an eye roll exactly,
but you couldn't call it *not* an eye roll, either.

He had done the same thing to her, issuing a silent rebuke. He
had expected to find her in a dress. She'd kept her jeans on, though,
in an attempt to make her guests feel more comfortable.

And anyway, Leo looked good. Although he was wearing jeans
and a black T-shirt, he had added a light blazer. But the sleeves
were rolled up. It was like his forearms *had* to be free. She stifled
a sigh.

"And what is it that you do, Mr. Ricci?" her father asked.

"I drive a cab, and I'm the caretaker of the apartment building
we live in." He gestured at his sister.

Her father rearranged his facial expression almost imperceptibly, but it was enough to convey disapproval. Marie's face heated.
She'd forgotten what a snob he could be, mostly because he rarely

encountered anyone who didn't run in their circles. But he had always been a little bit like this when her friends had come to the palace when she was in school.

"He was going to be an architect!" Gabby piped up.

What? She turned to Leo in surprise. He was making a dismissive gesture as he shot a quelling look at his sister.

Gabby ignored it. "It's true! He was partway through college when our parents died, and he had to drop out. But he knows so much about architecture. Like, *so* much."

Marie felt a little stab of hurt that Leo hadn't told her any of this, especially given their extensive chat about architecture in Madison Square Park. In fact, she'd expressly asked if he'd gone to university, and he'd said no.

"Yes," Leo said mildly. "The unexpected death of our parents required some rearrangement of plans."

A footman called Luis approached Gabby with two glasses on a small tray. One, rimmed in sugar, was light pink and full of tiny, fizzing bubbles. The other was some variation on hot chocolate, with a mountain of the kitchen's famous homemade marshmallows floating on the top. "For the young miss," Luis said, "ginger raspberry smash or hot milk chocolate with honey-caramel marshmallows."

Gabby's eyes widened. Marie's heart twisted as Gabby curtsied—to Luis—and took both drinks. Marie glanced at her father, who was reacting with predictable disdain.

"I think you're meant to choose one or the other," Leo said softly.

"Nonsense." Marie stepped forward and picked up the drink Gabby had hurriedly set back on the tray. "One's for now; one's for later." She set the hot chocolate on a side table and nodded at Luis to dismiss him. "I recommend starting with the raspberry, since it's lighter, and moving on to the chocolate. At least that's how *I* always do it."

Her father shot her a look. He knew that she'd never in her life had either of those drinks. Well. She shot him a look right back. She wasn't about to stand by while he embarrassed her guests.

"I notice that the palace seems to have central heating," Leo said. "When was that added? The walls are stone, aren't they? That must have been quite the project."

The question thawed her father somewhat. The palace was one of his favorite topics. "It's not as old as it looks. My great-grandfather had it built in the 1860s. He was a devotee of the Romanesque Revival movement. The palace was built with central heating—though the system has, of course, been upgraded since then."

From there, the conversation was easier, if not warmer. Leo—the *architect*; it boggled the mind—seemed genuinely interested in the history of the palace and asked intelligent questions. Dinner was a little awkward—Marie had requested a simple meal in the breakfast room, but her father had overruled her and ordered a four-course repast served in the formal dining room. She made a point of slowly picking up the proper utensil for each course so the Ricci siblings could see what she was doing. It helped that Gabby talked almost nonstop, and during lulls, Leo asked her father questions about the palace.

Eventually, they were done. Leo took a yawning Gabby to her room along with Frau Lehman, who seemed to have decided to take personal responsibility for Gabby instead of assigning a maid. Would they read stories? Talk about the day? Marie wanted to go with them, so much, to be part of whatever routine would unfold, but of course that wasn't her place. So, as they took their leave, she stumbled through an awkward good-night, hesitating over whether she should remind Leo of her invitation to go for a walk. Probably not. It was late, and no doubt he was tired, too. Anyway, she needed to talk to Max.

At her suite, she had her phone out before she'd fully closed the door. PhD????? We're out of touch for a few weeks and you drop this bomb?

> **Max:** Hey M, xo. How was NYC?

> **Marie:** Don't change the subject. Since when are you interested in doing a PhD?

> **Max:** Since I accidentally already wrote my master's thesis. But don't tell my father that. He thinks I still need the spring semester to finish it up. And this Christmas break. Definitely need to spend the break here and not there. Working v v hard.

She understood Max's desire to avoid Riems over the holidays. The duke was, to put it the way Max would, an unmitigated asshole. It was funny, though, to think of Max taking refuge at school when she had spent two years doing the reverse: wanting so desperately, after her mother died, to come home, but not being allowed to.

Marie: Well, we'll miss you at the ball. As for the PhD, I appreciate what you're doing, but don't do a degree you don't want to do.

Max: Don't take this the wrong way. You know I love you, but I want to do a PhD a lot more than I want to . . . do you. LOL.

Marie: No offense taken. Where is the turkey baster emoji when you need it?

Max: Right? Anyway, in all seriousness, I just thought this would buy us some time. It's not like I actually have to be good at PhD-ing. I can flunk out . . . slowly.

Marie: You have to get in, though!

Max: I'm the Baron of Laudon! I'm the heir to the Duke of Aquilla! I'm in!

Marie: Well, I can't pretend this isn't the best news I've had in a long time.

Max: Yeah, I heard it didn't go well with Gregory.

Marie: How does everyone know about this? Did a "Marie fails at America" memo go out?

Max: IDK, but I heard it from Mother. Anyway, re the PhD/reprieve, don't get too excited. The duke is NOT pleased. When I originally floated the idea, he said no, but apparently now he's thinking about it.

Marie: Is that why my father was there?

Max: I have no idea. But they made me Skype with them, and they seemed rather fixated on finding out if my sudden interest in the social history of the Blitz was genuine. I felt like I was being examined. Sebastian, of course, is hard at work in the mines and can do no wrong.

Poor Max. His younger brother, Seb, worked in the family mining business, though of course not literally in the mines. He was definitely the favored son. Too bad he couldn't have been born first.

Marie: The irony is I bet you could do a really amazing PhD on the social history of the Blitz if you applied yourself to social history as much as you apply yourself to other social activities.

Max: I'm sure I don't know what you're talking about.

Marie laughed. Talking with Max always made her happy. That was another irony. Max wouldn't make a bad husband, at least when it came to the compatibility part. It was the romantic part. The love part. The *sex* part. Having grown up with their families so close, Max was like her annoying brother.

Hence the turkey baster plan. But their underlying compatibility was why neither of them had provoked an outright confrontation with either set of parents. They both knew it could be worse. Much worse. So they rubbed along in denial while Max finished school.

Or, more accurately, kept going to school. Which, in addition to avoiding the marriage their parents had been talking about since they were children, would allow him to tomcat around, as was his wont, free from the prying eyes of his parents and countrymen.

Marie: You know exactly what I'm talking about. You're lucky you're only a minor royal, or your exploits would be all over the tabloids. If this were the nineteenth century, you'd be a rake.

Max: So since it's the twenty-first century, I'm what? A slut?

Marie: You said it, not me.

Max: You wound me.

Leo: Is that walk still on offer?

The simple question—and the identity of its sender suddenly appearing as a notification—sent a bolt of electricity through Marie, making her fingers clumsy as she pecked out an answer.

> **Marie:** Yes! The moon is almost full, so it's an ideal night for a walk.

> **Max:** What???

Oh, no. She'd seen Leo's message in the preview notification, and in her haste hadn't backed out of her stream with Max.

> **Marie:** Sorry, that wasn't for you.

> **Max:** Who was it for? Who are you going on moonlit walks with????

> **Marie:** We have guests for Christmas.

> **Max:** Guests? What guests?

> **Marie:** Someone I met in New York.

> **Max:** Oh. Okay. Who is she?

Marie hesitated over whether to correct him. On the one hand, he'd be like a dog with a bone if she told him about Leo, and she didn't need that kind of scrutiny. On the other, *his* exploits were legendary, and aside from a little good-natured teasing she didn't get on his case. She felt like this might be a "what's good for the goose is good for the gander" situation. But no. It was better to noncommittally agree.

> **Max:** And more importantly, is she single?

> **Marie:** You're more than a thousand kilometers away.

> **Max:** So? Maybe I *should* come home for Christmas.

All right. She could not resist.

> **Marie:** My guest is not a she.

> **Max:** WHAT.

She got up and retrieved a sweater from her armoire. By the time she'd pulled it over her head, he had exploded.

> **Max:** M! Explain! WHO IS HE?

> **Max:** HELLO?

> **Marie:** Good night, Max. xo

Chapter Nine

*L*eo wasn't sure what he expected. Maybe a horse-drawn carriage to pull up and whisk them away? He certainly hadn't thought they'd just walk out of the palace unaccompanied, but that was exactly what they did. Marie came to collect him from his room and led him through silent halls to the imposing marble entryway he'd glimpsed but not really processed when they'd arrived. But there was the big tree she'd talked about, and the fireplace, complete with stockings. It was impressive, even in the dim light of evening when it wasn't officially on display. But he could see what she'd meant about liking his homespun version better.

"Is that your mother?" he asked quietly, pointing toward a large painting of a woman with Marie's dark hair.

"Yes, but it doesn't really look like her. She was . . ." She stopped and contemplated the painting. "Happier than that."

It was true that the woman in the painting didn't look like a devotee of *Beverly Hills, 90210.*

Marie, however—and in contrast to earlier in the evening—*did* seem happy. She pushed open the huge, oaken front door, took a big breath in, and skipped down the stairs. It was like the outside air suddenly brought her to life. He followed suit—with the deep breath, not the skipping. The air was clean and bracing. It smelled like pine. "So you can just stroll out of the palace by yourself? What happened to that bodyguard guy?"

"Torkel's gone home for Christmas. We have other security staff, but to answer your question, yes, I can just stroll out of the palace by myself. It's not like New York where they feel they have to babysit me. The entire hill is fenced in—the gate we went through is the only way in or out by car. When we get to the village at the bottom, there's another gate, a smaller one for pedestrians. It's manned, but I've told them to let you and your sister pass freely."

"And what about the village itself?" he asked.

"Everyone knows me," she said, as if that was an answer that had anything to do with how safe she was there. But hey, if she wasn't going to sweat it, he certainly wasn't.

As they crossed the snowy grounds, Marie tilted her head back. Leo followed her gaze and had to swallow a gasp. He didn't think he'd ever seen this many stars. He'd headed off the audible gasp, but his astonishment must still have been apparent, because she said, softly, "It's beautiful, isn't it?"

"Yeah. It sounds stupid to say that you don't see stars like this in New York City, because of course you don't. But . . . you don't see stars like this in New York City." Or anywhere he'd ever been—no boat ride with Dani's dad out on Long Island Sound, no Boy Scouts camping trip.

"You know that rhyme, 'Star light, star bright, first star I see tonight'?" she asked.

"Yeah."

"My mother used to say that all the time—we used to spend a lot of time outside."

"What did you wish for?"

She didn't answer, just started walking. He followed. She pulled out a flashlight and aimed it at the road—they were walking down the same road they'd driven up.

"When I was younger, I used to wish for a sibling."

"I used to wish for a sibling, too, when I was younger—Gabby's fourteen years younger than I am." He'd forgotten about that. But some of his earliest Christmas-stocking wishes had been for a little brother or sister—though by the time Gabby finally arrived, his teenage self had moved on to Islanders-related wishes. "She was a bit of a surprise to my parents, I think." He was happy when they'd announced their news, and even happier now to have Gab. Life could be a lonely business, and having someone who shared your experiences and your blood made it a little less so. He suspected that growing up royal, despite its perks, was a lonelier road than average. The cage was gilded, but it was still a cage.

It occurred to him suddenly that despite the huge economic and social gulf between them, he had more freedom than Marie did. Or at least a different kind of freedom.

"My parents had trouble conceiving, then never managed to get pregnant again after me," Marie said. "Once I got old enough to understand that, I'd wish for frivolous stuff. A crush to like me back. A good grade on a test." She paused. "Now I wish my mother was here."

Her voice was so small. Leo wanted to grab Marie's hand but checked the impulse, saying instead, "What was she like?" A fan of *90210*, but he wanted to know more.

He could hear the smile in her voice when she answered. "She was a force of nature." Marie paused, trying, he sensed, to put words to complicated emotions. "She was like Audrey Hepburn in *Breakfast at Tiffany's*. She was fun and charming and always bursting with plans for some grand adventure. She'd throw an impromptu dance party and invite everyone from the village, or she'd take me to L.A. for the weekend and we'd go on star tours in disguise. She loved L.A., because of the American TV obsession."

"They say we live in the golden age of TV," Leo said. He didn't watch any himself—no time—beyond Thursday-night K-drama.

"Oh, but it wasn't *good* TV that she liked. No HBO for her. No, she was into the old, cheesy 1990s stuff of her youth. Programs you couldn't get on satellite or via streaming. She was always ordering DVDs. So that combined with the L.A. trips meant my vision of America was all these beautiful people with puffy, shiny hair hanging around by pools and having affairs with each other."

Leo laughed. It was so incongruous to imagine a European queen watching that stuff.

"Movies, too, though she preferred the serial format of TV." Marie was gathering speed, clearly happy to be talking about her mother. "But when my father would start getting cranky or stressed by work, she'd declare it family movie night. He would grumble, but he knew better than to refuse family movie night. We always watched in a small private parlor in their suite—you would call it a den, I think. She would order up a feast of all our favorite food, make everyone put on their pajamas, and we'd watch whatever silly movie she'd selected. My father always started off annoyed, and he'd sit at the far end of the couch. But by the end of the movie, they'd be all cuddled up. He was like a horse she had to break every few months. She'd get him back into a good mood. It was like she was . . ."

Marie's mother sounded lovely. Like a woman who cared for her family in little ways. Not that different from Leo's mom, really, except that she'd mostly done it with pasta. The princess had trailed off on her last thought, left off the final adjective she'd been going to use to describe her mother. He wanted, suddenly, to know what she'd been going to say. "It was like she was what?" he prompted softly.

"Magic. It was like she was magic." She waved a mittened hand in front of her face like she was erasing a chalkboard. "That sounds silly. She wasn't magic. She just knew how to handle my father. No one else could—no one else *can*."

"He loved her enough that he let himself be handled, maybe," Leo ventured.

"I think that's right," Marie said quietly. "Of course she *also* took after Audrey Hepburn in that she was lithe and graceful and beautiful and refined." She snorted. It seemed like a snort that was tinged with self-disgust.

"What?" Leo asked, genuinely confused.

"Nothing. It's just that life as a female royal is a lot easier if you're beautiful. My life would be so much simpler if I took after her in that regard."

"Hang on, now." He supposed what she meant was she didn't look like Audrey Hepburn—and she didn't. But Audrey Hepburn, or at least the *Breakfast at Tiffany's* version of her that he knew from watching the movie with Gabby, was not the be-all and end-all of female beauty.

"Oh, I'm not fishing for compliments. I know I'm not beautiful, and for the most part, I genuinely don't care. I don't have a long, graceful neck—fine. It's not a character flaw. But it's absolutely true that if you look the part, people treat you a certain way."

She didn't have a *long, graceful neck*? Huh? A long neck would look stupid on her. It didn't fit her proportions. "But you're—"

"Remember when I was hiding in that bathroom on that yacht?" Marie didn't wait for him to answer—she was on a roll. "I overheard Lucrecia and her friends talking about what a shame it was that I didn't take after my mother in terms of looks and grace. It's not enough for them to comment on what a professional disaster that party was? I have to be ugly, too?"

"Hey. None of that." That was objectively wrong.

She didn't seem to hear him. It was like she was talking to herself, now, rather than to him. "And it's almost like they see a causal relationship between the two things, you know? The Philip Gregory disaster order has nothing to do with what I look like, or at least I'd like to *think* it doesn't, but you'd never know it to hear them talk."

There were angry embers inside Leo, and her words were stoking them. "My point is, when you're a princess, beautiful is the baseline. If you're beautiful, people can look past that and judge the rest of your merits. If you're not, well, good luck."

He stopped walking. It took her a few steps to realize she'd gotten ahead of him. She shined the flashlight between them at chest height, its ambient light enough to allow him to see her face.

"Are you done?"

"Am I done what?"

"Comparing yourself to Audrey Fucking Hepburn?" Leo didn't bother tempering the annoyance in his tone.

Marie's eyebrows shot up.

"Look. I know I'm only here for a week, but I swear to God, if I hear you call yourself ugly again, I'm not going to be responsible for my actions. In addition to being possibly the prettiest human I have ever laid eyes on in the flesh, you're smart, so don't tell yourself things that objectively aren't true."

Her mouth fell open. Then she closed it. Then opened it again. He'd flustered her. Good. Maybe it would be enough to knock some sense into her. "Okay, point taken. I'm not *ugly*. On my best days I achieve cute. It's . . . It's hard to explain."

She *was* cute, with her rosebud mouth and those goddamn dimples, but apparently that was a bad thing? He would never understand this world of hers. "It's hard to explain because you're *not making sense*."

She huffed a frustrated little sigh. "There's a certain quality that the most popular female royals possess. Think of Princess Diana. Grace Kelly. Meghan Markle. There's a grace there that's hard to define except I can say I don't have it. Part of it is height. I'm five two." She chuckled. "But it's more than that. It's more just . . . ease. I'm awkward. I'm always worried about what I'm going to say next." She laughed again, but it had turned bitter. "And you should see me try to dance." She cut off the laugh with a small snort. "Which you will, if you come to the Cocoa Ball."

"I'm not going to the ball," he said reflexively. But he sort of understood what she was saying about ease and awkwardness. His first impression of Marie had been that she was snooty and formal. But he'd come to realize that it was a cover, a way of keeping people at bay. He did it, too, but with different qualities. Her snootiness functioned the same way his grumpiness did.

But it wasn't a crime to feel awkward in social situations. And he wasn't about to start agreeing with her because she'd muddled up all kinds of traits in her mind into some paragon she thought she had to aspire to.

So instead he baited her. "Dancing is not hard. Anyone can dance." He started walking again as he spoke, and she fell into step beside him. "Even me."

She took the bait. "Really? I don't know. I'm not picturing it. You all dressed up in a suit, cutting a rug? I bet you can't keep the steps straight any better than I can."

"Steps?" He laughed, suddenly seeing what the problem was, at least as it related to dancing. "Nah. You're overthinking." Before he could do the same, he grabbed the flashlight from her, turned it off, and stuck it into his pocket. He took her hand, spun around, and pulled her into his arms. Into a classic slow dance stance. "No need for steps. Just sway."

He started moving, willing her to move with him.

She did. It felt like a small miracle.

All that was audible was the crunching of the snow under their feet. His breath, heated from the fire stoked inside him by both her ridiculous take on royal beauty and the nearness of so much royal beauty, came harder than usual, made visible puffs of steam in the chilled air. She shivered, and he pulled her closer. "See? Easy as pie."

"This isn't the kind of dancing we do at the Cocoa Ball." She was a head and a half shorter than he was, and she was nestled so close to his chest that her voice came out muffled.

"No?" His came out all raspy. He would like to think it was due to the cold, but he feared not.

He felt her shake her head no against his chest. They kept swaying in the dark, and even though it was cold and they were swathed in layers of clothing, his body was lit up. Those angry embers inside him had diffused, sending heat to every inch of him. "Well, you must be dancing with the wrong people then."

That must have been the wrong thing to say, because she pulled away instantly.

"I am," she said. "I am dancing with the wrong people." She sounded sad. Resigned.

He didn't know what to do other than follow her down the hill. He thought about making a speech about how not-ugly she was, just to make sure she'd gotten that through her head, but the moment had passed.

MARIE HADN'T BEEN to the Owl and Spruce since before her mother died, but it was the same as always. The red fabric banquettes and dark wood walls of the village pub were comforting in their sameness.

She felt a little guilty that it had been so long since she'd seen Imogen, the proprietor and someone Marie had once considered a friend. After Marie left for university, they'd grown apart. And when she'd come back, it had been to a different life. A grieving father lashing out in anger even as he let his responsibilities— and the economy—slide. She had tried to take over as much as he would allow her. The new workload meant a lot of Marie's old connections—at least the ones that didn't directly benefit the crown—had been left to founder.

Imogen greeted her with genuine warmth, though, and somehow managed to clear out a snug for them. Imogen's father had been Irish, and he'd built the pub in the traditional style, including with a row of snugs—private booths with doors.

"Do you have time to join us for a drink?" Marie asked after she'd introduced Leo and they'd placed their orders.

Imogen smiled her cat-that-ate-the-canary smile—she always looked like she was up to something. "I most certainly do. I'll be back in two shakes of a lamb's tail."

Some of that awkwardness Marie had been referencing earlier settled on them once she and Leo were alone. The snug was big, and the large wooden table between them suddenly seemed an impossible gulf to bridge. She was tempted to make another speech about how she couldn't get caught up in anything with him as she had so awkwardly done when they'd kissed in New York. Even if Max managed to buy them some time, she was eventually going to have to get married. And even if Max managed to get *himself* entirely off the hook when it came to marrying *her*, whoever else her father might have in mind to take his place would be . . . not Mr. Leonardo Ricci of the Bronx. But as she'd learned last time, any speech she might be tempted to give on this topic was irrelevant. As Leo had told her himself, there was "no universe" in which he wanted to marry her.

Of course there wasn't. Her face still burned thinking about the rebuke. She'd only meant that she couldn't get involved with him in any capacity. She couldn't kiss him in the snow. She couldn't do anything that would put her in danger of losing her heart to him. But of course it had come out all wrong.

And then, completely disregarding her own advice, she'd let herself dance with him. If you could even characterize that hugging-with-minimal-moving as dancing. That would never be tolerated at a palace event, both because it wasn't dancing to begin with, and because it was too intimate. Eldovians didn't flaunt their emotions the way Americans did.

"These are cool."

Marie forced her attention back to the present, the present where she was having a friendly, platonic drink with Leo and *not* dwelling on their private forest dance. He was looking at some of Kai Keller's snow globes. Each of the snugs had an inset, glass-walled cabinet that displayed a selection of them.

"There's a carpenter in the village who's really talented. He mostly does residential work, but he started making snow globes a few years ago, as a lark. Imogen—she's the owner here—has been trying to convince him for years to start selling them."

"He should. The workmanship is amazing."

"Who should what?" Imogen slipped into the booth bearing a tray of drinks and sat next to Leo.

"Kai should sell his snow globes."

"Don't I know it." She shook her head. "Stubborn, stubborn man." She passed out drinks. "I took the liberty of bringing a few flights of our beer. We brew it here." Imogen gave a quick rundown of the four different varieties served in small glasses on a little board.

"I was surprised to hear you'd started brewing," Marie said as she sipped the seasonal offering, which was, of course, a cocoa porter.

"Yes, well, as my dad always says, 'Change or die.'"

Marie was about to ask a follow-up question—it seemed like there was a story there—but before she could get it out, Imogen turned to Leo and said, "So. Leo. How do you know our princess?"

"I was in New York last week, and he was my driver." Marie, trying to rescue Leo from a signature Imogen O'Connor interrogation, realized that her explanation was going to fall short. People didn't bring their drivers thousands of miles home with them for Christmas. "We struck up a friendship," she added, which, of course, didn't go terribly far toward clarifying things. People didn't bring their new friends thousands of miles home with them for Christmas, either.

"My little sister developed a massive crush on her," Leo said. "She's a little bit princess obsessed, so meeting a real one blew her mind. And we're on our own, so . . . Her Royal Highness was nice enough to invite us to the Christmas extravaganza here."

Leo's use of her proper title sounded . . . *wrong*. Like he was speaking the wrong language.

"Was she now?" She looked at Marie. Then back at Leo. Then at Marie again.

Marie sighed. She should have known better than to invite Imogen to join them. She'd forgotten how astute her old friend was. Probably all her years behind the bar—she'd tended it since she was a teenager, back when her father was still in charge—had sensitized her to unarticulated emotions. She had an abundance of what the Americans called emotional intelligence.

"Yes, and having realized that my father has turned into Ebenezer Scrooge, I decided to bring Leo here so he knows how to escape when he needs to."

Imogen flashed a smile that seemed on the edge of wicked as she turned her whole body to face Leo. "Well, you come by *anytime*."

The other thing about Imogen was that she was . . . Well, back in their school days, when everyone called her Minnie, they also called her boy-crazy.

A flare of jealousy, sharp and spiky, traveled up Marie's throat, but she kept her mouth resolutely closed. She could have no claim on Leo, and she would do well to remind herself of that fact.

WHEN HE GOT back to his room after tucking Gabby in, Leo sat down to eat some nonsoapy chocolates and deal with an onslaught of texts from Dani.

> Holy shit, Gabby FaceTimed me earlier and showed me her room. You really ARE in a Hallmark movie.

> But seriously, are you hanging in there?

> HELLO? Where are you? Have you been indoctrinated into an Alpine cult? Don't do that. I'd miss you.

He smiled and initiated a FaceTime call.

"Finally." Dani was sitting at the tiny desk in her bedroom, and she looked rumpled and exhausted.

"How's the book?" he asked.

"I need to have sex with a human."

He chuckled at the non sequitur. "As opposed to a not-human?"

"No! Gross."

"What's happening? I thought you were holed up writing?"

"I am, but it turns out that with you guys gone, I revert to living in my head, and a girl can only immerse herself so much in the stifling sexual and social norms of the nineteenth century before she starts thinking about the state of her life."

"So have sex with a human. Get on one of those apps you're always nagging me to start using."

"Ugh."

"You don't have to *date* said human. You're postlove; I get it."

"The thing is, I don't really *want* to have sex with a human. But I started thinking about how Vince has probably had sex with several humans by now. Dozens, even. And *then* I started thinking, damn, I shouldn't let him win." She rolled her eyes. "This is what too much Kate Chopin has done to me."

"So you don't want to have sex because you *want* to have sex; you want to have sex because you want to beat your future ex-husband at some imaginary sex-having game."

"That is . . . correct."

"Aww. My cousin broke you."

"Nah. Anyway, I'm playing mind games with myself. It's the stupid book. You're the one who should go on a date. This thing you have going with Giada isn't healthy. There's a reason you guys broke up years ago."

Here they went. One of Dani's favorite topics. "It's fine. It's . . . efficient." Seriously. Hooking up with an ex was great that way. They didn't have expectations of each other, yet they knew what worked. No fuss, no muss. Anyway, he hadn't seen Giada for months.

"Yeah, but meanwhile life is passing you by."

"When am I going to go on a date, Dani?"

"In any of the many hours per week that we spend hanging out together." She tilted her head and shot him a quizzical look. "But actually, you're kind of on a date right now, aren't you? A magical, palatial date with a princess."

"It's not a date. She's a nice person. She felt bad for us, so she invited us for Christmas."

"Yeah, but how do you *know* it's not a date?"

"You know what? I'm done talking about this."

"I'm sorry. It's the mind games. This book is giving me an existential crisis. Show me your room."

He reversed the phone and made for the bathroom. "Let me show you the soap I ate earlier."

Chapter Ten

The next day was surprisingly fun. Marie had been busy, holed up with her father, Mr. Benz, and some other humorless-looking men—Leo had seen them all filing into a room on his way out with Gabby. He supposed this was the cabinet she'd referenced.

Frau Lehman had arranged a snowshoeing excursion, and the two city kids had had a blast tromping along forest paths under the guidance of a guy who had met them at a stable on the palace grounds. He was a groom, Leo supposed, though like "footman," that was a job title that seemed like it should only exist in fairy tales.

Then he'd taken Gabby to the village, which in the light of day was basically a postcard. There was a central square with an enormous tree decorated in shimmering silver ribbons, and there was a little ice rink adjacent to the square. When Leo saw the latter, he resolved to come back with Marie. But then he thought better of it. Skating with the princess was a bad idea. So was slow dancing in the woods. Having snowball fights. Anything with the princess was a bad idea, basically.

Besides, he didn't know what her level of fame was here. Could she go skating in public without it being a big production? She'd seemed friendly with the woman who owned the pub, which was a bit of a surprise, but that seemed different from being able to stroll around in what was a bustling village.

Regardless, watching Gabby take in everything with wide eyes and unabashed delight was like a sedative. It made him feel calm. Like he could relax for a while. Logically, all his same worries—about their finances, about Gabby's well-being—were still there, but being outside his usual routine somehow made those worries feel physically far away. What had Marie called her time in New York? *A surprisingly refreshing break from reality.* It turned out it worked in reverse, too.

After poking around in a few shops, they settled in at the pub for a late lunch. They'd taken a seat at the bar because there was a giant gingerbread house set up behind it, where Leo guessed the liquor bottles would normally have been. Gabby had gravitated to it like it was her true north, and her effusive monologue had charmed Imogen, who was behind the bar.

"I can't take all the credit, or even most of it," she said. "I bake, and my friend Kai does construction."

"The snow globe guy," Leo said.

"The snow globe guy, but don't let him hear you say that. He fancies himself kind of a hard-ass." She had lowered her voice to a whisper, which seemed odd, but when she turned and said, "Kai! Are your ears burning?" Leo understood.

A big guy in a flannel shirt pulled out a barstool on the other side of Gabby.

"Kai," Imogen said. "Meet Gabby Ricci. She's a big fan of your work." She gestured toward the gingerbread house.

Kai seemed a gruff sort, but only a monster—or a stick-up-his-ass king—could be immune to the admiration of a kid like Gabby. He nodded at her and said, "Thanks."

"And this is Leo Ricci, Gabby's brother and a friend of Princess Marie's. The Riccis are visiting from New York for the holidays."

Kai nodded at Leo and at Imogen when she set a beer down in front of him unasked.

Imogen, he had learned, was a talker. Like Gabby. As the proprietor of what seemed to be the most popular establishment in the village, she knew stuff. He'd heard her dish and receive gossip since they'd arrived, and she'd made no bones about try-ing to pump him for information. She was nice about it, but he didn't blame her. It *was* kind of weird that someone like him would be here as a guest of someone like Marie.

But Kai was her opposite: silent, self-contained. "What's the pie today?" he asked.

"Pork and winter greens." Imogen nodded at Leo. "He's having it. Ask for a review."

Kai glanced at Leo's plate and said, "I'll have a club sandwich and potato salad."

Leo did chuckle this time. Kai was a man after his own heart: silent, decisive, and fond of flannel. "So." Leo nodded at the ginger-bread house. "A mansard roof? That's an interesting choice."

Kai shrugged. "Lots of the original buildings in the village have that kind of roof."

"That makes sense. I would have been tempted to go with a

gambrel in homage to all the barns I saw on the drive in, but you're right; mansard is better."

That got the guy's attention. He turned on his stool, eyebrows raised.

"Architecture school dropout," Leo said. "And nearly a decade on residential construction crews." He took a swig of his beer. "No experience with pastry, though."

"It's surprisingly not that different once you get the hang of it."

"You make the snow globes, too, I think?"

He nodded, and Gabby took over. "You do? The ones here?" When Kai grunted in confirmation, Gabby was off. "Oh my gosh, I love them so much! It's funny, because I have a snow globe at home of Cinderella's castle. You know the one from Disney World?" She didn't wait for an affirmative response. "It's a castle in the snow, the same as one of yours that I was looking at near the entrance. Right? A castle in the snow? But yours is *so* much better."

Imogen, having come back from serving someone else, leaned her elbows on the bar. "Kai's our resident artist." The artist in question rolled his eyes. "Oh, come on. He did all the built-in cabinetry in Marie's suite at the palace. After her mom died and Marie took on more royal duties, she moved into a new set of rooms and did a reno."

"I just did that as a favor because she asked me personally," Kai said dismissively.

"How do you two know Marie?" Leo asked, belatedly realizing it was kind of a dumb question. She was the princess of the country, after all. But it seemed like they actually *knew* her.

"We went to school together," Imogen said.

"You did? Regular public school?" He would have thought she'd have gone to some fancy private school.

"Her mother wanted her to have as normal a childhood as possible. Joséphine was from an old, noble, French family and had gone to posh schools in the States. She rebelled against the idea of Marie being shipped off to grow up away from her family like she had been."

Huh. That made sense, given what Marie had told him about her mother.

"And the village school is small. There's only a couple dozen kids in each grade, so all of us know Marie." She picked up a towel and started drying pint glasses. "We actually used to spend a fair amount of time together."

"Well, it's nice to see that she has friends. Normal friends." Wait. Had that sounded snobby? Maybe the king was rubbing off on him. "No offense. I mean that in the best possible way."

"None taken," Imogen said. "But we're not really friends."

"Oh." Leo was more disappointed than he should have been by this piece of news. It was just that he liked the meddling Imogen and the gruff Kai. They seemed like good folks.

She must have sensed his disappointment, because she cocked her head and looked at him without speaking for longer than he was comfortable with. "I wouldn't say we're *not* friends. We just don't really see each other much anymore."

"Maybe I'll bring her in again before I leave town."

"We would love that." She tapped the bar in front of Kai. "Wouldn't we, Kai?"

Kai grunted.

"We would *love* that," Imogen said again.

BACK AT THE palace, after Gabby was whisked off by Frau Lehman to help sample some of the recipes for Cocoa Fest—apparently they served some old standbys each year but also invented new, elaborate flavors—Leo was approached by the butler. He was carrying a sealed envelope—on a small, silver tray, for crying out loud.

But Leo's derision disappeared when the man said, "Her Royal Highness asked me to convey this message to you, Mr. Ricci."

She'd left a note for him. An actual physical note, which he found oddly charming, given that she could have just texted him.

> Leo, if you're not busy, will you come see me in my suite when you get back?
>
> —M

All that talking about Marie at the pub earlier, combined with the bulk of the day spent without her, made him . . . miss her. *Dammit.* He couldn't deny it. And worse, he didn't even really want to. Denial felt like too much work. That feeling he'd had earlier, of setting aside his cares, of letting the fairy tale of Eldovia take over? He was ready to surrender to it. He was on vacation, after all. So he just let himself be happy to be summoned.

The door to her suite stood ajar, so Leo rapped on it to announce his presence and pushed it open.

And found her in some other guy's arms.

Wait. No. *Other guy* implied things that were not true. Implied territory. A claim where there was none. He ordered himself to unclench his fists.

Marie hadn't heard him because she and the guy—no *other*,

just *guy*—were dancing. Music was playing, and they were doing some kind of formal thing he suspected was a waltz. At least, it looked like a Cinderella-at-the-ball sort of dance. The man was older. He had graying hair, wore a suit, and was saying something to Marie that Leo could not make out.

Once more, he had to make a point to relax his fists. He cleared his throat.

"Oh!" Marie tripped over her partner's foot and pitched forward—toward Leo. "Leo!" she exclaimed after he'd grabbed her and set her on her feet. She was pink. He wasn't sure if it was from embarrassment or from the dancing.

She was wearing a dress that looked like it was made out of men's suit material. It was gray and had a subtle checked pattern to it. It was belted around her waist and fitted snugly until it flared out and came to the middle of her calves.

It was a conservative dress.

It *should* have been a conservative dress.

It was making him crazy.

"Leo," Marie said, oblivious to the fact that she was driving him batty, "this is Jean-Paul Lavoie. Monsieur Lavoie, this is my friend Leonardo Ricci I was telling you about." She smiled at Leo. "Monsieur Lavoie has been my dance teacher since I was six. And I am afraid it's a thankless job. I have him come out every year before the Cocoa Ball to give me a refresher, and I don't know why he hasn't quit in a fit of pique. I'm hopeless."

Dance teacher.

Suddenly Leo's fists were completely chilled out.

"Nonsense, Your Royal Highness. You're very . . ."

Marie laughed, even as she raised her eyebrows at the older man.

". . . diligent," he finished, his eyes twinkling.

"Monsieur Lavoie cannot tell a lie," she said. "He's very honorable." She patted him on the back. "But at least I keep you in business."

"You are too kind."

There seemed to be a friendly familiarity between the two of them—an almost family-like vibe. Clearly, Leo had misinterpreted the scene at first.

Marie shook her head fondly at Monsieur Lavoie before turning to Leo. "So. Mr. Leonardo Ricci of the Bronx. Do you want to learn to dance?"

MARIE DIDN'T EXPECT Leo to agree. Leo was, understandably, sensitive about his background. She didn't want him to feel like he *had* to learn the waltz or any of the other traditional Eldovian dances they did at the Cocoa Ball. But if he *wanted* to learn them, she wanted to help. It was a fine line. She tried to express this sentiment as he walked toward her, bemused.

"There's absolutely no pressure. Most of the ball will be regular dancing. Like you would see at a wedding." Well, maybe that wasn't quite true—did American weddings feature the kind of slow dancing they had done in the woods last night? "But we also do some traditional dances, and some waltzes. Which you can just sit out. If you want. I'm not saying you *have* to sit them out. But if you want to learn, Monsieur Lavoie can help. But I didn't bring him here because I thought you needed him. I really do bring him in every year for a refresher." Oh dear. She was making a hash of this.

"I'm not going to the ball, though."

"Really?" Marie narrowed her eyes. "I thought you were kidding."

"Not kidding. Not going."

"Oh." Why was that so disappointing? She of all people should understand. She would skip the ball, too, if she could.

"So you don't have to be worried about your brutish American guest embarrassing you," Leo said flippantly.

"I wasn't worried about that!" But she could see how he would interpret her offer of dancing lessons that way. She geared up to apologize, but he was grinning.

"I know you weren't. I was just teasing."

Oh. She hadn't realized, which was too bad, because she enjoyed it when Leo teased her. He was in hitting range, so she swatted his chest. It was . . . disconcertingly hard. A memory arose suddenly, of resting her cheek against that chest last night. The cheek—just the one; her right—grew hot. "See? I didn't grasp that you were teasing. This is partly what I mean by saying I'm not a natural princess. I'm awkward on the dance floor *and* in social situations."

"Do not say such things!" Monsieur Lavoie seemed genuinely hurt by her observation. Poor Monsieur Lavoie. He was such a decent man.

"Listen to Monsieur Lavoie," Leo said as he jokingly wagged a finger at her and took a step back.

He was going to leave. Something was happening to her—to her whole body now, not just the one cheek. It was restless. Jumpy. Suddenly, remarkably, the idea of dancing didn't seem so horrible. Of being grounded by strong, sure arms.

When she was dancing, she always felt like she was under a spotlight. Alone under the glare of everyone's scrutiny, even though of course at balls she always had a partner.

With Leo, her jumpy body somehow knew, in a way that went deeper than her intellect, that she wouldn't be alone. That he would bolster her.

She wanted that. She wanted those forearms of his wrapped around her.

"Mr. Ricci," Monsieur Lavoie said to the retreating Leo, "even if you're not attending the ball, perhaps you would be so kind as to partner with Her Royal Highness? She would benefit from having a practice partner who isn't me."

Leo paused in his retreat and looked at Marie like he could see all the way inside her. That was all it took for the restlessness to return. It occurred to her that although she'd been thinking of Leo as the cure for this agitation, he was also the cause of it.

She opened her mouth to demur, to override Monsieur Lavoie and tell Leo to go.

But then she closed it.

Leo, still looking at her, linked his fingers, extended his arms out in front of him, and cracked his knuckles. "All right. Definitely not going to the ball, but let's do this."

Something spiked in her belly.

Monsieur Lavoie approached. "Allow me to show you the steps first, Mr. Ricci. I will take the lady's part."

Leo's sudden startled look made Marie smile. He was a good sport, despite the fact that he probably had not expected to end up twirling around the floor with an elderly Frenchman.

"You have a natural rhythm," Monsieur Lavoie pronounced as the two men came to a halt a few minutes later.

"Piece of cake," Leo said.

"Monsieur Lavoie is a retired professional ballroom dancer,"

Marie said. She had always found it easy to dance with Monsieur Lavoie, both because he counted quietly in her ear and because he took such a strong lead—her body simply had to go where he put it. It was never the same in the wild, though, and of course real dances were often also fraught socially.

"Her Royal Highness is not Her Royal Highness when you are dancing with her," Monsieur Lavoie informed Leo as he lined them up in front of each other. "She is your dancing partner. You lead. She follows."

Was that perhaps why her partners' leads never felt as strong as Monsieur Lavoie's? Because they were consciously or unconsciously deferring to her?

"Do not be intimidated by her," Monsieur Lavoie went on, and Leo raised an eyebrow.

If finding someone who would not fuss over her position was critical to the success of the dancing endeavor, Leo was her perfect partner.

Monsieur Lavoie put her right hand in Leo's left as Leo slid his hand around to her lower back and pulled her close.

And there it was. Those arms. Stepping into them was like lowering herself into a thermal spring in the mountains. Warmth where there had been cold, relief where there had been tension.

He had pulled her too close for a waltz, though, and Monsieur Lavoie wasn't having it.

"No, my dears, no!" He clapped his hands in two, sharp staccato bursts and stepped in to rearrange them. "Remember your frame." He put some distance between them and lightly slapped their arms, one at time. "Tension in the frame so that where you lead"—he pointed at Leo—"she goes."

There was that eyebrow again. Leo was enjoying this way too much.

But he certainly led. He got the hang of it quickly, and aside from a few early missteps, soon he was putting her where she needed to go. Like Monsieur Lavoie.

Except *not* like Monsieur Lavoie. Monsieur Lavoie's hands were not as big, or as warm, as Leo's. Monsieur Lavoie did not stare at her with his eyes burning with an odd mixture of heat and amusement. Monsieur Lavoie did not smell like spicy oranges.

Marie's stomach fluttered, but she kept moving.

She was lighter on her feet than usual. In addition to the strong lead, Leo was graceful enough for the both of them. He kept tension in his frame, but brought a kind of flow to the proceedings.

He made it feel easier.

Which, now that she thought about it, was true about him in general, whether "it" was a waltz or a meeting at a watch shop. Leo made *everything* feel easier.

After fifteen minutes, Monsieur Lavoie was showering them with delighted applause. "Shall we move on to the ländler?" Then, to Leo, he added, "It's a traditional Eldovian dance."

"It's hard," Marie said. "Think *Sound of Music*."

"I think I'll quit while I'm ahead," Leo said. "I was just telling Marie yesterday that in my book, dancing is swaying. I guess I was wrong."

"No," Monsieur Lavoie said, "not wrong." Marie was shocked. Not once in the eighteen years she'd been working with Monsieur Lavoie had he said anything like that. "Dancing is many things. For someone like the princess, it is a performance. Part of her job. That kind of dancing is highly choreographed. But in other contexts, dancing can be many other things."

"What do you mean?" Marie asked. "What else can it be?"

"Dancing can be joy. Comfort." He looked at her as if he'd recently uncovered a delicious secret. "Love."

"Well, that's not what's going on here," she said quickly. "None of those things." She was lying, though. Hadn't she just been comparing Leo's embrace to a hot mountain spring? Goodness, she sounded like a lovesick teenager.

A laugh bubbled up, like a jet in her imaginary spring. Monsieur Lavoie looked at her quizzically. She patted his arm. "I'm sorry. You know I appreciate you, Monsieur, but if I never had to dance again, I would be a very happy woman."

Yesterday, that would have been the truth. Today? She glanced at Leo. It was hard to say.

Chapter Eleven

*W*altzing is fun. Who knew?" Leo mused as they crunched along in the snow. Marie had asked him to come on a walk with her, saying she wanted to show him something before dinner. He hadn't had to be asked twice.

"I wouldn't go that far," Marie said.

"Oh, I've converted you to the swaying method, have I?"

She laughed. He loved making her laugh.

"No. It's just that dancing with you or with Monsieur Lavoie is different from dancing at the Cocoa Ball where everyone's attention is on me."

"Isn't there a cheesy song lyric about dancing like no one is watching?"

She scoffed. "Well, that's a pretty sentiment, but I've never in my life been able to do that."

Not even last night? He bit his tongue, though.

"You know who was a wonderful dancer? My mother."

"Ah, yes, your beautiful, graceful paragon of a mother."

She swatted him on the chest—for the second time this afternoon. He didn't hate it. So he kept poking. "I bet she danced like no one was watching all the time."

"She didn't." Marie grew serious, so he did, too. "She was extraordinarily graceful, but she was acutely aware of her position, and of the scrutiny that came with it. And even though she never let the outside world see it, it sometimes chafed. In public, she danced like everyone was watching her every move—because they *were*, and she knew it. She just made it *look* otherwise."

That struck Leo as incredibly sad. "Your father was king, right? She became queen because she married him?"

"Yes. She came from an old, wealthy family, so she was used to attention, but being a royal is different."

He marveled that anyone would choose such a life, especially if what Marie said about her mother chafing under royal scrutiny was true.

She must have anticipated his unspoken question. She said, softly, "He used to be more lovable. He used to be worth the sacrifices she made."

"What happened to him?"

"Her death changed him. It brought out the worst in him. He loved her terribly. I know it's hard to imagine if you're only meeting him today. I don't think any of us realized how much she stabilized him. Softened him. Until she was . . ."

Her voice cracked, and Leo felt like his heart did a little bit, too. They were walking on a path that cut through the woods—the hill the palace was situated on was crisscrossed with paths maintained for hiking and horseback riding and cross-country skiing. There were trees on either side of them, thickly lining the path even though they had shed their leaves for the winter. They'd been walking single file because the path wasn't quite wide enough for two people to walk abreast comfortably, but screw comfort. Leo shoved up next to Marie and slung an arm around her shoulders, but he kept them walking so it felt casual. Sort of.

"I kept thinking time would help," she said quietly, "but it hasn't. She died just before Christmas—on the twenty-second. I wanted to take the next term off, but Father made me go back to school." She huffed a rueful little laugh. "We actually had an enormous argument about it." Another laugh, this one even more bitter. "Of course, he won."

"What did he say?" Leo asked gently, not sure he wanted to know, because he feared that the answer might make him even more cranky the next time he had to see His Goddamn Majesty.

"He said that life goes on, that my wanting to be with him was just postponing us finding closure." Leo rolled his eyes, but made sure she didn't see it. "I went back to Oxford. I told myself he needed time alone, that we all deal with grief in our own ways." His heart broke to think of Marie, rejected by her father, alone with her sadness. "But the maddening thing was that I don't believe he addressed his grief at all. He just drowned himself in it. When I came home at the next term break, he was more brittle and short-tempered than ever. I try to do what he wants, to . . . be what he wants but . . ."

It was never enough. He knew how that sentence ended, because he could see her trying to manage her father, to smooth over his rough edges and placate him. "I'm sorry," Leo said, and he was. So much. At least he and Gabby had had each other to lean on. He didn't know what else to say, but Marie didn't seem to be expecting anything, so he let silence settle. But he kept his arm slung over her shoulders. They walked in silence for a few minutes until Marie shook off his arm. So that was the end of that little interlude. It was for the best—it had been feeling awfully cozy, and cozy was dangerous. Cozy was not something he could have in any permanent sort of way.

But wait, she'd pulled away because they'd arrived at their destination. A clearing. A big one, hidden deep within the woods.

"Wow," he marveled as he followed her in. "You'd never know this was here."

"Exactly," she said. "You said dance like no one is watching. This is the *only* place in my life where no one is watching."

He took a few more steps in and started to turn slowly, taking in the space. It was like a secret room in the woods. He didn't know if it was a natural clearing—Were those actual things? His city self didn't know—or if the trees had been removed. Either way, you could see all the way up to the sky, which was currently clear and blue and just starting to look like dusk was coming. He almost expected there to be some ancient druidic ruins here. He kept rotating, and—whoa. It seemed like there *were* ruins on one end? "What's that?"

"It's a log cabin. The start of one, anyway. Three-quarters of one."

It was indeed. He moved closer. Construction appeared to have been abandoned—the structure stopped at his eye level and lacked a roof. It had an opening for a door, though, so he ducked under it. "Wow." The interior was small. He had no idea if internal walls had been planned, but there were spots at which the structure jutted out, and he could well imagine small rooms or at least nooks to create separate uses within an open-concept great room.

Marie followed. "This was my mother's favorite spot, this clearing."

"Was it always here, or did someone remove the trees?"

"It was always here. Well, it was always here in my lifetime and hers. She's the one who had the network of trails put in on the hill, before I was born. Before that, there was just the main road. She hired a landscape architect, but she was very involved, tromping around and helping figure out what the best layout would be. They stumbled on this clearing, and she fell in love with it. She used to come here all the time, to get away from things."

"To dance like no one was watching—for real," Leo said.

"*Exactly*. She would drag my father out here, too, sometimes, and have picnics." A mischievous smiled bloomed. "Supposedly I was conceived here."

"Well, hot damn."

"She brought me here all the time. Some of my first memories are of sitting by the fire out here." Marie went back out the door opening and Leo followed her. "There's a firepit out here. Usually my mother and I would come by ourselves, but sometimes my father would come, too."

It was hard to imagine King Emil kicking back in the clearing, but Leo could totally see young Marie and the mother she had described doing so.

"She used to say it was our secret family place." Marie continued. "She would tell the palace staff that we were going for a walk, but we would come here. You were surprised that I'm allowed to come and go as I please. I told you about the fence but really, I think my mother is the reason I enjoy what freedom I have—she set those expectations." She spun in place, looking at the clearing as if she were seeing it for the first time. "Maman thought of this as a place where we could be a regular family. As soon as I was old enough to understand the concept, she swore me to secrecy regarding its existence."

"So why have you brought me here?" The question came out gruffer than he'd intended. But honestly, he was gobsmacked by this place. By the fact that she'd decided to show it to him.

"I figure you're safe."

Safe. He liked that idea. It stirred up something in his chest.

"You're leaving in a week," Marie said, "and I think it's safe to say you'll probably never be back to Eldovia."

He didn't like *that* idea. Not so much the idea of never coming back to Eldovia, although after the day spent in the village, the place had grown on him. But the thought of never seeing Marie again was . . . unsettling.

"I don't know." She seemed dissatisfied with her previous answer and kept talking. "I suppose the truth is that although I've kept coming here by myself, it's become a lonely place. It's meant to be a family place, but I don't really have a family anymore."

Leo was about to reflexively object, but Marie held up a hand. What she said next summed it up better than he could have. "Yes, I have my father. But I don't really have *my father* anymore. I have the king." He couldn't argue with that, so he said nothing. "As for why I've brought you here . . ." She shrugged. "I thought you would like this place. I thought I would like showing it to you."

I thought I would like showing it to you. Jesus. Her voice had gone all low and sexy. He wouldn't have thought it was on purpose—Marie was absurdly innocent in a lot of ways. But the phrase shifted the air between them. Charged it. *I thought I would like showing it to you.* He took a step toward her. "And did you? Like showing it to me?"

He loved that she didn't step back, didn't hesitate. Didn't do anything but stare him down and say, calmly, "Yes."

They stared at each other for a few beats before she surprised him by saying, "I'm vexed with you."

What? He'd thought they were . . . Well, he didn't know what. He forced himself to tune into what she was saying and found that he didn't like the way it felt to have Marie "vexed" with him. "Why?"

"You should have told me about architecture school. You had several opportunities when it would have been natural to do so."

"I'm sorry," he said automatically, though god knew why he was apologizing. He didn't owe her anything. "It's kind of a sore spot."

"Still. I thought we were friends, or . . ." She bit her lip.

Or what? She thought they were friends? Or she thought they were something else?

He'd been thinking about that something else, too. About that *or.* Fuck it. He'd been thinking of the gulf between them—the princess and the cabdriver—as a reason to keep his hands off her, but maybe that was backward. She was right. The princess of Eldovia and the cabdriver from the Bronx were never going to see each other again after this week. There had been sparks flying today, and between her snuggling up against him while dancing and being all coy just now, they weren't just coming from him.

So what the hell was he waiting for?

Leo had just enough coherent reason left in him to peel off his gloves first. He knew he was going to want to feel Marie. Her skin, her hair. *Her.*

Her breaths were shallow. Little bursts of steam emitted from her lips. His world shrank so those lips *were* the world. That rose-bud. That heart. He swooped in, but stopped just short of her mouth, so the steam from his breath joined with hers. Waited. Because although he had come, rather rapidly, to his "fuck it" revelation, that didn't mean she had.

He hoped she had. *Please let her have.*

There were only a few millimeters between them.

She closed the gap. It felt like a triumph. Belatedly, he remembered his hands. Or maybe his hands remembered her. They came down on her cheeks to ensure that she didn't go anywhere—no one was going anywhere for a very long time. He was going to feast on her.

It was different this time. This wasn't some impromptu kiss outside his building where Gabby might stumble on them. This was premeditated, and they were in her secret place in the middle of the goddamn Alps.

When his lips came down on hers, her mouth opened. So smoothly, so completely. As if this was choreography they'd been doing together for a long time. As if this was a dance she *knew* how to do.

He'd forgotten how amazing kissing could be, even—maybe especially—when it wasn't just the precursor to more. Kissing for its own sake, like you had all the time in the world, was pretty fucking great.

He could feel Marie relax as his tongue made its initial incursions. Even her head grew heavier in his hands. It was like she was shedding an invisible burden, surrendering it to him. He was happy to take it. Proud that she trusted him with it. That she thought he was, as she had said, *safe.*

So they stood there in the cold and kissed. Kissed like they were in a goddamned movie.

But it wasn't all heady emotion urging him onward; it was also pure, animalistic want. It was powerful, coarse, and highly improper. As he swept his tongue deeply through her mouth, he let one hand leave her face and slide down her back until he made contact with her ass. He encouraged her forward then, wanting her to feel what this was doing to him. Not that he expected anything to happen beyond this kiss, but he suddenly felt like the girl who thought she wasn't graceful or beautiful or *whatever* should *feel* decided evidence to the contrary.

As with the dancing, she went where he wanted her. She went *further*: she huffed a moan that seemed part arousal, part frustration and ground herself against his thigh. They were both wearing jeans, but he could feel the heat emanating from her through both layers of denim. *Fuck. Yes.* He had not imagined things going this far, but now he could not imagine stopping. He used his leg to grind back against her. Abruptly, she broke their kiss and let out another moan. This one was lower, longer, *dirtier.* This one was all frustration. She rocked her hips against his leg, and he thrust it harder against her core. Did it again, setting up a rhythm meant to encourage her to writhe against him. Let his face fall to her neck and whispered, "Yeah. Take what you need."

She sucked in a sharp breath, like she was shocked, but he was pretty sure it was a good sort of shocked.

If no one ever danced with the princess of Eldovia like no one was watching, it was safe to say no one ever talked dirty to the princess of Eldovia like no one was watching. "Yes. Keep going."

Another gasp. She liked this. He did, too, so he amped it

up—both the pressure and the dirty talk. "Use me to make yourself come."

And she did.

It was *astonishing*.

OH DEAR LORD. What had she *done*?

When Marie came back to earth, she wasn't sure which was the worse transgression, that she'd shown Leo her mother's secret hideaway or that she'd humped his leg like a dog in heat and had an orgasm in her mother's secret hideaway.

He was still holding her. They were both breathing hard.

He was a wizard. Those fairy tales Gabby so loved? Marie was in one now, and she'd been bewitched by an evil wizard with sexy forearms and a secret plan to ruin her. She knew how these stories went. Soon, she'd be locked in a tower. Or asleep for twenty years. She needed to get away from him.

Her face was on fire. She didn't want him to see her. So she buried her face in his neck. Which wasn't helping on the whole getting-away-from-him front.

He only let her rest there, mercifully out of his sight, for a moment before he gently pushed her back. Held her at arm's length. "Hey, hey." He studied her face for a long moment with those all-seeing, unnaturally pretty eyes, and though it should have been impossible, her face flamed higher. Hotter. Throbbed along with the juncture of her thighs, which was still tremoring with the occasional aftershock.

"Regrets?" he asked softly. "*Real* regrets, I mean. Not bullshit ones you think you should have. Because if so, I owe you an apology."

Real regrets. That was an interesting way of putting it. It reminded her of the dancing like no one was watching metaphor. Did she really, in her heart, regret what had happened? The prospect of him apologizing for it helped answer that question. She smiled sheepishly and shook her head. "No regrets. If there's any apologizing, it should be me to you for . . ."

Leo raised his eyebrows. "For what?" For a moment, he looked like he was trying not to laugh, but she wondered if she had imagined it, because a graveness washed over his face, a kind of serious intensity she hadn't seen on him before. "For grinding all over me and getting yourself off?"

Oh my. His words went straight to her oversensitive sex. She wanted to put it down to the fact that she hadn't had sex in the two years since university. She'd used her time at Oxford, away from the spotlight of royal life in Eldovia, to gain some experience. To have some fun—at least, until her mother died. Not that she had a bedpost full of notches, but she'd had some good times with a few boys. Still, even in those carefree years, no one had ever made her feel like this, and certainly no one had *ever* spoken to her the way Leo had.

She liked it. It was embarrassing but thrilling. How to answer? Her first instinct was to be all abashed and missish, because that seemed like the "proper" response.

But was it? In the sense that proper meant "right"? That sort of response felt weak.

No, she would own what had happened. She would own her own response to it. "Yes. For grinding myself all over you and getting off on it."

"Fuck, *Princess*," he bit out. Leo's face screwed up, and he sounded pained.

"I'm sorry if doing that was out of line, or if I was . . . using you."

"You *were* using me. I *told* you to use me."

"Right." Well, she was supposed to be owning this, wasn't she? So she lifted her chin and straightened her spine.

The gesture seemed to amuse him. He pressed his lips together like he was trying not to smile. "Let's just say no apologies are required."

"Good. So. Regrets: none on my part. You?"

He reached out and smoothed her hair. Plucked a leaf out of it. "Maybe just that we wasted so many days *not* doing this."

She felt the grin all over her body. She felt like her face might crack open. Like her *chest* might crack open—like it would *have* to, to let all the exhilaration inside her escape so she didn't burst. That he had enjoyed himself that much with her made her almost giddy. Not with the princess. With *her*. Even in her relatively carefree university days, away from the scrutiny of the palace, she'd never been able to fully trust that people—friends and lovers alike—were attracted to her and not to her position.

Leo had his head tilted up to the sky. "It's starting to get dark."

She had to revise her earlier claim of no regrets. She did feel a little bad that she had gotten off as a result of their hot, snowy interlude, but *he* had not. That was also unprecedented. In fact, she couldn't think of one time that had happened. In her experience, male orgasm was inevitable and female orgasm was an occasional, irregular bonus.

But Leo didn't seem fussed that his needs hadn't been attended to, and it was getting dark. And to be honest, she was enjoying the lopsidedness of the situation. This moment of selfishness. She busied herself smoothing her coat, still debating whether she should say something. Or attempt to . . . do something. But he was staring at the cabin with a contemplative look. "So what's the story with the unfinished cabin?"

"I told you this clearing was my mother's special place. Our family retreat. The summer before she died, she got the idea to build a little log cabin here. She was always getting these crazy ideas—everything from an ice cream buffet for breakfast to impromptu trips to the Riviera."

He smiled and held out his hand. She was used to people doing that with their elbows. She was used to resting her hand on a man's arm and letting him escort her into dinner or one of those infernal balls. But she wasn't used to holding hands for the sake of it. It seemed almost painfully intimate suddenly, which was silly given what had just happened.

She took his hand, hoping the mitten on hers would obscure the fact that it was shaking. "And it's not precisely true that no one else has ever been up here. There's a carpenter in the village. Kai—he made the snow globes at the Owl and Spruce."

"I met him today. I took Gabby for lunch, and he was there. He was . . . exceedingly silent."

She smiled. "Yes. So you can imagine that my secret is safe with him. And I went to school with him. I trust him." Leo led the way back onto the path. He walked a little ahead of her on the narrow path, but he didn't let go of her hand. "My mother presented the plan for the cabin to my father. She said it would make our clearing a more comfortable all-season retreat. He agreed easily."

"That's hard to imagine."

"It's hard to . . . overstate how different he was back then." Marie was having trouble getting the words out.

Leo stopped walking and turned to look at her without letting go of her hand. It was starting to get dark. He did that thing she'd come to recognize as a signature Leo move where he slouched so he could get right in her face and perform an assessment.

"He agreed," she said, pushing through the lump in her throat and rushing to get on with the story. "And she hired Kai, but what you saw was as far as he got. She got sick as the weather turned. She really wanted to see it finished, and Kai, God bless him, worked like a fiend. But in the end, she declined faster than the doctors predicted." She nodded toward the path to signal that she wanted him to start moving again.

He obeyed, asking, "And you didn't want to finish it after she was gone?"

"Oh, I did. More than anything. I still do. But my father won't hear of it. I took him out here and tried to convince him to let me keep going. I shoveled off the pond and brought our skates . . ."

"The bad memory you referenced when we were shoveling my place," Leo said gently.

"Yes." Marie still remembered the pain of that day. There was the fresh hurt of her mother's death but also the sharp sting of her father's reaction to the clearing. She had thought it would bring them together. But instead she'd lost her mother *and* her mother's place. "I was still naïve enough then to think that he might heal. That we might heal together. But he ordered construction halted. I tried to strike a deal with Kai to go behind his back, but my father found out and lost his mind. He issued a royal proclamation saying that it was forbidden for anyone to construct a monument to my mother."

"*What?*" Leo snorted.

"Mind you, it has no legal teeth. Though the mechanism still technically exists for the crown to issue royal proclamations, they're not actually enforceable. They're only used for things like proclaiming a day in honor of an athlete who medals at the Olympics, that sort of thing. And of course no one knew about the cabin. So the proclamation was targeted solely at Kai. Which Kai knew. So he backed down. Not that I blame him."

"Why no monument? What if someone wanted to put up a statue in the village or something?"

"I don't know. It's like he doesn't want to remember. He never even talks about her."

"It hurts too much," Leo said, and he said it kindly, like he understood, even though her father had been nothing but rude to him. Marie was glad Leo was ahead of her, glad she didn't have to look at him.

"I've always wanted to finish the cabin, but there's no way I'll find anyone to help me. Even if there was someone I could trust, no one is going to directly disobey a proclamation from their king. Not for something trivial like this, something that doesn't matter."

They'd reached the main road. Leo held up a large branch that was blocking their way so she could pass. He had to drop her hand to do so. She felt the loss.

"Hmmmm." He let the single syllable draw out, like he was teasing her about something. She didn't know what.

He laughed. Not *at* her, she was fairly certain, even though she was still confused about what was happening. It felt like a conspiratorial laugh. "It's too bad you don't know any architects. Or, technically, architecture school dropouts. You get what you pay for, I guess."

"Pardon me? You can't mean . . ." Could he? That was ridiculous. There wasn't enough time, for one, and—

"I do mean."

Marie was dumbfounded. Literally unable to speak. She had just been thinking how Leo made everything easy. This, she had to find a way to explain, was not something he could make easy. Not something he could apply his grumpy but relentless American can-do attitude to and just *do*.

"Look, Your Majestic Supreme Highness." He wagged a gloved finger at her. "This is my turf. I am the perfect person to finish this cabin for you."

Oh dear god, he was going to do it. He was *going* to make it easy. Both the job itself and her ability to trust him. Something fluttered in her stomach, something she hadn't felt for a long time. It was the same feeling she'd get when her mother would interrupt a meal, or, even better, dancing lessons, and proclaim it time for a trip to L.A.—or even just family movie night.

It was an unfamiliar feeling of late, but she recognized it all the same. It was excitement.

Marie wagged a mittened hand back at Leo. She was going to concede. Of course she was. But she was going to have fun doing it. "You're the perfect person for the job? I'm not sure how you figure that? I'm a little concerned about this *half*-architecture-degree business."

"Well, yes, but one, you don't need an architecture degree for this. That's just a little bonus. This is basically Lincoln Logs. I worked construction for years. Finishing this off will be a piece of cake."

She tried not to smile. "Very well. What's two?"

"What?"

"You said, 'One,' just now, implying that there was more than one reason you were the perfect person for this job."

"Right." A slow, almost evil smile blossomed. "Two is: I don't give a flying *fuck* about your father and his royal proclamations."

BACK AT THE palace, Leo hunted down Gabby and heard about her afternoon. She toured him around the kitchen and gave him tastes of all the hot chocolate she'd been helping make. He felt a little bad that he was only giving her half his attention, but two things were happening that were distracting the hell out of him. One, he was horny. That was what happened when you let a princess hump you in the woods. Two, doubts were creeping in. Again, a fairly standard outcome when you let a princess hump you in the woods.

After what felt like forever, Gabby was dispatched for a predinner bath—she had chocolate firmly lodged under her fingernails—and Leo went to his room and FaceTimed Dani.

He didn't even bother asking her about the book. He didn't even bother with *hello*. He dived right in—because he needed to have his goddamn head examined. "Marie and I got it on in the woods. Sort of."

Dani started laughing.

"What?"

"Oh my god," she choked out, barely able to get the words out.

"Will you shut it? I need advice, not mockery!"

"Okay, okay, sorry." She composed her face into an overly serious expression. "Shoot."

"What do I do now? Apologize?"

"Why would you do that?"

"Uh, because I defiled the goddamn princess of Eldovia in the woods. In *her* woods. In the woods surrounding her *palace*."

"Did she enjoy being defiled?"

"Well, yeah. I think so."

"Did she defile you back?"

"Actually, no." He shifted in his seat.

She snorted. "I fail to see the problem. Except maybe for your blue balls. Poor Leo."

"How can you not see the problem? I got Marie off in the woods!"

"So you're having a little holiday fling. Enjoy it. Try to get off yourself next time."

"Do you think she wants to have a fling with me?" Was that what was happening here? No. That didn't make any sense. "What would be in it for her?"

Dani cracked up. Threw her head back and cackled.

"What?"

"Are you really that dumb?"

Leo didn't know how to answer that. So apparently he really was that dumb.

"Have you ever thought about why Giada keeps fucking you even though you guys broke up years ago?" she asked.

"Because it's efficient?" he ventured, falling back on the word he usually used to describe his thing with Giada.

"Yeah, but she moved to Jersey City! She hauls her ass all the way to your place."

"Are you trying to say she has a thing for me?" Because she absolutely didn't. Their relationship had been brief, and it was ancient history. The sparks—those kind of sparks, anyway—were long gone. And he hadn't even seen Giada for the better part of a year.

"No! I'm trying to say that all signs point to you being good in bed, Leo."

"Oh." He was embarrassed. This was like talking to his sister about sex. "You know what? I gotta go," he said.

"Yeah, you do that." She smiled at him. "Bye, Leo. I would say, 'Be good,' but I think since you asked for my advice, I'll actually say, 'Be bad.'"

He needed to shower before dinner, but he had a bee in his bonnet about this, so he typed a text to Giada. **Hey.** He probably should have said more. She was going to interpret that incorrectly.

> I can't.

Leo chuckled. Yep. Actually, he shouldn't do this over text. That was a dick move, right? Even if they weren't really breaking up. They'd already done that, years ago. Still. He called her.

"Leo. I told you, I'm busy."

"Yeah, that's not why I'm calling. I just need to talk to you for a sec."

"Okaaay." Giada sounded skeptical, which was fair enough.

"I want to . . . break off this thing we have going. If we even have a thing going anymore."

"We don't have a thing going anymore. I met a guy like six months ago."

"Well, good for you." He meant it.

"He lives downtown."

"So no need to haul your cookies up to the Bronx anymore."

He'd been kidding, but she must have thought he was offended. "Leo, I'm sorry. Should I have told you? I didn't think we were—"

"Hey, it's okay. I met someone, too. It's just a temporary thing while I'm on vacation. But I didn't want to . . ."

She laughed. "Leo, you are honorable to a fault. I haven't seen you since last spring. You don't have to 'break up' with me." He could hear the air quotes. "*I* was planning to keep you in my back pocket in case things go south with Mr. Lower Manhattan, but you were always better than I was."

He wasn't sure he agreed with her assessment, but he just said, "Thanks."

"Send me a text every now and then, let me know how you and Gabby are doing, okay?"

"You got it. And if you're in the neighborhood visiting your parents, stop by and say hi if you have time."

"I will. And I'm not just saying that."

Leo felt like a weight had lifted when they hung up. Giada was a good person. But, Marie aside, he and Giada, who had been hooking up as exes for way longer than they'd been together, had been on autopilot for too long. Hell, most of his life was on autopilot. That was how it had to be. He had to make money and put food on the table. But still, it was nice to feel like he was moving on from something.

Chapter Twelve

King Emil was a real ass.

A real, royal ass.

He was insufferable and snobbish and generally a dick.

Which was one thing. But as dinner that night went on—and on and on and on—Leo started to understand that he was doing it on purpose. Emil's snobbery wasn't a defense mechanism like Marie's occasional bouts of prissiness were. He wasn't trying to cover social awkwardness or lack of confidence with a stiff upper lip.

Marie seemed to think it was grief driving him, but Leo was pretty sure it was just pure, unfiltered arrogance. Spite as sport.

He would have been able to handle it were it not for the way he treated Gabby. Yes, Gabby talked a lot. And perhaps *ladylike* wasn't a word you could apply to her. But she was a *child*.

Every time she got rolling on one of her monologues—and since they were four courses into dinner and counting, there had been a few of them—the king did this thing where he looked away and up. Like he was rolling his eyes but not quite. As soon as he could, he would interrupt and ask some question expressly designed to highlight the economic and social gulf between them. "And what exactly," he had drawled, "is a . . . Hatchimal?" when Gabby was in the middle of talking about how she'd grown out of liking some of the toys she used to be mad for. This, of course, had led to her enthusiastically explaining, with accompanying gestures, that Hatchimals were big eggs out of which animatronic stuffed animals hatched. "And after they hatch they go through all these different stages—baby, toddler, kid. You can tell which stage they're in by rubbing their tummies and seeing what color their eyes are."

"How . . . delightful." There went the king's eyes again. If you called him out, he would probably say he was noticing a cobweb on the ornate chandelier that hung above their heads, but they all knew what was happening here.

Well, the adults knew. Gabby wasn't sophisticated enough to understand that when the king stressed the word *delightful*, he intended to convey the opposite concept. But, judging by her furrowed brow, she could tell something was off.

Leo formed his hands into fists under the table. The only thing stopping him from pounding them on the table was Marie, who was clearly mortified, and whose repeated attempts to rein in her father were going ignored.

"They're really expensive," Gabby said. Leo didn't know if she was just doing her usual talking-to-fill-space thing or if, bless her, she somehow knew she was being talked down to and was trying to hit back without really understanding the context.

"Are they indeed?" Emil held his glass—a crystal goblet of red wine—up so that the light of the chandelier above glinted off it.

"Yeah, they're like sixty-five dollars at Walmart. But if you get the twins, they're even more expensive."

"My heavens."

"*Father.*" Marie's horrified whisper twisted something in Leo's chest.

But not enough for him to keep his mouth shut—it was hard to imagine any amount of twisting doing that when someone was insulting Gabby. "Yeah," Leo said, "I had to drive *a lot* of extra shifts—in my cab that I drive, for my job—to earn enough for that thing."

It was all he could think to do, to double down on his identity as the working-class guy from the Bronx. If the king was going to cast him in that role, Leo was going to play the hell out of it. He wasn't ashamed of who he was or where he'd come from. He stared defiantly at the king while he spoke, and eventually the fucker looked away.

"Oh, I forgot," Marie said suddenly, with an air of excitement. "I had an email from the UN High Commission on Refugees today!"

That got her father's attention. He put his wine down. "Oh?"

"Yes! They asked me to become a goodwill ambassador! Can you imagine?"

The king raised his eyebrows as if to signal that no, he could not imagine.

"I'm not surprised," Leo said. "By all accounts your speech was a smashing success."

"Were you there, Mr. Ricci?" Emil asked, his upper lip curling slightly. Strangely, that almost imperceptible curve was more effective than a full-on one would have been.

"No," Leo said, meeting the elder royal's gaze unflinchingly.

"But I googled it, and I read an analysis of it that said your daughter had 'exploded on the scene as an articulate and formidable presence in the realm of humanitarian policy.'"

So, yeah, he had google-stalked Marie. Big deal. Who wouldn't have, in his place? A princess offers you five thousand dollars a day to drive her around Manhattan, you do a little creeping.

"Anyway," Marie said, "if I agree, they suggest a trip to their center in Copenhagen to highlight their mission to create alternatives to camps with—are you ready for this?—Jessalina Angelo!" She turned to Leo. "She was one of my mother's favorite celebrities. She always wanted to meet her, but it never worked out. I know I shouldn't be focused on that aspect of things, because that's completely not the point of this work, but I can't help but be a little starstruck."

It was funny to think of Marie, an honest-to-God princess, being starstruck by the Hollywood action-star-turned-do-gooder.

"Ooh!" Gabby exclaimed. "She played the evil queen in that movie! So you could be like the good princess and she could be the . . ." She was overtaken by a huge yawn. She was so tired. It was late to be eating dinner—it was late, period.

"I'm sorry," Leo said, speaking only to Marie. "I think we're gonna have to bail on the rest of dinner. It's really late and Gabby needs to get to bed." He was tired, too. Exhausted, really. Lunch at the pub seemed like a lifetime ago. And in the interim, there had been waltzing lessons and the clearing and . . . making out with Marie in the clearing.

Thinking about the last item on that list suddenly had him feeling significantly less tired.

"Of course," Marie said. "We'll eat earlier tomorrow evening." When her father sniffed, she turned to him. "You needn't join us, Father."

"But Leo—" Gabby swallowed her protest when Leo shot her a withering look. She had probably been going to object to missing dessert, but it seemed to him that Gabby had Frau Lehman wrapped around her little finger—he took some comfort in the fact that it wasn't just him—so probably a quick in-room bedtime snack of the sweet variety could be arranged. Or there would probably be some nonsoapy chocolates in her room.

AFTER LEO HAD gotten Gabby to bed and retreated to his own room, it was almost eleven. Too late to text the princess, probably. They hadn't had a moment alone since they'd returned to the palace. He was a little relieved. He wasn't sure what the post-orgasm-in-the-woods protocol was. Hell, he didn't even know which fork he was supposed to use.

He had the vague idea that you were supposed to call the next day.

But that was assuming you and the woman in question went to your separate houses. It didn't account for what to do when you were staying at the woman's house.

And for when that house was a palace.

Well, whatever. He would worry about it tomorrow. For now he was going to . . . what?

He looked around, almost guiltily, at his posh surroundings. Someone had lit a fire in the hearth and turned back his covers. There was a tiny, foil-wrapped chocolate resting in the exact center of the pillow closest to the nightstand.

He knew what he wanted to do, but it didn't seem right.

Well, fuck it. He unwrapped the chocolate and after tentatively prodding it with his tongue just to make sure it *was* chocolate, he popped it into his mouth. It was dark and bitter and shot through with a mint flavor so intense it made his eyes water.

He shed his clothing and flopped down on the ridiculously cushy bed.

Stuck a hand down the front of his boxers and groaned in relief. It had been a very long evening.

He tried not to do it. Tried to turn his mind to something else—anything else. Any*one* else. Jennifer Lopez. So shoot him. JLo was from the Bronx. She was gorgeous. She did it for him.

Usually.

He could tell, though, that tonight there was only one thing that was going to work.

One image.

He could only hope he wouldn't be haunted by it for the rest of his miserable life.

He tightened his grip and let himself feel her breath on his cheek. The rush of it as she exhaled her surprise—and pleasure—as he whispered dirty nothings in her ear.

He let himself see her. Flushed and emboldened by her own power. Her Royal Highness Marie Joséphine Annagret Elena, Princess of Eldovia, making herself come as she ground all over his leg.

He muffled his shout by turning his head into that ridiculously fluffy pillow.

"You could at least try to be nice," Marie said quietly to her father after bidding the Riccis good night.

He whipped his head up from where he'd been refilling his wineglass—they'd kept up her mother's tradition of dining without servants hovering over them.

He was shocked. Marie had learned not to speak to him like this. After he'd sent her back to school and made clear that there would be no shared father-daughter grief, no strengthened emotional bond as the silver lining of her mother's death, there didn't seem to be any point in trying to say anything real to him. So she never corrected him or suggested that his behavior was anything less than impeccable or that his whims were anything less than gospel. It was easier to go along with what he wanted. It was almost never worth starting a row.

But that was before he started being cruel to her friends.

It hurt her, to see him like this. She'd told Leo that her mother had always tempered her father. Softened him. She was realizing now how much she had always believed that eventually, he would thaw. That things would get better between them. That beneath her father's gruff exterior, there was still a good man.

Like Leo.

But what if that wasn't true?

What if, without her mother, her father was just a big bully?

What if she never got him back?

"You'll tell the UN you're honored but you have to decline their offer."

She blinked at the change of subject. But, fine. They might as well have it out now. "No."

The king physically recoiled a little. Because if she never scolded him, she *certainly* never outright defied him. She wasn't sure what made her so bold tonight.

"You won't have time. We have to focus all our efforts on shoring up Morneau."

"Father." She sighed. "About that. I think it might be time to—"

"Mr. Benz reports that Marx is—"

"No." There it was again. How astonishing. "Mr. Benz does not report. *I* report." She had made a full report to her father and his cabinet this morning. "*I'm* the one who saw Marx."

"Yes, well, between him and Gregory, we need to focus all our energies internally for the foreseeable future."

"I can do both."

"So what I hear you saying is you want to throw open our borders to hordes of people who have no skills and—"

"That's not what I'm saying. I'm saying Europe has a refugee crisis. The *world* has a refugee crisis. It's not going to go away, and we—I—want to help."

He glared at her.

She glared back.

It's what Maman would have done.

She was being uncharacteristically bold tonight, but Marie didn't quite have the guts to say that out loud.

She wondered if he heard her anyway.

Chapter Thirteen

I can't see the phone when you hold it like that." Leo sounded peevish. He tried not to, but honestly, how was he supposed to copy Hair & There's tutorial if he couldn't see the damn phone?

Try to copy.

Leo was really bad at braids.

It shouldn't be this hard, with his years of construction experience. What were braids but building with hair? But he'd never gotten the hang of it.

Gabby heaved an extremely put-upon-sounding sigh.

He held his hands up like he was being robbed. "Okay, let's try again."

"Forget it," she snarked, letting his phone clatter to the dressing table she was seated at.

He closed his eyes. Started counting to ten in his head. He tried not to get into arguments with Gabby. She needed the stability of someone who supported her unconditionally. But sometimes she drove him batty. So, yeah, he was bad at even the most basic of French braids, forget the more elaborate creations she

coveted. Dani sometimes reminded him that they were still siblings. Still family. "And what is family," she said, "if not a bunch
of people who annoy the hell out of you a large proportion of the
time?"

He tried to comfort himself with Dani's words, but really,
the whole braids thing always gave him that borderline-frantic
feeling that he was fucking everything up. That no matter how
hard he tried, he would never be enough to replace the parents
Gabby had lost.

The worst part was Leo had thought they were post-braids—he
had thought *this* particular reminder of his inadequacy was behind him. Gabby used to want braids all the time, but she hadn't
asked at all this school year. He put it down to her getting older.
Well, that or the fact that Glinda and company wore their hair
down. Either way, he'd been happy for the reprieve.

When he finished counting and opened his eyes, it was to the
princess's reflection—he was standing behind Gabby and they
were both facing the mirror.

"Can I help?" Marie asked with a smile.

"We're good," he said automatically. And to Gabby: "What
about a regular French braid?" He could do those. Sort of.

"Fine," she bit out.

"Wait a moment." Marie stepped farther into the room. "What
kind of braid are you after? What about a waterfall braid? I'm
pretty good at those." She turned her head to display what Leo
could only assume was the braid in question. It snaked diagonally
back on one side of her head, except it was sort of like half a
braid—the pieces that were pulled through fell loose. Hence the
name, he supposed—it did sort of look like a waterfall made of

hair. "A staff member did this one because I can't do my own, but I can have a go at yours."

Come to think of it, Marie was probably the source of Gabby's renewed interest in braids. Though she hadn't worn them in New York, the princess seemed to favor braids here at home.

Marie came to stand next to Leo and made eye contact with Gabby in the mirror. "You don't have to keep the ends down like mine. We can do two braids like this." She sketched where the braids would go. "And then gather everything up in a ponytail or bun." She held her fist at the nape of Gabby's neck.

"Yes!" Gabby squealed.

"All right. Stand aside, big brother." Marie mock shoulder-checked him.

Her fingers moved with an ease Leo had never been able to achieve, try as he did to follow the instructions on the YouTube tutorials Gabby called up. Marie's fingernails were bare. They'd lost the ugly New York polish. Soon Marie was fastening the first of the two braids.

"You're really good at this," Gabby marveled.

"Well, I think I had my hair braided every day of my life until I turned fifteen. I'm not that good at doing my own hair, but I picked up a few things. I used to do Imogen's all the time when we were younger."

"Can you do Dutch braids?"

"I can. And you know what's fun?" She paused in her progress and used one hand to mime an imaginary braid diagonally across Gabby's head. "You do a side Dutch braid, but then when you hit the bottom, you do the tail as a fishtail."

"Oooh!" Gabby's mouth had formed an *O*, as if such a fantastical combination of techniques had never occurred to her.

"And we have a . . . woman who works here, Verene, who can do much more elaborate creations than I. I'll have her pay you a visit tomorrow."

Servant. That's what she'd been going to say. Not "woman who works here." Leo stifled a snort.

He watched in silence and thought about last night. He'd wondered if he should text Marie. He'd decided to put it off until tomorrow. Well, it *was* tomorrow. The day after he'd made her come in the woods. So he should say something, right? What, though? *I enjoyed getting you off very much, Your Royal Temptress, and look forward to being of service in the future?*

"There you are." The princess tied off Gabby's ponytail and patted her on the shoulder.

"Thank you!" Gabby rotated her head in front of the mirror so she could see the hairstyle from all angles.

Obviously, he wasn't going to say anything now, in front of Gabby. So Leo settled for addressing the immediate proceedings. "Thank you." He'd spoken softly, but it drew Marie's attention in the mirror. He was strangely touched by how easily—both from a technical perspective but also, like, emotionally—Marie had handled the situation. "I try, but braiding is not my forte."

She shook her head as if to disagree with him, but let the matter drop as she glanced at her giant watch. "I've come to check in on you. I'm afraid I have meetings again this morning."

Oh. Was this the royal blowoff? Okay, so maybe he didn't have to say anything about yesterday. Maybe she had already moved on.

That was fine. Good. A relief.

Right?

"No worries," Leo said. "Gabby and I are going to walk down to the village this morning, maybe go ice skating. So don't worry about us."

"However," she went on, "I have only one more morning of work—tomorrow—before we all break for the holidays, so I shall be a better hostess after that. I hope we will . . ." She sought Leo's eyes in the mirror. "Get to see each other this evening."

Okay then.

She turned pink.

Leo very much feared he did, too.

FOR GOD'S SAKE, Leo thought as he and Gabby approached a cabin in the woods a half mile or so out of the village, *this damn country really is a Hallmark movie come to life.*

The cabin was modestly sized but exquisite. It was double gabled, had a slate roof, and featured a wraparound veranda that probably doubled its square footage in the summer. A curl of smoke rose from a stone chimney.

And, more importantly, it was a *log* cabin—jackpot.

Its owner emerged out of another structure Leo hadn't noticed at first—an outbuilding of some sort. Semiobscured by a stand of trees, it was cruder in its construction but also made of logs.

So he had definitely come to the right place.

Kai scowled as he approached them. Imogen from the pub, when she'd given Leo directions, had told him Kai wouldn't be happy to see him. "He doesn't like visitors," she said. "Imagine Ebenezer Scrooge." She'd looked thoughtful then, as if contemplating a mystery. "If Ebenezer Scrooge spent all his free time making snow globes." Her face returned to normal as she shrugged, apparently done thinking about the contradiction that was Kai.

Leo didn't have a lot of time to get this done, so he'd decided to come right out with it. But then, he'd forgotten about the Gabby factor. Not that he gave one single shit about disobeying a royal proclamation or whatever, but there was no reason to involve Gabby in his plot. The odds were high she would end up compromising it somehow—the girl could not keep her mouth shut at the best of times, much less when there was a secret involved. So he tried to speak in code to Kai.

"Hey. I'm here because I'm going to be, uh, working on a project I could use some advice on." He hitched his chin toward Kai's cottage. "One you seem to have some expertise on. Or, you know, it's more that I'm *finishing* a project."

Kai's face twisted into a caricature of annoyed surprise. Well, at least he'd heard the code correctly.

"Let me show you something," he said gruffly, but he was speaking to Gabby. He didn't wait for Gabby or Leo to agree, just turned on his heel and headed back to the outbuilding, which turned out to be a workshop.

"Oooh!" Gabby cooed when she caught sight of a table covered with snow globes. "Can I look?"

Kai nodded and pointed past her to where a few projects were under construction. "You might be interested in those, too." He walked over to an elaborate wooden creation, picked up a small metal marble, and set it on top of the contraption. The marble started making its way down a little ramp before disappearing into the center of the structure and popping out on the other side. It was a marble run. Well, it was the Alps of marble runs. Leo watched, rapt, as the marble underwent an elaborate journey to the bottom of the structure.

Gabby was similarly delighted. "Can I try?" she asked, and Kai nodded.

Leo's heart squeezed. This was such a bittersweet age, this period between girlhood and womanhood. He hadn't imagined this . . . limbo.

Not that it took much to be enthralled by the craftsmanship of Kai's creations. Leo was, for the most part, not prone to thrall, but he was damn impressed.

Kai motioned Leo to the other side of the workshop, where there was a wood-burning fireplace. "What the hell are you up to?" he whispered.

"I'm going to finish the log cabin in the clearing."

"Who told you about that?" Kai wasn't bothering to disguise his annoyance, which, hey, Leo could appreciate.

"Marie. She took me there. And I told her I'd finish it."

"Why would you do that?"

Leo shrugged. "Why not?"

"You're asking for a world of trouble."

"Because of the *royal proclamation*?" Leo infused the words with the disdain he felt.

"No. Because you think you can just come railroading in here with your American arrogance, stir things up, and leave a mess for Marie to clean up."

Well. That was not at all what was going on here, but it was the sort of answer Leo could respect. So he tried again. Tried the truth, as uncomfortable as it made him. "That's not what I think. I think . . ." What? He didn't even know how to articulate to himself why he was doing this. "I think finishing it would help Marie. And, more practically, she spends a lot of time out there. A shelter would be good. And I'm not talking about building a minipalace. Nothing as nice as your place—I don't have the time for that or, frankly, the skills. I only want to raise it a little higher and add a roof."

Kai looked at him for a long time, his face unreadable.

"I don't need you to do anything. I have a plan for finishing it, but I need a lead on logs." Short of chopping trees down himself and dragging them in—which he'd actually given some consideration to doing, but a bit of research on his phone had illuminated the should-have-been obvious point that you had to debark and dry logs you were going to use in cabin construction—Leo didn't have a source. Kai kept staring at him. "Look. I have no local connections or knowledge. I just need logs. I'm estimating I need about eight more."

"Sixteen."

Interesting. "Why?"

"I was planning a saltbox roof, so there could be a loft in the back."

"Saltbox," Leo echoed, rejigging his mental image of the cabin.

"Yes. You Americans are good for something, it turns out."

A saltbox would mean they'd need to bring the back wall up higher, and that could indeed accommodate a small sleeping loft. It was a good plan. But . . . . "I don't have time for that. I'm leaving on the twenty-sixth. This is going to have to be quick and dirty."

"I was using a Scandinavian saddle notch on the logs," Kai went on. Ha. He was starting to crack. "That way it won't need any weatherproofing."

"Right. I saw that. But I was going to finish it with a dovetail notch."

"Amateur." Kai sniffed.

"But much faster." According to what he'd read, anyway.

"You can't just change the technique eighty percent of the way through."

He had the guy. He performed a shrug. "Not ideal, I'll grant you, but no one will be looking that high up. Most of it will be obscured by the roofline anyway."

Kai pressed his lips together like he had tasted something unbearably bitter. "I'll meet you there tomorrow morning. Be prepared to work."

Leo grinned. "You'll deal with the logs?"

"I'll deal with the logs."

"Thanks, man." Leo stuck out his hand.

Kai dropped his gaze from Leo's face to his outstretched hand, made another of his annoyed faces, and turned on his heel.

SHE WAS GOING to do it.

She *was*.

So why was Marie standing outside Leo's door like she was cowering in front of her father?

She had given a speech at the UN last week, for heaven's sake, a speech that had gone well enough that the United Nations had invited her to become a goodwill ambassador.

So certainly she could manage a minor personal matter such as this.

Honestly. She and Mr. Benz had spent the morning cooped up with a few allies in parliament trying to communicate the palace's priorities for the budget bill that would be tabled early in the new year. Then she'd called Max because she was losing her nerve—and at risk of backpedaling—when it came to the goodwill ambassador thing. She'd been hoping a little of his breezy confidence-bordering-on-overconfidence would rub off on her. And he had indeed given her a pep talk.

So she could do *this*. This was nothing.

She rapped on Leo's door.

"Gab." She heard him sliding the lock open. "I *told* you I'm gonna take a shower. I'll come get you when—"

He had opened the door a crack during his little speech, and when he realized it was her and not his sister, he stopped speaking.

"Good evening," Marie said. She could only see a slice of Leo's face, but it was enough to register that it was a smirking slice. "May I come in for moment?"

"Sure thing, Your Highest Splendidness."

When he swung the door open, he was naked but for a towel around his waist.

And a giant grin she was pretty sure the Americans would call "shit-eating." He waved toward a pair of wingback chairs positioned near the fireplace. "Have a seat." He overshot the chairs himself, and for a moment she thought he was going to the bathroom to get dressed, but he only grabbed a small box of truffles from the nightstand.

He held them out to her, but she shook her head.

Leo plopped down in the chair opposite hers and popped a chocolate in his mouth. She always ate those truffles in two or three bites. You could really savor them that way, notice the subtle textural differences between the bittersweet coating and the sweeter, softer filling.

But not Leo. He just popped the whole thing in his mouth like it was a piece of popcorn. He was sitting there with his legs splayed—not enough that she could actually see anything, but enough that the edges of the towel came away from each other.

"What can I do for you?" he said with his mouth full.

Was it her imagination, or did he let his legs splay a little more as he spoke?

And what if they had? That would be a sign her overture was likely to meet with success, would it not? She straightened her spine. "I am here with a proposal."

He raised his eyebrows.

She straightened her spine some more. "I propose we embark on a sexual affair for the duration of your time in Eldovia."

He choked. Pitched forward in his chair and coughed like a cat trying to expel a hairball.

"Oh my goodness!" She shot to her feet and crossed the short space between them. Once there, though, she didn't know what to do. "Are you all right?" she finished weakly.

The coughing tapered off and he gradually got himself under control. It occurred to her that this was the first time she'd ever seen Leo *not* in control.

She tried to retreat to her chair now that she was assured he was all right, but one of his hands shot out and grabbed her forearm.

"Say that again."

Had she not made herself clear? She didn't know how to be any more direct. "I propose we embark on a sexual affair for the duration of your time in Eldovia. That's what? Five more days?" The siblings were scheduled to fly home on Boxing Day.

Leo huffed a disbelieving laugh and let go of her in favor of running a hand through his hair. She took the opportunity to retreat. Which was, perhaps, not the wisest course of action given her aims. Retreating wasn't very . . . seductive, was it?

"Why?" he asked, finding her gaze when she was back at her chair.

"Because eventually I will have to marry, and it won't be someone I get to choose."

"You know this sounds like something from another century, right?"

"To you I am sure it does. I, however, have been aware from an early age that my eventual marriage will have to benefit my country. Ideally, I'll be fond of the person, too." She *was* fond of Max.

Should she tell Leo about Max? No. Max had no bearing on what she was proposing.

"What about your parents?" Leo asked.

"Their marriage was arranged by *their* parents."

"But to hear you tell it, they were in love."

"They were, but that came later." She gave a sigh of frustration. "The point is that I don't have an endless amount of time left, and I would very much like to . . . enjoy myself while I can."

"I see." He looked amused. She didn't know what to make of that. "And have you . . . enjoyed yourself before?"

"Are you asking if I'm a virgin?"

"Yep."

"Does it matter?"

"I'm sure as hell not in the business of deflowering any virginal princesses."

"You're not?" He didn't seem like the kind of man who would care about such antiquated notions of sexual purity.

"I know how that fairy tale ends. With me facing a royal firing squad."

She couldn't help but laugh at that. "Eldovia outlawed capital punishment in the 1950s."

"Still."

"Well, I'm not a virgin." Leo raised an eyebrow. "I . . . enjoyed myself while I was away at university."

"Oh, you 'enjoyed yourself,' did you?" He was teasing her, but not in a mean way.

She tamped down a smile. She had enjoyed herself. She'd set out to do so, in fact, just as decidedly as she'd set out to study engineering. "Eldovia is . . . it's hard to explain. It's like a small town where everyone knows me. Everyone thinks of me as the princess first and foremost. At Oxford, I'm sure people still thought of me as a princess, but I didn't have to see them in the village. Here, I can't just . . ."

"Hook up with someone casually?"

That was exactly it. "I thought of university as my last chance. But then . . ."

He grinned. "Then you 'enjoyed yourself' yesterday?"

"Yes." More than she had ever "enjoyed herself" at Oxford, in fact.

He *did* let his legs splay a little more—the term one saw on

American social media was *manspreading*, she thought—as he leaned back and grinned.

"Don't let it go to your head," she admonished but she couldn't help mirroring his smile.

"So I think what you're trying to say, Your Wickedness, is 'Leo, you rocked my world yesterday.'"

"That's not at all what I'm trying to say."

It was, though. It was exactly what she was trying to say.

"I see." He closed his legs and covered himself fully with the towel, which suddenly seemed like a lost opportunity. "I guess I misunderstood." He levered himself out of the chair and turned toward the room's armoire, but not before she caught a twinkle in his eye.

"I'm not sure I would characterize our interlude yesterday as 'world rocking,'" she lied, because she could tease him, too. "Still, as I said, it was enjoyable."

"But really, is 'enjoyable' a high enough bar?" he called from where he was standing, obscured by the open door of the armoire. "I'm assuming that what you're proposing would be a big freaking scandal if it came out. That seems like a lot of effort for 'enjoyable.'"

She bit the insides of her cheeks to keep from laughing as she pretended to give serious consideration to his argument.

"Not to mention Gabby. We'd have to figure out a way to ditch her."

"Repeatedly."

"Huh?" Leo stepped out from behind the door, and he was wearing a pair of jeans, which caused a curious little stab of disappointment in her chest.

She cleared her throat. "We'd have to ditch Gabby repeatedly."

"Because your intention would be to enjoy yourself repeatedly."

His chest was still bare, so she let herself look. Why not? Clearly they'd long ago abandoned any pretense of propriety. It was broad and dusted in the center with a smattering of dark hair. She ordered herself not to sigh like a lovestruck girl. "As much as I can."

He started walking, but instead of sitting back in his chair, he kept going until he came to a halt just in front of hers. She couldn't help but notice, given that she was eye to eye with it, a thin trail of that same dark hair starting at his navel and disappearing into the waistband of his jeans. Those jeans hung low on his hips, exposing V-shaped muscles.

"Tell me what you 'enjoyed' about yesterday," he said, drawing her attention as he made quotation marks with his fingers. He was standing so close to her—though not touching her, it had to be noted—that she had to tilt her head way back to see his face. "But use actual words, not this posh doublespeak. You're not allowed to use the word 'enjoy' anymore."

All right. She could do this. She'd come this far. "I liked the way you spoke to me."

It came out softer than she'd intended, and she half expected him to play at not being able to hear her, but he only said, "How did I speak to you?"

"You told me to take what I needed," she whispered, her face on fire. "You told me to use your leg to make myself come."

"Dirty talk," he said matter-of-factly.

"Yes, dirty talk." That was part of it. That was a lot of it. "But also . . ." He raised his eyebrows. It was hard to explain, even to herself. "You spoke to me like I wasn't a princess. Like I was a normal woman."

"Aren't you?" His expression turned quizzical. "A normal woman, I mean?"

She ignored the question in favor of continuing her explanation—it suddenly felt imperative that she finish. "And you concerned yourself with my pleasure," she said, finding that she was working out her feelings on the matter as she went. Being forced to articulate them helped unclutter her own mind. "But again, I got the feeling you didn't do that because of who I was. That it was more a matter of course."

"That is correct." His voice had taken on a stilted, almost formal tone. She might even use the word *posh* he had so recently sneered at. Which was why she was so shocked when that tone was used to deliver the next thing he said: "I might be a poor schlub from the Bronx, but I know how to fuck."

Marie gasped.

"And I know that the way to fuck a princess is exactly the same way you fuck anyone else."

Leo reached for her hand to help her to stand. He was the picture of gallantry, the gesture completely at odds with what had just come out of his mouth.

They still weren't touching—well, aside from her hand in his. He had taken a step back to make room for her when he tugged her to her feet.

"But not now," she said quickly. She had to get the necessary paperwork ready.

"Not now," he agreed. "I told Gabby I'd come find her after I showered."

"When, then?" She sounded needy. Maybe that was okay, though, because she *was* needy.

"After dinner," he said.

"Oh," she exclaimed. "After Gabby goes to bed."

"I think," he drawled. "This Hallmark movie is about to get *a lot* more interesting."

Chapter Fourteen

$\mathcal{D}$inner was, of course, interminable. Marie felt like an exposed nerve. In addition to being on edge about her father—she felt like she had to be on constant alert so she could smooth things over as needed—she could *feel* Leo's attention. It was heavy and palpable and . . . delicious.

Marie had thought having sex with Leo Ricci was going to be fun. It turned out that *not* having sex with Leo Ricci was also remarkably delightful.

"Will you pass the butter, please?" He nodded at the dish that was sitting between them. Though it was slightly closer to Marie than to him, it was well within his reach.

He did something with his face as she passed it. It was a smirk, but that wasn't, on its own, a sufficient descriptor. It was a smoldering smirk, though such a combination should have been impossible.

"Thank you," he rasped, as he let his fingers slide down her inner wrist before closing them around the crystal dish.

She started to worry that everyone could see the pulse in her throat. She felt like she'd swallowed a bomb. There was a ticking bomb lodged in her throat, pulsating shamelessly, a billboard advertising her desire.

Miraculously, no one seemed to notice. Well, no one besides Leo. He kept dropping his gaze to that exact spot. Which created a bit of a spiral in that his attention on that spot made that spot . . . more of a spot.

She was doing it, too, though. She couldn't stop looking at his lips. Which was silly. It wasn't like she hadn't seen them before. They were so . . . pillowy. Thick and lush, like a supermodel's. Lips that vain women the world over paid good money for. Especially the bottom one. She wanted to lick it. She wanted to—

She jumped when *he* licked it.

Probably because the soup—a beef consommé—was thin and therefore a little dribbly.

She sighed and forced herself to tune into the conversation. It was going remarkably well, which was good given that she was utterly failing in her attempts to stay on top of it. It almost seemed like her father was trying to be civil.

"I was so surprised when she came back home to find her mother gone, too," Gabby said. She was chattering about a book she'd found in the library, *Liesl*, a classic Eldovian novel from the nineteenth century about a girl who, through a series of unlikely plot twists, is forced to survive on her own in a remote part of the mountains for a summer. It was a beloved story that all Eldovians grew up on. Even her father had a soft spot for it, judging by the fact that he seemed to be giving Gabby's observation serious consideration.

"But in retrospect, don't you think there were hints?" he said.

"The way her mother gathered so many eggs that morning, for example."

Gabby nodded sagely. "I think you might be right."

Well, my goodness. A détente?

Marie darted a glance at Leo. He wasn't paying attention at all. To her father and Gabby, anyway. He was, however, paying attention to Marie.

He licked his lower lip again, did his smirky smoldering, and said, "Pass the salt, please."

So. Many. Fucking. Courses.

Soup. Salad. Fish.

And here Leo had thought the fish was it. Was the "main" course. But after that had come a plate of prime rib.

And cheese.

Some kind of apple strudel–type thing.

And, of course, chocolate.

He'd been worried he was going to end up catatonically full. That when it came time to get it up, instead of delivering the "Do me like I'm not a princess" goods, he was going to pass out.

Luckily—kind of—it was taking a hundred years to get Gabby settled.

She was yammering a mile a minute about the Cocoa Fest preparations she'd been allowed to help with and the book she and the king had talked about over dinner. Tomorrow, she was going skiing. Marie had arranged for Mr. Benz to take her to a gentle hill for lessons.

Which Leo was pretty sure meant Marie intended for them to spend a good portion of the day in bed.

"That Mr. Benz guy is kind of funny, actually," Gabby said.

"He is?" Leo didn't see it.

"Yeah, he seems so stuffy, but he brought me one of those marble things like we saw at Kai's. Oh, and there was this time when I was in the kitchen with Frau Lehman, and he came in, and . . ."

He zoned out. He tried not to. It was funny. Gabby used to talk all the time, when she was younger. But lately, at home, there were days where Gabby barely said two words to him. Days when he bent over backward to extract the merest morsels of information about her inner life.

Here, he couldn't get her to shut up. It was like Eldovia had unleashed her repressed inner chatterbox.

Which, normally, he'd be thrilled about. Normally, he would try to settle in and try to steer the conversation toward how she was doing. To find out how much and in which areas he was falling short. But not tonight. He kept looking at his watch. Initially, anyway. But then he checked himself. It was a real dick move to ditch your sister so you could go bang a princess.

A princess you were going to bang like she *wasn't* a princess.

Whatever.

Finally, though, Gabby went to sleep.

Leo detoured back to his room to take a shower. Which probably wasn't necessary as he had showered *before* dinner. He just . . .

Aww, *fuck*. He felt so much *pressure*.

Which wasn't like him. Leo wasn't a guy who got his undies in a bunch over sex. Sex was fun. Sometimes it was great. He generally took care to make sure his partner had a good time. But he didn't give it too much thought beyond that.

He would never admit it to Marie, because clearly to do so would be a royal mood killer of the first degree, but he was kind of worked up about doing it with her. Not because she was a princess. He didn't *think* so anyway—though he'd be the first to admit that he wasn't naturally talented at examining his emotions. But because of this whole thing where he was her last hurrah before she had to get married to some royal dickwad or other.

So, yeah, pressure.

He didn't like it. They needed to get this over with.

And when was the last time he'd thought *that* about sex? He was in the upside-down. But, of course, he already knew that. That had been true since they'd driven up the hill the first time and he'd spied the palace with its maddeningly asymmetrical turrets.

Leo paused in front of Marie's door, took a deep breath, and tried to find another emotion, something beneath his jitters. He closed his eyes and felt again her breath on his cheek as she moved over him in the woods. A shiver ripped through him as if he were back there, but he wasn't cold. It was excitement. Of the sexual variety but also just . . . the regular kind. He couldn't remember the last time he'd looked forward to something so much.

He rapped on her door, and she answered almost immediately, as if she'd been standing just on the other side of it.

She was wearing a white nightgown. Of course she was. He swallowed a laugh as he assessed it. It went to her ankles, though it was sleeveless. It looked like something Anne of Green Gables would wear, or Laura Ingalls.

Or, you know, the princess of a small Alpine country he'd never heard of a week ago.

"What?" she asked urgently. "What's wrong?"

Leo forced his face into submission. "Nothing." Even he knew it wasn't a good idea to laugh in a situation like this. And he wasn't really laughing *at* her. She was just so . . . herself. As much as he didn't want to be, he was charmed. Really fucking charmed.

What the hell had he gotten himself into?

Marie smiled shyly and gestured him inside. The gown, which he was still examining, laced up the front like a giant shoelace, which suddenly brought to mind her *other* white lace-up dress, the one she'd been wearing the day they met. An expanse of bare back. Creamy skin damp with sweat and painted with goose bumps.

A coil of desire twisted inside him, sudden and sharp.

Okay, this wasn't going to be so hard, after all.

She led him toward a seating area near a roaring fire. "We need to do some paperwork, I'm afraid."

Huh?

She sat on the sofa and picked up a sheaf of papers that had been lying on the coffee table. "I need you to sign an NDA."

Oh, hell, no. "*What?*" Also: there went the coil of desire.

"A nondisclosure agreement."

"I *know* what it is," he said peevishly.

"It's merely a formality. We have to do them in all sorts of situations."

"No." *Fuck that.*

"I beg your pardon?"

"*We* do them in all sorts of situations? Who is 'we'?"

That seemed to trip her up. She opened her mouth and closed it again.

"Well, I'm not signing it." Something was spiraling inside him again, but it wasn't lust this time.

Marie looked at him for a long moment. The fire had turned the light in the room a warm orange. She was glowing. She was gorgeous.

And he was *pissed*. Did she know him *at all*?

"There's no reason to take it personally."

"A nondisclosure agreement starts from the principle that I'm going to sell you out in some way. How do I not take that personally?" He didn't have a lot in this world, but he did have his pride. And he wasn't giving it up so easily. Even for a princess. *Especially* for a princess.

She followed. "You're too honorable, Leo."

Maybe so. If "too honorable" was even a thing. Regardless, a man had to hang on to what he had, and Leo didn't have a hell of a lot. "You want me to fuck you like you're a normal woman. Let me give you a little tip, *Princess*. I don't normally sign NDAs before I hook up."

She blinked. For a moment he felt bad, because she looked hurt.

But he was hurt, too.

He made an effort to gentle his tone, said, "Good night, Marie," and left.

Leo set out while it was still dark the next morning, thankful that Gabby was occupied for the day.

He had spent a largely sleepless night contemplating his life. Because that, apparently, was what he did now.

He continued to ruminate as he hiked down the hill. Had he been wrong to refuse to sign that damn NDA? What harm would it have done? He wasn't planning on selling Marie out in any way, shape, or form. He would never do that. So why wouldn't he sign a piece of paper *saying* he would never do that?

He just . . . couldn't. After all his mental wrangling, that had been his big conclusion. He couldn't even articulate why.

Which only served to ratify his second conclusion: he didn't belong here. He didn't know how to waltz. He didn't know anything about refugee policy. He still had trouble figuring out which fork to use. Those things—and NDAs—were part of a rarified world he was only visiting. He needed to not lose sight of that.

He *was* a guy who could build a log cabin, though.

So, apparently, was Kai. As Leo emerged into the clearing, Kai looked over from where he was standing, hands on hips, contemplating the cabin.

More importantly, next to Kai was a pile of perfectly straight, debarked logs.

"How did you get these here?" Leo had pondered the problem. The pathway that led to the clearing wasn't big enough for a truck. And he'd been sure he would beat Kai here this morning—it was only six A.M. Yet here was Kai *and* a bunch of giant logs.

"Christmas magic," Kai muttered grumpily.

"Well, thanks, man. I appreciate it."

Kai didn't say anything except, "Coffee?" He nodded at a large thermos.

"God, yes." Leo's early-morning departure from the palace—

like Cinderella fleeing the ball, except instead of a ball it was a royal booty call gone bad—had not involved coffee.

Kai, who was drinking out of an enamel mug, poured some coffee into the lid of the thermos and handed it to Leo. "I have an appointment at two this afternoon, so I have to be done by one. I thought I'd get an early start."

"You think we can finish the structure today?" There wasn't much time before Leo and Gabby went home. And, before everything had gone to shit last night with Marie, he'd imagined the unveiling of the cabin as a sort of Christmas present.

"Yes. I've already got half the logs notched. We just need to do the rest and build a tripod hoist. The actual raising of the logs will be fast."

Soon Leo was following Kai around as he did some kind of Grizzly Adams thing to decide which trees to cut for the hoist, which would help them lever the logs up to where they needed to be. He would walk right up to a tree, tilt his head back, and stare at it silently. Then, keeping his head in that position, he would walk a slow circle around the tree to examine it from every angle.

Leo had been unapologetically leaning into his modest city-guy persona in Eldovia. His pride demanded it. When the king made a martini "stirred, not shaken, with a twist of lemon," Leo drank his beer directly from the bottle, like he had at the Plaza. When Mr. Benz asked if he skied, Leo said, "I live in the Bronx in an apartment and don't own a car, so what do you think?" When presented with a goddamn NDA, he refused to sign it. It was a reflex, to show these people that he wasn't ashamed of his humble origins.

"This one," Kai said suddenly, tapping the trunk of a . . . tree. Leo had no idea what kind it was.

"What do you look for?" He hustled over to try to see what Kai saw. Though in the palace someone would have had to pry his pride from his cold dead hands, Leo didn't see any reason to cling to it here when there was something useful to be learned. He'd done a lot of time on construction crews, but he'd never really thought about the actual sourcing of the materials. That had always been someone else's problem.

"Just one that's long enough and fairly straight. So this one will work, and then we need another, similar one." Kai paused. "If you're looking for actual logs to use for a cabin, though, you want them to be about eighteen inches in diameter, and they need to be really straight."

"Good to know." It was. Not that he'd be building any log cabins back in New York. It was too bad. This was actually really interesting.

After they'd located their trees, Kai produced a chainsaw and they got to work felling them and building their hoist.

Soon, they were measuring and notching the rest of the logs. Leo was learning a lot. He'd read up on log cabin construction before approaching Kai, but there was theory and there was practice. To his surprise, Kai was tolerant of his questions, and even went so far as to start preemptively offering observations about what he was doing. As Kai had predicted, the actual raising and placing of the logs went quickly.

"SHALL WE CALL it for the day?" Kai asked when the last log was slotted into place. "We should be able to get the roof framed tomorrow if that suits."

Leo, whose stomach was growling audibly, was glad to agree on both points. "Rafters tomorrow, and underlayment?" Kai nodded. "And then what?"

"If we were purists, we'd make bark shingles."

"We're not purists. We're hurry-up-ists."

Kai did something with his mouth that wasn't a smile but was maybe less of a frown than his default expression. "Which is why I took the liberty of ordering shingles. If we can get the trusses done tomorrow, we should be able to do the shingles the day after. We just need to decide on pitch." He extracted a piece of paper from his pocket and handed it to Leo. "This is a 5:12. It'll make it easier on us—we'll be able to walk on it."

"This looks great." Leo glanced at Kai. He didn't want Kai to think that he was stomping all over his original plan. "A steeper pitch would look better, I know." They would need special equipment for a steeper roof, though. "And the saltbox idea was a good one. It's just that—"

"No. You're right. It was one thing when I was doing this before. But now that it has to be done in secret, I agree that we need to cut corners to hurry it up. You and Marie can make changes later, if you want. See how it ages."

"I won't be here. I'm leaving in a few days."

Kai looked at him silently for an uncomfortably long time before saying, "Right," and turning for the trees.

They trudged along the path in silence. Leo was exhausted, but in a good way. There was nothing like a day of physical work to get a man out of his own head, make him feel like he was doing more in the world than just taking up space.

When they reached the main road where they would part ways—Leo to go up to the palace and Kai down to the village his house lay on the far side of—Leo turned to Kai. "Thank you. I didn't expect so much help."

Kai shrugged, said, "Well, when we get drawn up on charges, you're taking the fall," and started ambling away.

Had that been . . . a joke? From Mr. Scrooge?

Chapter Fifteen

*L*eo hadn't been walking more than a minute along the main road before Marie appeared in the distance. She was wearing a bright red coat, and she looked like a beacon.

No, he corrected as she came close enough for him to see that the coat featured a fur-trimmed hood and that she was also carrying a basket, she looked exactly like Little Red Riding Hood.

Did that make him the big bad wolf?

As she strode up to him, with her cold-pinkened cheeks and her bright blue eyes, he very much wanted to eat her up. She had an ease about her out here, in the woods. She looked happy and free, and it was pretty fucking irresistible.

"Good afternoon," she said, smiling at him. "I thought I might find you here."

He eyed her, trying to find within himself some of the anger from yesterday. Some of what she called his honor, maybe.

He couldn't seem to locate any. All that physical labor must have wrung it out of him. He almost wanted to . . . smile at her, this woman who, just last night, had wounded his pride in a way that had felt mortal. He pressed his lips together.

"I'm done working for the day." She lifted her basket. "I brought lunch."

He smiled.

Dammit.

She glanced down the road behind him. "I thought we could eat lunch in the clearing."

"What's Gabby doing?" he asked. "Still on the ski trip?"

She looked at her watch. "They're probably done skiing by now." She smiled a cat-that-ate-the-canary smile. "But I asked Mr. Benz to take her horseback riding after lunch."

"I bet he loved that."

"Mr. Benz has an overdeveloped sense of duty that can be exploited, and I had an ulterior motive in sending him skiing with Gabby this morning."

"Yeah?"

"This morning we had a breakfast for the members of parliament. It's a social event, primarily, but we also use the occasion to push for our priorities in the upcoming session. Usually Mr. Benz attends." Marie's eyes twinkled.

He chuckled. "And let me guess. Your priorities are different from Mr. Benz's?"

"Well, some of them are the same, but I *might* have taken the opportunity to lay the groundwork for some of my plans with regard to refugee policy."

"Well, good for you."

"And what have *you* been up to all morning?" she asked. When he raised his eyebrows—she no doubt knew what he had been up to—she said, "May I see?"

Leo had been imagining waiting to show her the cabin—the big Christmas reveal. But screw it. She was here, she was practically vibrating with anticipation, and he could not deny her.

He tugged her basket out of her grasp and gestured for her to go ahead of him.

They walked in silence, the snow crunching beneath their feet the only sound as they made the turn onto the small, ungroomed path that would take them to the clearing. Apparently they were going to pretend that last night hadn't happened.

Which was fine. Denial worked for him.

She was walking in front of him, so she broke through the tree line into the clearing before he did. He heard her gasp, though, and, shit, that did something to his chest.

He emerged to see her running, literally running, toward the cabin. When he caught up with her, she turned to him, her hands clasped under her chin and her hood fallen.

"Oh, Leo, it's wonderful!"

She was overreacting. Despite today's work, the structure itself wasn't that different looking than it had been. It was just a bit taller, the newer logs a slightly darker color than the old ones.

But he'd be lying if he said her delight didn't please him. A strange, warm sensation began unspooling in his gut—it turned the corners of his mouth up, too, almost against his will.

She ducked under the doorway, and he followed her inside. The walls were now taller than he was, so the sense of being enclosed was magnified. It was going to be pretty damn cozy in here when it was done.

She continued a slow twirl, cooing over the space.

"We're doing the roof over the next two days," Leo said.

"We?"

"Kai," he said. "He's been a huge help."

Marie turned a mock-annoyed face to him. "So *I* can't get him to go against my father, but *you* can?"

He shrugged.

And continued to do that involuntary smiling thing.

"Are you hungry?" she asked.

That was probably what the warm feeling in his belly was. "I am."

She set her basket down and produced a blanket from it. He took it from her and spread it on the ground in one of the far corners. It was where he would put the kitchen if this was his place.

He sat back while she unpacked the basket, narrating as she went. "Cheese." She pulled out several hunks, each wrapped in wax paper. A long, skinny loaf of bread followed. "This was still warm when I raided the kitchens." She was like Mary Poppins, unpacking a seemingly endless feast from her modestly sized basket. Everything on its own was simple, but also kind of posh in its simplicity. There was some kind of deli meat, very thinly sliced. "This is a local variation on the Swiss Bünderfleisch—it's cured, dried beef," she explained. Next she produced mushroom sausage, plums, and walnuts. "And this," she said, unwrapping a large pastry of some sort. "I am not sure how to translate this. It's like a cake but also like bread. Like a sweeter croissant, perhaps. But our cook makes it with lemon curd inside, which isn't traditional, but my mother loved it, and I do, too!"

Marie's enthusiasm was infectious. Leo grabbed a knife from the pile of cutlery she was unpacking and sliced into the mystery dessert.

"You can't eat that first!" she scolded, her tone split between scandal and amusement.

"Can't I?" He extracted the slice and held it in front of him so they could examine it. He hadn't done a very good job—the lemon had been clustered in the middle and was now spilling out of the tip of his slice onto his fingers. There was probably some kind of royal protocol for cutting whatever this was.

He licked the lemon off his fingers, realizing as he did so that she was staring really intently at him.

So, even though nothing could come of it—except perhaps to demonstrate what she and her paperwork were missing out on—he made a show of it. Let his tongue drag over each finger individually. Really went to town on the last one—which didn't even have any lemon on it—biting down on it and letting his teeth scrape against it.

Marie was still staring at Leo's mouth when he was done, so he lifted the cake thing to it and took a bite. It was pretty fucking fantastic. Light and airy like the croissant she'd referenced, but sweeter. But with just enough of the tart lemon that the sweetness didn't become cloying.

It was so good he sort of lost his momentum on the whole "torment the princess" front.

Which is why he only half heard her when she said, "At least hold off on the sweets until I've unpacked everything." She rummaged around in her basket. "I've brought you the NDA."

The residual sweet tanginess in his mouth turned to ashes. "I *told* you, I'm not signing your NDA." He could maybe forgive her for asking the first time. It was habit for her, no doubt. But that she was going to try again was insulting. It made him feel like she didn't know him at all.

She produced a small, earthenware jar. It had a piece of light-blue checked fabric in place of a lid, affixed to the jar by a thin, blue ribbon. It looked like one of Dani's fancy hot fudge jars. "Here you are."

"What's this?"

"Open it and see."

He pulled the ribbon off and peeled back the fabric. The jar was full of small scraps of paper that looked like they'd been ripped by hand.

Well.

He looked up at her to make sure he was interpreting this correctly.

"I've given some more thought to the matter and have come to the conclusion that I owe you an apology."

He was shocked but also not shocked. He was starting to understand that there were two . . . well, not two versions of Marie, but two sides to her, maybe. There was the proper-bordering-on-prim princess who shouldered a shit-ton of duty. The wallflower who let balls and parties shake her confidence.

But there was also the woman who got into a stranger's cab with no money and only a vague idea of where she was going and ran after a ship belonging to a villainess. Who manipulated her butler-dude in such a way that she got what she wanted politically.

"I've been thinking about your question from last night," she went on. "When I asked you to sign this document and said, 'We do them all the time,' you asked me who 'we' was. It made me think that I didn't really know. Well, I do know. It's a generic 'we.' The royal establishment. But then I started thinking, there are only two members of the royal house of Accola, and I'm one of them. Why do I just mindlessly do what I'm told?"

"I'm not sure you do," Leo said, thinking back to the "version two" of Marie he'd just conjured in his mind. "I think you just *think* you do."

She cocked her head. "What do you mean?"

"Well, for example, you had quite the argument with your father about the UN appointment. That didn't look to me like doing what you were told. You got rid of Mr. Benz back in New York pretty handily, too. And you just told me you made him go horseback riding with Gabby today so you could get your way with parliament."

A slow, semi-self-satisfied smile blossomed. She liked his interpretation of things. "Well, I've come to the conclusion that insisting I make everyone I have any sort of meaningful interaction with sign a nondisclosure agreement suggests that I have bad judgment. That I don't know my own mind."

"That doesn't seem like you at all," Leo said, wanting the semismile to turn into a real one.

It did. "And if that's the case . . ." Marie picked up the jar and tipped it upside down. Little bits of paper scattered on the wind.

Okay then. Leo cleared his throat and tried to tamp down a spike of that same panicky excitement that had hit him outside her door last night. He wasn't sure what the destroyed NDA signified. Was he just witnessing a moment of emancipation? Or were they going to get back to what they'd been planning before she'd whipped out the document to begin with?

"So what now as it relates to . . . us?" she asked, verbalizing his thoughts exactly.

"You tell me." *And please tell me yes.* He had to adjust his position on the blanket. She was making him go half hard with her signature mixture of boldness and innocence.

"I'm unsure. Has the momentum been lost?"

He barked a laugh. She was so . . . primly herself. "No momentum lost here, Your Rebellious Highness." None at all. In fact—he shifted around some more on the blanket—momentum gained.

She looked skeptical. "I am fretting, though, that here I told you not to treat me like a princess and then . . ."

"You acted like the most princessey of princesses?"

She smiled sheepishly. "I'm afraid so."

"We're overthinking this. Here's how this is going to work. We are going to drop the princess/not princess distinction. I think it's less useful than it seemed. If you want to have sex, we're going to have sex the way you"—he pointed to her—"and I"—he pointed to himself—"have sex."

She liked that idea, judging by the way her eyes lit up. "And what way is that?"

He shrugged. "I guess we'll have to find out, won't we?"

"Now?"

"No time like the present." He wagged his eyebrows. "If you want to." *Please want to.*

"I want to, but I didn't bring any contraception."

I didn't bring any contraception. That was such a Marie way to say it. He smiled. "Well, we'll just have to do things that don't require contraception, then, won't we?"

She looked as shocked as if he'd suggested they run away and join a sex cult.

"Wow, you really have had some duds, haven't you? I'm glad the bar is so low." He was joking about that last part. The bar wasn't low. The bar—the very, very high bar—had nothing to do with her past lovers. It had everything to do with *her*. With showing this woman that she was desirable and that she deserved the best—and not because she was a princess.

Also, who was he kidding? He wanted to impress her.

Which he needed to not think too much about, or he'd freak himself out. When he'd said *We're overthinking this*, he'd meant it. The "we" part included. So he leaned forward—they'd both been sitting cross-legged on the blanket—intending to kiss her. But he leaned slowly. Despite what she'd just said, despite the shredded NDA, he wanted to make sure she was into this. In general, but also right here, right now.

In the queen's cabin in the goddamn Eldovian Alps—and what even *was* his life?

The little sigh of relief she exhaled into his mouth as their lips touched told him that she was. Her lips were cold. So was her face, he discovered, when he peeled off his gloves and settled his hands on her cheeks. So he set to work heating her up, letting his mouth slide lazily from spot to spot, taking his time at the corner of her jaw, the juxtaposition of impossibly soft skin over sharp bone doing something to him, before migrating back to her mouth and licking into it. Their tongues stroked together, lazily at first but then with increasing urgency. She grabbed his parka like she wanted to pick him up, or—

Like she wanted to use him as a handle to lever herself onto his lap.

"Oh god," he bit out as she straddled him. The sudden, exquisite pressure of her, even through all their layers of clothing was both welcome and insufficient.

"Leo," she whispered, trying to kiss him and unwind her scarf at the same time. "*Leo.*"

"Yes," he answered automatically as he helped her get the scarf off. "*Yes.*" He wasn't even sure what he meant. Was he answering to his name? It felt more like he was acknowledging something she wasn't saying, something his name stood in for.

She was grinding on him, like she had last time. He loved that she was doing it of her own accord, without the need for encouragement. Hell, he loved it, period. He thrust his hips up to meet her, and soon they were chest to chest—or parka to ridiculous red coat—rocking back and forth.

She started huffing short little pants that sounded familiar. She'd made those same noises last time, just before she'd come.

"Not yet," he said gruffly, his body protesting as he lifted her off him.

She protested, too, a little whimper of displeasure that went to his ego and his dick in equal measure.

Normally, he would have exactly zero objections to a woman dry humping him until she got off. But this wasn't what she wanted—or at least not the optimal version of what she wanted. He had listened carefully to her last night. She wanted him to talk dirty. She wanted to have sex.

And while they weren't going to get naked and fuck right here in the subzero woods, he did sort of feel like he needed to up the ante a bit from yesterday.

"Shh," he soothed as he guided Marie to lie on her back on the blanket, moving some of the food aside. He drew a focusing breath as he took in the sight of her, her cheeks pink, her pupils dilated despite the afternoon sun shining into the roofless cabin, her hair more out of today's braid than in, loose tendrils fanned out against the gray blanket.

Leo was at a loss for how to proceed. Not because he didn't have any ideas, but because he had *too many* ideas.

But that was actually an opportunity, in this particular instance, wasn't it, given what she'd told him?

He could just ask her.

He started undoing the buttons of her coat. "I can't decide what I want to do next. Should I make you come with my fingers or my mouth?"

She gasped.

He ignored her, peeling back the sides of her coat like he was opening a book. "I want to do both, but which do *you* think I should do?"

That got him another gasp but not an answer. He didn't know if he was hoping for an answer or a not-answer. Not having a clear direction was turning out to be an awful lot of fun.

He considered getting rid of her sweater, but it *was* awfully cold. So he settled for shoving his hands up it. He slid them under the band of her bra, too, and cupped her breasts. They were soft, but tipped with hard little nubs that he rolled gently between his thumbs and forefingers. "Oh, no!" she cried.

Shit. He pulled his hands off her immediately. How had he made that much of a miscalculation? He'd been sure she was enjoying herself.

"No." She reached for his hands and settled them on her bare stomach. "I don't want you to stop. I just didn't want to come too soon."

"Ah. And that would have been a problem because . . . ?" he teased.

"Because when you asked me if you should use your hands or your mouth, that is not where I imagined your hands."

God, she was too much. But she was right. It would be a shame if this ended before he got to feel her. So he went to work on her jeans. The scratching sound the zipper made as he lowered it echoed across the otherwise silent clearing.

She was wearing black lace panties. She didn't seem like the black lace panties type. She seemed like the white cotton nightie type. "Did you put these on for me?" This was a case where he wanted an actual answer. And he thought she would enjoy it if he pressed her on the matter. Their interests were aligned here.

"Did you put these on hoping I'd see them?" he goaded. He worked her jeans down over her hips, fully exposing the little scrap of fabric covering her mound. It had a tiny black bow on the front. He sucked in a breath. There was something . . . dangerous about that bow. It was small and shiny and it was a *bow*, for fuck's sake. It shouldn't have had that much power over him. But it caused an infusion of something that felt curiously close to too much, like a jet of water into an already full bathtub.

He covered the whole thing—the bow and the panties and *her*—with the palm of his hand so he didn't have to look anymore.

"Or maybe you were hoping I'd shove them out of the way and do this?" he rasped, sliding his thumb past the waistband and into her.

She bucked her hips, chasing his touch, and he gasped at the slick heat of her. Which was not the way he wanted to present himself to her. *She* was the one who was supposed to be gasping.

So he turned his attention to extracting the answer he wanted.

"Back to the original question. Which do you think?" He pulled the panties down farther, so they joined her jeans halfway down her thighs and maneuvered his body so he was looking right at the mass of short, springy curls. "Tongue?" he used a hand to part her folds, part of him wondering if actual steam would be emitted given the temperature differential between the air and . . . her.

A shudder racked her body—her whole body. It was sudden and startling and violent.

Had he pushed too far?

"Leo," she whispered again, all needy and trusting, and it almost undid him. She started shivering.

It was too cold to be doing this out here. So he pulled panties and jeans alike back up and arranged himself so he was lying on his side next to her, but he kept the one hand on her.

"Hands," he said decisively, using the hand *not* down her pants to reach over and grab one side of her coat and re-cover her. "Hands now, tongue later." From this angle he had his fingers pointing down, so he let three of them move exploratorily, making small circles near but not directly on her clit. He watched her closely, trying to assess what worked. He needn't have, though, because when he grazed the nub straight on, her eyes flew open, and she said, "Oh!" It rang out across the clean, cold air.

So he did it again. And again. He also allowed himself to

shamelessly press his erection against her hip, grinding harder with every "Oh!" she emitted—and she emitted a lot of them.

It took a while, but he judged that his best bet was to keep doing what he was doing. He felt like he was unraveling her slowly but inexorably. And he enjoyed the hell out of the process. It sounded stupid, but he felt almost honored to be witnessing this. He didn't get the impression that Princess Marie Joséphine Annagret Elena let go like this very often, much less in front of other people. Much, *much* less at the hands—literally—of other people.

He saw the level of trust involved and honestly, it scared him a little.

But not enough to stop.

And eventually the telltale panting started up again, and she was undone.

The more alarming part was that even though he hadn't come yet, he kind of felt like he had, too.

LEO WAS SUCH a good kisser.

Which was a somewhat strange thing for Marie to think given that he had done so much more than kiss her. It was just that she'd spent so much time admiring those pillowy lips of his. To have them on her was the strangest, most wonderful sensation.

Coupled with the fact that when they *weren't* on her, they said the most alarmingly delicious things.

It was like she had special, secret nerve endings that only Leo's mouth, with the things it did and the things it said, could light up.

"You okay, Princess?"

Oh. She was lying there like a crepe, flat and listless. Spent on account of the inaugural firing of all those newly discovered nerve endings. And, she realized with a surge of embarrassment, she'd just lain there the whole time and let him hover over her—let him dismantle her.

"What are you thinking?" Leo pressed.

He was worried. That she regretted their encounter, perhaps. There was nothing overt on his face to signal worry, but he was looking at her with the same intensity with which he had looked at Gabby in the rearview mirror of his taxi a week and a bit ago. A lifetime ago.

Marie was thinking that she could not abide this being the second time that she found release and he didn't. She couldn't just lie there and let him . . . do things to her.

She was certain she was going to enjoy doing things to him, too.

She wasn't sure how to start, though. Being with Leo already felt vastly different from her experiences with boys at university.

But she didn't have to think about it very hard before she realized she *did* know how to start. He had taught her that.

She lifted her hips, hitched her panties and jeans up, sparing a thought for how undignified this was and finding she didn't care, and sat up. "I'm thinking about what *I* should do to *you*."

He sat up, too. His lips twitched, and the intensity look receded. "Are you now?"

"Yes." She planted a hand in the middle of his chest and pushed him back down so he was on his back. "Do you have any thoughts on the matter?"

His lip twitch intensified, and her worry receded even more. "Oh, I have thoughts on the matter. Many thoughts."

"Let's hear them." She undid the fly of his jeans. How was it possible that this entire time, he'd been fully clothed? She'd like to blame the cold, and the temperature did make a significant degree of disrobing impractical. But in retrospect, it seemed unfair that while she'd been lying there with her pants down, *she* hadn't gotten to see *him* at all.

"I'd rather hear yours."

"I am struggling with the same dilemma that plagued you." She mimicked his earlier move, grabbing the waistbands of his underwear and jeans together and tugging. He lifted his hips to help her and soon she had his . . . manhood exposed.

His manhood. She laughed inwardly at herself. Was this a gothic novel? She was now, for the first time ever, looking at Leonardo Ricci's penis. He would probably call it his cock.

And it was a very nice cock. It was big and pink and circumcised. She'd heard that many American men had circumcised penises. The ones she'd seen up close had not been.

"What dilemma?" he prompted, his voice sounding a little put out, but not, she was confident, because he was genuinely annoyed.

"Oh, yes. I am pondering the hands-versus-mouth question you posed earlier."

"Princess." It came out like a warning.

"Yes?" When he didn't elaborate, she said, "I think hands, as you decided. It's rather cold out here, and I think perhaps the other is best left for more comfortable environs."

He did something then that seemed like a hybrid of a laugh and a groan, and she found she enjoyed inspiring such a sound. No. She didn't *enjoy* it. She loved it. Her whole self loved it, from her brain to her lungs, which were suddenly working overtime, to the spot between her legs that was throbbing anew.

"What are you thinking now?" He was still worried. Or worried anew, because he'd dropped the worry mask a moment ago when he'd expelled the laugh-groan. She was starting to understand how much Leo worried. How much, beneath his facade of breezy defiance, there was an ever-present hum of disquiet.

"I'm not thinking anything useful," she said. "I'm thinking too much. Overthinking, as you said a moment ago. So I'm going to stop doing that." She settled her hand lightly on his penis, noting that doing so made the resulting laugh-groan much heavier on the groan. She used her other hand to guide his hand so that it rested on top of hers. "Show me the way you minister to yourself, and I will emulate it."

"Oh my god," he said, but he did as she asked, curling his bigger palm over hers and guiding her hand. She got the hang of his preferred rhythm and pressure fairly quickly, and she expected him to turn the matter over to her, but he didn't. He was hard beneath her hand, like iron, and his hand above was scratchy, like sandpaper. The warring sensations, though limited to her hand, felt like they were engulfing her whole body. Moisture pooled between her legs, and her breath shortened to match his. A few more strokes and he was bucking into their joined hands. It was oddly, intensely erotic.

The only disappointing part was that it didn't take very long. She could have kept it up forever, watching his face twist in a gorgeous sort of pleasure that looked like it bordered on pain, knowing *she* had put that expression there, even as her own desire coiled up anew. It made her feel powerful.

And it had nothing to do with her identity as a member of the Eldovian royal family.

Which, in turn, made her laugh with delight.

"I'm glad you find my total and complete paralysis funny," Leo deadpanned. He did look rather done in, lying there as he was with one forearm resting on his forehead and his pants still down.

"You look thoroughly vanquished," she observed, flopping forward onto his chest and breathing in his spicy orange scent.

"I am." He groaned as his arms came around her. "I am thoroughly vanquished."

Chapter Sixteen

9 gotta find Gabby," Leo said as he put his dick back in his pants, packed up the uneaten food, and helped put the princess to rights.

Put his dick in his pants and helped put the princess to rights. Eff him, but that was something he had never imagined himself thinking much less doing.

He smiled.

Because he had a feeling it might be something he would have the opportunity to do again. As he buttoned Marie's coat up, his mind skittered back to the threat/promise of a blow job in "more comfortable environs." It kept replaying that sentence—and another one. *Show me the way you minister to yourself, and I will emulate it.*

When he'd first met Marie in New York, her oddly formal manner and way of speaking had annoyed him. Then, as he'd come to understand that in many cases it was a front for nerves or insecurity, he'd minded it less.

But now? Now, it drove him wild.

It made him stiffen again when he thought about it.

Marie looked at her watch. "I suspect the horseback riding will be done by now, but I'm sure Gabby is well looked after."

"I'm sure she is. She's loving it here. But I hadn't planned on being gone so long today. I haven't seen her yet."

"Let's go find her, shall we?"

"Your braid is a mess." He tried to smooth the destroyed hairdo, but it was no use.

She pulled off the elastic securing the bottom of the braid and combed her fingers through her hair. "It will just take me a moment to redo it."

"Why don't you leave it down?"

"You don't like the braids?"

"I do," he assured her, and it was true. The sometimes elaborate hairdos she wore in Eldovia were kind of like her white nightgown—maddening in their seeming primness. But he also liked her hair down. The way it had been in New York when he'd first been getting to know her.

Well, actually, what he liked best was her hair down *after* it had been in braids. It was the dishevelment he liked. It was being the dishevel*er*. He wasn't going to say that, though. So he pulled her hood up and said, "I like your hair all ways. You have good hair."

And good eyelashes.

And good lips.

Okay, enough. He nodded toward the path. "Shall we?"

"I'm sorry again about the NDA," she said quietly once they started walking.

"Forget about it." He had.

"The first boy I slept with took a picture of me sleeping in his bed and tried to sell it to the student newspaper—this was at university."

"What?" The fucker. "Did he succeed?"

"No. I called Mr. Benz, and he took care of it. I'm not even sure how."

Maybe there was something to say for meddling Mr. Benz after all.

"I hadn't had him sign anything—Mr. Benz had told me, when I left, to make sure anyone who might 'be in a position to compromise me or my reputation' signed an NDA. But I was afraid of insulting him."

Shit. "Write me up a new one. I'll sign it." He contemplated asking her for the name of this dude, but checked the impulse. What was he going to do? Hunt him down vigilante-justice style?

"I don't want you to. I just wanted to explain."

"Princess, I appreciate the trust, but now I'm going to have to insist on signing one." He had been thinking about the document as an affront to his pride, as a symbol of the gulf between them. He hadn't been thinking of it from her point of view, about what she risked when she made herself vulnerable to men who might turn out to be dickheads.

"No," she said decisively. "It's good to reevaluate one's habits periodically. Actions one performs by rote that may not . . . be serving one anymore." He was ramping up to object again, but she cut him off. "Let's find Gabby, shall we?"

BACK AT THE castle, Frau Lehman reported that Gabby had enjoyed both skiing and horseback riding, that Mr. Benz had taken to his bed exhausted, and that she had escorted Gabby to the library to borrow a book, then tucked her into her room for a rest.

Except Gabby *wasn't* in her room when Leo and Marie poked their heads in. "I bet she's back in the library," Leo had ventured, and yep. When they appeared, she sprang up from where she was sitting on an old-fashioned-looking sofa surrounded by haphazard piles of books. She was holding an equally old-fashioned-looking volume in her hands. "Oh my gosh, Leo! Look at this!" Her cheeks were rosy and her eyes bright with excitement.

"*The Red Fairy Book*," he read aloud from the faded gold-leaf lettering on the battered cover. "Andrew Lang."

"It's in English, unlike a lot of the rest of the books in here, and it's full of fairy tales I've *never heard of*!"

"Yes," came a posh voice from behind them. Leo didn't have to turn to know it was King Emil. He braced himself for a royal damper to be put on what had, so far, been an incredible day. "Remarkably," the king drawled, "it turns out your Disney schlock *isn't* the sum total of the world's folklore."

"*Father*," Marie said.

Emil ignored his daughter and turned to Gabby. "Miss Ricci, I must ask you not to use my library if you're going to treat its contents so carelessly."

Leo sighed and turned back to his sister, the princess of clutter. On the one hand, he couldn't really argue with the king. Gabby's room at home was a complete sty. And that was saying something, because it wasn't like Leo had the highest standards himself on the domestic front—it was another arena where he constantly felt he wasn't keeping up.

"Oh!" Gabby turned red and started stacking books like she was on speed.

On the other hand, King Emil could go fuck himself.

Leo turned to say as much, but Marie had her father by the elbow and was in the process of yanking him out of the room.

Well. Okay then.

"He's a royal jerkface," Leo muttered as he helped Gabby put the books back on the shelves.

Gabby giggled, which had been his aim, but then said, quietly, "Frau Lehman said I could use the library."

"Yes," Leo said. "But did she say you could treat it like your own personal property and mess it up like this?"

"No. She said I could borrow one book and take it to my room, which I did . . . but then I came back." She hung her head. "I'm sorry."

"I'm not the one you need to apologize to, kiddo." As much as he hated it.

MARIE INVITED MR. BENZ to stay for cocktails and dinner. He was startled by her invitation but accepted, as she'd known he would. Instead of seeing it as an invitation he was free to refuse, he would regard it as his duty. She was using him, shamelessly, as she had that morning. It wasn't something she normally did, and she vowed not to make a habit of it. But she hoped his presence might act as a buffer between her father and the Riccis. Not that Mr. Benz was known for his sparkling, upbeat personality, but she didn't have a lot of options here. Anyway, he was often so wound up this time of year that it might have the side effect of doing him some good.

To her surprise, though, they didn't really need him.

Gabby marched straight up to her father and said, "Your Majesty, I would like to apologize for using your library uninvited and for treating it disrespectfully. I got carried away with my enthusiasm for some of the books I found there, and I lost track of my manners. It won't happen again."

She performed another of her little half curtsies—Marie really needed to impress upon her that she didn't need to do that—and turned to Leo, who nodded very slightly, as if signing off on the statement of remorse.

Her father remained silent, staring at Gabby.

"Miss Ricci," Mr. Benz said, "if you would be so kind as to inform me what sorts of books you like, I will see to it that—"

The king held up a hand, silencing his equerry, and Marie suppressed a sigh. This was exactly why she'd invited Mr. Benz. He had a talent for smoothing things over, especially where her father was concerned. But if her father wasn't even going to let him speak, he might as well go home.

"I accept your apology, and I offer you one of my own," her father said, and Marie was certain that hers was not the only jaw in the room that dropped. "My reaction to your presence in the library was out of proportion."

She could see that Gabby, who had so clearly rehearsed her apology with Leo, had not covered what to do when presented with one of her own. The correct response, of course, was to murmur her acceptance. Instead, her eyes went wide and she spent a long moment looking like a fox at the culmination of a hunt before blurting, "No biggie!"

Marie had to stifle laughter. She would bet her kingdom—her literal kingdom—that no one had ever said "No biggie" to her father before.

The king, to his credit, did not react. He turned to Mr. Benz.

"Miss Ricci is a devotee of fairy tales and yesterday she encountered a volume that contained some stories that had, heretofore, been unfamiliar to her."

"Ah." Mr. Benz nodded. "Miss Ricci, are you aware that His Majesty is himself the author of an English translation of a collection of traditional Eldovian fairy tales?"

"You *are?*" Gabby exclaimed.

"Mr. Benz exaggerates the situation. I studied comparative literature in my undergraduate days. I undertook a project collecting some of the traditional tales of these mountains, mostly passed down orally in German. Since I was doing it anyway, I thought I might as well translate them into the languages I already spoke. They aren't formally published."

Marie could see that this news both astounded and delighted Gabby. The girl remained silent, though, probably afraid of saying the wrong thing.

"My father used to tell me fairy stories when I was a girl," Marie said to Gabby. She turned to her father. "Remember? I never wanted to go to sleep. Maman would insist, but sometimes you'd wink at me, and then you'd sneak back into my room later and tell me another."

He smiled. A real one. "I'd forgotten that." His expression became quizzical. "I think of your mother as the rebellious one, but we did deceive her from time to time with our bedtime stories, didn't we?"

"Yes!" Marie agreed. "She *was* the rebellious one. But not when it came to bedtime, for some reason. I never could puzzle that out."

"She was strict about your bedtime because she and I watched TV together after you went to sleep." Father smiled in a way Marie might have characterized as dreamy, though *dreamy* didn't seem like a word that should ever describe her father.

As if to prove her point, he shook his head and cleared his throat as the smile disappeared. "Miss Ricci, perhaps we can strike a bargain. I do much of my work in the library."

What work? Marie was tempted to ask, but she knew better than to disturb this rare moment of goodwill.

"Therefore, I prefer not to be interrupted," he went on. "Perhaps we can agree that you may borrow whichever volumes you like, but you'll need to find another place to read them."

Marie was amazed. She hadn't seen her father give way to anyone in years. She wasn't sure if the fact that this someone was an eleven-year-old and not, say, a member of parliament who held an opposing view, made it more or less remarkable.

Either way, dinner was less fraught than last night's.

And the best part of it was when it was over. They parted ways with good-night greetings, but when she said hers to Leo, he licked his lips and said, "Yes, I think it *is* going to be a very good night."

THE TEXT ARRIVED an hour after Gabby had gone to bed. Would you like to come to my suite and see Buffy?

Leo: Buffy? Is that a euphemism?

Never in a million years would Leo have pegged Princess Marie as the type to name her vagina.

Marie: What would that be a euphemism for?

> **Leo:** Do you really need it explained to you?

She sent him a photo of a DVD set of *Buffy the Vampire Slayer*. It made him laugh out loud as he typed **Yes, I would like to come to your suite and see Buffy**. And hopefully a few other things of the noneuphemistic variety as well.

> **Marie:** Buffy was one of my mother's favorites. We watched it together when I was a teenager. I've been rewatching it recently.

When Leo arrived, Marie ushered him past the sitting room he'd been in before—the room in which they'd conducted their dancing lessons. On its far side was a small hallway.

"It's a whole apartment in here," he remarked, registering that she was still dressed in the jeans and blazer she'd worn at dinner. He'd been hoping to see the white nightgown again. Or maybe the black panties.

Or maybe both?

She was confusing.

"Yes and no," she said. "My suite is not like the large-scale apartments in the famous British palaces, which are effectively self-contained residences. It's merely a semiformal sitting room, where I receive personal guests, and a few other rooms." She gestured at an open doorway as they passed it. "This is my office." He peeked in. It was a small room dominated by a large desk and a wall of built-in shelving. That must be Kai's handiwork. Leo would have called the room fancy—the walls were papered in an elaborate floral pattern and the desk was as ornate as they came—but it was strewn with papers and books. He would even go so far as to call it messy. Which surprised him.

"This is the small parlor." She gestured into the next room as they continued down the hall. "I think perhaps you would call it a den."

A glance inside confirmed her interpretation. There was a sofa on one wall and an entertainment system ensconced on the opposite one nestled in a perfectly sized built-in shelf—probably more of Kai's work. "We can watch in here, or . . ."

He raised his eyebrows.

"Another option is to watch in my bedroom. I have a small television in there."

Was she propositioning him? It was hard to tell. She might just be genuinely—and innocently—inviting him into her inner sanctum.

Heh. Her *inner sanctum*. Was it just him or did everything tonight sound like innuendo?

"I also thought it would be the more efficient option in the sense that if we want to have sex, we're already in the bedroom," she said almost brusquely.

He burst out laughing. Well, that solved that.

"I've said something wrong." There was a hint of dismay in her tone.

"No. Not at all." He made a shooing motion down the corridor. "I vote for the bedroom."

"Would you like me to have something sent up to eat? My suite doesn't have a kitchen. Are you hungry?"

He winked and said, "I am hungry, but not for food."

It was one hundred percent cheesy but one hundred percent true.

Thankfully, one hundred percent cheesy plus one hundred percent true worked on princesses of bonkers Hallmark-style Alpine countries.

She perched on the end of the bed in front of a small TV mounted to the wall. "As it relates to Buffy, I'm in the middle of season four, which, frankly, is the long slog on Riley."

"The long what?"

"To my mind, be Team Spike or be Team Angel—I suppose. I don't really get the latter, but I respect it. But Riley? That's like being pro-beige."

"I have no idea what you're talking about." He was, however, aware enough to understand that the princess was talking about American pop culture—and was talking circles around him. It was amusing.

Ignoring him, she picked up the remote and started the show.

The opening sequence seemed to be a girl engaged in hand-to-hand combat with vampires, but she would stop every now and then to trade banter with them. "What *is* this?"

"It's about a high school in California that happens to be built over the hellmouth, and all manner of vampires and other unpleasant creatures need to be slain, but handily one of the students happens to be the Slayer. It's like being the chosen one, and . . ." Marie trailed off, perhaps because she had registered the confusion on Leo's face. "This isn't the best show to pick up in the middle." She hopped off the bed and opened a cabinet underneath the TV to reveal rows and rows of DVDs, most of them titles he was vaguely familiar with but had never seen. "Let's watch something else. You pick."

"You've seen these all?"

"Yes. I grew up watching several hours of TV a night."

It was hard to wrap his mind around. It was so incongruous with the idea of her as a princess, as a highly educated person who did things like address the United Nations.

"I learned English in school, of course—everyone here does. But I learned *idiomatic* English mostly from 1990s television." She pulled out a disc called *The Nanny* and held it out to him with her eyebrows raised. "What do you think?"

He put his hand over hers and guided the disc back to its place on the shelf. "I think I didn't come here to watch TV."

She said, "Oh," but she said it on a shuddery exhalation, and that was all it took to make him hard. "I have secured prophylactics." Marie spoke initially with the utmost seriousness, but then she cracked a smile.

Jesus, Mary, and Joseph. The way she talked. *Why* did it drive him so wild?

Well, whatever, he didn't feel like examining it right now. He felt like going with it, allowing the rush of affection her earnestness—which was somehow, paradoxically, also very sexy—inspired to propel him toward the bed. He heaved himself onto the mattress, leaning back against a mound of fluffy pillows and crooking a finger at her.

She flashed him a shy smile, but she came. He was sprawled on the bed, and she kneeled between his splayed legs, but she didn't touch him.

He eyed her, all bundled up in her "casual" clothing that wasn't casual.

He wanted to see her. All of her.

And he wanted her to see him.

So he sat up, inserted his hands into her blazer, and pushed it off her shoulders to reveal a white blouse done up with what seemed like a hundred buttons. They looked like tiny pearls. "That's a lot of buttons you've got there, Princess," he said, surprising himself with how low his voice had suddenly gone. He spared a moment to take off his shirt while he pondered this maddening little engineering problem.

She looked down. "It's not very practical for our purposes, is it?" She started working on the buttons, her small, nimble fingers entrancing him as they moved with the same efficient precision she applied to so much of her life.

He *also* liked disrupting that precision. So even though it risked coming across as brutish, he reached out and applied his own brand of efficiency to the one-million-buttons problem and ripped the last several of them open. He used enough force to make her gasp—he was pretty sure no one had literally torn off Princess Marie's clothing before—and to send some of the buttons over the edge of the bed where they made satisfying *pings* as they hit the wood floor.

Her eyes opened wide—and sparked. Taking a hold of one side of her now gaping blouse with each hand, he pulled her on top of him. She shrieked as she toppled and smiled so widely she practically blinded him with her dimples. Those fuckers were lethal.

He only had a moment to admire them, though, before she kissed him.

Her kiss was familiar by now. It started softly, her lips moving against his gently, but rapidly escalated until she was sighing into his mouth, opening for him and moaning as his tongue shamelessly slid inside, stroking hers. They kissed for a long time, and he got more and more wound up. He had to make himself pause, remember his larger mission: to see her.

So he tore his mouth from hers, relishing the little moue of displeasure that resulted. He fumbled with the clasp at the back of her bra, and once he had it unhooked, pushed her back so she was sitting astride him. She was backlit by soft lamplight, and she was *perfect*. Teardrop-shaped breasts with small, pink nipples at their tips made his jaw slacken like he was a god-damned caveman.

"I want to see all of you," he rasped. "Will you let me see you?"

Without hesitation, she pushed herself off him and started wiggling out of her jeans. "I want to see you, too."

Sliding his own jeans over his hips to free his aching cock was an enormous relief. So much so that he groaned and closed his eyes, needing to stem, for a moment, the sensory onslaught. When he opened them, she was naked and was crawling back from the edge of the bed. She was small and lithe and perfect.

"Oh, Princess."

She climbed right back on top of him, except this time there was nothing between them, so it was her, the slick, soft heat of her, that slid against his thighs as she straddled them. She tilted her head and did that thing where her brow knit—just a little, almost not even enough to notice—as she braced herself on his chest and leaned forward.

"What are you thinking?" he asked, suddenly feeling like she was trying to see into his soul or some shit.

She leaned a little closer, and her attention intensified. "I'm thinking how much I enjoy looking at this lip." One of her hands floated up, and she rubbed her thumb over his lower lip, letting its tip make an incursion into his mouth. "Sometimes I want to bite it."

He huffed a startled chuckle. *Startled* was the word of the day, apparently. She was constantly startling him.

"So why don't you then?"

She leaned forward and did just that—and he was startled anew.

He'd been expecting a little nip, and that maybe she'd then soothe that nip with another kiss, but no, not his princess. She did exactly what he'd told her to do—she *bit* him. Not hard enough to draw blood, but enough to hurt.

The quick infusion of pain was a jolt to his system. It ratcheted up his need. He growled and flipped them. Covered her with his body and took control. He dragged his mouth along her throat, enjoying the feeling of her pulse thundering under his lips.

She threw her head back and moaned, arching her chest. He reached for her breasts, and the sound she made as his hands made contact was half relief, half dismay. She was so soft. But also so hard. He'd thought her nipples had gotten so hard earlier because they'd been out in the cold, but it turned out it was just her. He adored the way the little nubs grew sharper and sharper as he twisted them gently between thumb and forefinger.

"Leo," she gasped. "Leo."

"You like this, Princess?" Experimentally, he twisted a little harder.

"Yes!" she cried.

"What does it feel like?"

"It feels like . . . too much but also not enough." She wiggled underneath him until she was splayed open beneath one of his thighs. "And, when you touch me there"—she nodded at the nipple he was still working over—"I feel it here." She ground up against him. She was so slick, so warm, he suddenly felt like he would die if he didn't get his hands or his mouth on that incredible softness. Not wanting to stop with the nipple onslaught she seemed to be enjoying so much, he replaced one hand with his mouth, which made her jerk.

"Shh," he soothed, before he refastened his mouth over a perfect pink peak. He sent his now-free hand between her legs, parting her folds and stroking her. After a few minutes, she was restless again. It took a moment for him to register that she was trying to get out from under him. With regret—sharp, metallic regret—he rolled away, panting.

She crawled over to a heavy oaken nightstand, yanked open a drawer, produced a box of condoms—*prophylactics*, to use her term—and tossed it at him. He sucked in a breath as he was overcome with . . . something. Lust, yes, but not only that. His chest felt light. It felt like . . . joy?

Okay, enough of that. There was no call for melodrama. He was just really glad she wasn't calling a halt to the proceedings.

"Well?" she said, drawing him from his uncharacteristic bout of self-examination.

The impatience in Marie's tone made Leo smile. It made him feel like a million bucks, actually. He tore open the box, then an individual condom packet, and sheathed himself.

He reclined on the mound of pillows against the headboard and held out a hand.

"I'm meant to be on top?" she asked.

"You're meant to be whatever you want, but if you're on top you'll have more control."

Her eyes widened and a slow smile blossomed. She took his

hand, and he had the sudden, absurd notion that he was helping her into a carriage that would take her to a ball or some shit. She reached for his dick with her free hand and he groaned just at that. She kept hold of his hand with her other hand, and slowly, slowly, guided him inside her.

"Oh, fuck, you feel good," he ground out, and she let loose a needy moan. "You're so wet, I fucking love it."

She started moving, and soon they'd established a rhythm, a slow, steady . . . dance, almost. That, along with the fact that she hadn't let go of his hand, sort of reminded him of when they'd actually been dancing.

Except dancing hadn't made him feel like he was going to explode. He tried to slow himself down, but it was no use. The pressure gathering was an unstoppable force.

So as with the dancing, he moved her where he wanted her. He slid himself down on the bed so he was lying flat, taking her with him. She'd been sitting up, grinding herself on him, but he pressed on one thigh to indicate that he wanted her to straighten her legs and lie on him. "C'mere," he said gruffly, and she did, tipping forward until she was stretched out on top of him, those maddening, sharp little nipples scratching his chest. He slid himself down a bit, aiming to line up their bodies so her clit made contact with the base of his dick. Another of her moans told him when he'd hit a good spot, and he let one hand settle heavily on the curve of her ass to keep her in place. "Rock yourself on me."

She did, burying her face in his neck. The hand that was still holding his pressed his own down on the bed next to his head, her fingers laced in his. Pinned down by the princess.

There were worse places to be.

He rocked in sync with her, resisting the urge to thrust in opposition to the movement of her hips and letting his free hand slide back and forth over the curve of her ass.

"Leo," she panted against his neck.

As with the times she'd come before, her breathing changed. Her fingers tightened around his, and a shudder ripped through her as she came. He could feel her inner muscles spasming around his dick. He couldn't hold himself back anymore. His hips had taken over, and they were going to move. With a groan, he snapped them up, a big, almost involuntary thrust that turned her moan-in-progress into a surprised-but-delighted yelp. It only took one more thrust, and he was emptying himself into the condom.

She pushed herself back up, and he grabbed the base of the condom, thinking she was going to climb off him, but she just sat there grinning at him, her face red and her braids mostly undone, looking both thoroughly fucked and thoroughly self-satisfied. She lifted their entwined hands, and suddenly, he didn't want to let go. So he pulled her hand back. Brought it to his lips and kissed it.

"You are a very interesting mixture of qualities," she informed him as she took her hand back—he had to let her—and slid off him.

"What do you mean?"

"You are very chivalrous, but you have such a dirty mouth."

He shrugged. He liked sex and he had manners. He didn't think that was such a remarkable combination.

Marie flopped down on her back next to Leo. "I can't usually come with a man."

"You mean from just dick?"

She sputtered with laughter and turned her head toward him. "No. I gather that's not that unusual? I meant with a man at all.

From his ministrations—regardless of which appendage is being employed. Yet that was the third time with you, so clearly I was mistaken."

"So what you're saying," he asked, to make sure he had this right, "is that you can rub one out but you don't come when you're with a partner?"

"That might not be how I would phrase it, but yes. Usually when I'm having sex, I get the same feeling I do when I have to dance in public—like I'm the object of too much scrutiny to fully relax."

He took that in as he stared at the—gilded—ceiling. He couldn't have wiped the grin off his face if he tried. It was stupid to get such a boost from something as mundane as making a woman come. In addition to being good manners—literally, the least he could do—in his experience, reciprocity usually meant better, more frequent sex.

He supposed he was disproportionally pleased by the princess's praise because it had been so long since he'd done anything that felt like more than merely surviving. And even then, he usually ended up feeling like he was falling short.

Regardless of his feelings on the matter, though, Marie should know that expecting an orgasm out of sex was not an outlandish demand. "What the hell were those Casanovas from your past doing? Besides selling you out to the school newspaper?" She made a noncommittal murmur. He could imagine what they'd been doing. "I'm no rocket scientist, but even I know that most women can't come from a guy just hammering away at them with his dick."

"Hmm."

He rolled onto his side. "What?"

She smiled. "I'm thinking about the image that conjures. A

man hammering away at a woman with his dick. I think I'd like to try that."

"It's supposed to be a negative example."

"Still. A little controlled experiment might be fun, no? Besides, I am confident you would find a way. You seem to have a talent for multitasking."

He shook his head. "You are something else, Princess."

"I SHOULD STOP calling you that," Leo said, examining Marie from above—he'd propped his head on one hand, and she was flat on her back. She wasn't sure she could move her limbs yet.

"No you shouldn't," she said automatically.

"But the whole point of our thing is that I don't give a shit that you're a princess. So why do I keep calling you that?"

"It's a term of endearment, I think." Was that the right word? She was conscious of the fact that she didn't want him to feel trapped, as though she had expectations of him, but she liked him, and she was pretty sure he liked her, too. "I think you would call me Princess if I was a . . . banker. Or a teacher."

"That's . . . true." He looked surprised at that interpretation.

"I think it's also a little dirty, sometimes. I think you like the idea of sullying me."

"Hmm." His brow furrowed. "That's also true." He tucked some hair behind her ear, and the gesture felt almost unbearably tender. "But not because you're a princess."

"No," she agreed. "Because I'm a little . . . wound up."

The confusion left his face then, chased off by a wicked smile. "Yes. And I enjoy unwinding you."

"So don't stop." *Please don't stop.*

"Unwinding you?"

"Unwinding me, yes, but calling me Princess, too. I like it when you call me Princess."

"Okay. But you know I'm not going to do it *now* because that would be too much like obeying a royal proclamation, right?"

She laughed. "Of course."

He kept his fingers in her hair, playing with it, undoing the putting-to-rights he'd done a moment ago.

"Thank you, Leo."

"Are you thanking me for having sex with you? Because I can assure you, it was my pleasure."

She was, but really, she meant it more holistically. "For everything. For coming here. For putting up with my father. For the cabin."

"About that. I'm not going to be able to get more than the rudimentary structure done before I leave. But if you can get it past your father, you could have Kai put in windows and floors. And we're leaving a spot where a wood-burning stove could vent."

Marie hated to think of Leo not being around to see the finished cabin. She was going to furnish it in the summer, too, she'd decided, her father be damned. Make it fully functional. Maybe she'd even figure out a way to spend a night there.

"How did you get interested in architecture?" she asked, suddenly curious.

He rolled over and stared at the ceiling. She, having got control of her limbs, rolled onto her stomach and propped her chin on his chest, worrying belatedly that maybe she was getting too cozy. But his arms came immediately around her and he started playing with her hair again as he spoke.

"I told you I used to work construction?" She nodded. "It was what my dad did. So he would get me on his crews in the summers, when I was in high school. I thought it was interesting. The way a building comes together physically from what starts out as a plan on paper—and before that, just an idea in someone's head. I always assumed I'd follow him into the business full-time, but when he got wind of that he read me the riot act. Pointed out all his injuries and maladies—it was true that his back was all screwed up from that job. He said he hadn't worked so hard his whole life so his kids could do manual labor. He marched me into the high-school guidance counsellor, and before I knew it I'd been set up to job-shadow an architect."

"And you liked it."

"Yeah." He smiled. "It was all the stuff I loved about buildings, but also all this problem solving, you know? How to make the most of a site. How to incorporate what people said they wanted but also what you thought they needed. How to do all that and make it look good. It sounds dumb, but it kind of reminded me of a real-life video game."

It didn't sound dumb. It sounded exactly like Leo. "So what happened?" She recognized that as the wrong question the moment it was out. "Well, I know what happened."

"Yeah. I mean, *yeah*. But it wasn't . . . just that."

"What was it?" she asked gently.

"I was the first person in my family to go to college. It was a big deal for someone like me to be in architecture school."

"That's good, though, isn't it? You should be proud of yourself."

He blew out a breath. "There wasn't a day that I didn't question whether I belonged there. If I should just give up."

"Of course you belonged there. They admitted you, didn't they?"

"Yeah, but I was barely hanging on. I worked my ass off for middling grades. I tried, but it was just . . . never enough." He laughed, but there was no mirth in it. "Which actually turned out to be good practice for what came next."

"What does *that* mean?" she said sharply. She hadn't meant it to come out like a rebuke, but she hated to hear him talk like this.

"It means Gabby. I try with her, but it's never enough."

"Leo! That's objectively not true!" She had seen the love between the siblings. She had *envied* it.

"It is, though," he insisted.

"Give me one example."

"Braids."

"I beg your pardon?"

"She always wants braids, and I can never get them right."

"Oh, Leo." He was breaking her heart. He didn't see how wonderful he was. "Girls need love, not braids."

He swung himself off the bed without answering. He didn't seem angry, but clearly he didn't want to continue this conversation.

She asked one more question anyway. She couldn't help herself. "Do you ever think of going back to school?"

"I don't see how I can swing it until Gabby's much older." Leo darted a glance at her but looked away quickly. "As it is, we get by, but barely."

She was certain it hurt him to admit that. Leo was proud—though there was no shame in what he was saying. She was absurdly pleased, though, that he regarded her as a person he could say such things to. She resisted the urge to offer to pay for his school, or to help them in some way. He was only confiding in her because he trusted she *wouldn't* react that way.

"My mother used to talk about the accident of birth," he said thoughtfully.

"You mean like unplanned pregnancy?"

"No. The randomness of the life circumstances a person is born into."

"Ahh. Meaning some people are princesses and some people aren't?"

"That's one way of looking at it. But I meant more that even though some shit has happened lately, I have a good life. I wouldn't trade my life for anything."

"I know," she said. And that was what was so great about Leo Ricci.

They stared at each other for a long moment, him standing and her on the bed. She knew he had to go back to his own room eventually, but didn't want him to leave yet. "Leo?"

"Yeah?"

"Will you stay a little longer?"

"Yeah."

"If you stay past midnight, it will be the twenty-third." She wasn't sure why she was still talking. He was already sliding back into bed. "It will be the day *after* the anniversary of the day my mother died."

"I know, Princess. I know."

Chapter Seventeen

$\mathcal{L}$eo got to the cabin site late the next morning, having inadvertently slept in. He'd had a hard time extricating himself from Marie's bed last night. It had been ridiculously cozy there, and he didn't just mean her puffy, soft bedding, but the cocoon effect of talking late into the night. About real things like his aborted academic career and her mom's death. But also about silly things like how the kitchen staff had allowed Gabby to invent her own cocoa flavor for the Fest, and they had been testing variations on her butterscotch s'mores creation.

He'd been so . . . relaxed. Profoundly relaxed. Being so had thrown into sharp relief how *not* relaxed he had been for such a long time.

By the time he'd finally heaved himself out of bed and sneaked back to his room, it had been three o'clock. He was bleary-eyed today, but, paradoxically, the relaxation effect endured. His steps were light as he hiked into the clearing.

The roofing materials were all in place, neatly stacked near the structure itself. Kai, however, was not present. Well, Leo had done his share of roofs back in the day. By the time he had the ladder set up and started shuttling shingles up, Kai appeared.

With a horse.

Pulling a cart.

This country was bananas. Though the single horse and narrow cart did explain how he had gotten the materials to the site via the paths.

Leo raised a hand in greeting. "What's this?"

"I brought you a stove."

"What?" But sure enough, there was a black iron stove and pieces of a chimney in the cart.

"I thought you could use one."

"For what?"

"Do you really want me to answer that? Or should I just say that I stopped by yesterday afternoon intending to put in a couple hours of work but ended up finding the cabin occupied."

Leo winced. Not that he minded being caught, but he didn't want Marie's private business broadcast all over the place. "Listen. Whatever you think was going on—"

"None of my business."

He could trust Kai. Leo didn't quite know how he knew that, but he knew. "Thanks, man." He started toward the cart to help unload it, but the horse made a . . . horse noise at him. He didn't know the word. It did, however, cause him to jump like a soft city boy.

"You just happen to have spare wood-burning stoves lying around?" he asked Kai as the horse did some kind of aggressive snorting thing again. Whinnied, maybe?

"Hey," Kai said mildly, "don't look a gift horse in the mouth."

GABBY CHATTERED THE whole way to the cabin. Marie had to interrupt her as they turned off the main path to the smaller one that would take them to the clearing. She stopped walking. "I need to ask you a favor."

"Oh, anything!"

"What I'm about to show you is a secret. No one can know. Especially not my father." Gabby's eyes widened. "Or Mr. Benz."

"I do solemnly swear to keep whatever you are about to show me a secret," Gabby intoned with exaggerated seriousness.

"Thank you." As they cut through the brush, Marie told Gabby an abbreviated version of the history of the cabin.

"And my brother is helping you?"

"He is."

"Yeah. He does stuff like that."

Gabby was lucky to have Leo. He *did* do stuff like that. All the time, in big ways like cabins but also in small ways. Marie thought back to the cardboard mantel in the siblings' apartment. She wished Leo could see himself the way his sister did.

"How do you know when a boy likes you?" Gabby suddenly asked. The question alarmed Marie a bit. Could Gabby tell what was going on between Marie and Leo? Marie felt herself flush. She'd never had the poker face required to inoculate her against the Lucrecia von Bachenheims of the world.

"Because I like this boy at school."

Right. Marie had forgotten how handy the self-absorption of youth could be. "I'm not sure I'm the best person to ask."

"Well, I can't ask Leo."

She probably could, but Marie didn't say that. "Dani?"

"She just tells me that boys are no good and that I should wait until I'm thirty to date."

Marie wanted to laugh. "Well, some people say that when a boy likes you, he's mean to you, which seems counterintuitive."

"Some people say that. Do *you* say that?"

"It's hard for me to speak from experience. People don't act normally around me. People aren't generally mean to princesses." Lucrecia von Bachenheim excepted.

"I see your point. But, like, say you're not a princess. What does 'mean' actually look like, if a boy is being mean to you because he likes you? Like, he might put humiliating pictures of you on Instagram?"

"No!" That had not been at all what she'd meant. But then, she'd been thinking more along the lines of hair pulling, but this wasn't the 1950s, was it? "I think more like he teases you. Gives you a hard time. Maybe he has a nickname for you."

Princess.

Hmm.

"That doesn't sound very mean," Gabby observed.

Marie thought of the many not-mean things Leo had done to her last night. "I think you're right." Her limbs felt restless suddenly.

"What do you do if you're pretty sure someone likes you and you don't like them back?" Gabby asked, oblivious to Marie's jumpiness. "That's my actual question."

"Is this about someone in particular?"

"You don't know him." She heaved a melodramatic sigh.

Of course she didn't know him. Marie had to stifle a laugh. "Try me."

"His name is Alex. He played the Cowardly Lion." Marie tried to conjure an image of that character but came up blank. "I wish he would get some actual courage and ask me out so I could say no and we could be done with it."

"Is he a nice boy? Maybe you should give him a chance."

"But don't you think I would know if I liked him? I mean, I like him. He's fine. I just don't *like him*-like him. I feel like when you *like*-like someone, you know."

"How do you know?" And who was the one giving the advice here?

"You're constantly aware of where they are," Gabby said. "Like, literally in the sense that you probably have his class schedule memorized. But also, when you're in the same room, you're kind of . . . hyperaware of him."

For some reason, Marie thought back to that last night in New York, at the Riccis' apartment, when she was fixated on the inch of space between her forearm and Leo's. But, no. This was about Gabby. "So there *is* someone you like."

"You don't know him, either," Gabby said quickly and sped on ahead, signaling the end of the conversation—which Marie had to admit had been delightful.

Also, perhaps, illuminating for her own purposes. To a worrying degree.

When they emerged into the clearing, Marie forgot about her worries because the cabin was . . . done?

Almost, by the looks of it. Kai and Leo were on the roof, which was still unfinished on the one end. Her heart sped up with happy excitement. When Gabby took off running, exclaiming, "Oh my gosh! This is the best thing ever!" Marie had to agree.

"Hey, kiddo." Leo waved to Gabby from the roof and looked around like he was looking for someone else.

Stupidly, it wasn't until his eyes landed on her and he grinned that Marie realized *she* was that someone else. "Good morning!" she called.

The men came down from the roof and Marie showed Gabby around. She filled her in on the history of the cabin, telling her about her mother's plan for it to be a family retreat. "I can almost feel her with me when I'm here," she said, her voice catching a little.

She didn't want to grow maudlin, so she cleared her throat and flashed the men a smile. "Gabriella and I are going down to the pub for lunch, and we thought you two might want to join us."

Leo looked at Kai, who nodded. "Lemme show you one thing before we go."

That thing turned out to be a wood-burning stove, which the men had just installed.

"This place is so cozy!" Gabby was turning in circles inside the small cabin, oohing and ahhing over it as if it was as magnificent as the palace itself.

"So now it'll be all warm and toasty in here," Leo said, ignoring Gabby and staring rather intensely at Marie. "If you know what I mean."

She felt the blood rush to the surface of her skin. "I do surmise your meaning."

"Let's go eat," she said as her face flamed. "Are you hungry?"

She realized too late that she'd asked that same question last night.

"I am," Leo said, not even bothering to disguise how hard he was checking her out, "but—"

"Let's go, then!" she exclaimed before clearing her throat and adding a more refined, "Shall we?"

He winked. "We shall."

LUNCH WAS GREAT. The pub crowd, headed up by Imogen, was a lot of fun. Unstuffy fun. Even Kai had thawed a bit, pulling out a drawing and asking Leo's opinion on his expansion plans for his workshop. Imogen kept dropping by and sitting with them for little stretches in which she and Marie would get to yakking like old friends—which he supposed they were.

Soon the two of them were organizing an impromptu hayride for the village kids. And Leo was stupidly happy to learn that Gabby was being included. In fact, Imogen's niece, who was a little older than Gabby, was bussing tables since she was on break from school. But in reality she was spending more time with Gabby talking about the fact that they had the same favorite You-Tubers than she was actually working.

"You can take them, right, Kai?" Imogen asked.

Kai looked at Leo. Leo knew he was thinking about their plans to finish the roof this afternoon. He made a dismissive gesture. "It's almost done. I can finish it."

"*What's* almost done?" Imogen asked.

"Nothing!" Marie glared at Leo. *Shit*. He should have been more careful.

"Okay, you all think you can keep a secret from me, but you're forgetting that I basically run this village—no offense, Marie—so—"

"Would you like to come to dine at the palace tonight?" Marie asked suddenly. If the aim had been to divert Imogen with a new topic, she succeeded, because it turned out that yes, Imogen definitely wanted to come to dinner at the palace. "You remember when I used to eat with you up there when we were in school? Your cook used to make the most amazing spätzle."

"I'll see what I can do to influence the menu," Marie said.

Kai was dispatched to rig up a cart for the hayride, and soon Leo and Marie were waving at the departing group as Marie hung up the phone with Mr. Benz, whom she'd directed to pick up Gabby at the end of the ride and take her back to the palace.

Which left . . .

"Hey, Princess, you wanna see my chimney up close?"

Leo started the snowball fight this time. But he started it with a softball of a snowball, one aimed to get her attention more than anything, she thought.

As if he hadn't had enough of that in the last hour they'd spent "examining the chimney."

Marie blushed just thinking about it, but she also prepared to retaliate. She did not acknowledge his hit in any way, instead concentrating on quickly forming her own weapons. She fired off two shots—direct hits.

"Damn, why are you so good at that?" Leo shouted as he bent to gather snow.

She moved behind a waist-high stone wall that, in the summer, bordered a rose garden. "I told you, I have a talent for winter activities!" She ducked and missed an incoming missile.

They played for a few minutes, him getting a hit for every half dozen or so of hers. But he was advancing slowly on her. He was indifferent to her hits. They would make him laugh or cry out in mock indignation, but he kept walking toward her. He even stopped launching his own snowballs. He just kept coming, like a superhero immune to a rain of bullets from mere humans.

Eventually she stopped, too. Stood up straight—she'd been crouching behind the half wall. Waited. He'd been wearing a grin as he approached, but when he got within a few feet of her it slid off his face. She felt her own disappear, like she was his shadow. He looked almost angry, though that couldn't be right.

She felt cold and hot at the same time. Like her skin didn't know what to do. The air was, objectively, cold. But she was heating up from the inside.

Leo didn't pause when he reached the half wall. He wasn't looking at it, but he seemed to know it was there. Without breaking stride, he pressed one hand on the top of it and leapt over it, landing softly on his feet, like a cat. He shook off his gloves, letting them fall to the ground as he took the final step toward her, planted his hands on her cheeks—which did not help with her skin-temperature confusion—and without ceremony, lowered his mouth to hers.

Marie wobbled. Leo made her knees not work. She grabbed him to bolster herself, winding her arms around his neck as she kissed him. He kept hold of her cheeks and pressed his tongue against the seam of her mouth. She opened. Of course she did. Leo had opened her up already, in so many ways. Would she never not open when he asked?

He emitted a low growl as he swept inside, licking deep into her mouth. She never wanted it to end. She pulled him tighter, went up higher on her tiptoes, and feasted on him, this man who had grown so familiar to her. Familiar and . . .

The hair on the back of her neck rose as a prickling sensation overtook her. And it wasn't a good kind of prickling; it wasn't Leo-induced prickling. She pulled away, registering how flattering it was that he resisted. Growled again. But when she pulled back harder, he let her go. She turned, feeling like someone was watching them.

All she saw was the blank facade of the palace. So it was fine. Probably.

But they needed to be more careful. She liked to think if a staff member had happened to be looking out the window just then, they would keep what they'd seen to themselves, but the fact remained that she shouldn't be kissing Leo out in the open like this.

"Sorry," he said. "I got carried away."

"No, I'm sorry. *I* got carried away. I suddenly realized I can't be seen kissing you like this."

"Right." He stooped to pick up his gloves, which had landed rather far from them. She smiled to think that this was the first time a man had been so wild to touch her that he had shed his items of clothing so decisively.

She stopped smiling to think that it would probably be the last. She and Max had agreed that they wouldn't get in the way of each other's "discreet social lives," but the reality was it would be easier for him to carry on in that manner than it would her.

And she was certain she'd never meet anyone else like Leo.

He was all business as he stood and started brushing the snow off her coat with one hand and straightening her hat with the other. But, seeming to think better of it, he stopped abruptly and stepped back. "You probably can't be seen like this, either."

Leo was right. There had been an intimacy to the gesture, to the act of putting her to rights—putting her to rights after he'd mussed her up. He'd acted like both were his right, and she liked it way too much.

She took over the job of fixing herself and started walking toward the palace, overcome with a kind of inexplicable sadness. She told herself to snap out of it. It was Christmas Eve tomorrow. She and Leo and Gabby would attend Cocoa Fest. It was the happiest day of the year in Eldovia. "You're sure I can't convince you to attend the ball tomorrow?"

He sighed. He really didn't want to go. Which she understood. She didn't want to go, either. She backpedaled. "I'm sorry. I'll stop haranguing you."

"Is it really going to be that bad?"

She shrugged. How silly was it that she was dreading a ball? A beautiful, glamorous night filled with wonderful food and endless champagne. Most people would kill for an opportunity like that. "Can I come to your room after?"

He smiled. "You sure can."

Chapter Eighteen

*L*eo kept his hands off Marie as they made their way back to the palace. It was harder than it should have been. He wanted to . . . Jesus, Mary, and Joseph, he wanted to do *everything* to her, and not just the dirty stuff. He wanted to brush the snow off her coat and stroke her cheek and . . .

Goddammit.

So it was just as well that she'd put a stop to their post-snowball-fight make-out session.

That she'd put him in his place.

So, yeah, time to go inside, take a cold shower, and remember what this was. And what it wasn't.

Remember who he was. And who she was. And the vast gulf between them.

As if the universe had decided to help him in this quest, they were met in the foyer by the king.

"Marie." It was a single word, but it was shellacked with ice. "May I have a moment?"

"Of course." She stiffened. It reminded Leo of the way she had done just that in his cab ten days ago—a lifetime ago. She turned the fake dimples on him. "I'll see you at cocktails, Leo?"

"Yes."

"Mr. Ricci." The king turned his head ever so slightly toward Leo, as if turning it the full amount so he could look Leo straight in the face was too much effort. "If you're looking for your sister, I believe you will find her in the kitchens, tidying up after having dropped a tray of crystal mugs on the floor."

Well, shit. In any other circumstance, he would have felt badly. Would have apologized and offered to pay for the damage. But since the king's aim here was clearly to make him feel inferior, he wasn't going to do that.

"Father!" Marie stage-whispered. "She's helping with the preparations for tomorrow."

"Helping?" the king echoed. "Is that what you call it?"

"Well," Leo drawled, turning up his accent as much as he could. "I guess you can take the kid out of the Bronx but . . ." He performed an exaggerated shrug and turned on his heel.

"Leo!" Marie called after him. He turned. It wasn't her fault her father was an ass. "I'll see you at cocktails?" she asked again, like she was worried he wouldn't show.

She looked miserable. He shot her a quick smile. "Wouldn't miss it, Princess."

Hopefully her father would think his use of the term "princess" was literal.

And hopefully she would understand that it wasn't.

He was tempted to go to the kitchen to clean up Gabby's

mess—literally—but he headed for his room instead and Face-
Timed Dani. Surprisingly, his need to talk about his goddamn
feelings was more urgent than his need to find his sister.

"What's up?" Dani said when she picked up.

"Oh, you know, just showing my working-class roots, defiling
the princess, the usual."

She laughed. "Are you getting defiled in return now at least?"

"I am indeed."

"So why do you look so annoyed?"

Because he didn't want it to end.

"Anyway, the defiling has to stop." It did. Things were getting
all muddled. He was supposed to be having a fun little fling.
Make-believe. Which was aided by the fact that he was in a fucking palace.

He was *not* supposed to be losing his head. Which was clearly
what had happened to him back there in the middle of their
snowball fight. Something had flipped inside him. What had
been silly and fun had turned inside out, with no warning, and
suddenly he'd *needed* to kiss her. To touch her. He would have
Incredible-Hulked anything that stood in the way of that singu-
lar goal.

"Why does it have to stop?" Dani asked. "Seems to me it's a
major perk of your little vacation. Or maybe it's even the *feature*
of your vacation."

"Because it's not going to get any easier to stop as time goes
on. Tomorrow's the big ball—and no, I'm still not going," he said,
anticipating her question. "Then it's Christmas, and then we're
heading home."

He didn't want to go home.

Well, he did and he didn't. He didn't want to go back to sitting on his ass in a cab for twelve hours a day. But he could certainly do without this "Your sister broke the palace crystal, you plebeian" bullshit.

"But why do you have to stop, period?"

"What do you mean?"

"Why don't you invite her back to New York? In the spring, maybe."

"I can't do that."

"Why not?"

Because . . . Well, shit. He couldn't think of a damn thing.

"You're adults. It sounds like you both know this can't be a long-term thing, but why not extend the fling if you're both enjoying yourselves and as long as she's . . . free? What's the word? Not betrothed. Ha! What is even your life, Leo?"

"I know. She apparently has to marry 'strategically,' whatever that means."

"What *does* that mean?"

"I have no idea, but I'm not it."

"Do you want to be it?"

Did he? Leo always sort of vaguely imagined himself married, but . . . later. After Gabby was grown up and they were less on the edge financially. But anyway, whatever happened, even if he did get married someday, it sure as hell wasn't going to be to the princess of Eldovia. "No," he said, in answer to Dani's question.

"Want to try that again a little more decisively?"

"I am decisive."

"Okay, you know what? I'm taking back my extend-the-fling advice. You're in too deep here, and no offense, Leo, but there is no universe in which the heir to the throne of Eldovia is going to entertain being with you in any real way."

"I *know* that." Shit. That had come out way too defensive-sounding. He tried again. "Look. I'm having fun. I'm not used to that. It's probably the leisure as much as the fling. It's been so long since I've—" Shit. He suddenly felt like his voice was about to crack.

"I know," Dani said softly. "You deserve some fun. Just don't get yourself hurt in the process, okay?"

They hung up, and goddamn it, the seed had been planted. He couldn't stop thinking about Dani's idea that he invite Marie back to New York. She might not even have to make a special trip if she was taking the UN ambassador gig. He still had that fifteen grand. He could put a chunk of it aside so he could afford to take a week off. If she came when Gabby was in school, they could get up to all sorts of fun during the day. Sexy fun, yes, but also, New York in the springtime could be great. They could rent a boat in Central Park, go to the cherry blossom festival in Brooklyn. And Dani could take them out to her parents' place on Long Island.

People did this, right? It wasn't that different from what he and Giada had had. There was just more distance between Marie and him, both geographic and social, than there had been between Giada and him. But a booty call was a booty call. And Dani was right. They were both enjoying themselves, so what was the harm?

"What the hell do you think you're doing?"

Marie blinked as she stood in the doorway of the library, where her father had silently led her after so rudely dispatching Leo. Father hadn't even waited for her to close the door before lashing out.

She eased the door shut and tried to think what was happening. Had he found out about the cabin somehow? How was that possible? The only people who knew were Leo and Kai, both of whom she trusted absolutely.

Had Gabby let it slip? She sighed. "Look, I can explain—"

"Anyone could have seen you. Out in the open like that."

Out in the open? *Oh*.

"It's shameful. *You're* shameful."

Tears rushed to the surface. She had *never* heard her father like this. He could be cruel, yes, but usually in a passive-aggressive way—like the way he'd treated Leo and Gabby so often the past few days.

She knew what he was referring to, though. *He* had been the source of her sense that she and Leo were being watched earlier.

"The duke, duchess, and their sons will arrive tomorrow morning. What if they'd come today? What if they'd *seen* you?"

"Max is coming?" She would be so happy to see him. "But I thought he was in Cambridge for the holidays."

"Max has had a change of plans."

"But—" Did that mean he *wasn't* doing a PhD? She was afraid to ask.

"I don't know why I've indulged you for so long. It's time for your guests to leave. Mr. Benz has booked a late-night flight out of Zurich and has arranged a car to take them. They'll need to be ready by six." He sat at his desk and opened a newspaper, clearly done with her.

"No." Marie had to swallow the gasp she nearly emitted. It was getting easier to say no to him, but still, she had surprised herself there.

He whipped his head up—he was surprised, too. "I beg your pardon?"

She had defied him a bit, before, as it related to the goodwill ambassadorship, but this was different. This was personal. But she'd be damned if Gabby went home before Cocoa Fest. Leo had been so kind to Marie in New York, driving her around, buying her treats, opening his home to her when she was alone. She refused to repay that generosity by letting her father run him out. "Tomorrow is Christmas Eve. They're not leaving tonight."

"Yes, they are," he said with exaggerated patience, like she was a child.

She was determined to stand her ground. "The whole point of them being here is to experience an Eldovian Christmas. Gabby's worked so hard on the festival. They're staying." Should she say more? She thought back to her father's appalling treatment of Gabby the other night at dinner. Yes, in fact, she should. "And what's more, you will stop insulting them."

"That sounds remarkably like a threat," the king snapped, not even bothering to conceal his anger. "Let me give you a little tip, my girl. Threats are more effective when you clearly state the consequences. I will stop insulting your guests, or what?"

Marie channeled her mother's quiet certainty as she lifted her chin. "Or I will stop doing your job for you. I will stop jumping when you issue your orders and leave me to try to execute them without letting me have any meaningful input."

She watched a bunch of different emotions go to war on his face. Shock, anger, and, finally, hurt.

It was the hurt that weakened her resolve. Softened her. "All I'm asking," she said gently, "is that they stay through Christmas and that you stop harassing them. It's unkind. They're alone at Christmas." *Just like we are.*

The hurt was gone from his face. That was something at least. But he almost looked like a stranger now. She thought she'd seen the hard version of her father. The man whose grief had changed him into a more austere version of himself. But this version was worse. It was frightening in its blankness.

"I will make you a deal," he finally said. He spoke with eerie calmness. "Your friends stay until Boxing Day as planned, and I announce your engagement to Maximillian at the ball."

"No."

There it was again. How remarkable. Such a little word, but so powerful.

"I don't want to marry Max."

"You don't want to marry Max," he repeated. She would have expected him to revert to the anger he'd displayed a moment ago, but his tone was strangely mild—and then he threw his head back and laughed at her.

Marie sucked a breath in as tears rose to the surface.

"Did you have someone else in mind, then?" he said, making her feel like a child. "Someone else lined up?"

"I—" Of course she didn't. What had Leo said? There was "no universe" in which he wanted to marry her.

Father kept looking at her, his eyebrows raised, impatience written on his face.

"I don't wish to marry anyone at present," she finally said, disappointed that she hadn't managed to hold on to her mother's commanding tone. That the tears she was trying hard to suppress were so obviously, so mortifyingly, apparent in the quavering of her voice. He sighed. Looked at her for a long time. "I'm sorry, but this is the way of things for us." He flashed a small, cheerless smile, her sad king. "To hear it told, your mother didn't want to marry me, either." The smile widened, but turned false. "And look how that worked out."

She wasn't sure if he meant that it had worked out fine, because they'd been happy, or if he was referring to the wreckage her death left behind.

Regardless, the anger—the cruelty—had gone from him. For now. Her mind churned, trying to work out an escape, but it was moving slowly, mired in the heartbreak and embarrassment of having been mocked by her own father. *Did you have someone else in mind?*

"Need we announce the engagement at the ball?" she said carefully, falling back on the strategy of postponement, rather than outright defiance, that she and Max had always relied on. If they could just get through the holidays, perhaps there was a solution yet to be discovered. "Won't it draw the focus from the holiday celebration?"

"On the contrary, it will enhance the celebration. And who knows, perhaps it will do us some good to have a pleasant memory to associate with the holiday."

Did he mean that last bit sincerely, or was he merely manipulating her to get what he wanted? Regardless, Marie didn't know what else to say, so she turned away from him. She needed to get out of this room. Maybe then her brain would work properly. She could call Max, and—

"And . . ." her father said, drawing her attention just as she'd reached the door. When she looked over her shoulder, he looked . . . She wasn't even sure. He almost looked contrite, but that couldn't be right. "I'll take a look at your UN proposal."

She wanted to tell him that it wasn't a proposal. It was a *plan*. A plan she had sent him a copy of as a courtesy. Because she was accepting the UN ambassadorship no matter what he said. But it seemed wiser to save that fight for another day.

So she sought the only concession she could think of that might be within her grasp, given that he'd softened a bit. "You'll be civil to all our guests tonight, including the Riccis, who will stay until Boxing Day as planned?"

Whatever she thought she'd seen on his face was gone. It was now blank. But he said, calmly, "Yes."

"Very well."

She turned, aware anew of how lonely she was. Leo had managed to distract her from it for a while, but in a few days he would leave and she would be more alone than ever.

A sad princess to go with the sad king?

Maybe it was inevitable. Maybe this was how it happened.

WHEN MARIE CAME to Leo's room late that night, she seemed off. Sad.

"Hey, Princess, what's shaking?"

She smiled at him, but it was a fake one. He couldn't abide that. He led her to one of the chairs by the fire. "What's wrong?"

She shook her head as she sat. "It was just . . . a very long day."

He sat in the companion chair, wishing the room had a sofa so he could sit closer to her. "You had a fight with your father, didn't you?" Oddly, the king hadn't been as much of a dick as usual during cocktails and dinner. Leo had put that down to the fact that Imogen had joined them, had thought perhaps His Majesty tolerated commoners of his own nation better than

New York interlopers. And Marie and Imogen had seemed to have a good time, reminiscing and teasing each other, though he had wondered if Marie's good cheer was a little forced.

She sighed and slumped lower in her chair. "Are you a mind reader?"

"No. I just know you." It was a bit startling, given that they'd only met ten days ago.

Marie tilted her head and regarded Leo with a puzzled expression. "You do, don't you?"

"Yeah, I know all your tells. You lift your chin like this"—he demonstrated—"when you're feeling cornered."

"I *do*?"

"Yeah. And you have a fake smile and a real smile, and I fucking hate the fake one."

A startled laugh bubbled out of her, and he pointed at her in triumph. "See, that there's the real smile. That's better. So, yeah, you can't fool me. What happened with your father? Spill it."

"There's really nothing to tell." She hesitated in a way that he was pretty sure indicated she was holding something back. "We don't see eye to eye on many things."

"The watches?"

She huffed a bitter laugh. "We haven't even talked about that since we officially broke for the holiday."

"The UN thing?"

"Yes, but I've decided I'm doing that anyway. They asked me, not him. He makes the decisions about the Morneau brand because he runs the company. And I don't have an official seat on his advisory cabinet even though I do most of his work since my mother died. But I don't need his permission for this."

"Good for you." Ambition looked good on her.

But then why was she so dejected?

And another why: Why did he care so much? She clearly didn't want to talk about it. He redirected. "You wanna go back to your room and watch some *Buffy*?" Maybe it would relax her, and he could find out what she was so upset about.

"No. What I want is . . ." Marie sat up straight, the way she sometimes did when she wanted to exert authority, but that didn't seem like what was happening here. It was more like—

Oh.

She was taking off her sweater. She pulled it over her head, threw it on the floor, and reached around to unclasp her bra.

"You want to look at my chimney some more?" he said, hoping to make her smile by invoking the silly innuendo they'd used earlier in the day.

She produced a "prophylactic," out of her pocket, and his body reacted in predictable ways. She also ignored his question. "What I want is for you to say filthy things to me, and then I want us to do those things."

Oh, eff him. He had created a monster. Not that he could take credit. She had created herself. He'd just done a little encouraging.

All right, then. Following her lead, Leo took off his T-shirt. She raised her eyebrows as if she were not impressed. He chuckled, unzipped his jeans, and took his already-at-attention dick out. Raised his eyebrows right back at her and let himself drink her in. The only sources of light in the room were the bedside lamp he'd been reading by and the fire, so she was painted in a soft warm glow. Her breasts were as gorgeous as always—white and pink and . . . perfect.

She cleared her throat.

Right. She'd wanted him to talk, and here he was getting all moony over her breasts. "Take off your pants." She did. And as she began to shimmy out of them, he added, "Underwear, too." She started to move toward him once she was naked, but he held up a hand to stop her. "Sit back down." She pouted a little. He stroked his dick and said, "I thought you wanted to talk."

She sat.

"So what do you wanna do, Princess?" he said while he took his pants the rest of the way off. "You want to open your legs and I'll come over there and eat your pretty pussy? I can guarantee you that's the only way you'll ever get me to kneel in front of you."

Her breathing had grown audible. She was so delightfully easy to wind up. Or unwind, to use the word she had the other day. "Nobody talks to you like this, do they?"

"Just you," she whispered.

Damn right.

Her pupils were blown, and she was staring at his mouth. He no longer regretted the lack of a couch in this room. There was something intensely erotic about sitting in armchairs facing each other, her naked and him nearly so. He let his teeth scrape across the lip she was fixated on and was rewarded with a little whimper that went straight to his dick.

"Or maybe," he said, "you want to come over here and ride my dick and bite my lip some more."

She inhaled sharply, bent her arms, and used her elbows to squeeze her breasts, as if they ached. He was pretty sure that signified a direct hit.

"So why don't you do that, then?"

She expelled a soft little sigh, and he tried to keep a hold of himself as she let her teeth slowly scrape her lower lip. Another sigh—it sounded almost like she was relieved. "Come on, sweetheart. Slide that condom on my dick and then get on here and bounce around."

And she did.

And she almost killed him—him and his smart mouth. Real big talker he was, goading her like it was something he could deliver on. Like he could just sit there while she "bounced around." After she straddled him, sank down on a moan, and started moving, he realized he was going to blow pretty quickly. Well, hell, he might as well go down talking, since she seemed to like it so much. So he let loose a steady stream of dirty talk as he thrust upward, trying to keep with the rhythm she was setting. "Oh, fuck, Princess, you feel incredible. I'm not going to last very long. You're gonna make me come way too fast. You think you can catch up with me? Because I want to feel that tight pussy clenching all around my dick. I want you to give it to me. I want—"

Her breath shortened, which was her warning sign. He pushed back against the incredible pressure building inside him. He wanted to be able to watch her when she came. He slid his hands up to her breasts, and she went still. He heaved upward and his dick started pulsing just as the clenching he'd asked for commenced. And fuck him, had anything ever felt so good in his life? She moaned as pleasure washed over her. He did the same, letting it pulse all through him, spread through his limbs like a narcotic. He'd thought before that she sounded relieved, and he felt that too, suddenly. It was the physical release, but not just that. It was also . . . her.

She slumped forward onto his chest, and he put his arms around her. They stayed like that for a long time, their ragged breathing and the crackling of the fire the only sounds in the room.

Eventually, she started to shift like she was preparing to lever herself off him. He didn't want her to go. Not yet. So he stood, taking her with him. She squealed and laughed and wrapped her legs around him and let him carry her to the bed. He used one hand to hold on to the condom as he eased her off him and laid her down. After ditching it, he slid under the covers next to her.

"Are you going to finish the roof of the cabin tomorrow?" she asked quietly.

"Yeah. I intended to today, but then a princess showed up and spirited me off to lunch. I'm planning to get up first thing and finish. I only have probably another hour's worth of work, so I'll be back for all the cocoa nonsense."

"Thank you, Leo." She propped herself up on his chest and looked at him intently. "You don't know what this means to me."

"I do know."

She smiled. It wasn't the fake one, exactly, but it was a wistful one. "I wish I could do something for you."

"Well, I'm pretty sure you just gave me the best sex of my life." Her face lit up. "Really?"

He probably shouldn't have admitted that, but . . . "Yeah." He stopped short of floating the come-to-New-York-in-the-spring idea. Because, ultimately, Dani was right. He needed to not get himself in too deep.

"I was thinking about the concept of pleasing people, actually," she said.

"Yeah?"

"It's going to sound odd to compare these two things, but bear

with me. I was thinking about how, since we started . . ." Marie
screwed up her face like she was having trouble spitting out the
words.

"Ah, come on," he teased, playing with her hair. "You can say it.
You can't make me do *all* the dirty talking."

She rolled her eyes. "Since we started having sex."

"And here I was hoping you'd say 'fucking.'"

"Regardless, the point is, I've found myself wanting to please
you. Wanting to do exactly what would give you the most pleasure. This evening for some reason I was thinking about how unusual a position that is for me to find myself in. I mean, in normal
circumstances, not sexual ones."

"You don't have family that allows it."

"Correct. I would love to make my father happy, but I can't. My
mother, though . . . Here's the other memory. In the spring, there
are wildflowers everywhere around here. She loved them. When I
was young, I used to go out every day and pick some for her. I even
did it as an adult. Not as often, but from time to time. And I remember on my first trip home from Oxford in the spring, after the
Hilary term in my first year, I was being driven up to the castle
and they were in bloom. So I asked the driver to stop, and I picked
an armful. It was such a simple thing, but it made her so happy."

He could see what was missing in her life. Well, there were a
lot of things missing in her life. Dancing like no one was watching.
Pastrami on rye. But the larger point was that she was, elementally,
alone.

"My whole life is arranged so that I'm surrounded by other
people whose entire jobs are to make me happy," she said.

"And do they?"

"They make me comfortable."

That was a nonanswer. But really, the nonanswer *was* a sort of answer, wasn't it?

"*I* never get a chance to make *anyone else* happy," she went on. "That's what I'm trying to say. Happiness—whether you're experiencing it or creating it for others—is important. And happiness and comfort, it turns out, are not the same things."

"You know what would make me really happy right now?" *If you agreed to come to New York and see me. If this didn't have to be it.*

"What?"

"If you would say 'fucking.'"

Marie cracked up, which had been Leo's aim. He knew it didn't address anything she'd said, but all that stuff about wildflowers and happiness? He got what she was saying, but he was not the person who could fix any of that for her, not in any sort of permanent way. So he stuck with what he *could* do. "Come on. It's not that hard. 'Leo, I enjoyed fucking you very much.'"

She swatted his chest. "Oh, stop it."

She didn't really want him to stop it, though. He could tell from the way her eyes danced. He performed an exaggerated sigh. "Well, okay. I guess I'll just lie here all unhappy-like."

She heaved herself onto him so she was lying directly on top of him. Scooched herself up so they were nose to nose and announced, "Leo, I enjoyed fucking you very much." But she did it in that semiprissy princess tone he loved to hate and hated to love.

Ah, shit. He was so screwed.

Chapter Nineteen

*W*e thought, if anyone can think of a way out of this, it's you," Max said.

Marie's heart was hammering. She'd called Max last night after her confrontation with her father, and Max had suggested that when he arrived this morning, they jointly speak to Mr. Benz. Maybe, he'd reasoned, the equerry would see a way out of the engagement where they could not. She hadn't had a lot of hope but had reasoned it couldn't hurt. The man was a master courtier. He knew the politics of the country, the country's nobility. He knew Morneau. He knew the family. He knew *everything*. What was the worst that could happen?

She just hadn't expected to be so nervous. Before, when she and Max had talked about the impending engagement, she'd been . . . bummed, as the Americans would say. Bummed but resigned. Now, though, she felt like she was back at the United Nations, about to step onstage. Panic was unspooling inside her, edging into despair, even.

"Have you told your father you don't wish to marry?" Mr. Benz asked after they'd laid out their concerns.

"Yes." Marie had to fight to keep her voice even. She had told him, and he'd mocked her.

"We've been trying to postpone the inevitable for *years*," Max said, idly sipping a cup of tea, clearly not feeling the same dread she was.

"Indeed," Mr. Benz remarked.

"I've already done my master's thesis," Max said. "I'm just pretending I need more time."

"I'm aware."

"You are?" Max aimed an astonished face at Marie. That had shocked him out of his languor.

"I told you he knows everything."

"I was going to suggest that you at least try making your case directly to His Majesty," Mr. Benz said, "but His Majesty doesn't . . ."

She could tell he'd been going to say something he'd thought twice about, probably something he'd decided would come across as disloyal. So she filled in the blanks for him. "Listen to reason? Care about what I want? Have a heart anymore?"

He sighed. "It's true your father has not been himself since your mother's passing."

"We all miss her. But it's been three years. I can't keep doing this." Her voice was rising, and she could hear the hysteria creeping in, but she couldn't control it. "I can't keep doing his work as well as trying to do the work I *want* to do. And I can't marry the wrong person!"

The wrong person.

That suggested there was a *right* person to marry, didn't it?

Oh dear god. That's what was different now. That's why she was so upset.

She *did* want to marry Leo, even though there was "no universe" in which *he* wanted to marry *her*.

She was in love with him.

Her stupid, naïve heart had opened right up to him. Marched right over to his rough-gentle hands and laid itself inside them.

Marie gasped. Audibly and mortifyingly. She wanted him *so* terribly.

She reminded herself, though, that she was accustomed to not getting what she wanted. She closed her eyes and pressed her knuckles against her eyelids, hoping the pain would make the sobs that were about to come recede.

"Aww, Marie." Max came over to her and tried to touch her arm. She didn't want that. She didn't want *him*. She shook him off.

She had to get a grip. Max aside, there was no scenario in which she was going to marry Leo. She had to stop conflating the issue of the engagement with . . . the fact of Leo.

Marie pulled her fists off her eyes and straightened her spine. "I'm sorry. I lost my head there for a moment." She turned to Mr. Benz. "I'm sorry I bothered you with this nonsense. If you'll excuse us for a moment, I'd like to have a word with Max before we join everyone on the grounds." Max's family was scheduled to join Marie and her father for a walkabout, to take in Cocoa Fest. She'd invited Leo and Gabby, too. She needed to fill Max in—to prepare him, at least, for the possibility that her father might be horrible to the Riccis. And she needed him to back her up in making them feel welcome.

And then there was the ball. *The fucking ball*, which was what Leo would call it.

As Mr. Benz left, Max approached cautiously. "You want to tell me what's wrong?" He held his arms out like he wanted to hug her. She let him this time, burying her face in his shoulder—the wrong shoulder—and saying, "I fell in love, Max. That's what's wrong."

FUCK IT. HE was going to do it. What was the worst that could happen? She'd say no thanks. *Leo, I am not interested in a transatlantic booty call.* And he would move on. Go home. Where he belonged.

The decision made him feel oddly light.

Oh, who was he kidding? What was making him feel oddly light was the idea of her back in New York. Boats and fucking *cherry blossoms*. Getting it on in his rickety double bed while Gabby was at school.

Leo hadn't felt this light in a long time. Possibly, he had lost his mind and that was what was making him feel so light, but hey, he was going to run with it.

He should have waited for her to respond to his knock. But that stupid lightness was propelling him, making him hurry, like he was a balloon filled with helium skittering along a ceiling.

Marie was in her sitting room. His eyes went right to her. They always did. "It's my turn to make a proposition, Princess."

"Leo!"

The problem with the way Leo's eyes immediately went to Marie when she was in a room was that there was a delay in registering the presence of *anyone else* in the room.

Like, for example, the guy she was hugging.

The guy she was guiltily jumping away from.

"Leo, this is my friend Max. Maximillian von Hansburg. The von Hansburgs are close family friends, and they're here for the festivities tomorrow. Max, this is Leonardo Ricci."

"Ah, he of the moonlit walks," Max drawled as he stuck out a hand for Leo to shake.

Leo ignored the hand and surveyed its owner. Max was dressed in a suit. A skinny gray one, but instead of a normal tie, he was wearing his shirt open with a scarf thing tied into it. Was that an ascot? Leo had never seen one in person, but he was pretty sure that was it. The dude was wearing an actual fucking ascot.

"Max, hush," Marie said. "This is not your business."

"It is if you want to keep taking those moonlit walks, my friend," he said to Marie.

"What?" What the hell was this guy on about?

Max retracted the hand that Leo had not shaken and switched to beckoning him over to a chair near the fireplace. "Marie and I were settling in for a plotting session on how to avoid our parents' matrimonial machinations. Join us."

"Max!" Marie nearly shrieked, and Marie was not a shrieker. At least not in this sort of circumstance. And "matrimonial machinations." Did that mean what he thought it meant? Leo eyed the pair of them. The hand that hadn't been beckoning him was now resting on Marie's lower back with a familiarity that suggested that yes, "matrimonial machinations" meant exactly what he feared it did.

"You should have told me," he said quietly. He'd thought it was going to come out like a yell—that's what he'd intended—but he had to settle for a shaky whisper. His lungs felt like they were working overtime yet couldn't seem to suck in quite enough air.

"Leo." Marie rushed over to him. "There's nothing between Max and me. There never has been."

"That's right." Max came over, too, looking alarmed, and Leo's fingers flexed. He wanted to punch this guy even though he understood with his higher brain that that would achieve nothing. "Marie is like a sister. We've been plotting ways to postpone this engagement for years. It's almost a hobby of ours."

"You've been engaged for *years*?"

"Well, not technically," Max said. "That will happen at the ball tonight, unless we can—"

"That's not what he means, Max," Marie said quietly. She met Leo's gaze unflinchingly, which he had to give her credit for. "Yes. Max and I have known for years that our parents wanted us to marry. Our fathers are friends and want to unite the two houses."

Unite the two houses. Was this the Middle Ages?

They must have read the derision on his face. "My family, the House of Aquilla—my father is the Duke of Aquilla—have extensive mining holdings," Max said.

His father was a duke? So this guy would be a duke when his father kicked the bucket? Like Marie would be Queen of Eldovia someday?

"We could supply trace minerals for the Morneau watches," Max went on. "Our fathers have been talking for years about joining forces."

"So why don't they just fucking join forces? Why do they have to—"

He'd been going to say, *Sell off their children*, but what was the point? Leo already knew these people were different than he was. He'd been reminded in a thousand little ways since he got here.

And more to the point, why the fuck did he care? Because he wasn't going to get his stupid springtime in New York with the princess? It was always going to end at some point. As Dani said, better to end things now, before he got hurt.

Except it was too late, wasn't it? He was already hurt. So much that, apparently, his lungs had stopped working. He was literally panting now. It felt like his chest was being punctured by a million tiny needles.

He had fucked this up big-time. He'd let this woman get to him.

He'd flown across an ocean and eaten excruciating five-course meals. He had endured passive-aggressive abuse from her father—like Dani used to have to do with her in-laws. And he wasn't even married to Marie—or engaged to her. He'd done that part *voluntarily*.

He'd built a fucking log cabin for her.

"We're going to use a turkey baster if it comes down to it," Max said, and oh fuck, Leo doubled over.

"Max!" Marie whisper-shouted.

"What?" Max protested. "I'm trying to say that if we can't avert this, you guys can come to some sort of arrangement. I'm certainly not going to get in your way. That's always been the plan, hasn't it? We do what we want on the side?"

Oh god, they were talking about making him a royal mistress. A master? Whatever. No *fucking* way.

But good, actually. That additional little bit of info was enough to tip him from hurt to *angry*. To *royally fucking pissed*, actually.

He didn't know what had happened with him and Marie, but

he did know that he was never going to be her dirty secret on the side while she was married to someone else. Leo didn't consider himself a practicing Catholic. But he still believed in enough of that shit to know that when you stood in front of a church—or a judge or whatever—and vowed to love and honor someone, *that was what you did*.

So, no. He was done here, even though it hurt like hell—which made him madder than he otherwise would have been because it wasn't *supposed* to hurt. It was supposed to be a vacation fling. A "surprisingly refreshing break from reality." The anger was growing, eclipsing the hurt. It was allowing him to finally breathe. Leo straightened, let the air saturate his lungs for a few breaths, and looked Marie in the eyes. Hardened himself to the pain he saw there and said, "It was always going to end anyway."

It looked for a moment like her face was going to crumple, but she got control of herself, lifted her chin, and said, "Right."

He should have left then, but that prissy princess chin-lifting, directed at *him*, pissed him right off. He wasn't standing for that shit. "You should have told me," he said again, but this time it came out properly. Like the angry accusation it was. For fuck's sake, they had lain in bed and bared their goddamn souls to each other—he'd thought. He'd told her about maybe wanting to go back to school, and she'd told him about her mother. She'd told him that he was the only person who saw the real her.

"Yes," Marie agreed, "I should have told you." Her face did crumple then.

"I'm going to take Gabby to Cocoa Fest now." Leo spoke to the side of her head—she'd turned it away in what he was pretty sure was shame. "She'll want to watch you get ready for the ball tonight if you're still willing." He didn't have it in him to deny the ball-obsessed Gabby that. Marie gave a little nod. "We'll be out of your hair tomorrow morning." They were scheduled to leave mid-day on the twenty-sixth but no way were they staying that long. He would go back to his room now and book flights for tomorrow morning. And a car to get them to the nearest airport. It would probably cost all of the fifteen grand he'd earned from his driving gig, but that was fine. Suddenly he wanted more than anything to wash his hands of all this. To be left with nothing that reminded him of her. To have none of her blood money left.

"You can't leave on Christmas," she protested weakly.

"I can, though," he said, not unkindly but forcefully. "I can do whatever I want."

She burst into tears, and he turned and fled before he did, too.

Chapter Twenty

*C*ocoa Fest really was something, Leo had to admit. He and Gabby walked the palace grounds sampling peppermint cocoa and black cherry cocoa and Nutella cocoa and Gabby's own butterscotch s'mores cocoa. Each flavor really was served out of a giant cauldron manned by a member of the palace staff—Gabby's featured a sign that credited her as the "chef"—and there were tables set up with elaborate toppings ranging from homemade marshmallow fluff to candied orange rinds to half a dozen flavors of whipped cream. It was all so extravagant that Gabby didn't notice Leo was not himself. He managed to walk around and nod at the right times and generally act like a person whose heart had not been splintered into a million pieces a few hours ago.

He was relieved when, after doing a lap of the festivities, Gabby agreed to his suggestion that they walk down the hill and see what was going on in the village. He'd seen Marie and the king and Max walking around the grounds with an older couple he could only assume was the duke and duchess and a poshly dressed guy who looked a little like Max. That was probably Marie's future brother-in-law. Leo didn't want to see any of them. He didn't trust himself to see Marie again and not lose his shit.

The village square was abuzz with carnival games and ice skaters. The aroma of roasted nuts wafted through the chilled air, joining the smell of hot chocolate emanating from stands that were selling it out of more traditional urns than the palace cauldrons. It was snowing gently, the fat, white flakes making the whole scene look like a movie set. It was the Hallmark movie he'd teased Marie about, except he was pretty sure Hallmark movies didn't end in heartbreak and ruin. Of course, they also didn't feature as much fucking as had happened the past few days, so clearly he was on the wrong channel.

"Gabby!" It was Imogen's niece from the pub, along with a couple of younger boys Leo didn't recognize. "You want to come skating with us?"

Gabby introduced him. They turned out to be Imogen's nephews, whom Gabby had met on the hayride a couple days ago. "Can I, Leo?"

"Sure, kiddo." He handed her a few euros, and she ran off to the skate-rental stand. He looked around for a place to sit and watch and spied Imogen working a booth out front of her bar.

"Hello!" she called as he approached. "Can I interest you in some hot buttered cocoa?"

"Sure." She had set up a small outdoor wooden bar complete with stools, so he collected his mug and went to sit on one. He watched her hand off cocoa-serving duties to someone else and make her way over to him.

"Gabby and I are heading home tomorrow." He hoped. He was a little worried about the forecast: this snow was not supposed to stop anytime soon. "Thanks for all the hospitality while we were here."

"I thought you were staying through Boxing Day. I was going to invite you all down for a little post-Christmas party I usually hold for close friends. I close the pub at five on Christmas Day and we all kick back and toast the fact that we don't have to drink, discuss, or look at cocoa for another twelve months."

"Yeah, well . . . our plans changed."

"Did you and Marie break up?" she said softly.

"We were never together," he said automatically.

"But you kind of were, weren't you?"

Leo sighed. There was no point in lying—to her or to himself. "Yeah. We were." He wasn't really sure how it had happened, but it had. "Did Marie say something about us?" God, listen to him. He sounded like a teenager.

"No. It was obvious, though."

"It *was*?" That was mildly horrifying.

"To anyone who really knows Marie. It was easy to see how lighthearted she was around you. I think our princess has been alone—existentially alone—for a very long time. Since her mother died, certainly."

He sighed again. "Will you . . ." Fuck. What? What was he trying to say? "Will you take care of her when I'm gone?"

"I will." She smiled. "But you could also just . . . not leave? Merely a friendly suggestion."

"Maximillian von Something of the House of Whatever has arrived, so, yeah, I pretty much have to leave."

"Ah. I see."

Imogen didn't *sound* like she saw, though. "They're engaged. It's being announced at the ball tonight." He hated how indignant he sounded. He cleared his throat. "I'm supposed to just stick around for that?"

"I don't know if it's sticking around for *that* so much as sticking around for *Marie*. She hates that ball. She would probably appreciate having an ally there."

"She's getting married to someone else." What part of this did this woman not understand?

Imogen nodded sympathetically, but then she winked. "Unless someone rewrites the ending."

IN THE END, it was Max who made Marie brave. Marie had made good on her promise to invite Gabby to witness the ball preparations. They chatted while Verene did Marie's hair and makeup. Gabby clearly had no idea what was happening between Marie and Leo, but she had been informed they were leaving tomorrow, and she was *not* pleased about it.

"I don't understand what the big hurry is. There's supposedly a party at the pub on Christmas night after it closes, and Imogen's niece invited me to sleep over afterward."

Marie was going to miss Gabby's babbling so much.

"Wow, that lipstick is so pretty!" Gabby moved a little closer to get a better view. "Is that an actual paintbrush you're using?"

"Ahem." Max appeared in the doorway of her dressing room.

"Max," Marie said, meeting his gaze in the mirror while Verene murmured "Good evening, Lord Laudon."

"Lord!" Gabby exclaimed.

"Gabby," Marie said, "this is my friend Max. Max, this is Gabby Ricci, Leo's sister."

"Are you a prince?" Gabby asked.

"Alas, no. A mere baron." When her face fell, Max added cheerily, "Future duke, though, if that helps."

"What can we do for you, Max?"

"I need a word with you."

Marie eyed her half-made-up reflection. "Now?"

"Yes."

She raised her eyebrows. Easygoing Max never insisted on anything, never showed up uninvited into a space as private as her dressing room. "All right."

Verene stood. "Miss Gabriella, let us step out for a moment. Would you like me to apply some of this lipstick for you?"

After Verene and Gabby left the room, Marie rose and moved to join Max on a sofa by the fireplace. She said, "What's on your mind?"

"We can't do this."

"What? The engagement?"

"Yes. It's madness."

"Excuse me?" Max had always been cheerfully resigned to their turkey-baster-and-open-marriage plan. "I appreciate you trying with Mr. Benz earlier, but since when have you thought this was anything other than a strategic union we'd resigned ourselves to?"

"It still is that for me, but it's clearly not for you, so we've got to call it off."

"But it's not like I'm going to marry Leo."

He shrugged as if that *wasn't* the most preposterous idea he'd ever heard.

"*Max.* I can't marry Leo." Could she? *No universe*, right? That's the phrase that had been echoing through her head during the confrontation with her father.

"Let me ask you, why did you agree to marry me in the first place?"

"I don't know that I did agree. It's more that I went along with it."

"All right, then why did you go along with it?"

"I—" Because going along with things was what she did?

But . . . was that true anymore? Marie thought back to last night, when Leo had listed off all the ways she hadn't bent to her father's—or Mr. Benz's—will.

"I'll tell you why *I* went along with it," Max said. "Because I like you. I like you better than most people. I'm never going to meet anyone I want to marry. Since I *have* to marry, it might as well be to you."

"I *know*." She tried not to let the frustration she felt come through in her tone. Max was only trying to help. "We've talked about all this."

"It's all the same to me," he went on, as if he hadn't heard her. "But it's not all the same to you. Not anymore."

It wasn't. It wasn't the same at all. There was theory, and there was . . . Leo.

A sob started to rise through her chest. She tried to swallow it—there was no point in crying—but Max knew her too well. He scooted closer and took her hand.

"I'm not going to pretend I understand this love business. But I can grasp it intellectually, and I know you well enough to know that now that you've had it—even if it can't work out with Leo—you can't settle for . . ." He grinned. "My sorry ass."

"What am I going to do, though, if he doesn't want me? Just not get married?" Could she do that?

He only shrugged again. She glared at him. She needed real advice here.

He sobered. "Don't you at least think the first step is to get out of marrying me?"

"I have no idea what my father will do. What if he . . . kicks me out?" She couldn't quite bring herself to say *disown*.

"Does it matter? You have money."

She did. Her mother had had a trust, held independent of any of her father's family money. She'd drawn on it for their impromptu trips to America. She used to say, "It's my money. I can do what I like with it." Marie had forgotten that. Her mother used to say that rather vehemently, too. Defiantly, almost. As if someone had objected to the way she was spending it.

And Marie knew who that someone was, didn't she?

Her mother had bequeathed that money to Marie. It wasn't a lot. Maybe a hundred thousand euros. But that was more than the average person had. It was enough to rent somewhere to live and tide her over until she figured out a way to make more.

"Max. Could I . . . get a job?"

He sniffed. "I can't imagine why you'd want to, but, yes, of course you can. You can do anything you want to, Marie." He still had her hand, and he give it a quick, hard squeeze. "I'll help you. You can stay with me in Cambridge until you get on your feet if you need to." Her skin started tingling. The idea felt simultaneously so ludicrous and so obvious. She'd never had a job. But she'd given a speech to the UN that had been heard and applauded by some of the world's most powerful people. She was a mechanical engineer by training, too!

What had Imogen said that first night in the pub? *Change or die.* But . . . "What about *your* father, though?" In some ways, Max's father was worse than hers. Father hadn't always been the remote, uncaring man he was now. The duke, by contrast, didn't seem to care at all about Max and Sebastian except in terms of what they could do for the dukedom.

"You worry about your father, and I'll worry about mine."

"Max. You can't just—"

"Listen. I'm prepared to get stubborn here. We both know I'd make a miserable husband, but I flatter myself that I'm a decent enough friend, so hear this." He lifted Marie's hand and kissed it before letting go of it. "This is just a courtesy call, really. *I'm* not marrying *you.* After all, despite all appearances to the contrary, this *isn't* actually the nineteenth century."

She studied his face, her kind, loyal friend.

"I'll go out there and make a scene all by myself if need be. The part I can't help you with is the next part."

"And what part is that?" she asked, though she knew the answer.

"The part where you don't let go of love without a fight." He smiled at her. "The part where you talk to him. The part where you try to keep him. The part where you let *him* decide he doesn't want you instead of making that decision for him."

"Even if it costs me everything?" Again, though, she already knew the answer. She just wanted to hear Max, her oldest and truest friend, say it out loud. Help her really *hear* it. Bake some

courage into her for the enormous detour this evening was now
going to take.

"It won't cost everything, though, will it? Because all this"—he
gestured around the room—"isn't even remotely everything, is it?"

"No, it's not," she whispered. "*He's* everything."

"All right." He stood up and gave her his arm. "Let's do this
then."

Leo cracked a beer in his room while he waited for Gabby.
Actually, it was his second beer. He had pulled the velvet rope
in the corner and asked the dude who appeared at his door a
few minutes later for "some beer" and had received in return a
six-pack in a silver ice bucket. It was—of course—cocoa porter.
This fucking place. But it was from Imogen's pub, so he couldn't
be too annoyed. Imogen was all right. He was going to miss her.
Kai, too.

This was the first time he had used that stupid bell. He'd
thought the whole concept was kind of gross. He was on vacation
and in possession of nothing but time to spare, so he could use his
legs to go out in search of whatever he wanted.

Of course, mostly what he wanted while he'd been here had
been Marie.

It was sort of morbidly amusing, though, that he was finally
availing himself of the bell on the eve of his departure. Going out
with a bang—or, rather, a polite, understated ring.

He looked at his watch. His cheap watch from Target with
the beat-up leather strap. He felt a little bad that he and Marie
had never talked through what had happened on the whole Morneau front. She'd been holed up working those first few days, so

she'd probably broken the bad news about Philip Gregory to the cabinet she wasn't a member of. But how had they reacted? He'd never asked.

But no. He checked himself. It was not his job to solve the princess's problems anymore. And more to the point, it never had been.

He'd only been looking at his watch to check the time. Where the hell was Gabby? She was supposed to come to his room after watching Marie get ready for the ball, but she should be here by now.

He eyed the remaining four beers.

Well, fuck it. He didn't have to drive anywhere. He didn't have to do anything except roll himself and Gabby out tomorrow morning and into the car he'd ordered to take them to Zurich.

Two more beers and forty more minutes later, Leo had to revise that thought. Maybe he had to get off his ass and go looking for Gabby. And somehow not see any evidence of the ball-in-progress.

Could he pull the bell again? Order up his sister? The thought amused him. *Hello, yes, could you kindly bring me another six-pack, and while you're at it, I'm in the market for an extremely talkative eleven-year-old girl. She's—*

There was a rap on the door. Finally.

He only lurched a little as he made his way over to answer it. He wasn't drunk, just tipsy. "I was about to come looking for you. Are you all packed, because I—"

It was not Gabby.

"Good evening, Mr. Ricci."

It was Mr. Benz.

"What's wrong?"

"Nothing at all." Mr. Benz had a clothing rack on wheels with him, which he proceeded to roll into the room.

"Where's my sister?"

"She is safely ensconced in the library."

"It's Christmas Eve. I can't have my sister hanging out by herself."

"It's merely a temporary measure, and I assure you she is quite happy. I sourced a few rare volumes of folklore for her." When Leo tried to protest some more, Mr. Benz held up a hand. "I can only solve one problem at a time, Mr. Ricci, and right now I'm here about yours."

"I don't have a problem." Well, actually, he had a lot of problems, but none that this guy could solve.

"On the contrary." He swept into the room. "You're about to let Marie make the biggest mistake of her life."

"Hang on now. There's no letting or not letting Marie do anything." Leo thought back to Marie bossing Mr. Benz in his cab, that first day in New York. "You of all people should know that."

He sighed like Leo was a dim-witted child. "Mr. Ricci, Marie is on her way to the ball, where she is about to do one of two things: let Maximillian von Hansburg be named as her fiancé or abdicate the throne."

"What the fuck?"

Mr. Benz shot him a look Leo couldn't decode, but it was probably disapproval.

"Sorry," Leo said with a sneer. "I beg your pardon. Is that better?"

"No," Mr. Benz said mildly. "I believe the problem with this family is that it needs to confront some questions of the 'What the fuck?' nature."

Leo couldn't have been more shocked if he tried. But he was also annoyed. And more than a little confused. "Will you stop speaking in code?"

"Yes. Marie loves you, and I believe you love her. Is that correct?"

Yes. Leo couldn't say it, though. He could only sigh and close his eyes in defeat.

"What's more, I believe you're good for her. I believe you—and your sister—are good for this family."

Leo's brain was moving slowly. "Hang on, rewind. Marie loves me? Did she tell you that?" What was happening in his chest? It felt like one of those giant cocoa cauldrons had been upended inside him. There was a hot, churning sensation in his chest, and it hurt like hell.

"I know Her Royal Highness better than anyone else does. She might not like to think so, but since her mother has been gone, it's true." He paused. "Well, present company excepted."

"She loves me enough to *abdicate*?" And was that even a real thing that happened in the world? And what did it actually mean? Where would she go? Would she be literally out on the street? What would happen to the UN thing? And what about her father? She loved him so much, even if he was terrible. She shouldn't lose both parents if she didn't have to. Leo of all people knew that.

Panic. That was what the hot churning sensation was. Pure, unadulterated panic. Marie couldn't throw over her whole life for him. He wasn't worth it.

Was he?

Something Marie had said to him popped into his head. *Girls need love, not braids.*

"I believe she does, yes," Mr. Benz said calmly. "But for that to happen, it would probably be helpful for her to know that you loved her in return, would it not?"

"Are you *trying* to get her to abdicate?" What was *happening* here? This was Mr. Benz. Stuffy, proper, by-the-book Mr. Benz.

"No. In fact, her cousin who's next in line for the throne would make a perfectly horrible monarch. I am simply trying to say that it has been a long time since anyone has seen past the role Marie occupied and appreciated her for who she is."

The cauldron boiled over. And Leo hadn't been wrong before; he *was* panicking. But there was also something else in the middle of that roiling mass. It was small and quiet and unfamiliar, but if he concentrated very hard he could tell what it was. Hope.

Also maybe a little bit of pride. Real pride, not the kind that was always getting wounded here in the palace. Leo had spent a long time thinking he wasn't enough. For college. For Gabby. He was forever feeling like he and Gabby were barely getting by. They *were* barely getting by financially, and for the rest of it—the emotional shit—he had to lean so hard on Dani.

But was it possible that he hadn't seen that he had other things to offer? All those things people called him: Honorable, chivalrous. A good brother.

He was also, to hear it told by both Mr. Benz and by Marie herself, the only person in the world who looked at Marie and saw past the princess.

That was not nothing.

It was possible that was everything.

"She can't abdicate," Leo said, working out his thoughts as he spoke. "She'll lose any chance at repairing her relationship with her father. And even though I personally could give a flying fuck that she's a princess, doesn't all the stuff she cares about, like the UN ambassador thing, kind of require her to be in a prominent position? Like, to use her princessness for good?"

"Well, perhaps there is another solution," Mr. Benz said with that same maddening mildness. "But I suspect that for it to be located, someone may have to make a rather dramatic gesture. May have to shock it into being. A metaphorical shout of 'What the fuck?' if you will."

Leo was starting to understand. He pointed to the clothing rack. "What is that?"

"Formalwear."

Holy shit. He got it now. "I have to go to the ball. I have to go *now*."

Mr. Benz didn't smile per se, but one corner of his mouth turned up slightly. "I was hoping you'd say that."

He whipped a phone out of his pocket and started barking orders into it. No old-school bell pulls for Mr. Benz. Or any fairy godfather magic wands, for that matter.

After he'd made several calls, he looked at Leo. They held each other's gazes for a moment, sudden, unlikely allies. Leo felt like he was in the eye of the storm. The cauldron had overflowed. It was temporarily calm right now. But he had heard Mr. Benz summoning Verene, asking that several pairs of shoes be brought up, commandeering a shaving kit.

Shit was about to get real.

"How come everyone calls you Mr. Benz?" Leo asked suddenly.

"Because that is my name. Well, actually my name is Trauttmansdorff-Benz, but that's rather a mouthful."

"But *everyone* calls you Mr. Benz, whereas Torkel is Torkel and Verene is Verene. I feel like if you're going to fairy-godfather me into a prince, I should know your first name."

"It's Matteo."

"All right then, Matteo. I need to tell you one thing."

Mr. Benz—Leo couldn't actually think of him as Matteo, it turned out—raised an eyebrow.

"I am a little bit drunk."

Mr. Benz rolled his eyes.

"So maybe you should add coffee to that list of stuff you ordered."

Mr. Benz sighed. Poor Mr. Benz.

Chapter Twenty-One

*A*s Marie paused on the threshold to the ballroom, she tried to appreciate it objectively. The palace staff had worked hard to transform the cavernous space into a gorgeous, glittering winter wonderland. A forty-foot tree decorated to the hilt anchored one end of the dance floor. Holly and pine garlands hung on the walls and from the crystal chandeliers that studded the space.

The guests were gorgeous, too, decked out in frothy formal dresses and tuxedos and military whites. Max, at her side, patted her arm and Marie turned to smile at him, her best friend, her coconspirator. He was dressed exactly as the occasion called for, with his baronial adornments and a sash over his suit. But there was always something about Max that winked at the formality of any proceeding. His hair was a little too tussled, his posture a little too relaxed. *Rakish* truly was the word.

It was really too bad she couldn't dredge up any romantic feelings for him.

But on the other hand, pity the poor woman who ever did, because Max wasn't just rakish. He *was* a rake.

"Are you sure we shouldn't just do it now?" Marie whispered, scanning the room for her father as they slipped in through a side door—they'd opted not to make a grand entrance via the stairs at the front. As resolute as she was, she was literally shaking from nerves and just wanted this all to be over so she could go in search of Leo.

"Quite sure," Max said, nodding at people as they walked to their table, which was about halfway back. Her mother had always insisted that they—the royals—mix with other guests rather than sit at a more traditional head table, and they'd continued the practice after she was gone.

Marie and Max had decided that instead of talking to their parents immediately, they would corner them after dinner—before the dreaded announcement was to be made—so there was less time for a protracted discussion. They were counting on the desire to avoid a public scene to work in their favor. Marie fully expected a *private* scene to follow later, but they would deal with that when the time came.

Dinner was excruciating, not least because Lucrecia was at their table. But it wasn't the usual kind of excruciating. There were the typical Lucrecia barbs, but Marie found they didn't stick like they used to. She tried a new strategy: cheerfully concurring. Yes, her mother had been so graceful and lovely. Yes, it was remarkable that Marie had chosen to study engineering instead of a more traditional field like history or literature. She was happy to agree with her former tormenter because she realized suddenly that none of what this woman said *mattered*. None of it was *true*, and more to the point, Marie had people in her life who knew that. Who saw the real her.

No, the excruciating part was the interminable wait until it was time to put their plan into motion.

"Now?" she whispered to Max as they watched her father get up from his table—he was at one closer to the front with Max's parents and some other senior nobles and parliamentarians. He was headed for the dais where he would traditionally make a toast to open the dancing. She and Max had hypothesized that this was where the big announcement would come.

"Yes. Now." Max rose and pulled her up with him. He was going to talk to his parents while Marie intercepted her father—a simultaneous, two-pronged attack at a moment where appearances were important—to their parents, at least. "Break a leg, M," Max whispered, and he was gone.

Her legs quivered but she forced herself forward, suddenly worried that they hadn't timed it right, that her father would beat her to the dais.

She had to get there first. Her father was wending his way through the tables, stopping every now and then to return a greeting someone made as he passed. She decided to take a shortcut through the empty dance floor.

The click of her heels on the parquet floor thundered in her ears. Marie had no idea what she was going to say. She had decided that rather than rehearse a speech, she would speak from the heart. She hadn't taken into account that the organ in question was going to feel like it might pound out of her chest. She hitched her floor-length skirts up so she could pick up the pace without stepping on them. Adrenaline made her clumsy, though. Adrenaline and high heels. As she reached the center of the dance floor, she stumbled. Pitched forward awkwardly but managed to right herself after a few lurching steps.

She heard gasps. She was drawing attention. "Oh my god!" she heard someone exclaim. All right, yes, she was embarrassing herself, but really, who cared? She took a fortifying breath and continued toward the front.

The expressions of shock from the crowd continued. "Can you believe it?" she heard someone murmur as she passed. She was starting to get annoyed. So she'd stumbled. It wasn't a crime.

"Look at him!" came another voice.

Look at *him*? Was Max drawing attention, too?

Marie turned, looking for the source of everyone's marveling and—

All the air whooshed out of her lungs. She was getting that floaty feeling again, like at the UN. Like she was full of helium and if she wasn't very careful and very deliberate, she might take flight, just float up to the chandelier above her head that was functioning like a spotlight. Because there was Leo, perched halfway down the majestic, red-carpeted staircase at the front of the ballroom.

How surprising. But also how *not* surprising. Wasn't Leo always there when she needed him? He looked extremely annoyed— which made her smile, because he looked so much like himself, despite the very un-Leo-esque tuxedo he was wearing. He scanned the crowd, either not realizing or not caring that everyone was all aflutter about his sudden appearance, until his gaze landed on her.

The room went quiet. It was as if they were watching a movie, and they all knew they'd reached the denouement. "Would you care to dance?" Leo's voice echoed across the vast space between them, but it was low and sure. As if his question was mundane and not the most remarkable thing anyone had ever asked her.

"Yes," she said, her voice also sounding remarkably steady. "Yes, I would."

The music started before either of them moved. It was the same song they'd practiced to. She spared a glance for the band—and found Mr. Benz standing behind the bandleader.

How extraordinary.

Leo started coming down the stairs, and he looked exactly like he had two days ago, after the snowball fight. He looked like a predator. He also looked like a prince.

The tuxedo he was wearing was free of adornment. Leo Ricci didn't do adornment. He didn't have to. It was more the way he carried himself, confident—bordering on entitled, almost. Focused.

Focused on her. So intensely. No one could mistake that look. That stride. He was staking a claim. He was coming for her.

Earlier, she'd been focused on not making a scene. But she hadn't known that *this* kind of scene was an option. Her entire body tingled as he jumped down the last few steps, landed like a panther, and began crossing the floor, oblivious to the lights shining on them and to the crowd watching in silent astonishment.

She half expected him to ravish her right there, but he merely swept her into his arms. They slid into the steps as if the whole thing had been choreographed.

"What I'm trying to do here," Leo said immediately, speaking low so only Marie could hear, "is the royal version of throwing you over my shoulder and carting you away so everyone knows you're mine."

Yes, that's *exactly* what it had looked like. The sensations she'd had before, that she was about to float away, that she couldn't get a breath in, started reversing themselves as they twirled, picking up speed. She felt strong and sure and calm. She knew these steps. She knew this man. "I love you!" she blurted. "I don't want you to go home. Or if you're going home, I want to go with you."

Leo grinned. "I love you, too, Princess."

"I was just on my way to tell my father that I'm not going to marry Max."

The grin grew self-satisfied. "I think by now that point has probably been made. But just in case . . ." He pulled her against him abruptly, ending the waltz, breaking the frame that Monsieur Lavoie had drilled into them. His arms banded around her and his lips came down on hers, brushing a light kiss against them. He kept their bodies moving in a slow dance, like in the woods. She smiled against his lips as they swayed.

She could feel everyone's attention on them. The silence in the ballroom gradually gave way to whispers, and then cheers—yes, cheers; how remarkable! She pulled her lips from his. He grunted like he wasn't happy about that.

"Are we dancing like no one is watching?" she asked.

He laughed. "I suppose we are."

"My father might disown me. But I'm prepared for that." She was. She had been since Max's big wake-up speech. She'd been prepared to walk away from all this without knowing if she would be able to build anything with Leo. But knowing she *did* have Leo made her big declaration of independence even sweeter. It made her braver.

He looked over her shoulder. "If we all sit down and talk about this like adults—"

"Your Majesty! Your Royal Highness!"

She turned. Whoever had spoken was extremely upset. It was . . . "Frau Lehman?" The housekeeper was not dressed for the ball, and the drama with which she'd burst in suggested something was terribly wrong.

Frau Lehman hurried over to them, arriving at the same time Marie's father and Mr. Benz did.

The housekeeper looked positively horrified. Marie took the older woman's hand, wanting to offer comfort. "What's happened?"

"It's Miss Gabriella. She's missing."

"No, she's not. She's in the library," Leo said. He turned around to confirm with Mr. Benz. "Right?"

They'd discussed a plan for Mr. Benz to make sure Gabby was comfortable and to convey a message that Leo—and, he had hoped, Marie—would join her later for a private Christmas Eve celebration. He'd even ordered up some of her butterscotch s'mores cocoa.

"Indeed. I left her there an hour ago."

"Yes," said Frau Lehman, "and you told me to join her. But when I arrived no more than ten minutes later, she was gone." Frau Lehman's voice was rising, bordering on hysterical.

Just his fucking luck. Gabby had wanted to come to the ball so desperately, and look, here she was making a big splash with her absence. "Then she's in her room."

"She's not!" Frau Lehman cried. "She's not *anywhere*! I've had everyone who's not in here looking for her. We've covered the whole palace. I've got Thomas leading a group of men in searching the grounds now. But it's snowing so heavily, and it's so cold!"

Leo was starting to get scared, but he ordered himself to be calm. Children didn't just disappear into thin air at royal palaces. That only happened in fairy tales.

But—*shit*. Shouldn't waltzing with princesses at Christmas balls also be something that only happened in fairy tales?

"She wouldn't have gone outside in this weather, would she?" Marie asked. "There's nowhere she . . ."

The thought arrived in Leo's head the same time it appeared to have landed in Marie's.

"Oh, Leo," Marie breathed. "Do you think?"

"Yes," he said brusquely. He didn't know whether to be relieved— he knew where Gabby was—or scared shitless. Frau Lehman was right. It was cold, and it was snowing something fierce.

"Let's go," Marie said.

"Would someone care to enlighten me as to what is going on?" the king asked.

Marie's eyes darted around like she'd only just become aware of their surroundings, her father included. Leo couldn't blame her. They'd been dancing in a bubble. In their own fairy tale for two.

"I'm sorry, sir," Leo said. "My sister seems to have run off, but I know where she is, so if you'll excuse me . . ."

"You think you can come storming in here, make some kind of . . . declaration with regard to my daughter, and just leave?"

He already was. He spun on his heel, part of his brain registering that the king's words had been delivered in a surprisingly neutral tone. Almost like he was curious rather than angry. But whatever. He didn't have time for this now.

"Wait!" Marie called. "I'm coming with you."

She caught up to him outside the ballroom. It was a relief to be out of there. God, he wanted to kiss her again. She was wearing a shiny, royal blue dress. It was as fluffy as the cake-topper dress, and it matched her eyes. Her hair was loose around her shoulders. She looked incredible. She looked *edible*.

She also could not come with him. He shook his head. "I'll be back as soon as I can."

Her father burst out of the doors, but she ignored him. "There's no way I'm not coming with you! This is my fault. I'm the one who showed her."

"You can't." Her father could not discover the cabin.

"Showed her what?" the king demanded. "What are you talking about? Where is Gabriella?"

Leo wasn't about to let the cat out of the bag on Marie's cabin. He hitched his head at the king. *This is why you can't come.*

Marie shook her head, rejecting Leo's silent message. "I don't care if he finds out. I *want* him to find out."

Leo sighed. There was no point in arguing. There wasn't time.

Mr. Benz rushed over. "I have a car ready out front if that will help."

Leo nodded, and he didn't bother protesting as the king and Mr. Benz got into the car with them. No one spoke. Leo watched Marie as they wound down the hill. She was sitting forward in her seat, as if she could will the car to go faster, and when they'd gone as far as they could, she said, sharply, "Here."

Leo was out of the car before it came to a full stop. He led the way to the path, shining a flashlight Mr. Benz had given him and tamping down the snow as best he could with his stupid dress shoes—Mr. Benz had pressed coats on everyone but they were all still wearing their formal footwear—so that the people behind him would have an easier time. When they had to turn off the formal path, it was slower going, but his fear propelled him forward. It was snowing too hard for any footprints to be visible, but he kept up a steady chant in his mind, like a mantra: *She'll be there. She'll be there. She'll be there.*

He burst out into the clearing and only vaguely registered the king's astonished "Dear god!" Leo was panting from the effort of running through the snow by the time he ducked through the doorway.

And there she was. Curled up into a little ball, asleep in a corner.

She *was* asleep, right?

"Gabby!" he shouted.

She woke instantly, surging to a seated position, her eyes wide.

Leo sagged against a wall, rage and relief at war inside him. Rage won. "What *the hell* are you doing out here?"

"I'm sorry!"

Marie was there, suddenly, with Gabby, pulling her to her feet and hugging her. Which Leo supposed he should have done first, but he was mightily pissed.

"I got so sad in the library all of a sudden," Gabby said in a small voice. "I started thinking about Mom and Dad. And then I started thinking about how you"—she pulled out of Marie's embrace and looked her in the eye—"said that when you came here it made you remember your mom in a good way. I thought it might work for me, too."

"Oh, sweetheart." Marie looked devastated as she hugged Gabby close again.

Leo's heart was breaking. His poor, brave sister. The anger

started to drain out of him. He had the absurd notion, all of a sudden, that even though he'd thought he was finishing this cabin for Marie, maybe he'd actually been building it for Gabby. Or *also* building it for Gabby. Because although it was cold in here, it was significantly less so than outside. And it was dry—no snow was getting in between those logs, thanks to Kai's insistence on the Scandinavian saddle notch. "And then when I got here," Gabby went on, "I realized I'd made a mistake." Her voice was muffled by Marie's body, but she seemed determined to finish her explanation. "The snow had gotten so deep. I was worried that I wouldn't be able to find my way back to the road. It wasn't as cold in here as outside, and I thought it might be safer to wait here, at least until it stopped snowing."

She had made the right call, but Leo was still . . . what? Pissed? Relieved? Heartbroken?

All of the above.

Marie hugged Gabby again, and Leo walked over and wrapped his arms around both of them.

"I'm sorry, Leo," Gabby said quietly as Marie extricated herself.

"Don't say anything," he heard Marie say, quietly but with conviction. "Now is not the time." She was talking to her father.

He'd forgotten about the king, but of course there he was, looking around at the small cabin that had been started by his wife and finished by his daughter in direct defiance of his wishes.

Leo sighed. There was still the matter of . . . his whole future to deal with.

But then he looked at Marie, and she looked at him, and she smiled. And it was okay.

It would be all right, whatever happened. Gabby was safe.

Marie loved him. It was Christmas Eve. They'd figure every-thing out tomorrow.

Mr. Benz appeared with a blanket and wrapped it around Gabby's shoulders. "The forecast doesn't show any sign of this letting up, so I suggest we depart as soon as we can."

It was hard going, but soon they were back in the car, all of them cold but unharmed. Gabby was *clearly* unharmed, judging by the barrage of questions she let loose about the ball. What was everyone wearing? How was dinner? What did they have for dessert? Were the decorations as pretty with the ballroom full as they'd been with it empty?

"Kiddo," he whispered into her ear.

"Yeah?"

"Hush."

She did, and he regretted his intervention. Without her chat-tering, the silence became charged.

"Father," Marie said, just when Leo was about to open his mouth and say something that would probably have turned out to be ill-advised.

The king held up a hand as they pulled up to the palace steps, and never had Leo been happier to see the fancy old pile of rocks. Emil waited until they'd all piled out of the car and were in the grand foyer before speaking. "We will all visit our rooms and change out of our wet things, after which we will reunite in the ballroom."

"Father," Marie said, "I really think, after all that's happened—"

Ignoring her, he gestured for Frau Lehman, who came scur-rying up murmuring apologies as she enveloped Gabby in a hug.

Leo knew that wasn't right. Apologies were due in the other direction. "Gabby, do you have something to say to Frau Lehman?"

She hung her head. "I'm sorry I ran off. You must have been very worried." She lifted her head and looked the rest of them—the king, Marie, and him—in the eye, one after another. "You all must have been."

The king said nothing, merely turned to Marie and Leo. "I'll see you back in the ballroom shortly."

"Father! You can't pretend that none of what has happened tonight matters! You can't just—"

The king was already halfway across the foyer, speaking in a low voice to Frau Lehman, who had Gabby by the hand.

"I think he can, love," Leo said, a little impressed at the king's relentless ability to ignore reality. To ignore his daughter. "But we don't have to do anything we don't want to. Come on, let's go get changed and find Gab. It's Christmas Eve."

"You know what?" Marie wasn't looking at him. She'd turned to face the direction of the ballroom. "I *am* going back in there. I'm going to abdicate."

"*What?*"

"When you came into the ballroom, I'd been on my way to tell my father I wasn't going to marry Max. I hadn't been using the word 'abdicate,' even in my head, but I was—I am—prepared to if need be. I'm *not* prepared to go back in there and pretend that nothing has changed. If he can't see that—if everything he saw tonight wasn't enough . . ." She shrugged. "Then I guess I need to make my point more explicitly."

Holy Mary, mother of God. "Okay, hang on now." Leo took

Marie's hand and started towing her toward his room. She resisted. "I'm cold," he said. "I need to change first." He could give a shit about being cold, but he needed a moment to gather his thoughts, and he wasn't above manipulating her sympathies to get it.

Inside his room, he shut the door. "You can't abdicate." He rummaged around in his stuff until he found a pair of jeans.

"I can, though. I can do whatever I want." She laughed incredulously, like the idea was equal parts astonishing and delightful.

"Marie." Leo flung his wet dress pants to the side and jammed his legs into his jeans. "Listen to me—"

"No. *You* listen to *me*. Do you want to be with me or not?"

"Yes, of course." He gentled his voice. "I love you. I just think we can leave this for tomorrow. We can talk to your father tomorrow. And if you need to . . ." Jesus, he couldn't even say the word. "Maybe there's a way to do this that doesn't result in you losing your father."

"I already lost my father. He used to be my father the king. Now he's just the king." Her voice hitched and she swallowed. When she spoke again, it was in a whisper.

"Leo, I don't want this life anymore. Not like this, anyway."

He took her in his arms. "All right, love." She was shivering. He tightened his hold on her. "But does it have to be now? Are you sure you want to go busting in there breathing fire?"

"You did!"

He chuckled. "Yeah, you got me there."

She pulled away from him and looked him in the eyes. "I think sometimes you need to make a grand declaration. You have to say things in a way that ensures they'll be heard."

He still didn't think *she* needed to do it that way, though. She'd be the center of attention, which she hated. She'd embarrass herself.

"I'm done letting people tell me what to do. I'm done playing princess. I've spent the last few years doing exactly what my father wanted me to, the way he wanted me to, my own wishes be damned, and—"

He cut her off with a kiss. When she put it like that, it was a no-brainer. He thought he'd been protecting her by trying to talk her out of abdication, but he could see now that what she needed wasn't his protection, but his support. He pulled away. "Okay, let's go. You want to stop by your suite and change first?"

She looked down at herself. The bottom of her gown was wet, the deep blue looking navy. It was muddy in spots, too, and there were a few twigs stuck to its hem. "No, no, I do not. In fact, I think this is perfect for the task at hand." Her gaze flickered to him. "I think we're perfect."

He didn't look any more respectable than she did, with his jeans and bare feet—which he proceeded to stuff into his sneakers. The two of them looked like Prince and Princess Ken and Barbie torsos had been mistakenly stuck on top of rag-doll legs.

He held out his arm. "Then let's get this show on the road. It's Christmas Eve. We have other places to be." Namely, cozied around the fire with Gabby, getting Marie an airplane ticket so they could all get the hell out of Dodge tomorrow.

As they approached the ballroom, Leo caught a flash of yellow. A flash of yellow that looked like a dress on a small person who had just disappeared through the double doors into the room.

"Was that *Gabby*?" Marie asked.

Oh fuck him. Was this night ever going to be over? He picked up their pace. "Well, we're already going out with a bang." And this way Gabby would get her wish to see the ball, if only for a moment before they were all thrown out on their nonroyal asses.

"I think that was one of my old dresses," Marie said, puzzlement in her tone.

When they started down the stairs, Gabby was about halfway across the dance floor, in the same spot Marie had been in when Leo had burst through these same doors earlier. And she had everyone's attention, just as Marie had. Including the king's. Emil was on the dais, dressed in a plain tuxedo. *No spare bullshit king outfits clean, huh, Your Royal Asshole?*

"Ah, good," Emil said mildly. "We're all here." He raised his eyebrows at Marie and Leo as they reached the edge of the empty dance floor. "Though I can see that Miss Ricci is the only one who followed my directive regarding attire." He turned his attention to Gabby. "Miss Ricci, will you please do me the honor of joining me up here? I would be delighted if you would dance with me later, but I have a few words to say first."

"Hang on now," Leo said. He wasn't about to stand here while the king insulted or embarrassed his sister. He had stood for that shit all week, and he was done. He dropped Marie's hand and started forward as the king extended his arm to Gabby and she took it.

"Mr. Ricci." Mr. Benz stepped into Leo's path.

Marie, following Leo closely, managed to dodge Mr. Benz. "No, Father, *I* have something to say." She started toward him.

"Get out of my way, Benz," Leo growled. The equerry was surprisingly nimble as he got in Leo's face like an NCAA shooting guard.

"Mr. Ricci, would you agree that despite what I'm sure are my many faults, I am a passable student of human nature, especially when it comes to this family?"

"What?" Why couldn't this dude talk like a normal person? And why wouldn't he get the hell out of the way?

"Do you trust me, Mr. Ricci? Have I led you astray yet today?"

"Other than losing my sister, you mean?"

Mr. Benz didn't even blink. "Other than that, yes."

"No," Leo had to admit. And really, he couldn't blame Benz for Gabby's disappearance. She'd managed that all on her own.

"Then I suggest you listen to His Majesty."

"Oh, shit." Leo cursed as the crowd closed around Marie. He leveled a death glare at Mr. Benz that finally made him step aside and Leo started pushing his way through the crowd to get to Marie. He was determined to at least be by her side as she said her piece.

"Ladies and gentlemen," the king said, which at least made Leo's journey easier because everyone stopped looking between him and Marie and turned their attention to the front. "Thank you for coming this evening to the one hundred and seventieth annual Cocoa Ball. You may recall that traditionally, I would welcome you with my beloved Joséphine by my side." Marie sucked in a breath as Leo reached her side. "She is three years gone, but . . ." He paused and cleared his throat.

Leo was listening to the king but watching Marie. Astonishment washed over her features.

The king's voice broke as he added, "I miss her every day, but perhaps the most at Christmastime." A sympathetic murmur broke out through the crowd, and Marie gasped. "But life goes on, does it not? Family goes on. Which is why I'm so pleased to be able to make an announcement today of a royal suitor for my dear daughter, Marie."

Leo grabbed Marie's hand and squeezed. "It doesn't matter," he whispered. "He can say whatever he wants. It doesn't mean anything."

She turned to him, her eyes bright with unshed tears. "That's right. He'll say what he's going to say, and I'll say what I'm going to say, and then we'll go to New York."

Aww, shit, he loved her. His brave princess who was so unassailably herself, even when it was hard. Even when it was about to cost her everything.

"I'm not even gonna make you shovel when we get home," he whispered. "You can order me around, like Gabby does." He was saying that to make sure she knew that she was his. That she had a home with him. But he actually got off on the idea of Miss Prim having the run of the place. Of doing her bidding. In all ways. It was going to be—

"Ladies and gentlemen, please welcome Mr. Leonardo Ricci of New York."

—perfect.

Marie emitted a strangled, muffled shriek and went from holding Leo's hand to clutching his arm like she was drowning as the room broke out in cheers.

"Mr. Ricci, I owe you an apology," the king said when the applause died down.

Well, shit. This was *not* how Leo had seen this story ending.

The king's face softened. "And you, too, my Marie." He cleared his throat. "But you'll be getting those later." Emil's voice took on a more regal tone as he went back to addressing the assembly. "For now I would like to introduce you to my friend Miss Gabriella Ricci. Miss Ricci and I will be joining our happy couple for a dance, and I invite you all to do the same."

Leo turned to Marie and saw his own shock mirrored on her face. And happiness. There was happiness there, too. "I guess we gotta dance, Princess."

She blinked rapidly but managed a bewildered smile. "I guess we do."

As the orchestra struck up another waltz, Leo took Marie into his arms the way Monsieur Lavoie had taught them, but she wasn't having it. She wound her arms around his neck and pasted herself onto him. Burrowed into his chest.

"I'd rather dance your way," she whispered.

As they swayed, his mind started to reel. How was this going to work? Where were they going to live? Was the king really going to be cool about this? But he forced those thoughts back. Concentrated on the woman in his arms. His love.

He'd fallen in love with a goddamned princess.

He couldn't hold in a laugh.

She tipped her head back to look at him. "What's so funny?"

"This. Us. Everything."

"We do have a lot to discuss, don't we?"

"Shh." He pressed a finger against her lips. He had no doubt her mind was swirling with all the same questions his was. "We'll figure out the details later, because that's all they are—details. It's Christmas Eve."

"Let's get this silly dance done with and go celebrate," Marie said.

"I don't know." Leo peeled her off his chest and locked his arms into the frame position. "I kind of feel like dancing."

"Like *waltzing*?"

"Yeah, I mean, look." He nodded down at their feet as they picked up speed and glided effortlessly across the floor. She followed his gaze and they both laughed at the picture they made, her muddy, wet dress brushing against his jeans-and-sneakers-clad legs. "You're so good at it now."

"Only with you."

"Damn right, Princess." He winked at her as they twirled under the chandelier in the ballroom in the goddamn royal palace of Eldovia with Gabby and the king and the entire country looking on. "Damn right."

Epilogue

Four months later

$\mathcal{L}$eo picked Marie up at LaGuardia in the cab. He wasn't actually driving it that much anymore—he was busy getting ready to move to Eldovia at the end of Gabby's school year—but he thought it might amuse Marie.

When she emerged from Customs, his nerves flared. He had been a borderline basket case all day. When she threw herself into his arms, he was a little worried that she would feel his thundering heartbeat, but she didn't seem to notice. She just hugged him and laughed—and cried a little, too. He could sympathize. He was so freaking happy to see her. His small, strong princess. Back at the cab, his own eyes were suspiciously watery as he opened the passenger-side door for her and got her settled. When he came around his side and got in, she grabbed his right arm with both hands and hugged it.

"You don't need this arm to drive, do you?" she said. It was the first thing she'd said—their embrace before had been silent—and her voice dragged against some tender, inner part of him, like fingers massaging a scalp. It felt so *good* to hear her in person and not through a phone speaker. He almost groaned.

"Sure don't," he said, reaching his left hand over to put the car in gear. He switched it to the steering wheel as she clung to him. Once they'd gotten going, he glanced at her. "You better stop looking at me like that. I'll get a big ego."

She rolled her eyes affectionately and let go of his arm.

"Hey now." He really *didn't* need that arm to drive, especially if the alternative was using it to touch her, so he grabbed her hand and laced his fingers through hers.

She sighed happily, and they drove in silence for a while. They talked every night, so it wasn't like they had actual news to catch up on. But the silence made space for more nervousness. He blew out a breath. Actually, it was more like terror at this point.

It wasn't like this was going to be a surprise. When a man was named a "royal suitor" to a princess and was preparing to move his entire life to the goddamn Alps to be with said princess, everyone knew how the story was going to end.

He ordered himself to chill. He wasn't going to do it until they were off the expressway, just in case things went to shit—so he asked her a question he already knew the answer to. "How's your father?"

"He's well! He's thinking of hiring a management consultant for Morneau, if you can imagine!"

It was in keeping with Emil's retreat from being a complete and total dick. He was still a snob, but he seemed like he was trying, both when it came to Marie and to Morneau. "Well, hey, if he wants to spend a small fortune to have someone to tell him to

sell his goddamned watches online, I guess that's his prerogative."
He smiled and winked, though, to show he was teasing. To show
that he was trying, too.

"And Gabby?" she asked.

"Losing her mind with excitement—both to see you and for
the big move."

"Really?" Marie asked, and he could hear the concern in her
voice. He shared it. Gabby assured him she was over the moon
at the prospect of moving to Eldovia, but he worried. It was another big life change for her to absorb. But she and Marie had
grown close, and, remarkably, she and Emil had taken to writing
each other letters. His arrived with a ridiculously elaborate wax
seal. Gabby didn't let Leo read them but assured him they were
corresponding about books.

"Really," he assured Marie. "Your father has apparently informed her that Mr. Benz is going to help her purchase her own
horse." He snorted. "*I* have informed her that she's going to have
to do a lot of chores to pay for the beast's upkeep. She's less happy
about that." He wasn't trying to be a stick-in-the-mud, but he was
determined, as they transplanted themselves into Hallmark-land,
that his sister not forget where she'd come from.

"What else?" Marie asked, giving him that look again, the one
that made him feel like he was the king of the world in a way that
had nothing to do with literal royalty. "Tell me everything."

They were getting closer to home. He'd gotten off the expressway, and they were inching along in traffic on East Tremont.

He could not put this off any longer. Talking to kids was easier in
cars. He remembered thinking that the day he met Marie. Surely
the same logic should apply to talking to princesses in cars, but oh

Jesus, there went his heart again. He cleared his throat. "Nothing to tell, Princess, but I do have something to ask."

"All right," she said. "Or as you Americans say, 'Shoot.'"

"I tried to think how to do this. Probably you deserve a bigger production. I mean, *of course* you do. But I couldn't figure out what that would be. *Where* that would be. The cabin, obviously, but we're not in Eldovia. And I didn't want to wait. And it's the wrong season for the ice rink at Rockefeller Center. So, *then* I thought—"

He cut himself off. Listen to him. He sounded like Gabby on one of her babbling streaks. This was not the impression he was going for here, at this moment that was supposed to be . . . everything. All right. Take two. "You remember when we first met? When I was driving you around in this cab?"

"Of course." He could hear the smile in her voice. He glanced over, and sure enough, the dimples were out.

"This is where it all started," he said. "And this is probably the last time I'll ever drive you around in this cab." He took a deep breath. "So I thought this was the place I should ask you my question, which is: Will you marry me?"

She gasped like he'd announced he was taking her to a special screening of *90210*. Which meant it was a good gasp. A happy one.

He grinned. "You can't be surprised. It's not like—"

"Yes!" she shrieked. "Yes, of course I'll marry you, Leo!"

His grin became a laugh. He couldn't help it. It just . . . bubbled up and out of him. "Open the glove compartment."

"What is this?"

It tickled him how genuinely shocked she seemed about the proposal and about the tiny box he'd stashed in the glove compartment. People had been doing this for centuries. He hadn't invented any of this.

"Oh," she breathed when she opened the box.

"It's my mom's engagement ring. So it's probably, like, negative carats—my parents were broke when they met." It was a white gold band with a small diamond in the middle surrounded by little chips of aquamarine. In other words, nothing special. "Turn it over."

"AR and VM," she said, hunching over to examine the ring. "Oh! And LR and MA! That's us!"

"Yeah. I had us added." He felt sheepish all of a sudden, like maybe he should have shown her before he had the engraving done, rather than assume she'd want to wear it. "I figured you have access to literal crown jewels. How can I compete with that?"

"You can compete with that by not competing with it," Marie said quietly. "By giving me something like this, something from your family. From your heart."

Leo swallowed to get rid of the lump that had risen in his throat. "Well, you have that, too, Princess."

They were home. "All right. Enough of this." He looked at his watch. "Gabby's gonna be home from school in an hour, and then it's going to be all grilled cheese sandwiches and nonstop chatter, and tomorrow you have your meeting at the UN first thing so . . ." He let his gaze rake over Marie's body and waggled his eyebrows to make sure she got his point.

"So we should make the most of that hour?" She was out of the car before he had cut the engine.

He caught up with her and grabbed her hand. "I mean, yeah.

While we can, you know? I'm imagining that as soon as the news gets out, there's probably going to be a shitload of royal wedding protocol unleashed."

"Probably," Marie agreed cheerfully. "I'm sure it will provide hours of fodder for you and my father to argue over."

"I am prepared to lose all those arguments except one." Marie raised her eyebrows inquisitively as they mounted the stairs. "I want Dani to be my best man. Best person. I know that's probably 'not done,' but I don't give a shit. I'll let your father win on everything else. You can dress me up and put me in a pumpkin carriage and I'll sign whatever papers he wants me to, but Dani's not negotiable."

"Of course it's not. Dani will be your best man, and Max will be my maid of honor. My father will lose his mind. It will be epic. It will be—"

He cut her off with a kiss, pressing her against the inside of his door as he let her bag fall to the floor. Fuck, he had been waiting *forever* for this, to hear her sigh into his mouth as her jaw went slack. To feel her wind her arms around his neck and lean into him and kiss him like she had no plans of stopping.

She lit him up like all the lights of an Eldovian ballroom at Christmas were suddenly flipped on inside his chest. As she moaned softly, trying to rock herself up against him, he started to feel a little frantic, like he couldn't get close enough to her. But he forced himself to take a step back, shedding his coat as he did so and assessing the problem of how to most efficiently divest her of her clothing. Gabby *was* going to be home before they knew it. So they could either stand here and make out by the door forever or they could get on with it.

Marie was dressed in her princess gear. Her coat was a sort-of trench coat, but it sloped out at the bottom like a skirt and featured a wide belt tied tight over two rows of buttons. He un-wrapped the belt and started on the buttons. So many buttons. But that was kind of her signature thing, wasn't it? He persevered even though his fingers were made clumsy by lust. She talked while he worked. "You still have your Christmas stockings up!"

"Yep." It was April, but he hadn't taken the cardboard mantel down.

Finally, he slid the coat off her shoulders to reveal . . . a pink suit-dress thing that featured approximately one million buttons. "Are you kidding me?"

Marie looked down, bewildered.

He rolled his eyes and started on them. She laughed, belatedly catching up. "This wasn't the right thing to wear, was it?"

"Gabby's going to be home in"—He looked at his crappy watch. He had, so far, refused her attempts to give him a Morneau—"fifty-one minutes."

She raised her eyebrows. "Well, you'd better pick up the pace then, hadn't you?"

He picked up the pace.

"Really, Leo," she pressed. "Why do you still have your Christmas stockings up?"

"Because," he said, not caring—much—that what he was about to say was going to make him sound like a giant sap. "I didn't want to take them down until my Christmas wish came true."

"And what was your Christmas wish?"

"Would you believe me if I said I wished for a naked princess in my apartment?"

The dimples came out. "I would not."

Finally done with the suit buttons, he paused with one hand on either side of the blazer. "If I open this to find you have a shirt with buttons on underneath, I swear to God . . ."

She batted his hands away and took over, shrugging herself out of the jacket—she was wearing a silky camisole underneath that was blessedly button-free—and unzipping her skirt. "What did you wish for, Leo?" she said as she hopped on one foot to get out of her tights.

"I *told* you. And look, it's coming true."

She snapped her fingers at him. "Hadn't you better start on your own buttons?" He was wearing a flannel shirt. "And you are such a liar. You did not wish for me naked in your apartment."

Instead of doing what she said—he would, but not just yet—he picked her up. She shriek-laughed but wrapped her legs around his waist. "You're right." He walked them down the short hallway to his bedroom. "I actually wished for you naked in my *bed*." He lowered her carefully until she was within safe "tossing" distance and let go, which earned him some more delightfully shrieky laughter. He mock scowled at her from above. "So now we have achieved one-half of that wish."

"You did not wish for me naked in your bed," she insisted, even as she shimmied out of her camisole and underwear.

And there she was, Her Royal Highness Marie Joséphine Annagret Elena, Princess of Eldovia, naked in his crappy IKEA bed, flashing her dimples at him and wearing his mother's engagement ring.

He had to not think of it like that, though, because it would freak him the fuck out. So he tried again. There she was, *Marie,* naked in his bed, flashing her dimples at him and wearing his mother's engagement ring.

She was right. He hadn't wished for this. But only because he would never in a million years have thought it was possible. He opened his mouth to tease her some more, but something caught in his chest and he ended up making a mortifying sort of choking sound.

"Oh, Leo." Marie lifted her hand and pressed her palm against his cheek. "What did you really wish for?"

"You," he said without hesitation, though it came out all raspy. "I wished for you."

"Not a princess?" she asked. She did that sometimes, sought reassurance about why he was with her. He would gladly give it, as often as she needed.

"No," he said sharply. But then he gentled his tone. "I wished for *you*. Just you."

And he leaned down to kiss her until she believed it.

Four months later

"Holy . . ."

Leo shot Dani a look as the car pulled up to the palace, and she finished her thought with "Cow."

"It's okay," Gabby said cheerfully. "I know what you were going to say, and that's pretty much everyone's reaction when they first see this place."

Leo and Gabby had gone to meet Dani's plane in Zurich. She'd finished her summer teaching and they'd lured her to Eldovia for a visit. He was so excited to see her. He and Gabby were settling in fine. Gabby was passing the summer holidays reading, learning to ride, and having sleepovers with Imogen's niece. Leo, to his great surprise, seemed to have stumbled onto a little side gig building log cabins with Kai. It seemed his half an architecture degree wasn't going to go to waste after all. He genuinely liked the work, and it made him feel like less of a kept man.

Still, he'd missed Dani. It was going to be awesome to have someone from home to hang out with for a while.

"You should see it when Marie or her father arrive home after a trip," he said as the car pulled up. "There's a lineup of literal servants here."

Dani snorted. "I guess I only rate a princess." She waved at Marie. "And who's that dude?"

It was Leo's turn to snort. While in theory he understood that Max was Marie's best friend, and that he was a good guy, he still had trouble with the fact that in another universe he would have been Marie's husband. Her platonic husband who totally didn't appreciate her. It boggled the mind. He hadn't known Max was going to be here. Last he heard, Max was in the Riviera romancing a Hollywood starlet.

"Dani!" Marie exclaimed, and the women embraced. She pulled back and performed introductions. "Daniela Martinez, this is my friend, Maximillian von Hansburg. Max, this is Leo's good friend Dani."

"I thought you had a . . . date," Leo said as Dani and Max shook hands. He wasn't sure how to phrase it. *I thought you were trying to get with a B-list American celebrity on a yacht off the coast of Monaco* felt a little too uncouth, even for him.

"Yes, well, it turned out that the young lady in question had a, ah . . . prior engagement she'd forgotten about with a gentleman friend of hers who walked in on us . . . engaging." He made a face of fake contrition.

"Max is a slut," Marie said matter-of-factly to Dani.

"A slut and a *scholar*," Max said indignantly. He turned his attention to Dani. "As, I understand, you are, too, Dr. Martinez." Then he suddenly looked genuinely contrite. "A scholar, I mean. Not a slut."

Dani didn't have time to process any of this because Canine Max started barking from inside the car. She turned and accepted the travel crate from the driver. "Would it be all right to let him out here?"

"Of course," Marie said.

Soon, he was yapping and jumping around so excitedly he was practically levitating.

"Max!" Dani said sharply. "Sit."

Max—the dog—started yapping even louder.

Max—the duke-to-be—said "I beg your pardon?"

Marie laughed. "Max, meet Max."

"Well, I'll be damned." Max narrowed his eyes in mock indignation. "I'm not sure I approve of this. If I'm going to have a dog named after me, I'd much prefer it to be a manly dog. A hound of some sort, perhaps."

"Can dogs *be* manly, though?" Dani asked. "Aren't they just . . . dogly? Anyway, I just met you, so he's not named after you."

"How long are you here?" Max asked Dani.

"A week."

"Can I take you to dinner? Tomorrow perhaps?"

Leo chuckled. You had to admire Max's direct approach.

"Nope," Dani said cheerfully.

You had to admire Dani's, too. "Dani's post-men," Leo offered, enjoying watching her shoot Max down.

"Well, isn't that too bad for the men of the world," Max said, but he actually seemed sincere. He'd dropped his signature bored-aristocrat tone and he was looking at Dani with curiosity.

"Actually," Marie said, "here's one more introduction to make." She turned to Dani. "Best woman, meet man of honor." And to Max she said, "Man of honor, meet best woman. Dani's here for a visit but also for a dress fitting."

"Well," Max drawled, "isn't *this* going to be interesting?"

"Leo, this is amazing!" Dani turned around, taking in the interior of the cabin in the woods.

"It is, isn't it?" Marie beamed.

Leo waved off the praise, but he was pretty proud of the place. It was why he'd wanted to bring Dani here before showing her the palace. He and Kai had reverted to the original plan for a sleeping loft, but they'd also extended the main floor so there was a cozy little den and an office alcove where Leo worked on his drawings.

"Leo and Marie basically live here," Gabby said.

"Really? How'd you manage that?" Dani asked.

He wasn't really sure. They'd just . . . started staying over more and more and so far, the king had not objected. There had been a few pointedly raised eyebrows when they showed up for breakfast in their outerwear, clearly having hiked up from the cabin, but he hadn't actually said anything.

In fact, the only thing Emil had expressly said about the matter

of Leo and Gabby moving to Eldovia was that he expected everyone at the palace for dinner each night at seven. Leo had been expecting peevish demands regarding protocol and behavior. He'd
been prepared to sign the mother of all prenuptial agreements.
But it seemed like the king, while still his cranky, slightly snobbish self, was trying. Their dinners were less frosty and, when the
conversation turned to books—he and Gabby had formed a little
book club of sorts—almost pleasant. Gabby, it seemed, was working her magic on him. Or something was. Maybe it was just more
of the fairy-tale mojo that seemed to have infected Leo's life.

Speaking of the king . . . A knock at the cabin door heralded
the arrival of a palace worker—Leo refused to call them footmen.
"His Majesty requests the honor of your presence for cocktails in
the green parlor so he may welcome Dr. Martinez and the baron."

"Well," Max said, picking up Dani's bag, "that is not a summons
to ignore."

"I can carry that myself." Dani tried to tug the bag from him.

"Nonsense. You devote yourself to your doggy companion"—he
looked at Canine Max, who had calmed down but took the baronial attention as his cue to start yapping again—"and I'll carry
this."

"We are going to have the *best* drinks," Gabby said, skipping
ahead of everyone as they made their way across the clearing. "I
got to help make them. They have rosehips in them. And mine
has a mixture of 7Up and pomegranate juice. You guys get sparkling wine."

Leo grabbed Marie's hand as they brought up the rear. He let
everyone else's chatter wash over him as they strolled. Gabby was
still talking about the drinks. Max was trying to impress Dani by

telling her about his master's thesis. Leo deliberately slowed their pace—not enough that they'd fall too far behind, but enough to put some distance between them and the others.

When they reached their spot, he planted his feet and tugged on her arm, stopping her progress.

"Leo!" she protested, but she didn't mean it. They always stopped here on the way to or from the cabin. This was the spot where they'd danced in the woods that first night. He liked to mark it. He pulled her in with a flourish, as if they were contestants on a cheesy dance TV show. She came, easily, as if everything had been choreographed for them long ago. He paused, watching Dani and Max and Gabby recede a little farther into the distance. Summer was short in Eldovia, but it was at its peak, and soon the leafy trees swallowed them.

This was what he did now, what he was learning to do. To carve out a little time and space for them to be Leo and Marie instead of the princess and the taxi driver.

"Leo," she whispered, and her breath against his cheek made him shiver.

"Hmm?"

"Dance with me."

"Yes," he said. "Yes." And he pulled her closer and danced in the woods with his love.

Acknowledgments

*O*nce upon a time I idly thought, *Hey, what if I did a Hallmark-style Christmas book?* I am so happy I have an agent, Courtney Miller-Callihan, who responded by saying, "What if you *did*?!" And I'm so happy I have an editor, Elle Keck, who raised the bar by saying, "What if you did *three* of them?" And lo, this series was born. I am so grateful to Courtney and Elle for their enthusiasm and hard work.

The idea for this book really started, though, with my dad, who is possibly the world's biggest fan of cable-channel holiday movies. One of the major joys of the Christmas season for me is getting his play-by-play analysis via text. So one day, I thought to myself, *Hmm . . . Maybe I should try one in book form.* Unfortunately for my dad but fortunately for my existing readers, what I ended up with was more aligned with the Jenny Holiday brand than the Hallmark brand. This means that even though I would prefer he not read this book, Dad will in fact read it. (He will also make the rounds to stores in his city to make "adjustments" if it's not facing out on the shelves.) We just won't talk about Those

Parts. I knew all those emotional sublimation skills I picked up in my Minnesota youth would come in handy someday.

Thanks also to my friend Marion Kuhn for the German language help. I learned a lot about German (non) swearing!

And as usual, thanks to my readers, both old and new. You're the best!

Keep reading for an exclusive excerpt from
Max and Dani's fairy-tale Christmas romance,

DUKE, *Actually*

Winter 2021

*W*hen Dani Martinez woke up Friday the twenty-first of December, she thought, *It's going to be a good day.*

And then she thought, *Liar.*

But whatever, just because it was the last Friday of the semester and she was about to be inundated with a hundred essays on *The* (Not So) *Great Gatsby*, it didn't necessarily follow that today was going to be *bad*.

So she hadn't done a lick of Christmas shopping, forget the fruitcake she was supposed to have started weeks ago. That didn't mean this particular day was *automatically* going to suck.

And just because the cherry on top of December twenty-first was going to be the departmental holiday party at which she would "get" to see her still-not-quite-ex-husband with his trade-in trollop didn't mean—Ah, forget it. This day was going to be *crap*.

Her phone dinged. It would be Leo. Because of the time difference between New York and Eldovia, they often talked early in the mornings New York time. Dani missed Leo and his sister, Gabby, something fierce, missed being able to go across the hall and just walk into their apartment and have coffee in the mornings. Sometimes, before she was caffeinated, she forgot he wasn't there anymore. And then it would hit her anew: her best friend lived in Eldovia now, where he was *engaged to a princess.*

Eyeing the slumbering ball of fur next to her, Dani did a slo-mo roll to grab the phone from the nightstand—she wanted the ball of fur to stay slumbering until she'd had coffee.

The text was not from Leo. Hey, it's Max von Hansburg. Marie gave me your number. I'm in New York for a few days. Can I take you to dinner tonight?

Max. Human Max. Max was Princess Marie's best friend. Human Max was also Marie's ex-fiancé. Marie and Max's past was like a telenovela, complete with conniving royal parents, arranged marriages, and elaborate balls. Leo had crash-landed in the middle of it, getting swept up in a gender-swapped Cinderella story that had made even Dani's stone-cold heart defrost a degree or two.

Dog Max did one of his signature snore-snorts, and Dani swallowed a laugh. She even had Cinderella's animal companions, except hers didn't help with the tidying.

Max: Or lunch?

The Cinderella thaw in Dani's heart did not extend to Human Max, who, in addition to being a baron, was also an insufferable man-whore. She considered the various ways she could decline his invitation. In the end she just went with No.

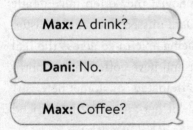

Max: A drink?

Dani: No.

Max: Coffee?

Dani: Coffee is a drink.

Max: So that's still no?

Dani: Yes.

Max: Yes that's still no, or yes you'll have coffee with me?

Dani: Listen, dude. Or should I say listen, duke?

Max: Baron, actually. My father has to kick the bucket before I attain dukedom, and I can report that he is in excellent health. He climbs a literal mountain every day.

Dani: Okay, but here's my point: I am post-men. As I told you last summer. Repeatedly.

Max: Yes, meaning you don't want to date, correct?

Dani: Right.

Max: But what about Leo? You talk to Leo all the time. You flew across the Atlantic to visit him.

Dani: Leo's my best friend.

Max: I rest my case.

Dani: What the does that mean?

Max: Leo is a man.

Dani: Your powers of observation are astounding.

Max: My point is, I don't want to date you either. I just want to hang out with you.

Hmm. Not sure what to say to that and seduced by the smell emanating from the Greatest Invention of All Time, aka the programmable coffeemaker, Dani carefully pushed back her covers and conducted a stealth army-crawl out of bed. For some reason, minute shifts in the mattress were enough to wake Dog Max, but once she was out of bed, she could turn on the radio and have a dance party and he'd be oblivious. She padded to the kitchen.

Dani: Why do you want to hang out with me?

Max: I like you.

Dani: Why?

Max: Because I get the sense that you don't give a shit that I'm an almost-duke.

Dani: That is correct.

Max: I would even go so far as to say that my almost-dukeness works against me.

Dani: Still correct.

Max: I like that about you. You're normal.

Dani: Is that a supposed to be a compliment or an insult?

Max: You don't want to hang out with me. Therefore I want to hang out with you. I'm like a kid who wants what he can't have.

Dani: So in this scenario I'm like a toy you want.

Max: No, you're just a cool person I would like to spend time with since I happen to be in your city.

She almost cracked as she took her coffee back to her bedroom to try to figure out what to wear that telegraphed "It's just a normal day, a day in which I continue to be unbothered by the fact that my husband is boning Undergrad Barbie, tra-la-la." *You're just a cool person I would like to spend time with.*

When was the last time someone had said anything like that to her? Well, never, because grown-ass adults did not speak like that, so openly and without guile. Her limited interactions with Maximillian von Hansburg—she'd met him last summer on her visit to Eldovia—suggested that he did, though. He told the truth. And even though that truth was often about his many and varied romantic and sexual conquests, there was something refreshing about his cheerfully relentless honesty. Max was a fuckboy, basically—a fuckbaron?—but he was a remarkably self-aware one.

Max: So there's no scenario in which you'll get together with me.

She was strangely tempted, but . . .

Dani: No.

She opened the closet and pulled out her standard day-to-evening black dress. She could wear a blazer over it for teaching, then take the blazer off and jazz the dress up for the party to make it more festive.

How, though? Scarf? No. If she added a scarf to the retro-silhouetted dress, she would come off a little too Rizzo from *Grease*—although maybe some Rizzo energy was exactly what the situation called for. She needed a statement necklace. And she needed that statement to be: *Eff you very much, Vince.* No, actually, that wasn't right. The message she wanted to send was more: *Sorry, what was your name again? I have moved so far on that I can't quite remember.* If only she had an accessory that would communicate that.

Oh, hang on. She grabbed the phone.

> **Dani:** On second thought, there might actually be a scenario in which I want to get together with you today.

> **Max:** I wait with bated breath.

> **Dani:** Any chance you want to be my plus-one to my departmental holiday party, at which my soon-to-be-ex-husband Vince will be in attendance, as will his new girlfriend, who is a former student of both of ours and who is twenty years younger than he is?

> **Dani:** Is your soon-to-be-ex-husband the main character in a Philip Roth novel?

She laughed out loud.

> **Dani:** He might as well be.

> **Max:** The answer is yes, but I have questions.

Dani: Of course you do.

Max: Question the first: Is this like one of those elaborately complex rom-coms where we're pretending to be in love to make your ex jealous?

Dani: Let's leave it vague. If pressed I'll call you a friend. But if you wanted to very obviously find me the pinnacle of wit, that would be fine.

Max: It will be a stretch, but I'll try. Question the second: Am I myself or am I pretending to be, say, a visiting scholar of feminist literature who is therefore extra suspectable to your pinnacle?

Dani: You're yourself.

Max: Ah. So what I hear you saying is that in this one very specific scenario, you actually find it convenient that I'm an almost-duke.

God damn him.

Dani: God damn you.

Max: I might even go do far as to say that you're using me for my almost-dukeness.

Dani: She's twenty years old. He told me she was his Lolita. That she saw the real him and that in order to take his writing to the next level he needed someone who could be a "helpmeet." When I said we were each other's helpmeets, he said there can only be one helpmeet and one help-ee in any relationship.

Max: What time am I picking you up?

Dani: Five. I'll meet you there—it's a building on campus but not mine. I need to look up the address. I'll text it to you.

Max: Dress code? Formal? Business casual?

Dani: Duke-ish casual.

Max: Got it. Prepare to be the pinnacle.

Dani smiled, dove onto the bed, and prepared to be love-bombed by the other Max, who genuinely thought she was the pinnacle. As he did every morning, he acted like waking up next to her was the greatest joy of his life, going from dead asleep to vibrating with happiness as he hurled himself onto her lap. "Good morning, my love," she cooed, burying her nose in his fur as she hugged him.

Maybe today wasn't going to be quite as crappy as she'd feared.

MAX WAS SUPPOSED to meet Dani at the faculty club on her campus, but since he arrived half an hour early, he had his driver drop him at the English building.

This was going to be fun. He hadn't been lying—he did like Daniela Martinez, not least because *she* didn't seem to like *him*. That wasn't something that happened. It wasn't that everyone liked him. He wasn't that conceited. But he rarely encountered someone who didn't at least *pretend* to. Sparring with Dani last summer when she'd come to Eldovia to visit Leo had been a breath of fresh air in a remarkably stressful time.

"Oh, I beg your pardon," he said when he ran into—literally—a student standing outside her office.

A boy wearing sweatpants and a sweatshirt with a picture of a ram on it looked him up and down. "No prob, man."

There was also a girl in line, ahead of the boy, and she said, "Are you looking for Professor Martinez?"

"I am."

She snapped her gum at him, but not in a way that seemed hostile. "Get in line."

He did. He hadn't wanted to be late, and not knowing how long it would take to get to the Bronx from his Midtown hotel, he'd budgeted too much time for the journey.

After a minute or so, another boy came out of Dani's office, and the girl went in. Ram Boy shuffled down the wall so he was closer to Dani's open door.

"Are you enjoying Professor Martinez's class?" Max inquired.

"I guess," the boy said flatly.

The girl emerged, having only been in there a minute, and

Ram Boy went in. Max edged closer to the open door so he could eavesdrop.

"Hey, Professor M, I need you to do me a huge favor." *I need you to do me a huge favor.* Something about the way he phrased that, like a command, rubbed Max the wrong way.

"And what would that be?" That was Dani's "I am not impressed" voice. Max smiled. He was acquainted with that voice.

The boy proceeded to make a weak case involving a diving meet, a book forgotten on the team bus, and a thesis all worked out but just not quite down on paper yet. Dani proceeded to systematically dismantle him, but subtly enough that the kid wasn't understanding the full extent of the burns he was sustaining.

It was hot.

Dani was hot.

Interestingly, that was a fact Max could note with detachment, which was another new experience. All the years he'd spent assuming he was going to marry Marie had also been spent, he would freely admit, slutting around. He and Marie had agreed that their marriage would be in name only and that discreet "extracurricular" activities would be allowed, necessary even. Still, he'd viewed the last several years as his last gasp of singledom and therefore of freedom and had conducted himself accordingly.

So when the world offered itself to him, he took. And when you were an obscenely wealthy baron, you had a lot of offers.

What you *didn't* have a lot of was refusals. But Dani, having made her disinterest in him clear from the moment she'd arrived on Eldovian soil, was a rare woman. Wickedly smart, deliciously witty, insanely beautiful, and *not interested*. There were no hard-to-get long games being played. Leo had told Max a bit about her ugly divorce, and Dani herself had used the phrase *post-men* more than once.

She was a goddamn delight.

To Max's surprise, even though the boy was wilting under Dani's questioning about the thesis he supposedly had all worked out—it didn't seem he had actually read the book, which sounded like it was meant to be *The Great Gatsby*—she suddenly granted him a forty-eight-hour extension and abruptly dismissed him. "Happy holidays," she said so flatly she might as well have been saying, "Good riddance."

It was such an unexpected turnabout that Max, who had been lounging against the wall, stood up straight, startled.

"Are there any more students out there?" she asked the boy.

"Students . . . no," the boy said, making brief eye contact with Max as he breezed by in possession of an extension he did not deserve.

When Max stuck his head into Dani's office, it was to find her peeling off a blue blazer to reveal a formfitting pinup-girl dress that looked like it belonged on Bettie Page instead of a literature professor.

"Oh!" She jumped.

"My apologies. I didn't mean to startle you." He smirked. "I'm merely here to ask for an extension."

She rolled her eyes in lieu of greeting him, sat at her desk, and pulled a small mirror out of a drawer. "You're early," she said to her reflection.

"My thesis is all ready to go." He sat on the guest chair and, as she started applying a deep burgundy lipstick, revised his previous assertion that he could appreciate Dani's hotness from a purely intellectual perspective. "Want to hear it?"

"I guarantee you I already have."

"None of the characters in *The Great Gatsby* have any inner life to speak of, making what is admittedly a masterfully written book into a mere melodrama."

She glanced at him with one lip painted. The contrast between the dark red of the finished lip and the pale pink of the natural one certainly was something. "An interesting line of thought."

He thought she was going to say more, but when she merely returned to her lips, he asked, "Why did you give that kid an extension? He was bullshitting you. And does he know you at all?"

One eyebrow rose, though she was still looking at her reflection instead of at him. "Do *you* know me at all?"

"I'm thinking the way to get an extension from Professor Martinez is to level with her. Own the fact that you screwed up—with time management or laziness, or what have you—present a plan for fixing your screwup and state your terms."

Ah, that cracked her. She put the mirror down and really looked at him for the first time. *Almost* looked like she might smile. "Did you hear the student before him?"

"No."

"She asked for a twenty-four-hour extension because she works two part-time jobs and she fell asleep at her computer last night."

"Did you grant it?"

"I did. I told her to go home and take a nap and to take another week with the paper."

The fact that he had been right about how to handle Professor Martinez when you were a wayward student was strangely, sharply satisfying. "Why?"

"Because she shows up to class prepared and has never asked for anything. Because I see her working at the Starbucks in the lobby all the time, and if that's only one job of two, that's a little sobering."

"So why does Diver Boy get an extension, too? I wouldn't have pegged you as such a pushover."

"I have a hundred essays to grade in the next two weeks, so it doesn't really matter to me when they come in. And frankly, it's not worth the bad reviews on my student evaluations."

Hmm. It was hard to imagine Dani getting "bad reviews." And her unexpectedly blasé response to the boy's request created a disturbance in the mental picture Max was painting of her.

"You ready?" she asked as she stood, and his appreciation of her dress—and her lips, and her *everything*—grew even less intellectual.

"You want to give me any background about the ex-husband—did you say his name was Vince?—or the new girlfriend?" he asked while he tried not to be too overt about his escalating appreciation.

"Neither of them have any inner life to speak of, so nah." She did flash him a little smile then. It was pleasingly conspiratorial. "I'm sure you—" Her speech came to an abrupt halt and her body froze except for her eyes, which traveled rapidly up and down his body.

He looked down at himself. "What? Not duke-ish casual?" The New York trip was a short one, so he only had the one suit with him. He'd almost worn it without a tie, but in the end he hadn't been able to make himself do it. If a man was wearing a suit, he should wear a suit—all its pieces, not some haphazard, choose-your-own-adventure version of it.

"It was a pun on business casual," she said.

"I got that. Is this not business casual? You Americans with your dress codes. You put words together that either don't mean anything or contradict each other and call it a 'dress code.' I *could* have worn my frock coat complete with ceremonial sword."

She cracked a grin, a full unreserved one, and he was unbecomingly excited to have been its source.

"You look fine. Let's go."

ALL EYES WERE on Dani as she entered the English Department holiday party, but for once it wasn't because of her status as jilted ex-wife of the inexplicably popular Professor Vincent Ricci, who had left her for a perfectly average twenty-year-old named Berkeley.

Or it wasn't *only* because of that. To be fair, it probably started because of that. Vince and Berkeley coming out as a couple a hot minute after Berkeley formally dropped out of school had been the biggest news to hit the department since the dean's office reclaimed the faculty lounge and gave it to the economists for an econometrics lab. Poor discarded Dani, replaced by a younger, tauter model.

But it only took a second, once everyone got a load of Max, for the narrative to shift.

Because Max, in his duke-ish casual, looked a lot more than "fine." He was a sight to behold, especially in contrast to the men in this crowd, who were "dressed up" in their Dockers and "no-iron" shirts that actually needed ironing. Max's tallness and slimness was accentuated by the tailored blue suit he was wearing like it was a second skin. Like it *was* casual. With his icy blue eyes, his dirty blond hair slicked back into a pompadour, and his angular face, he looked like that Swedish actor from that vampire show, all sharp angles and cool cobalt. And the best part was it wasn't all empty good looks. With his rapid-fire wit, he could eat these people for breakfast if he wanted to.

She hoped he wanted to.

He must have noticed everyone's attention—it was hard not to; this crowd was not subtle—because he laid his palm on her lower back. In any other circumstance, she would have shaken him off. He didn't press or push, though, just stood serenely while everyone gaped at them. After a few beats of that, he said, "Shall we go to the bar?"

Dani caught the eye of Sinead, who she supposed was her best friend in the department. The only youngish woman professors without tenure, Sinead and Dani had leaned on each other a lot in the early years, forming a kind of battlefield bond that had never gone away even as they'd found their stride and gotten busy with research and relationships.

Sinead raised her eyebrows in a way that was meant to communicate *Holy shit, girl.*

Dani raised hers back and hitched her head slightly to send a return message: *Meet us at the bar.*

Max's hand stayed resting lightly on Dani's back as they made their way through the crowded room. She said a few hellos to colleagues as they passed, but she didn't stop. Better to let them wonder.

"Hel-*lo*," Sinead said as she sidled up to the bar. "Don't you look smashing?"

"You, too." She really did. In fact, she was wearing a blue suit, just like Max, except hers was tailored to hug her curves, and she wore an open-necked white silk shirt under it.

Dani kept introductions brief. "Max, Sinead. Sinead, Max."

They ordered drinks, and as they waited for them, Sinead flicked Max's blue, black, and red checked tie. "Burberry?"

Max raised an eyebrow. He probably wasn't used to people touching his clothes. Or commenting on labels. Both were probably exceedingly low-classy. "Indeed." He reached over and flicked the cross-body briefcase Sinead wore. "Vuitton?"

Dani rolled her eyes. These two dandies were perfect for each other.

"Knockoff," Sinead said cheerfully. "I'll be paying off my student loans until I die."

"Ah, yes, the puzzling American tradition of bankrupting young people before they even begin their careers."

"Hang on." Sinead pointed at Max. "You're the duke."

"Baron, actually," Max said.

Sinead had been leaning against the bar, but suddenly her posture changed. "Incoming."

Dani looked over her shoulder, took stock, and whispered to Max. "The guy on his way over here is the chair of the department and also of my tenure committee. We care about his inner life. His inner life needs to grant me tenure." Max made a vague noise of acknowledgment.

"And, bonus!" Sinead whispered. "He seems to have collected Vince and Berkeley, too."

"*Berkeley*?" Max barked an incredulous laugh. "Is that Lolita the Helpmeet's name?"

"It is indeed," Dani said, choking back her own laugh—his mirth was contagious. "But ugh, all three of them at once? I'm not ready for this."

"Sure you are," Max said as the bartender set their drinks on the bar. He put a fifty-dollar bill in the tip jar and handed the women their drinks. Before picking up his own he rolled his shoulders back and straightened his spine like he was preparing for battle. "This"—he winked at Dani—"is going to be fun."

About the Author

JENNY HOLIDAY is a *USA Today* bestselling and RITA-nominated author whose work has been featured in the *New York Times*, *Entertainment Weekly*, the *Washington Post*, and National Public Radio. She grew up in Minnesota and started writing at age nine when her fourth-grade teacher gave her a notebook to fill with stories. When she's not working on her next book, she likes to hang out with her family, watch other people sing karaoke, and throw theme parties. A member of the House of Slytherin, Jenny lives in London, Ontario, Canada.